Another

2 0 0 1

novel by
yukito ayatsuji

YEN
ON

NEW YORK

[Another 2001]
[Yukito Ayatsuji]

Translation by Nicole Wilder
Cover art by Shiho Enta and Kumi Suzuki

Another 2001
© Yukito Ayatsuji 2020
First published in Japan in 2020 by
KADOKAWA CORPORATION, Tokyo.
English translation rights arranged with
KADOKAWA CORPORATION, Tokyo,
through TUTTLE-MORI AGENCY, INC., Tokyo.

English translation © 2022 by Yen Press, LLC

Yen On
150 West 30th Street, 19th Floor
New York, NY 10001

Visit us at yenpress.com · facebook.com/yenpress
twitter.com/yenpress · yenpress.tumblr.com
instagram.com/yenpress

First Yen On Edition: December 2022
Edited by Yen On Editorial: Maya Deutsch
Designed by Yen Press Design: Wendy Chan

Yen On is an imprint of Yen Press, LLC.
The Yen On name and logo are trademarks of Yen Press, LLC.

Library of Congress Cataloging-in-Publication Data
Names: Ayatsuji, Yukito, 1960- author. | Kiyohara, Hiro, 1981- illustrator.
| Wilder, Nicole, translator.
Title: Another 2001 / Yukito Ayatsuji ; illustration by Hiro Kiyohara ;
translation by Nicole Wilder.
Other titles: Another 2001. English
Description: First Yen On edition. | New York, NY : Yen On, 2022.
Identifiers: LCCN 2021062843 | ISBN 9781975336011 (hardcover)
Subjects: LCGFT: Horror fiction. | Light novels.
Classification: LCC PL8675.Y38 A8513 2022 | DDC
895.63/6—dc23/eng/20220121
LC record available at https://lccn.loc.gov/2021062843

ISBNs: 978-1-9753-3601-1 (hardcover)
978-1-9753-3602-8 (ebook)

10 9 8 7 6 5 4 3 2 1

LSC-C

Printed in the United States of America

Another

2 0 0 1

~To Dear M.F.~

Another 2001
CONTENTS

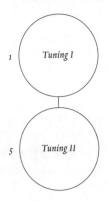
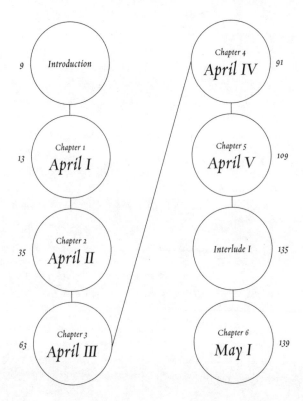

Part 2
............*I.A.*

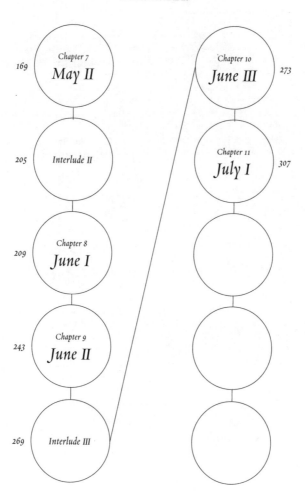

Part 3
............*M.M.*

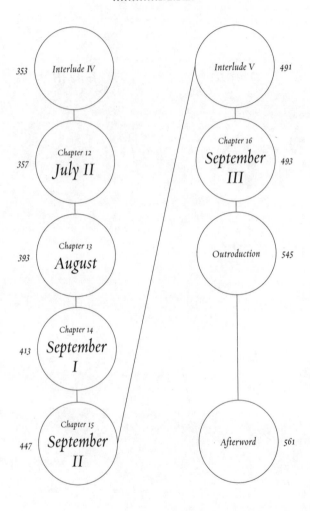

Another
2 0 0 1

Tuning I

The year was 1972. According to the Japanese calendar, it was Showa 47. **In other words, the incident took place _twenty-nine years ago_. That spring, a _certain student_ in Grade 3 Class 3 at Yomiyama North Middle School died.** It happened after the start of the new semester, just as they were approaching their fifteenth birthday. There's been a lot of speculation at school over what really happened—whether they died in an airplane crash or a train accident, but...the truth is, they lost their life in a home fire, right?

Seems that way.

The whole family went up in the blaze. The student's parents, plus their brother, who was one year younger.

That's right.

The student's name was Misaki.

That's what they're called in the rumors, but they don't specify whether they were a boy or a girl.

Misaki...is correct.

All right.

His full name was Misaki Yomiyama. And he was a boy.

Misaki Yomiyama...

. . . .

From the time _he_ was in Class 1, he was an outstanding student, a strong athlete, and talented in art and music. To top it all off, he was handsome and easy to get along with. He was popular, beloved by students and teachers alike. Heh, when you sum it all up like that, it sounds kind of fake.

But supposedly, it was the truth.

Yeah. So…when they heard the news, everyone was awfully shocked, and there was a lot of grieving. People couldn't accept that someone so popular had passed away just like that. Neither his classmates nor his homeroom teacher could face the facts. And so…

Everyone meant well, but they coped with his death in the worst possible way. **That is to say, they *pretended* that Misaki was alive.**

Right.

It started with the idea that his passing was a lie. They couldn't accept it. They didn't want to. Before long, it escalated into the delusion that Misaki had never expired. That he was still alive—look, he's *right there…*

. . . .

Misaki's right *there*, like he always has been. He's still with us. He couldn't have died… **All the students of Class 3 insisted that he was "still alive." And once they started, they kept up the charade. All the way to graduation day.**

. . . .

Even their homeroom teacher played along, you know. She pretended, just like everyone said, that nothing had happened to him. That, at least in her classroom, he continued living on as a member of the class. They left Misaki's desk right where it was, spoke to him *as if he were there*, played with him, walked home with him…they all *pretended*.

. . . .

But that was—that way of doing things was a mistake, you see. They should have come to grips with it and accepted that *death* is *death*. And yet…

. . . .

There was this photograph, a commemorative picture taken in the classroom after the graduation ceremony. Everyone who looked at the image was shocked—in the corner of the class photograph was something that should not have been. There stood Misaki, face as pale as a corpse, smiling just like everyone else. **That was when it all started, twenty-nine years ago...**

This was the incident that triggered the mysterious "phenomenon" that began to hound Grade 3 Class 3 the following year.

Yes, the "phenomenon"...and the inexplicable "accidents" that accompanied it.

I see...

....

....

....

......So?

So what?

So the "phenomenon" probably hasn't ended, not even after what happened *three years ago*. It'll probably begin again. It could be that you'll end up in Class 3 this year. And maybe...

Ah...but even if you start worrying now, there's nothing we can do.

Nothing we can do?

....

...You should be careful. And if by some chance it happens again—

Sure. But you know, if it does, I'll be...

Tuning II

○ 1998 School Year List of Deaths (Considered to Be) Due to "Accidents"

April   Misaki Fujioka......Cousin to Mei Misaki, a student in Grade 3 Class 3. The younger sister of a set of twins.

May   Yukari Sakuragi......Grade 3 Class 3 student. Class president.
Mieko Sakuragi......Yukari's mother.

June   Sanae Mizuno......Grade 3 Class 3 student. Takeru Mizuno's older sister.
Ikuo Takabayashi......Grade 3 Class 3 student.

July   Shouji Kubodera......Grade 3 Class 3 homeroom teacher. Japanese language instructor.
Tokue Kubodera......Shouji's mother.
Atsushi Ogura......Grade 3 Class 3 student. Yumi Ogura's older brother.

August   Manabu Maejima......Grade 3 Class 3 student.

Izumi Akazawa......Grade 3 Class 3 student.
Shigeki Yonemura......Grade 3 Class 3 student.
Takako Sugiura......Grade 3 Class 3 student.
Junta Nakao......Grade 3 Class 3 student.

Kensaku Numata......Administrator at the Sakitani
Memorial Hall. Ikuo Takabayashi's grandfather.
Miesko Numata......Same profession. Kensaku's wife.

Part
1

. . . . . .

Y.H.

Introduction

Hey. What did you think about all that talk the other day?

The other day... Oh, you mean what happened at the "handover ceremony" with the outgoing graduates?

Yeah. Do you believe their story?

I'm not sure.

You don't?

I have my doubts.

Every year, around this time in March, they hold a "handover ceremony" like that one. The outgoing third-years in Class 3 pass the torch to their incoming counterparts.

They do that once the rosters are set—once they know who will be in that group at the start of April.

The school administration is also aware of the situation and immediately delivers the news to the students who are going to be placed there, without waiting for the official announcement in spring. It's not just a problem for the students, after all.

Come on—that's totally crazy...

I do remember hearing the rumors, though.

About the **cursed class**?

Yeah. Didn't you?

I haven't heard a thing about it.

That's because it's supposed to be some kind of secret, yeah? They say bad things will happen if they go around telling everybody.

Even if someone told me, I'd have a hard time buying into it right then and there.

So you don't think it's true?

What about you? Do you?

I can't say for sure.

See? Besides, there weren't really any "accidents" last year and the year before that, so…

Apparently, the year before we started school here was an *"on year."* They say all sorts of disturbing incidents took place. And a lot of people…

Died. They died.

When you put it like that, it sure sounds scary.

Sure does. But…

But?

But I just can't get myself to take it too seriously, all that talk about how there's really a **"curse" or whatever.**

I see how you feel, but…

You didn't get the impression that even the outgoing students weren't entirely convinced?

Is that how they seemed?

Yeah, to me, I guess…

Hmm.

Doesn't the whole story about **such-and-such happened to Misaki from twenty-nine years ago** sound kind of fishy anyway?

Mm…it kinda does.

Like some sort of *game* the graduates have kept going to frighten the incoming class.

Mm-hmm. I mean, it would be great if that was all it was.

There's another meeting at the end of this month, huh?

Yeah. They said it was a **"strategy session"** or something.

Man, what a pain.

There are some people who take it pretty seriously.

Guess it would be bad if we played hooky.

Yeah, it doesn't seem like something we can skip.
I heard the homeroom teacher will be there, too.
I think I remember hearing that.
Ugh, guess there's no getting out of it.

†

Last year and the one before that—the 1999 and 2000 school years—were fortunately "off years." As the century draws to a close, we hope there is a chance that the phenomenon is also *finished*. It's possible that this year, nothing will happen, either. That's what some of us believe, at least...

...and yet, we have no proof it's going to let up.

If it is still active, and this year—the 2001 school year—happens to be an "on year," we must be prepared. We'll need to set up countermeasures like last time. That is why I have asked all of you, who will be joining Grade 3 Class 3 this April, to gather here today.

There are two important things that we need to discuss.

The first is the selection of our **"countermeasures officers."**

The second thing is determining who shall bear the burden of playing **the "*non-exister*," which is essential for the success of our contingency plans in the event that this is an "on year."** We have to settle that.

Apparently, people used a variety of different methods to select both the countermeasures officers and the "non-exister" in the past. But this year, we've set up this meeting to hear as much input from you all as possible on how things should play out...

....

....

....

...Well then, let's begin, shall we?

As I've just explained, if we see any signs that this year is an "on year" once the new semester starts, then at that time, we—

—Excuse me, teacher.

Yes? What is it?

I wonder if that's enough?

What?

I mean, **is that really the only countermeasure we need to take?**

What do you mean?

Um, well, the thing is, according to what I heard, three years ago—in 1998, when it was an "on year"…

…………

…………

…………

…So I was thinking, this year, **wouldn't it be better to set things up like that from the beginning? Wouldn't that be safer?**

I see… Well, obviously, the best outcome would be for this year to also be an "off year." But we should do everything we can regardless…

Your proposal is worth considering. What do you think, everyone?

Chapter I
April I

1

Spring had arrived. I had finally finished moving into my new place, and tomorrow I would start the new semester as a third-year student.

I say I'd finished moving, but it wasn't that big of a deal. In terms of distance, I didn't go more than a hundred meters horizontally and maybe a few dozen meters vertically. It was a pretty modest relocation. Practically the only things I'd needed to transport were my personal belongings...

We didn't hire movers; instead, I just carried my things, bit by bit, in cardboard boxes over several days. And for the things I couldn't carry on my own, Mr. and Mrs. Akazawa were kind enough to help me out.

Unit <E-9> on the fifth floor of the six-story apartment building, the "Freuden Tobii"—this was my new place.

The tidy little one-bedroom felt empty even after I'd moved in all my things. It was too spacious for a single middle school student. Of course, I was grateful for the Akazawas' kindness, but it seemed like kind of a waste.

Mrs. Akazawa had offered to help me get set up, but I turned her down.

"Thank you. But I'll be fine."

Both the *thank you* and the *fine* had been genuine.

After finishing dinner at *the main house*, I headed back alone to my very own apartment.

The first thing I did was open up my large sports bag, the last piece of luggage I'd carried over that day. From it, I pulled out a black-painted wooden box that was wrapped in a bath towel. I opened the lid and quietly checked its contents.

Inside was a single doll.

A beautiful girl wearing a black dress. She was about forty centimeters tall and belonged to the category known as "ball-jointed dolls." Among all my possessions, she was perhaps the most precious.

For the time being, I stored her box in a corner of a bookshelf that didn't yet hold any books, and then—

I wandered out onto the veranda.

The cool evening air of early April was still chilly against my cheek, and my breath came out white.

There were only a few lonely stars in the sky. I was sure there was supposed to be a full moon that night, but it was obscured by clouds, so I couldn't see it.

Placing both my hands on the railing, I straightened my back. Then, taking quiet, rhythmic breaths, I looked out over the landscape.

It was a little past eight o'clock, and darkness had already descended over most of the town.

In the foreground was the Yomiyama River, flowing downstream. Here and there, I could make out clusters of streetlights. Those gaudy, shimmering globs illuminated the other bank of the river.

That must be the shopping district in the Akatsuki neighborhood.

It had been two years and seven months since I'd *returned* here. This small village among the mountains—Yomiyama.

I've been told that I was born in the maternity hospital here in town. I'd lived here in Yomiyama City for less than a year. After that, my family moved to a seaside town called Hinami, where we stayed until the summer of my sixth grade in elementary school.

I say that I used to live here, but that was when I was a baby, so it's not like I remember the place. There was nothing nostalgic about my return. Instead, it felt like a foreign country. The unfamiliarity had made me anxious initially, but…over the last two years and seven months, those feelings had also gradually faded.

…However—

I turned away from the Yomiyama night stretching out before me and looked down at my feet. Without meaning to, I let out a long sigh, then tightly shut my eyes.

But starting tomorrow—

Depending on the situation, I…

My eyelids still squeezed tightly shut, I sighed again, this time deliberately trying to release the tension, when—

I heard a hollow electronic tone ringing inside the apartment.

Oh, my phone?

2

Could it be a call from her? I thought, picking up my chrome-plated cell phone. My heart started to beat a little faster.

Unfortunately, my hopes were immediately dashed. An unregistered number was on the display.

"Heya, Sou? It's me, Yagisawa. My cell phone's busted, so I'm calling from my landline."

Nobuyuki Yagisawa.

He was my classmate—we went to the same middle school, Yomiyama North Middle School (North Yomi for short). For the past two years, we'd been in the same class, and now we knew we would be in Class 3 together for our third year as well. Yagisawa and I had a *certain something in common*, and ever since identifying it not long after we met, we had maintained a pretty special friendship.

"What's up?" I asked, reminding myself that calls from *her* were few and far between anyway… "Something must be going on if you're bothering to call from your house phone."

"Nothing's really up—just…aren't you anxious? I mean, tomorrow we finally start the spring semester."

"Hmm. You scared?"

"Duh! I keep imagining what might happen. But, like, I also keep telling myself that the worst-case scenario probably won't pan out."

"You've always said that, haven't you?"

"I'm an optimist at heart," Yagisawa replied.

"Well, you don't need to be afraid for me, then, do you?"

"Come on now—I wanna hear you say you're glad to have your best pal by your side!"

Despite his claims to the contrary, I could hear the *fear* welling up in his voice. I tried to tell myself that I was probably just reading too much into things.

"When I think about what could happen," Yagisawa continued, "I worry that you must be under some awful pressure right about now."

"Oh? Well, you don't need to be," I responded in the calmest tone of voice I could muster. "I'm telling you, I'm fine. I'm not having a hard time at all."

"............"

"Anyway, we'll have to see how things are tomorrow. Optimism is good, but...you know all about it, right?"

"Yeah."

"And you're okay with the worst-case scenario? You know we can't back out halfway through."

After a brief pause, the voice on the other end answered, "Y-yeah." He sounded a touch overwhelmed.

"All right, bye," I said and hung up the phone.

About an hour later, I got another call. This one was from Mrs. Akazawa.

"Ah, Sou? I forgot to tell you—make sure you come down to our place for breakfast tomorrow. You mustn't oversleep and skip it, you know."

That seemed to be her main reason for ringing me up. I answered with an obedient, "Yes, ma'am."

"And make sure to bring your laundry to me every day. You've got your own bath in the apartment, so you can use that whenever you please."

It seemed like all sorts of things were weighing on her in spite of having just said good night not two hours earlier.

"You're not feeling lonely by yourself?" she asked soberly.

"I'm all right. I'll be fifteen this autumn, you know." I answered her just as seriously.

"Feel free to ask for help if you're having trouble with anything... okay? You can always talk to us. If it's urgent, you can ask Mayuko. She lives right above you."

"Sure. Thank you, Auntie."

Ever since three years ago—since they'd started looking after me in September of 1998—the Akazawas had been really good to me. They'd done their best to treat me kindly despite my...complicated situation.

Of course, I felt very grateful to them. But the truth was, their concern and kindness could feel constricting at times.

"All right then. Good night, Sou."

"Good night."

"Sou" was the name that my actual parents gave me. My surname was "Hiratsuka" at the moment, but I would probably replace it sooner or later.

I was thinking of changing it to "Akazawa." It seemed like a real possibility, but I hadn't settled on it just yet.

3

My personal relationships were a bit complicated, but basically—

The Akazawa family, who had been taking care of me in Yomi-yama, used to be major landowners in the Tobii neighborhood long ago. The patriarch of the previous generation (though he was still alive) was a man named Hiromune Akazawa, who had three sons. The oldest was Haruhiko, the middle was Natsuhiko, and the youngest was Fuyuhiko. The person who I referred to as "Mr. Akazawa" was his oldest son, Haruhiko, and "Mrs. Akazawa" was his wife, a woman named Sayuri.

This couple—the oldest son and his wife—lived with their father, Hiromune, who led a quiet retired life in his old age. Their house had stood on the same plot of land in Tobii for a long, long time—their home was practically the definition of *old-fashioned*.

The Akazawa household had taken me into their custody two years and seven months back. I was no longer welcome in my previous home in Hinami, the Hiratsuka house...they'd driven me out.

Just a minute's walk from the Akazawa family house stood the Freuden Tobii. The Freuden was an apartment building under the management of Natsuhiko, the middle brother. Details aside, the important thing to know was that he'd allowed me to live in one of the apartments there since the start of April.

During our phone call, Mrs. Akazawa (aka Sayuri) had mentioned someone named "Mayuko" living above me, which referred to Natsuhiko Akazawa's wife. They occupied the penthouse. I thought of them as "Mr. and Mrs. Akazawa" as well, though calling them that could make things confusing.

For me, the important thing was—

The last of Hiromune Akazawa's three sons, Fuyuhiko, was none other than my biological father. But he had passed away fourteen years prior, just after I'd been born. I had only found out much later, after starting middle school, that he'd taken his own life out of grief.

4

I opened up most of the other cardboard boxes that I'd used to transport my stuff. By the time I'd finished putting away the bare necessities, it was almost midnight.

Tomorrow was the opening ceremony, so I didn't have much of anything to put in my school bag. I pulled my uniform and a shirt out of a box and hung them up on hangers. With that, all my immediate preparations were more or less complete.

I was living alone in a studio apartment, but it was only a temporary arrangement.

My room had neither a television nor refrigerator, and since I had a cell phone, there was no need for a phone affixed to the wall, only an Internet connection for my computer.

After taking a shower break, I opened my laptop PC on the living room table and booted it up. I had one purpose in mind. All I wanted to do was check my e-mail, but—

There were two new messages.

The first was from *Yomiyama Town News*, a free newsletter that was sent out twice a month—largely pointless regional affairs and local notices. I'd discovered it about a year ago and subscribed to its mailing list for some reason.

The other was from Shunsuke Kouda.

We'd been classmates back in our first year of middle school and were also members of the biology club. This April, he would become the club president. Naturally, he was also friends with Yagisawa, who had called me earlier.

The program for the coming year's club activities comprised the majority of the e-mail's content. Shunsuke was always a very meticulous kind of guy, so it wasn't hard to imagine him writing and sending a notice like that. However—

At the very end of the e-mail, there was one line that made me gasp in surprise.

> I'LL BE PRAYING FOR YOUR SAFETY.

In principle, the *special circumstances of Grade 3 Class 3* were supposed to be kept a secret from outsiders. Nevertheless, it seemed like Shunsuke had heard something about it. Although to be honest, it would have been more surprising if he hadn't heard anything at all…

I looked over this second e-mail, then picked up my cell phone, which was sitting beside my PC. Other than the phone call from Mrs. Akazawa—Sayuri, that is—no one else had contacted me.

Letting out a little sigh, I turned my gaze back to the computer screen.

No calls, not even an e-mail. I had expected at least that. From *her*. From Mei Misaki.

Mei—I wonder when the last time I talked to her was.

Once at the start of this year… No, I had two chances to speak with her.

We'd exchanged a few words over the phone just after New Year's.

The other time was around the start of February, in person, when I'd visited "Blue Eyes Empty to All, in the Twilight of Yomi," the doll gallery in the neighborhood of Misaki.

Back when we'd met in February, we talked for a while about *the accidents*. I was close to starting Grade 3, so I'd asked her if there was any possibility of avoiding *them*.

Several days after the graduation and school closing ceremonies had ended, when I knew that I was going to be a member of Grade 3 Class 3 in April, I'd worked up the nerve to call her. However, no matter how many times I rang, she never picked up. I even tried going to the gallery in Misaki once in early April, but there had been a CLOSED sign on the door…

I assumed she'd gone on a long vacation with her family or something. Even if that wasn't it, she would be starting her third year of high school in the spring. She had her own present and future problems to worry about and must have had a lot on her plate…

I'd decided to send her just a single e-mail, a report of sorts.

To tell her that the hunch she'd had way back then was on the mark. That my Grade 3 class was going to be Class 3, like she had surmised.

Of course, I didn't include a plea for her to do something about it. Even if I was in Class 3, it remained to be seen whether this was going to be an "on year," after all.

I sighed again and was about to close my PC when it happened.

Suddenly, I heard a slight noise. It was the notification tone for an incoming e-mail.

Reflexively letting out a small "*ah!*" I gripped the mouse again. Then I turned my attention to the e-mail software display.

The message was untitled. But the sender was…

"Oh!"

I let out another involuntary noise.

The name of the sender was "Mei M."
Mei Misaki!

> DEAR SOU,
> SCHOOL STARTS TOMORROW, DOESN'T IT?
> BE CAREFUL.

I didn't exactly feel happy when I read her message but rather a kind of meager relief. As I stared at her words on the display, an image of her—of Mei Misaki—appeared in my mind's eye. But for some reason, I wasn't seeing her as she had looked when I'd seen her back in February—rather, I'd pictured her as a fifteen-year-old girl, on a summer day three years ago, with her left eye hidden behind an eye patch...

"...I'll be fine," I whispered quietly to myself.

I pursed my dry lips and straightened my back up as best I could.

"I'll be fine. I'll do everything right."

5

Since moving to Yomiyama, I would get up every morning at around 6:30 unless I was sick or worn out. I would always set an alarm just in case, but it was rarely necessary.

Although I was an early riser, I wouldn't immediately get out of bed.

Instead, I'd lay there on my back, staring at the ceiling for several minutes while checking my breathing, my body temperature, my heartbeat. As I lay there, I'd focus my consciousness on the *undeniable fact that I was alive right then.*

I'm sure that it's because of what happened to me three years ago, an aftershock of that bizarre experience. Even in a new location, this process that I went through between waking and rising remained the same as ever.

"All right," I muttered to myself, nodding and sitting up.

I am alive.

In the year 2001 of the Western calendar, April the 9th, that was a fact.

Mm, okay.

I got dressed, left my apartment, and locked the door behind me.

Beside the entrance was a small plate on the wall that displayed the room number, <E-9>, beneath which was a metal frame for inserting a nameplate. I wasn't really sure what I should write there, so for the time being, I'd left it empty. My mailbox in the entrance of the building was the same.

Yesterday, Sayuri had apparently gone to speak to the tenants in the two apartments on either side of me so that they wouldn't think me suspicious. I rarely got any mail, and even if something was to come for me, it would go to the Akazawas' house like it always had, so that wouldn't be a problem.

In this apartment building, the first-level rooms were all *A*s, the second-level rooms were all *B*s, and so on... The letters indicated the floor. Most of the other apartments on E, the fifth floor, had nameplates; unlike <E-9>, most were configured for families.

As I headed down the deserted early-morning hallway toward the elevators, I happened to glance over at unit <E-1> across the hall. Like my own apartment, <E-9>, it also lacked a nameplate beside the door...

...This place.

Suspicion flickered through my mind.

Here?

This apartment...

In that moment, just for an instant, the whole world went black.

There came a low, reverberating thumping just beyond my hearing—I felt it rather than heard it.

It was like...this is a weird metaphor, but it was like someone standing *outside of this world* had just clicked a camera shutter to capture the scene. Or maybe as though someone had fired off a strobe light. Regardless, it was a bizarre thought, one that left me just as quickly as it had arrived.

I don't really need to worry about anything. It was just a second, after all. Less than that, even. I was probably just paying too much attention to my own blinking is all...

The suspicion that had flickered across my mind a moment earlier was already evaporating.

"Mm. All right, then."

Nodding, I reshouldered my bag, then pushed the elevator call button.

6:50. Still plenty of time before school starts.

6

After stopping by the Akazawa house and eating my fill of breakfast, I still had plenty of extra time before I needed to report for school.

"All right, I'm going."

Nevertheless, in my most indifferent voice, I announced my departure to Mrs. Akazawa and left the house. Kurosuke (a black tomcat, estimated to be about eight years old, who had been in the care of this household for longer than I had) walked as far as the gate with me, meowing the whole way.

He's seeing me off... No, that can't be it.

I almost never went straight from the house to school. A direct course took me only fifteen minutes even if I was dragging it out, so as long as the weather wasn't awful, I liked to take a kind of detour and stroll down the Yomiyama River floodplain. I enjoyed the time alone. I'd started doing this on a whim one morning last summer, and, well, it had become almost like a routine—

The flow of the Yomiyama River was very calm that morning. Perhaps because we hadn't had any heavy rain for a while, the water level was so low, it seemed like I could cross the river on foot.

Although the sky was slightly overcast, it wasn't too cold out. My outfit, a student uniform with long sleeves and a stand-up collar, was just perfect. But when a cold wind blew past me from time to time, I would reflexively hunch my shoulders against the chill.

As usual, I strolled lazily along the small path that followed the riverbank. Partway down, there was a small group of stone benches, and I took a seat on one of them.

I gazed over at the opposite side of the river and saw a row of beautiful cherry trees stretching down the bank. They were just past full bloom. Before long, the petals would start scattering in the wind, which would be even more impressive.

I put my thumbs and index fingers together to form a rectangular frame, then peered through it at the scenery. I imagined the *click* of a shutter. I really would have liked to snap a picture if I'd had a camera on me, but as it was, I was content to capture the image with the one in my mind.

Kweeh!

I heard the call of an animal.

Shifting my gaze, I watched the owner of the voice alight on a little island that had formed upstream. It was an unexpectedly large bird.

White feathers, a long neck, and long legs…a heron?

That was my first thought, but no, it was different from the white herons I sometimes spotted along the bank. This bird was larger, and on closer inspection, its feathers were more of a bluish-gray than white. A black band stretched from its forehead around to the back of its head, and its wings were spotted with black speckles here and there… *Still a heron, but a blue heron maybe?*

It was the first of its kind that I'd seen here.

I unconsciously stood up from the bench, and as I lined the heron up in my imaginary viewfinder, an idle thought struck me.

Someday…I'd like to get myself a genuine single-lens reflex camera and travel to all sorts of places, taking all sorts of photos. That's always been in the back of my mind, for sure. Like Teruya…

Teruya Sakaki, my uncle on my mother's side, who'd died three years ago.

When I'd first started middle school in Yomiyama, the Akazawas had advised me to join an after-school club…and despite his influence, I'd chosen the biology club over the photography club.

But I had never felt that I'd made the wrong decision. At the time,

I'd been thinking that *I had to follow in Teruya's footsteps* in my own way—and that was what I'd chosen. So…

"…It's not time yet."

My vision could wait a bit, at the very least. I wasn't at that stage of my life yet.

There were things I had to do first. There were challenges I had to overcome.

I sat back down on the bench and closed my eyes softly.

The sound of the flowing water, the feeling of the wind brushing my skin… It felt somehow unreal. When the bird called out again, it, too, seemed distant.

I kept my eyes closed like that for a little while. When my mind grew calm, I left the bench behind.

The blue heron was no longer anywhere to be found; in its place, a group of smaller white birds was flocking close to the river's surface.

Before long, a pedestrian bridge called the Izana Bridge came into view. It was an old structure, just wide enough for two people to squeeze past each other, and the wooden support pillars and hand-rails looked kind of suspect. I got close enough to get a good look, then went back to the path along the riverside.

"Hiratsuka?"

Someone was calling out for me.

"Hiratsukaaa!"

The voice was coming from about ten meters behind me on the same path along the river. I could make out someone waving at me.

Is that…?

It was a girl wearing the North Yomi uniform. Her long hair fluttered behind her as she jogged over to catch up with me.

It is…

Hazumi—Yuika Hazumi.

I remembered being in the same class with her when we were in Grade 1. We were in different classes in our second year, but this year we were going to be in Class 3 together. We'd hardly ever had a real conversation, but I knew her name and face well enough to recognize her, of course.

Nevertheless, I didn't stand there and wait for her. I started walking away alone.

Why is she here right now?

I thought her presence was a little fishy, but…well, it wasn't a question I wanted to waste time answering.

"Ah!" Hazumi caught up with me, making flustered noises. "Wait for me, Hiratsuka!"

I stopped when she bade me to wait. I mean, it wasn't like I was going to make a break for it.

Hazumi reached me before long. The boys in her class had propped her up as a "beauty" ever since Grade 1. Whether I agreed with their assessment or not, I couldn't deny that she had delicate, handsome features. She possessed a fairly mature presence for her age.

She was about the same height as I was, average for a guy my age. Her chest-length hair had a brownish tint, but I couldn't tell whether it had always been that way or if she'd dyed it.

"I'm talking to you, Hiratsuka!" Yuika Hazumi exclaimed, staring at me anxiously. "Why? Why did you keep on walking even after I called your name?"

Her words seemed somehow childlike, at odds with her typically grown-up demeanor. When I didn't respond, she tilted her head slightly and asked again, in an immature manner, "Hey, why are you ignoring me? I heard that you walk along the dry riverbed every morning super early."

Hmm? Is that true? She went to the trouble of finding out when I come here and followed me?

"Hey, Hiratsuka…"

"It's just a *habit*," I answered as indifferently as possible, without looking at her.

"Nothing is set in stone yet, but when we go to school today, if…?"

"If…?" I mumbled the word back at her.

"Ummm, I mean…" She paused for a second or two. "*…If there aren't enough desks and chairs in the classroom?*"

"That's right. At that point"—I turned to look at her—"we'll know, won't we?"

"Yeah." Hazumi nodded meekly but quickly put on a smile and turned to me. "So, look, I just thought I would say thanks ahead of time."

"And you came all the way out here to say it?"

"I did." Her cheeks were slightly red. She was probably flushed from running to catch up with me.

"That's… Well, I appreciate you making the effort," I replied.

"In either case, we'll find out soon, but *if it happens*, I just wanna say thanks in advance."

That was all the conversation I wanted to have with Hazumi at that moment. She seemed to have more she wanted to say, but it would have felt awkward to walk to school together or something, so—

"Well, see you around," I announced before turning to continue my trip down to the riverbank.

"Later," she replied.

Before I walked off, I paused to add one more thing. "Oh, and Hazumi? If you don't mind, from now on, would you please call me Sou? I don't really like being called by my last name."

7

I arrived at school at 8:45.

The opening ceremony was scheduled to start at nine.

There was a bulletin board hanging beside the entrance to Building A, the central edifice that housed the principal's office and all the staff rooms, where the class rosters for the new semester were posted. Printouts with all the class lists for each year were also being distributed. The staff had already conveyed the information about Grade 3 Class 3 to anyone it affected, but just in case, I checked to confirm that my name was indeed listed there. Then I headed for the gymnasium, where the ceremony was being held.

We got into rows, sorted by our new class assignments…and I did my best not to make eye contact with the other students. I avoided looking at Yagisawa, who had called me the night before, and everyone else who I would share a class with from now on. I had met them all for the first time at the "handover ceremony" and "strategy session" held back in March.

I didn't make eye contact and obviously didn't speak to anyone... Instead, I stood in the back of our row, mostly letting my mind drift away from the teachers making speeches up onstage, passing the time allotted for the ceremony in a daze. I was there in body, but not in spirit.

Once the opening ceremony was over, all the students headed for their classrooms. Grade 3 Class 3 was on the third floor of Building C.

By the time I stepped foot into the room, more than half of the other students were already inside. However, there was none of the usual racket that you would expect in such a situation, just a few small groups whispering to one another. Everyone else was silent...

Nothing was written on the blackboard. Even though it was the start of the new semester, one of the fluorescent lights in the ceiling was already flickering and failing... Beneath the erratic illumination, the orderly lines of desks and chairs seemed somehow ominous.

No one made a move to sit. No one set their bags down on the desks, either.

"Let's take our seats for now, everyone," called out one of the girls. She was articulate, with a crisp, sharp voice...

Could it be? Who does that voice belong to?

—Thud.

My heart gave a low reverberation, and the world went pitch-black for a split second. Then I remembered. *She* was one of the students who had been selected as a "countermeasures officer" at the "strategy session" in March...

"Sit in cardinal order according to what's written on the printout... Actually, you know what? Close is good enough, so let's all just take a seat somewhere, please."

At her urging, a few of the students obediently started to move. The reaction from most of them, however, was to uneasily tilt their heads and stare at one another.

But for some reason, a few shot glimpses in my direction. Yagisawa, who had been so sure that the "worst case" wouldn't come to pass, was one of them, along with several others. Casually glancing around, I could see that Hazumi, who I had encountered that morning by the river, was also peering at me. She looked like she wanted to say something.

Ignoring them all, I took up a position near the back of the classroom, beside the door.

Just in case it happens...

That's right. It would be dangerous for me to sit down with everyone else so soon.

At the moment, it wasn't yet clear whether I would need to conduct myself with that level of caution. It hadn't been established whether such strict *rules* were in place. But...

I'd made up my mind to take every precaution.

Eventually, our teacher arrived.

By that time, fewer than half of the students had taken their seats.

"Good morning, everyone," greeted our homeroom teacher, Ms. Kanbayashi. (Female. Approximately age forty. Main subject was science. Probably single.) She placed both hands on the lectern as she addressed us. "Well done making it through the opening ceremony. I'm sure you've all been feeling...apprehensive."

The tension in the room was palpable. It was perhaps even greater now than it had been when we'd met in March.

And it wasn't just us students. Naturally, our instructor was also anxious. Maybe even so strained that she wanted to make a break for it.

Pushing the bridge of her delicate metal-frame glasses back up her face with one finger, Ms. Kanbayashi surveyed her silent pupils.

"Anyway, all right, everyone, please have a seat. You can sit wherever you like."

She gave the same instructions as the countermeasures officer girl. The students who had been hesitating to sit down did as they were told. Only I refrained from moving, opting to remain standing near the door in the back of the room. I'd intended to stay that way until the end, and of course, my teacher grasped that as well.

And then the *situation quickly became clear*—once everyone except for me was seated.

Every desk and chair that had been set out in the classroom was occupied. The numbers were exact. In other words, there was no place for me, the sole person who remained standing, to sit. There was *one desk missing.*

"Ah..."

A quiet, trembling noise fell from Ms. Kanbayashi's lips as she stood at her podium. In response, many of the students made similar sounds...expressing a variety of emotions.

Yuika Hazumi was sitting behind the very last desk in the row closest to the windows. While everyone else stared straight ahead, pointedly avoiding looking in my direction, she alone turned my way.

I nodded silently at her.

Next, I looked toward Ms. Kanbayashi at the podium. She noticed my gaze and gave me a small nod while averting her eyes, so I left the classroom without saying anything. I had to fulfill the role that I had taken upon myself. *I would be the class "non-exister" this year.*

Yagisawa's optimistic observations had been too hopeful after all. Just because there had been two "off years" in a row didn't mean that it was *over.* Just because we had entered the twenty-first century didn't mean it was *over.* There would be no end to this.

The peculiar "phenomenon" that had beset this class since the death of Misaki twenty-nine years ago was happening again, twenty-nine years later...and so. Just as I had always suspected, *this year*—2001—was an *"on year."*

8

"Everyone had the best of intentions when they started dealing with it in the wrong way. Misaki's death, that is." I recalled the words that Mei Misaki had spoken when we'd met back in February. "Death is death, and they should have come to grips with it. If only they had accepted the truth... But instead..."

That was apparently what had started it all.

Misaki, *who was supposed to be dead*, appeared in the class's graduation photo. That was when the mysterious "phenomenon" had started happening to Grade 3 Class 3 of North Yomi Middle School. The incidents began the following year.

The first sign of trouble came in April, when there had been one too few desks in the classroom at the beginning of the new semester. The reason, they say, was because—

"There was an extra student in the class...and nobody knew who."

I'd known a bit about the "phenomenon" even before I entered middle school. I had heard about it from Uncle Teruya before his passing three years ago.

Still, back in February, when I was about to advance to the third grade at North Yomi, I'd felt the need to confirm everything all over again. That's why I'd enlisted the aid of the girl who had experienced an "on year" in her own Grade 3 Class 3—Mei Misaki.

"There's no way to know who the 'extra person' is. No matter how you investigate or who you ask...everything related to the class, from the roster to the records that the school and city hall keep, even the memories of people associated with the class...they're all *altered somehow, changed to agree that the new student belongs there.*"

Altered records.

Rewritten memories.

"There are 'on years' and 'off years' for the phenomenon...which means it's not guaranteed to happen every year. It's typically happened at least once every two years so far, but it's unclear whether there's any kind of regularity to it. Even if you end up in Class 3, there's no problem if it's an 'off year.' But if it happens to be an 'on year'—"

"The 'accidents' start happening, right?"

"Right. In the years when there's an 'extra person,' the class will suffer a series of unthinkable disasters. Every month, at least one person, up to many 'related individuals,' will succumb—they'll be pulled down into 'death.'"

Deaths by accident, illness, suicide, homicide...all sorts. According to the rules extrapolated from all the past incidents, the phenomenon could apparently affect "blood relatives two degrees of separation or closer to active members of the class." That meant the students themselves, plus their parents, siblings, and even grandparents.

I'd asked why having an "extra person" in the class induced these "accidents."

"Because the true identity of the 'extra person' is the 'casualty,'" Mei had answered.

Her explanation went like this:

"I suspect that the incident with Misaki twenty-nine years ago kicked it all off. Ever since, Grade 3 Class 3 at North Yomi has been somehow close to 'death.' I think the class attracts the 'casualties.'

"One result of the group's proximity to 'death' is that the 'casualties' are able to slip in unnoticed. You could also argue that the class gets closer to 'death' with each 'casualty' that appears.

"Because of that, it becomes *easy* for everyone connected to Grade 3 Class 3 to *die*, and 'death' swallows them up."

Formally, the school refused to officially recognize the existence of these strange "phenomena" and aberrant "accidents." There was probably no way that a public institution like a middle school could openly confront something so unscientific as a "curse." In the past, however, the administration had discreetly attempted a number of "countermeasures."

For example, they had tried changing the classrooms around. The thinking was that the "curse" was probably connected to the *physical location* of Grade 3 Class 3. Tragically, this hunch had ended in failure. The "phenomenon" and "accidents" occurred regardless of where Class 3 was placed.

In another instance, the staff tried renaming the classes from Class 1, Class 2, Class 3, and so on to Class A, Class B, Class C. This, too, had been a failure. The "phenomenon" and "accidents" still struck the students in Grade 3 Class C.

One year, they tried omitting Class 3 altogether and reconfigured the groups as Class 1, Class 2, Class 4, Class 5, and Class 6. But this resulted in tragedy as well. The "phenomenon" simply skipped over the missing Class 3 and afflicted Class 4 in its stead, and the "accidents" started anew...

After trying various approaches, a little over ten years ago, the school finally discovered an *effective "countermeasure."*

"To offset the 'extra person,' the class designates someone to serve as a 'non-exister.' By doing that, the room goes back to *the amount of people it should've had.* The numbers balance out, you see. It's like the 'nonexistent' neutralizes the harmful influence of the 'extra person,' who isn't originally supposed to be there."

That was how Mei had explained it.

"If all goes well, the 'accidents' won't start up, even during an 'on year.' There are actually a number of instances where this 'countermeasure' worked out successfully, and no one ended up dying. So ever since that was discovered, every year, Grade 3 Class 3…"

Class 3 started holding the aforementioned "strategy session" at the end of March. The meeting that Ms. Kanbayashi had facilitated—

First, the group elected at least one countermeasures officer. They would be in charge of dealing with any trouble surrounding the "phenomenon." Next, the class selected a candidate to shoulder the burden of being the "non-exister," in preparation for the possibility that it was an "on year"…

…The "non-exister."

Despite being a member of the class, they would be treated as if *they didn't exist.*

Their classmates, their homeroom teacher, and the rest of their instructors would ignore the selected individual all year long, as though they weren't even there. From the start of the first semester, up until graduation next spring.

At the meeting, the staff asked us who would undertake that important duty this year in case the worst came to pass.

If no one volunteered, the class would hold a discussion to decide, and if they still couldn't reach an agreement, they would draw lots. The specifics of how they determined the "non-exister" differed from year to year, but that was the basic selection process—

"I'll do it."

I had raised my hand without hesitation at the meeting.

"I'll take on the role of the 'non-exister.'"

34   yukito ayatsuji

Every person in the room had turned to me with eyes full of surprise, as well as a mix of other conflicting emotions.

"Are you sure?" Ms. Kanbayashi seemed shocked, too. "Is that really okay...?"

"Yes." I straightened up, aware that everyone was looking at me, and answered, "It's fine."

Starting in April, I would carry out my duty as the "non-exister" in our class for a year. If we could avoid any "accidents" by my doing so, then—

—Then in that case, I'm happy to do it. I'll never flinch or run from what needs doing.

I had made up my mind about this long ago, assuming the situation would arise.

It was no big deal to me. Considering my firsthand experience with "nonexistence" three years prior, I didn't mind playing the part of the "non-exister" now with everyone's consent and cooperation.

I can do this—I'd insisted to myself.

I can do this. I'll do it right. I can handle it.

...But still—

After I volunteered, there had been an unexpected development.

"Excuse me, teacher."

The person who spoke up was none other than one of the newly selected countermeasures officers, a female student named Etou. Making no attempt to conceal the anxiety and fear in her expression, she threw out a question, eyes shining darkly.

"I just wonder if that's enough. I mean, is that really the only 'countermeasure' we need to take?"

After further discussion, we decided that *we would make one major modification to our strategy this school year.*

Chapter 2
April II

1

After the opening ceremony, it was time for the first homeroom period with the new class. But as my title implied, it would be best if the "non-exister" *wasn't* around for it. With that in mind, I had made a timely exit.

There was still an issue weighing on my mind, but I convinced myself that if what I knew about her was true, she was sure to do a good job.

There's no need for me to follow her every move, and my starting to act all weird will only complicate things. I wonder if I should just go home for the day.

I felt a bit rudderless after leaving the classroom.

Everyone else was still in the middle of homeroom, so there wasn't a single soul wandering the school corridors—

Trying to shuffle along quietly, I made my way to the stairwell. I hadn't decided to go home.

How about I try going out on the roof—for some reason, that was what I set my mind on.

The steel door that led onto the roof was painted a cream color, and as usual, a piece of paper reading NO UNNECESSARY ACCESS had been stuck to it with masking tape. The half-hearted prohibition was scrawled out in red ink.

Something told me that few students actually heeded its injunction.

I opened the door, and on the other side of it, naturally, was no one. Just the dreary, filthy concrete roof of a three-story municipal building. The iron railing that wound around the edge was grimy as well, stained reddish-brown with rust.

I walked up to the railing overlooking the athletic fields and did some light stretching.

It was still partly cloudy, as it had been earlier that morning. When I looked up, I saw several ebon birds flying low across the sky.

Crows.

Kaah, kaaaahhh... As I listened to their cries, I recalled something—

Oh yeah...

There was that old superstition.

"If you hear the calling of crows on the roof, make sure to step back inside with your left foot when you reenter the building. If you don't, you'll soon meet misfortune."

It was a rumor that I had heard from somebody not long after starting school here, and there was another one like it.

"Once you start the third grade, be careful not to fall on the road up the hill behind the school's rear gate. If you do, you'll flunk your high school entrance exams."

Of course, I didn't put any stock in either jinx. They were the sort of thing you heard here and there, the so-called "Seven Mysteries of North Yomi." More people than I would have expected seemed to take them seriously, but to me, all these alleged mysteries seemed like common ghost stories.

To be honest, I'd already gotten more than my fill of unscientific, occult tales of "ghosts," "psychic phenomena," "curses," and the like three years ago, but—

There was only one exception: namely, the "phenomenon" affecting Grade 3 Class 3, which I was now facing head-on.

There's no way I can dismiss this as "unscientific" or "occult"...

The bell rang, signaling the end of class, and I started seeing the figures of students flow out of the school building below me. But I decided to stay up on the roof alone for a little while longer. I considered going to peek into the biology club room later but decided against it for today. It would be better to alert Shunsuke Kouda, the club president, of my situation by e-mail or phone call.

So then…

Just as I was considering my next move, the cell phone that I carried in the inner pocket of my uniform jacket started vibrating with a call.

"So it was an 'on year,' huh?"

The person who abruptly inquired this was none other than Shunsuke Kouda.

"Uh, yeah," I answered as indifferently as possible. "Word gets around fast."

"I just heard from Keisuke."

"Oh."

Keisuke was the name of his twin and younger brother. And this younger Kouda brother was a member of Grade 3 Class 3 this year.

Any information related to the phenomenon was supposed to have been kept secret from "outsiders," but I wasn't surprised that Keisuke had already spilled the beans to Shunsuke.

"What're you gonna do about club activities?" he asked me.

There was a problem with that. "I told you before, didn't I?" I responded. "Morishita is in Class 3, too."

"Ah, right."

There were three third-years in the biology club. Shunsuke and I were two, and the third was a boy named Morishita.

"Say that he came into the clubroom—I would have to act as the 'non-exister.' I wouldn't be able to say a word to anyone else there."

"But he's been, like, a ghost member for half a year. He doesn't ever show."

"Guess we'll have to wait and see for a little while."

"You think so? —Mm, you're right."

At that moment, I could almost see Shunsuke gripping his phone and blinking his small eyes behind his thick wire-rimmed glasses.

"Well anyway, swing by the clubroom sometime soon. There's some stuff I want to discuss with you."

"Sure thing."

"All right, see you soon. I wrote this in my e-mail yesterday, too, but I'm praying for your safety."

"Thanks."

We hung up, and as I put my phone back in my pocket, another crow cawed, high up in the sky.

Well then, which foot should I step on when I go back inside? Deliberating over the question, I turned to go.

2

I left the school building, then headed for the back gate, which was on the south side of the sports field. Though I didn't encounter any of my new classmates from Grade 3 Class 3 on the way, I'd gone a few paces outside the gate when—

"Hiratsuka."

Someone called my name, and I stopped in my tracks.

I immediately knew who was addressing me, since this was the second time she'd done that today.

That voice—

"Hiratsuka…um, I mean, Sou?"

It was Yuika Hazumi.

She had been standing by herself beside the barrier. She wore a slightly awkward smile and was tilting her head somewhat nervously.

"Ah, hey," I answered, also rather clumsily.

This should be okay. We're technically not on school grounds anymore.

With that in mind, I asked, "What's up? Why are you here?"

At this, Hazumi quickly walked up to me and answered, "I was waiting for you."

"…For me?"

"You were on the roof just a minute ago, weren't you?"

"Uh, yeah?"

"I could see you from down here. So I thought maybe I could meet you if I hung around a bit. You leave from this gate when you're going straight home, don't you, Sou?"

"Yeah." I nodded and looked her in the face.

She seemed surprised and cast her eyes down and to the side.

"...So?" I asked again. "What's up?"

"Well, I wanted to talk some things over with you. I mean, this is my first time dealing with something like this."

I'm sure that's true. You're probably anxious. I could sympathize.

"Here." Hazumi pulled something out of her bag and held it to me.

It was a single sheet of white paper, folded in half. I took it and opened it up.

"Ah...when did you get this?" I asked, still gazing down at my hands.

"Earlier, in homeroom," she replied. "The teacher left them on her podium for us to take home with us. So I grabbed one for you, too."

After I'd left early, Hazumi must have stayed behind until homeroom ended.

"I wonder if that's all right?" I asked, just to be sure. "No one's supposed to talk to me or say my name, so what about that?"

"Well, I didn't do either, so it's all right."

Her voice was bright, but she still had her head tilted uneasily.

"But," she continued, "it sure does feel weird when you get right down to it."

"I'm sure everyone else thinks the same," I responded. I took another look at the sheet of paper that I had taken from her.

It was a class roster for Grade 3 Class 3. Teachers always passed out these kinds of documents during homeroom at the start of the semester, but...

Even at a glance, I could see that this year's roster differed from that of a normal class. It listed students' full names, addresses, and phone numbers in order of student ID number. But in the middle of the list, there was a row that had been crossed out with double lines, redacted—

"A roster for an 'on year,' huh?"

They hadn't crossed out the row after printing it, either. It was clear that it had been obscured in the digital copy as well. Evidently, just blacking it out with a marker didn't cut it.

"The school prepared two versions in advance. The 'on year' version and the 'off year' version."

Yep, that sounds like Ms. Kanbayashi.

I had taken her science class back when I was a first-year.

To put it kindly, she's very serious and precise. To put it unkindly, she's boring and inflexible. But at least that means she's probably fit to handle being the homeroom teacher for Class 3 during an "on year."

"Ms. Kanbayashi's not my favorite," Hazumi continued, almost as though she was talking to herself. "She seems a little cold. I mean, you can't tell what she's feeling."

"I don't think she's a bad person, though. Actually, if she can be dispassionate like that, then I think…"

It's easier that way.

I can't really handle people who go through emotional highs and lows, foisting their feelings onto everyone around them. Even if those sentiments happen to be things like enthusiasm and positivity.

I glanced down at the sheet in my hands.

A class roster made for the 2001 school year, Grade 3 Class 3, in an "on year." The two redacted lines contained my full name, Sou Hiratsuka, along with my address and phone number. Deleting them was reasonable; that way, everyone in class would be sure about the identity of the "non-exister" from today until the graduation ceremony next March. And also—

There is another name on this class roster that has been redacted in the same manner, struck through with double lines—Yuika Hazumi.

3

"I wonder if that's enough?"

One of the students had raised this question at the "strategy session" last March.

"I mean, is that really the only 'countermeasure' we need to take?"

The girl named Etou voiced her opinion.

She'd brought up what had transpired three years earlier—during the 1998 school year. Her older *cousin* had been in Grade 3 Class 3 that year, and Etou had heard the story after the fact.

1998 had been an "on year," so they'd taken the "countermeasure" of designating a student as the "non-exister." Due to unforeseen circumstances, however, the strategy hadn't worked out, and the "accidents" started in full swing. Whereupon they added a new emergency "countermeasure"—namely, they'd tried *adding a second "non-exister."*

Nobody could say whether this "additional countermeasure" had actually succeeded or not, because even after designating a second "non-exister," various "accidents" continued to befall the class, and several more "related individuals" wound up losing their lives. And yet, the "accidents" ceased at the end of summer vacation, even though they'd been expected to continue until March of the following year. Perhaps the "additional countermeasure" of designating two "non-existers" had achieved some kind of effect in the end.

And so—that's what Etou had proposed during the meeting.

She suggested having two "non-existers" from the beginning of the year.

Previously, the "countermeasure" of a single "non-exister" had been enough to prevent the "accidents," provided everything went well. By that logic, it followed that implementing double the "countermeasures" would also double the chance that they would succeed.

Even if, for instance, one of the "non-existers" caved under the pressure and abandoned their role partway through the year (something that had apparently happened once before), as long as the second "non-exister" fulfilled their duties, the "accidents" would never start. It was effectively a form of "insurance."

"I mean, is that really the only 'countermeasure' we need to take?"

In short, the real meaning behind Etou's question was that *choosing just one* "non-exister" made her anxious, so she wanted the class to try taking *additional* "countermeasures" right from the beginning of the school year.

Ms. Kanbayashi had reacted by saying that the motion was "worth considering," then asked the students for their opinions. The students were just about equally divided between those in favor and those who shied away from responding. Strangely enough, not a single person had spoken up to oppose the idea, so—

A major change would be added to this year's "countermeasures"—there would be two "non-existers."

By that point, I had already volunteered to be the "first," but choosing the "second" hadn't been so easy... In the end, we decided it via a lottery using playing cards. The class counted out a number of cards equal to the number of students, making sure that one was a joker—the person who drew the wild card would be selected. Everyone, including the previously elected countermeasures officers, was required to participate in the lottery. And so—

The person who'd pulled the card to become the second "non-exister" was...Yuika Hazumi.

4

"You know, if I'm being honest, I still can't believe this is all happening..."

Hazumi and I chatted as we walked along the path up the hill beyond the back gate.

"Hmm?"

"I mean, I found you this morning to wish you good luck, in case the worst came to pass, but I never thought it would really..."

"Happen?"

"Yeah. But no matter how you slice it..."

"It's undeniable that there weren't enough desks and chairs, right?"

"I keep thinking that it must have been some kind of fluke, that there just happened to be too few."

"No way... If you don't believe in this stuff, then why did you accept being a 'non-exister'? It's certainly not going to be much fun."

"Well..." Hazumi struggled with her answer. "That's, um, because I drew the joker."

"If you really didn't want to do it, I think you could have put your foot down during the meeting."

"That would... I mean..." She left it there.

It wasn't that I didn't understand how she felt. Even after the "handover ceremony" and "strategy session" back in March, incredulity and disbelief were probably the most realistic reactions for a normal student. However—

"Are you going to be all right, Hazumi?" I inquired, putting some intensity in my voice. "We've got to take this seriously."

"Huh?"

"This *thing* with Grade 3 Class 3, it's not like the rest of the Seven Mysteries or the other legends around town. It's a real phenomenon that's been happening at this institution for the past twenty-eight years."

Hazumi stopped walking and nodded, confusion plain on her face. "Y-yeah." But then she immediately shook her head slightly and added, "I've heard that, but...but how do I say this? Without actually experiencing it myself—"

"If you wait for that, it'll be too late," I interrupted, my tone growing strict. "If our 'countermeasures' fail, and the 'accidents' start occurring...people will die. No, really. A *lot* of people will die."

"............"

"You know, I've heard the stories directly from people who actually went through it. So..."

Actually, I'd heard everything from Uncle Teruya, who'd passed away three years ago. Fourteen years earlier—in 1987, he was a member of Grade 3 Class 3 at North Yomi. That year had been an "on year," and many people had been "dragged into death" due to various "accidents." Teruya had watched it all happen...

"Capisce?" I stared straight into Hazumi's eyes and reminded her of the stakes. "We have to take this seriously. This isn't a game."

The look of confusion faded from her visage, replaced with a humble expression. Then she nodded again, slowly, and broke into a childlike smile the next moment.

"I understand. And I'll be all right. Let's do our best together, Sou."

5

After that, we continued on, chatting about this and that. It mostly consisted of me answering Hazumi's questions.

"They say that the 'extra person' who is added to our roster is already deceased; is that true?"

"Yeah. Moreover, that dead person, 'the casualty,' is apparently *one of the 'related individuals' who died in a prior 'accident.'*"

"So they're a ghost? Or a zombie? In that case, it seems like they would be easy to spot."

Although Hazumi must have heard the answer to this sort of question during the general explanation we'd all received at the "handover ceremony" in March, she didn't seem to have fully grasped the nuances from just that basic rundown. I had no choice but to go over it again.

"They're different from a ghost in that they have a physical body and different from a zombie in that they are truly *among the living.* It's as though they've been *resurrected.* By all appearances, they're no different than any other living thing. Even if they were to undergo a health exam…if a curious doctor inspected them, they could never tell the difference. And the 'casualty' themselves has absolutely no idea that they're already deceased."

"Even their families can't tell? If a kid who passed a long time ago rose from their grave, you would think they'd notice!"

"You're right on that front—but apparently, they can't tell."

"But there's so much evidence…"

"It's because all the records and memories related to that person are somehow altered or modified. Right up until the 'extra person' disappears after the graduation ceremony."

"…………"

"That's why nobody notices, and why we can't confirm their identity. It's a very peculiar 'phenomenon' in that way."

"Phenomenon?"

"Uh, yeah, phenomenon. It's not a 'curse' or 'spell,' you know. *It's a 'phenomenon' nobody's to blame for*—at least that seems to be the accepted theory."

That piece of information didn't come from Teruya—I'd only learned it after his death. Shortly after the incident, during summer three years ago, Mei Misaki and one of her classmates from Grade 3, Koichi Sakakibara, had explained this to me.

I'd heard the same thing from Mr. Chibiki, the head of the school's "secondary library," who'd concurred with that assessment when I visited him on Mei's suggestion. Mr. Chibiki, however, preferred to use the label of "supernatural natural phenomenon."

I was mulling over this sudden recollection when—

We emerged onto the path that led along the Yomiyama River.

The peaceful flow of the water was no different than it had been this morning. Moreover, the chill of the wind was somewhat more temperate than it had been earlier.

"That sheet we were looking at before…" Hazumi pointed at her backpack, which she had hanging from one shoulder. "The class roster already has the name of the 'casualty' on it, right?"

"It should," I replied.

"Hmm." She pouted slightly. "I still can't quite wrap my mind around it… Oh, but it's all right! I'll do my part to play the role of a 'non-exister.'"

It sounded like she was trying to put me in a good mood, to reassure me. She followed up with a short sigh.

"Tomorrow morning is the entrance ceremony, right? Second and third grades only have homeroom class, but what will you do, Sou?"

"Stay home."

"I guess they can't scold you for it, huh?"

"Ms. Kanbayashi goes without saying, and all the other teachers also know about the situation and are playing along, so…no."

"Yeah, it's kind of incredible."

I debated going to the riverbank, but I was with Hazumi, so I gave up on that idea. As we continued slowly down the path, I suggested, "How about we go over the rules again?"

"Rules?"

"The guidelines for 'non-existers.'"

"Ah, those!"

Hazumi put up her index finger and tapped it against the middle of her lips.

"Generally speaking, we need to avoid speaking to anyone in our class while we're at school. That includes Ms. Kanbayashi."

"That's right."

"But it's okay to talk with students from other classes."

"Yes."

All it took to avoid misfortune was for the students of Grade 3 Class 3 to agree on a "non-exister." This understanding hadn't changed since the school had first implemented the current set of "countermeasures."

"What we have to be careful about is courses with teachers other than Ms. Kanbayashi. It's fine for us to have normal contact with those instructors if we're away from our classroom, but not when they're actually teaching. That's because we'll be in the same place as our classmates. During that time, all the teachers know that they should, for instance, avoid making us read aloud by calling on the students in seat order."

"So they aren't allowed to address the 'non-existers' during instruction, right?" Hazumi asked.

"That's exactly it."

As far as I knew, the teachers had their own set of rules to follow, which differed from the guidelines that had been passed down to the students over the years.

"And we have to sit out during gym?"

"Well, we obviously can't participate in group sports like baseball or soccer. And sitting out would be preferable even for solo sports like running and swimming."

"Good thing I hate PE."

"That about does it for the basic rules when we're at school," I told her.

"Um…so that brings us to the next question. We can talk to other people in Class 3 once we leave the school grounds, right?"

"Honestly, I've heard some people say that we shouldn't ever speak to them, even outside of school, but apparently, the current rules allow it."

"It would be way too hard to keep that up all the time."

"The thing is—"

I hedged my last statement.

"—even if you're off campus, the 'non-existers' need to stay 'non-existers' during school events, like field trips or class outings. Making the right call in those situations can be tricky, so I think it's safer just to avoid any contact with Class 3 whenever possible, even outside of school. Especially on the way to and from campus. It pays to be cautious then."

"Seems like it'll be rough with all these things to keep in mind."

"Sure will… Ah, but becoming a 'non-exister' is totally different than being bullied and ignored in class, you know. Don't forget that, okay?"

"—Mm."

Hazumi nodded and gave another short sigh. Then she asked me something.

"Sou, why did you put your hand straight up during the 'strategy session' in March?"

"Oh, back then…"

I mulled it over for a second, then gave her a harmless, ineffectual answer.

"Well, it was because I thought I would be suited for the job."

"What made you think that?"

I tried to change the subject without addressing her follow-up question. "Since you're becoming a 'non-exister,' you'll have to deliberately act like no one else can see you. In a way, it's almost like becoming a ghost. Can you handle that?"

"—I'll do my best." Hazumi nodded and brushed down her hair, which was being thrown about by the wind. "I'm sure it would be impossible by myself, but as long as you're with me, Sou..."

"One more thing. This isn't limited just to us 'non-existers,' but we're supposed to keep the special circumstances of Grade 3 Class 3 a secret from outsiders. Even with family—you can't be irresponsible and confide in them."

"Sure. The teachers told us that at the meeting in March."

"They said that revealing too much invites disaster, right? It sounds like it's not totally prohibited, but I'm sure it's smart to follow the guidelines as best we can."

Hazumi said she understood, but I actually thought that we probably didn't need to be too concerned about this stipulation. Mei had said as much, too. She'd dismissed it as one of those bits of "common knowledge" that develop out of an overabundance of caution.

"Come to think of it, are you in any clubs?" I asked Hazumi, suddenly concerned.

"Not right now." She shook her head slightly. "But I was in the drama club until last year. I've already quit, though."

In that case, I don't need to worry. There's no chance she'll slip up and interact with a classmate during club activities.

Around that time, the Izana Bridge, the pedestrian bridge I had crossed that morning, came into view ahead—

"Oh, I almost forgot—" I realized I had forgotten to tell her something.

I guess we'd better talk it over now.

"Listen, Hazumi, there's one more thing..."

The moment I spoke up, however, she started making a statement of her own.

"You know, Sou, you..."

We both shut our mouths at once, locked in a kind of stalemate. The flock of birds that had settled on the river's surface flew off together, as if startled by something. As their movement caught my attention, Hazumi seized the moment and kept talking.

"Um, so, about your address that was on the class roster I gave you earlier..."

"My address…? Oh."

I immediately guessed what she wanted to bring up.

"There was a Tobii address written for you, and after that it said 'care of the Akazawas,' right? Um, is that the same Akazawa family that, well…"

"My address has been the same ever since first grade. You just noticed today?"

"Uh, yeah."

"You want to know why I'm in the 'care of the Akazawas'?"

"—Yeah."

"It's a little complicated," I confessed. "I've been staying at their place since I was in sixth grade of elementary school. The Hiratsuka family home is in Hinami… There were…a number of reasons I had to leave."

I didn't want to tell her all the details. Hazumi seemed like she still wanted to drill me on the subject, but I pretended like I didn't notice and turned away from her.

"So then, the Akazawas…"

We were just coming up on the bridge when she started working up to another question. I could get home by continuing to follow the path by the river, but I came to a halt and told her, "I'll leave you here today."

"Huh…?" she said, confused.

I looked away from her again. "I've got an errand to run over that way," I said, gazing across the bridge.

I was a bit concerned about the thing I'd forgotten to mention earlier, which I had been just about to tell her, but… *Well, I guess it's probably all right. I don't have to tell her right this second. I can bring it up to her tomorrow or after normal classes start.*

"Okay then. See you later."

I waved casually and strode across the bridge.

Hazumi stood there waving back at me, her hand low in front of her chest. Suddenly, a strong gust of wind tossed her long hair into her face, obscuring her expression the moment I turned back.

6

BLUE EYES EMPTY TO ALL, IN
THE TWILIGHT OF YOMI

The sign, with its cream-colored letters painted onto a black background, hadn't changed since my first visit three years ago, during autumn.

Standing out front of the first floor of a mixed-use building situated on a corner of the quiet residential neighborhood of Misaki and facing out toward the sloping street, the sign marked the entrance to a doll gallery with an eccentric name.

I hadn't been lying when I'd told Hazumi that I had something to do, but that "errand" was, well... Let's just say I didn't exactly have plans to meet up with someone or anything like that. I'd simply wanted to drop in at the gallery—

A short distance from the entrance was a large, elliptical display window. This showing area had been adorned with the same doll (the upper half of an eerily beautiful girl) since I'd first visited. But when I swung by last February, she was gone. Someone had paid her full price and taken her home.

I felt kind of lonely without her there, but I imagined that Kirika, the artist who'd made her, was probably overjoyed that her creations were selling. Although depending on the doll, she probably felt something like loneliness when they went, too.

Now there was nothing in the window where the eerie torso had once stood. It was still empty.

Today there was no CLOSED sign hanging up. Just as I was about to enter, I decided to stop for a second and make a call. From my cell phone to hers—to Mei Misaki.

There was no response.

Mei lived on the third floor of this building. The second floor, Studio M, belonged to the doll artist Kirika—Mei's mother.

She wasn't picking up. Evidently, the girl who hadn't hesitated to point at my phone and call it an "awful device" didn't have hers within reach at the moment. *Or maybe...*

I wasn't even sure whether Mei would be home at this hour, since she was in high school. But there was a reason I'd come all this way...I wanted to inform her of the situation facing this year's Grade 3 Class 3 straightaway. And I wanted her thoughts on the matter.

After deliberating over what to do for a moment, I pushed the doors open and went inside.

The doorbell tinkled with a dull chime.

It was the middle of the afternoon, but the inside of the gallery was wrapped in a dusky gloom. The instant I set foot inside, it felt like light had disappeared from the entire world.

"Welcome," came a familiar, muffled voice.

From across a long, thin table immediately to the left of the entry, behind an ancient cash register, sat an old woman with white hair, dressed in dark-gray clothes that almost blended into the gloom of the gallery.

Her glasses were fitted with dark-green lenses. Pinching the temple piece between her fingers, she stuck her neck out over the table and stared at me.

"Oh, it's Sou!"

Mei called this woman Grandma Amane. She was Mei's great-aunt on her mother's side, and she was always here, welcoming the customers.

"Hello," I greeted her quietly.

Grandma Amane moved her wrinkled mouth in a chewing motion. "Yes, hello. You've grown, haven't you, Sou?"

I feel like she says that every time I come here.

I'd first visited this gallery three years ago in October. Back then, I was still just an elementary school sixth-year, so I was much shorter—my voice hadn't even settled yet. So yes, it was true that I had grown.

"You're a friend to the shop, so you don't need to pay. Are you going to see the dolls?"

In front of the register was a small blackboard with the words

GALLERY ENTRY—¥500 written on it in yellow chalk. Student viewings were typically half price, but I'd gotten a "friend discount" ever since my first visit, so I'd never paid for entry.

"Um, actually—"

I did enjoy looking at the dolls and paintings on display. *But that's not why I came here today, so...*

"Did you come to see Mei?"

"Yes." I nodded intently. "I called her phone, but it didn't go through, so I came in. Is she at school?"

"She's upstairs," Grandma Amane told me. "But she can't see you today."

"Huh?" I reflexively tilted my head. "Why...?"

"She's been stuck in bed sick since the day before yesterday, you know."

Sick? Maybe the flu—I see.

"Seems like her fever hasn't gone down yet, either. I wouldn't want you to catch it, so I can't let you go upstairs, all right?"

"—I didn't know."

I glanced up at the gallery's dark ceiling and took a deep breath.

"Thank you very much. Um, well, please take care."

"She's young; you don't have to worry. I'll tell her you came by, Sou."

"Ah, sure. Please do, thanks."

I bowed politely and left the shop.

I'll give it a few days, then try to reach her again.

—Although...

If she's got the flu and a high fever, she must be in pretty rough shape. So why did she go out of her way to e-mail me last night? That thought began, ever so slightly, to unravel the thread of tension that had been stretched tight ever since that morning.

Stepping outside, I cast my gaze once again on the sign, BLUE EYES EMPTY TO ALL, IN THE TWILIGHT OF YOMI. The words *Blue Eyes Empty to All* naturally recalled the color of Mei Misaki's left iris, of her "doll's eye."

7

Even now, I still occasionally had the dreams.

They'd started before I came to town—when I'd still been living in my family home in Hinami. I would have terrifying visions, nightmares born from fragments of the experiences I was having at the time.

They were usually set at Lakeshore Manor near Lake Minazuki. Uncle Teruya had lived there alone while he was still alive—

Teruya's older sister—my mother, Tsukiho, in other words—changed her surname to Hiratsuka when she remarried ten years ago and had a daughter, Mirei, with her second husband—my step-father, in other words. Since I didn't fit into this new household, I would often go to stay at Lakeshore Manor. Uncle Teruya both worried about me and doted on me, treating me more like a little brother than a nephew, and filled me in on all sorts of things I hadn't known before. I loved him. He'd had a library filled with so many books that I couldn't have read them all even if I spent the rest of my life at his house. I'd loved spending time there by myself, too. However...

The spring of three years ago brought Uncle Teruya's sudden death. The night of his twenty-sixth birthday. Suicide. A long time coming. And—

The beginning of a series of unusual incidents.

My memories of that time were...bizarre. Any normal person would think I was delusional. Usually, I kept them shut away in a little box that I had created in a corner of my mind, but it wasn't like I could completely forget about them. And there were some memories that I could never completely contain, no matter how hard I tried. If I cracked open the box, even just a little, they would come rushing back in vivid detail.

And that little box was the source of my nightmares.

Sometimes, when I was sleeping, the seal on the container would break, and all the things that had been stuffed away would come spilling out...

...For example—

Once, I dreamed I was in the back garden of Lakeshore Manor, taking a knee in the dirt. Stretching out before me were rows and rows of crosses, made crudely out of scraps of wood (—like that scene from *Forbidden Games*, an old French movie...). One of these crosses was much newer and larger than the rest. I don't know what I was thinking, but I reached out to that cross with both hands. But when I grabbed the horizontal bar and tried to pull it out of the ground...suddenly—

The earth right in front of the cross split open, and a bloody human hand pushed its way out of the dirt. It was exactly...it was just like the famous shocking final scene from an old horror movie I had borrowed during my first year of middle school.

The hand that had emerged from the dirt grabbed me by the ankle.

I let out a shriek.

Then, one after the other, the rows of crosses burst from the ground and toppled over. The fallen objects proceeded to blacken, as though they had been scorched, before turning into ash and blowing away in the wind.

Giant crows appeared in the sky. Flapping their huge wings, they let out piercing shrieks, spitting up streams of dark blood. That very same fluid began to gush from my mouth as I continued to scream. The blood became rain, and the rain begat a flood. I struggled and sank, and there at the bottom of the deep sea of blood, I would finally awaken from the dream.

Or how about this one—

I would start out the dream in pitch-black. There wasn't even the slightest glimmer of light; it was literally total darkness... Then suddenly, I would notice a bad smell. The more aware of it I became, the worse the stench got...and as soon as I thought I couldn't stand it anymore, a meager light would fill the inky black. Then I would see it—

A corpse.

Somebody's dead body, resting on a filthy sofa.

Rotten skin. Rotten flesh. Rotten innards... Uncountable swarms of squirming insects.

This corpse is me—I would think as I stared at it.
I'm here, deceased.
I'm dead, and I've transformed into this ugly, disgusting thing. I—
I am the "casualty" after all. And it's not anyone else. I and I alone am the "casualty," the person who will send everyone to their doom. It's me. I'm the one…
Then, when I was at my wits' end and about to shriek—
Bang!
An intense noise would shake the entire world. The corpse would crumble and lose all its shape, as though it had been bludgeoned by an invisible ax. Together with the sofa, it would dissolve into a viscous black liquid and melt into the darkness. Then it would spread out around my feet and climb up my body, inching slowly from my legs toward my mouth…and just as I was about to let out a voiceless scream, I would awaken from the nightmare with a start.

Today, I'd also had one of these dreams.

After staying through dinner at the Akazawas' house, I'd gone back to my apartment and laid down on my bed, where I unfortunately dozed off. It was really just a few minutes, but during that short snooze…

A low rumbling sound came from somewhere.

I immediately realized that it was the vibration of my cell phone set to silent mode. That was probably what caused me to open my eyes.

As I sat up and reached for my phone, which I'd tossed on the desk, the buzz of the incoming call stopped. I checked my voice mail and saw that Yagisawa had tried to reach me.

Last night, he told me his phone was busted, but I guess he got it fixed already.

He'd left a message.

—*Heya, it's Yagisawa. Thanks for playing your role; it's a tough job. I think it's okay for me to contact you like this, as long as it's after school hours. My optimistic prediction may have been wrong, but let's do our best and try not to dwell on it. I'm sure it'll be fine. Right? Talk to you later.*

Hmm, as laid-back as ever, I see. I smiled knowingly but decided against calling him back.

Sure, it was after school, so I wouldn't be breaking the rules by reaching out to him now. But as I had gently reminded Hazumi, my "number two," it was best to avoid as much contact with our classmates as possible even when we weren't on campus.

If I tried keeping up with my friends like normal outside of school, then I might slip at some point when we were there... It would be all too easy for an accident like that to happen. That's how I saw it, anyway, so that would be my policy going forward.

Even under these circumstances, I wasn't going to return his call.

I wouldn't ignore everyone who rang me up or refuse to answer everyone who spoke to me, but I was at least going to actively avoid making contact.

—Yeah. That's probably best for the time being.

8

I got up to wash my face and looked at myself in the bathroom mirror.

It had been two years and seven months since I'd arrived in Yomiyama. I could see that my features had changed a lot in that time, but my face was still pale and small, and I looked kind of androgynous depending on the angle. My underlying complexion was still the same. And though my voice had definitely gotten lower, I still didn't have much facial hair growing in yet...

I washed my face with cold water to bring myself back to my senses after my nap. Just as I considered taking a full shower, I remembered that I had no soap or shampoo in my bathroom.

Come to think of it, I didn't even have a toothbrush and toothpaste at the sink. I'd forgotten to bring them when I moved. This morning, I had gone to the Akazawas' house and brushed my teeth while I was there, but I had yet again forgotten to bring any toiletries up to my apartment.

Maybe I can get them tomorrow.

I looked at the clock. It was past nine.

It's getting a little late, but…

I'm gonna go get them.

I'd made up my mind. As I left the apartment, I stuck my cell phone in my jacket pocket with my keys, thinking nothing of it.

But just as I was about to push the elevator call button in the lobby, an incoming call brought my phone to life.

Deliberately suppressing my excitement, I picked up with a short, "Yes?"

"Ah…Sou?"

A weak, hoarse voice answered me.

"Mei?"

I'd seen that it was her from the display, but I couldn't help confirming it regardless.

"Mei, is that you? Um…ah—"

As I searched for the right words, I heard her coughing on the other end.

"Are you all right? I heard you had the flu, so…"

"Grandma Amane told me you came by the gallery," she responded before coughing again for a while.

"Uh, are you…okay?"

"Sorry. My fever has come down a bit, but I'm still…"

"You should take it easy."

"Don't worry. I don't think I'm gonna die or anything."

What the…? Don't say it like that! It's bad luck!

"Why did you go out of your way to come visit? Was it what I think it was?" she asked.

I answered immediately. "That's right. Today, after the opening ceremony, we had homeroom, and—"

"It's an 'on year,' isn't it?"

"Yep."

"I see."

"And, um, I'm also this year's 'non-exister.'"

"So you went and did it, huh?"

When I'd visited her back in February, I'd revealed my intention to take the position if the worst occurred.

"I—" Unconsciously gripping the device in my hand ever tighter, I responded, "I can't run away from this responsibility, so…"

"Mm-hmm."

"Oh, and Mei? Actually, this year is a little…"

Just as I was about to tell her about the "additional countermeasure" of having two "non-existers," she burst into another coughing fit on the other end of the line. I trailed off and reconsidered.

"It seems like speaking is hard on you, so…I'll call you back later, after you're feeling better," I told her, then added, "but thanks for reaching out."

Mei had to be feeling pretty bad, because all she could manage was a hoarse "understood" before our conversation came to an end.

However—

No sooner had I hung up and put my phone back in my pocket with a sigh than the door to unit <E-1> by the elevator (the room I'd mentioned earlier that didn't have a nameplate) flung open.

9

It moved so suddenly that I leaped back, but there wasn't any particular reason to be surprised. This apartment also had someone living in it, and *she* just happened to be stepping out at the moment.

The woman who came out of <E-1> was someone I knew very well—

"Oh, Sou!" she said once she recognized me. "Perfect timing. Would you give me a hand?"

She was clutching garbage bags in both her hands. Three in total.

"Help me throw these out, please?"

"Huh…ah, s-sure."

She was dressed casually in a baggy blue sweatshirt and jeans, so it took me a second to place her, but that face and that voice…there was no doubt about it. That was *definitely her*.

We'd seen each other earlier that day, at school, in the Grade 3 Class 3 classroom. She was the girl who had instructed the students who were unsure about sitting down, *"Let's take our seats for now, everyone."* The girl who was serving as one of the countermeasures officers that year—

"My room was a total mess. I had so many things I didn't need," she told me, shoving one of the bags into my hands. "I promised I would take care of keeping the place clean, but…man, it turned into a dump before I knew it."

Although she was speaking casually, her voice was still energetic and articulate. "You're going to be living up here alone for a while, aren't you, Sou?"

"Yeah, I am. Probably until about June."

"Well, the main house isn't far, so I'm sure you won't want for anything." She zipped past me and pushed the elevator button. "You can come talk to me anytime you're having trouble, whether that's with everyday stuff or with what's going on in class…okay?"

"Uh, sure. Thanks."

We rode the elevator down together to the first floor. Then we tossed the garbage bags into the collection box for the apartment building, which was off to the side of the bicycle storage room entryway.

"Thanks for your help. See you around," she said, lightly brushing her hands together as she looked my way. "Going out now?"

"Yeah, just for a bit."

"Where to? Got some errands?"

"Uh, well…"

When I candidly answered that I was going to retrieve my toiletries, she responded, "Oh, well, you can use what I have at my place."

"Huh? But—"

"I've got extra soap and an extra toothbrush set. And you can use my shampoo, too."

"But…"

"It's already after nine. I bet they go to bed early over there."

"Ah…"

"Don't be shy. *We're cousins*, after all."

"—Mm."

The way we acting in the classroom and the way we were acting now—it was completely opposite. But that was appropriate, considering our relationship. The two of us were indeed related.

Until the Akazawas took me in three autumns ago, we'd never had the opportunity to meet. But ever since then, we'd spent a fair amount of time together, since we were both around the same age… though this was the first year we'd been in class together.

I wonder what I should call her during school? I pondered, but it was a little late for that.

I guess I should use her family name. Calling her by her first name seems somehow wrong, even though I do it all the time normally… Though as a "non-exister," I wasn't in a position to speak to her then anyway.

"How long have you been living in that room?" I asked as we rode the elevator back up.

She tilted her head to the side as she thought. "Um…since the summer of our second year, I think."

"Why? There's the penthouse upstairs."

"I've got my reasons. Plus, Mama and Papa usually give in to my selfish whims."

"Do you hate them or something?"

"No, nothing like that."

Her prim expression softened somewhat as she glanced at me out of the corner of her eye.

"Living in my own space is easier because I don't have to take anyone else into consideration. I mean, don't you think so, too, Sou?"

"Sure, I suppose."

"Besides, once I go to college or whatever, I'm going to kiss Yomiyama good-bye and start living alone. I'm kind of practicing for that while I'm still here…get it?"

College, huh?

I hadn't even had the chance to think about those kinds of future questions at all. Getting out of this mess was my primary concern.

I've got to make it there first…

When we got back to the fifth floor, she quickly rushed into unit <E-1> and brought out what I needed.

"Thanks," I replied as I accepted them, and then—

"Tomorrow's the entrance ceremony, but…are you even going?" she asked, her expression suddenly serious.

"I wasn't planning to," I answered.

She nodded, still wearing a grim expression. "Yeah, there aren't any classes yet, so not showing up is the right thing to do."

"Yeah."

"We're supposed to select the class reps and everything during tomorrow's homeroom, but I can fill you in later on what you need to know. After that, you can tell me if there's anything you think will be a problem. Of course, that's after classes are over and we come home, yeah? I'm sure it's really tough, but since you're a 'non-exister,' you've got to do it right…"

"I know. I'm fine," I snipped clearly, then stiffened my lip. "You won't catch me speaking to anyone at school. Not even to my dear cousin."

"Good luck. We all have to do our best."

"Yeah. All right, thanks for these. I'll bring the shampoo back later."

"Tomorrow's fine. Good night."

"Night."

I walked to the entrance of my apartment, then turned back toward the elevator. I could see her silhouette on the other side of the lobby, about to shut the door.

The lights that lined the corridor ceiling suddenly began to flicker. They stopped right away, only to be replaced by a low throbbing. The world went black, as if someone had turned out the lights. But an instant later, it ended, fast enough for me to forget it had ever happened.

I stood there staring at the now-closed entrance to room <E-1>. I turned over everything I knew about her in my mind.

She was my classmate in Grade 3 Class 3 at North Yomiyama Middle School, one of the countermeasures officers for this school year. *She's my cousin, and we're the same age.* In other words, she was the daughter of the second son of the Akazawa family, Natsuhiko, and his wife, Mayuko, who lived in the penthouse of this apartment building.

Her name was Izumi—Izumi Akazawa.

Chapter 3
April III

1

"Oh, Sou. What are you doing here?"

Just as I was setting out from the bicycle parking at the apartments, someone called to me. It was my aunt Mayuko, the other Mrs. Akazawa. The tension around her eyes reminded me of Izumi's expression the night before. She was staring at me from the porch off the front entrance of the building, making a slightly puzzled face.

"You're going to school now? By bicycle?"

It was 10:30 in the morning. Even though class was starting late today because of the entrance ceremony, it was still too late to be leaving. On top of that, I lived close enough to walk there, and the rules forbade commuting by bike anyway. Hence, it was only natural for Mayuko to be suspicious.

"Izumi left a long time ago. What's going on?"

"Oh, um…"

I mumbled some noncommittal noises from astride my bicycle.

After finishing breakfast at the Akazawa house, I'd gone back up to my room to kill some time and change out of my uniform and into my normal clothes. It should have been very obvious that I was not, in fact, heading to class at all.

"Today I'm a little, ummm…under the weather. Izumi is going to let the teachers know for me."

"Oh, you're not well?"

"Yeah, just a little... Oh, but I seem to be improving already, so I thought I might go to the bookstore or something."

"Oh?"

Despite her slight frown, Mayuko didn't ask me any more questions. Instead, she simply told me, "Be careful and have a good time," and smiled faintly.

"Um...would you mind keeping this a secret from Auntie Sayuri?"

"Hmm? Why?"

"I would feel bad about making her anxious. The main residence is going through a lot right now."

Hiromune Akazawa, the family patriarch who lived in the house with his oldest son and his wife, had been in poor health since the end of last year. Because of his situation, they were renovating the old house to make it more accessible. The construction work had also spurred my temporary move into the Freuden Tobii.

"You don't have to be that considerate..."

Mayuko stopped whatever she was about to say next, then glanced over her shoulder at the doors into the building.

"By the way, Sou?" She came up beside me and lowered her voice. "You're in the same class with Izumi this year, right?"

"Uh, yes."

"Is there some kind of, um, special problem going on there?"

"Ah..."

My hands, gripping the handles of my bike, were suddenly sweaty.

"Why...do you ask?"

"I can sort of...tell."

We weren't supposed to reveal too much about the situation at school, even to our families. That was one of the "rules," and I was sure that she—Izumi Akazawa—was faithfully upholding them. Nevertheless, Mayuko must have sensed that something was amiss in the way her daughter was speaking and behaving...right?

But unfortunately, I was in the same boat and also wasn't at liberty to talk about the situation. Not to Auntie Sayuri or Uncle Haruhiko, either. In fact, I hadn't said a word about the "phenomenon" or the "accidents" to them. To say nothing of the fact that I had to play the role of a "non-exister" in class as a "countermeasure" against it all... As far as I was concerned, I had no intention of speaking about any of that, even if it didn't risk inviting supernatural retaliation. The Akazawas weren't my real parents, so if I brought up the situation, it would inevitably make them even more anxious about me than they already were...

"There's not really anything going on," I answered, trying to feign impassivity. "Yesterday was just the opening ceremony anyway."

"Are you sure?" Mayuko asked, looking yet more concerned. "Listen, you probably haven't heard, Sou, but there have apparently been some pretty bad rumors going around about Grade 3 Class 3 at North Yomi for a long time."

Ah, I get it. She's been picking up on them.

"What kind of things have been getting around?" I tried to probe for more.

"How do I put it...? I heard that the class has a lot of dangerous accidents and incidents. And sure enough, three years ago, there were all sorts of..."

She put her palm to her forehead and pressed a thumb to her temple. After holding that pose in silence for a while, she finally shook her head slowly and lowered her hand.

"...Oh, I feel sort of strange. Sorry. Don't worry about me."

But a shadow of some terrible loneliness and sadness had fallen across her face.

"I'll keep quiet about today to Sayuri. But I don't want you to worry so much, okay? It's not good for you."

Mayuko smiled faintly again and ran a hand through her shoulder-length hair. It was shockingly white for her age—she was only in her mid-forties, so much younger than her sister-in-law Sayuri.

"You should come up to our place for a bite to eat sometimes. I'm sure that Natsuhiko and...Izumi would also be happy to see you. Okay?"

2

I wasn't riding my bike to school, and I wasn't headed for a bookstore, either—I was going to the library. Specifically, the public library in the nearby neighborhood of Romero, which sat on the grounds of a public park known as Daybreak Forest.

When I'd lived in Hinami, I had access to the library at Lakeshore Manor, so I never wanted for reading material. Not only had its shelves been lined with children's manga and novels, but I could get recommendations from Uncle Teruya or go digging on my own. Because of that, I'd ended up reading tons of books that were maybe a little too challenging for an elementary schooler. That's how I came to the hobby, and nothing much had changed since my move to Yomiyama.

I regularly frequented public libraries. When I'd first started middle school, I primarily made use of the school library, but it had become insufficient over time.

Today, as usual, I returned a number of volumes that I had borrowed and checked out a few new ones.

Now that the school entrance ceremony was complete, normal classes would begin the next day. Naturally, as a "non-exister," I couldn't talk to anyone if I attended, so I would be spending a lot of time alone. I figured it would be essential to go ahead and get some books I hadn't read.

My errand finished, I left my bike parked in front of the library and wandered through the park alone.

It was fine weather, more springlike than the day before, and there was no wind. The warm sunshine felt nice.

It was early afternoon on a weekday. Throughout the largely deserted park, I spotted elderly people sitting here and there on benches, their backs rounded. I could also see a few mothers taking walks with babies in colorful strollers…

I reflexively averted my eyes from the women pushing their strollers.

Whether I wanted to remember or not, looking at them made me recall the face of my own mother, Tsukiho, who lived far away from here…but I didn't pity myself or feel overly sentimental. Three summers ago, she had chosen to protect her present and future as "Mrs. Hiratsuka" by sending away the son who she feared could threaten that life. That was not difficult to understand.

I didn't think she was an awful mother. Rather, I now saw that she was a weak woman. I couldn't do anything about that. And so…

I wasn't particularly hurt by it.

I walked through the promenade in the center of Daybreak Forest Park, lined on both sides with splendid cherry trees in full bloom. When I emerged on the other end, I could make out Yumigaoka Mountain in the distance.

It was the highest point of the mountain ridge, which sat along the east side of town. Turning my gaze to an adjoining hill, I spied a familiar building—Yumigaoka Municipal Hospital.

The thin, wispy clouds floating against the background of a broad blue sky and the straight lines that made up the hospital building— the combination was kind of interesting.

I formed an imaginary viewfinder with my thumbs and forefingers, then snapped the imaginary shutter. Just then, cherry blossoms came twirling into the frame, fluttering down across the shot and grazing my lens.

I narrowed my eyes, stretched as hard as I could, and stared up at the sky high above me.

As long as I can spend my days like this… It was a peaceful, unblemished spring afternoon.

I wish this would go on forever.

Tomorrow, and the day after that, and the day after that, I'm not going to school. I bet that's probably the best way to make sure that the "countermeasures" take effect.

It's not much trouble for me to be alone. I'm sure that I have the most experience in that realm, more than any of my classmates. Yeah, I'll just stay like this…

The next moment, my cell phone began vibrating in my jacket pocket.

Who can that be? Yagisawa again? I guess class must be over for the day already.

I looked at the display, expecting something like that, and found myself unintentionally sucking in breath.

The name of the caller on the screen was "Tsukiho."

A call from her? Now?

I felt conflicted. In the end, I ignored this call from my mother.

—So you're a third-year already, Sou? Mirei is, too. A third-year in elementary school.

When I listened to my voice mail after she hung up, this was the message she had left:

—Sayuri said you're doing well. Ummm...oh, are you going to the clinic like you're supposed to? Uhhh...do you have enough spending money? If you need more, just tell me. I'd like to come visit if I have the opportunity, too...

Once every month or two, she called me like this, as if she had just remembered that I existed. Speaking timidly in a frail voice, her calls were always the same. And then at the end, she would always finish with the exact same line.

—I'm sorry, Sou.

Ah, you don't really have to... I don't want you to apologize.

Although I was only a fourteen-year-old junior high student, still a child in the world's eyes, I had a pretty clear picture of the sort of "grown-up problems" that she was facing. I'd been pretty upset back when she'd first sent me away from home, but now, more than two years later, I was no longer interested in blaming anyone. And yet—

"Man...forget this..."

As I stuck my cell phone back in my pocket, I glanced up again at the outline of the hospital on Yumigaoka.

The "clinic" that Tsukiho had mentioned was in that building— officially, the Yomiyama Municipal Hospital Psychoneurological Department. I'd been going there regularly for counseling ever since my arrival.

Come to think of it, this coming Saturday is my next appointment, I think.

I didn't dislike my attending physician, Dr. Usui. I even trusted him to a certain extent. But…recently, I hadn't exactly been feeling much of a need to go.

Maybe I'll make up an excuse and skip this time…

3

"Sounds like the renovations on the house are really going to get underway next week," I said. "I imagine they'll do most of the work during the day, when I'll be at school. So I feel kind of bad that your folks went out of their way to set me up with this apartment. They said it was important, considering I've got high school entrance exams coming up, but still, somehow I can't help but feel guilty…"

"Oh? I don't think you need to be that worried about it," Izumi replied.

"What do you mean?"

"The place is gonna be a mess during the construction. Plus, there's everything that's going on with Grandpa," Izumi explained.

"Well, that's—"

"He always was a stubborn guy, but he's getting harder and harder to please these days… Mama says so, too. And with his body in *that* bad of shape, it would be all sorts of difficult to live with him."

"That's… Well, yeah."

"And hey, having you take refuge up here for the time being is easier on Auntie Sayuri, too. It has to give her peace of mind."

"I wonder."

"This room was empty anyhow. And Mama was all for it."

That night, I was chatting with Izumi Akazawa.

After dinner, I'd gone back to my apartment, and then she showed up at my door a little after eight. She'd come to deliver a report on the state of Grade 3 Class 3 earlier that day.

Izumi was dressed casually, as she had been the night before, and stepped into my apartment without hesitation. Standing across from me at the living room table, she pushed a can of oolong tea into my hands.

"Delivery."

Then she set a sturdy paper bag that she'd brought with her on the table and plopped down in a chair.

"This is a complete set of your new textbooks. And I stuck your class schedule for the first semester in there, too."

When she told me that, I unconsciously let out a small noise of surprise. "Ah…"

It was the start of a new semester, so obviously the students would be receiving new textbooks. And since classes started the next day, there would be a schedule, too. And yet, all of these commonsense things had completely slipped my mind. I had been trying to conduct myself with as much composure as possible and without any mistakes, preoccupied with the special circumstances of our class.

"Thanks for going to the trouble." I thanked her earnestly.

Izumi answered with a short, "Sure!" and then immediately launched into her report. "After the entrance ceremony, we had a long homeroom just like every year and chose class reps and officers and stuff. A boy named Yagisawa and a girl named Tsugunaga got picked as the representatives."

"Yagisawa is a rep?"

Somehow, I wasn't expecting that.

With his long, unruly hair and round, tinted glasses, Yagisawa had quite an eccentric look for a middle schooler; he didn't seem like the class representative type at all. Indeed, during first and second year, not a single person had endorsed him for the position, and yet…why now?

It was a total enigma to me, but Izumi's explanation readily revealed the answer. "Yagisawa put himself in the running. And there weren't any opposing candidates or any objections to his eligibility."

But why did he volunteer in the first place? I'll have to unearth his real motives later.

"Let's see, and that girl, Tsugunaga, she's…"

"Tomoko Tsugunaga," Izumi clarified. "Is it your first time in the same class with her?"

"It is." I nodded.

"It's mine, too, but she's serious, speaks clearly, and seems attentive to small details... All in all, I think she's not a bad person to have in charge. She's the type I would want for countermeasures officer."

Izumi opened the pull top on the oolong tea she had brought for herself and took a huge swig.

"Yagisawa is a friend of yours, right, Sou?"

"I guess. We've been in the same class ever since our first year."

Also... I was about to continue, but I stopped myself this time. Somehow, I felt like explaining further would be a pain. The thought of it just bummed me out.

"The atmosphere in the classroom was tense and nervous, as you'd expect," Izumi told me, dropping the tone of her voice a little.

"Once I start attending tomorrow, I'm sure everyone will be even more anxious, huh?"

"I mean, it is everyone's first experience with this. It seems like there are still some students who just don't believe it or can't bring themselves to believe it's happening."

"I guess that's probably also unavoidable."

"But the thing is, in order for the 'countermeasures' to be successful, we need everyone's cooperation," Izumi said, eyes flashing. "They can choose to take stock in it or not, but we need to get everyone to be diligent about following the 'rules.'"

"How's Hazumi?" I asked, suddenly concerned. "Did she go to school today?"

"She wasn't in the classroom, no."

After responding, Izumi immediately continued. "But I saw her by the gate to campus on my way home."

"Hazumi?"

"Yeah. Apparently, she skipped the entrance ceremony and homeroom, then waited there until the end of class. She also picked up her textbooks from a friend who brought them out to her."

"Oh, really?"

"And it sounded like she stood there chatting with that friend about this and that for a while... She was outside the grounds, so it's not a violation of the guidelines."

"No, it sure isn't."

But considering the potential risks, it's probably not the most responsible course of action, either, I thought, anxious. From the way she was speaking, I could tell that Izumi also felt the same sense of danger.

"I spoke to her, too, you know, back there," Izumi told me.

"To Hazumi? About what?"

"About you, Sou."

"Me?"

"She asked to confirm that you hadn't gone to school today."

"Hmm?"

"That was the first time she and I had ever exchanged words, but the fact that she went out of her way to ask me must mean she thought I was someone who was close to you, right?"

"Probably."

Recalling the way Hazumi had been acting the day before, I nodded. "She saw that my address was listed 'in care of Akazawa' on the class roster and seemed pretty concerned about it."

"I explained everything to her. I told her we lived close by and were cousins. She also seemed worried about how you would get your textbooks, so I assured her that I would bring them to you."

As I sat there talking face-to-face with Izumi, I got the sense that we were more like siblings than cousins. And even though we were the same age, I had an overwhelming feeling that she was my older sister…but I'm sure that was thanks to her personality and disposition, along with the strange circumstances we'd found ourselves in.

Though not particularly headstrong, Izumi was a fast thinker, and she had the physical dexterity to match the quickness of her mind.

As for me, no matter how deliberately I endeavored to do things, they just didn't turn out how I wanted.

After that, my conversation with Izumi turned away from school issues and switched over to what was going on with the Akazawa family. From there, we circled around to the matter of my retreat to the new apartment.

"I know that you're always considering the needs of others, but you ought to let Auntie Sayuri and Uncle Haruhiko do a little bit more to take care of you."

Even with her telling me so directly, it wasn't like I could just cheer-fully agree. It was I who was most vividly aware of the *irregularity* of the events that had led to my stay with the Akazawa family, after all.

"Auntie and Uncle were really happy when you came to stay with them, you know. Mama told me."

But still...

"They were pleased? Why?"

"You know. Auntie and Uncle had two daughters, but both of them got married and left home as soon as they were grown. And they both moved really far away, too."

Of course. I had heard this story before.

The older daughter married an employee of a famous trading com-pany and, if I remembered correctly, was currently living in New York. Meanwhile, the younger daughter got together with a marine biologist she met in college, and they'd made their home in Okinawa.

"So you see." Izumi's gaze suddenly softened. "When the family settled on you coming here, they felt like they were getting a new son. Regardless of the circumstances that brought you here, they're really happy to have you."

"Is that...so...?"

Even with her explaining it to me, I still didn't think I could take it all seriously. Whether or not she knew my inner feelings, Izumi took another big swig of her oolong tea, then let out a little sigh.

"There's not much chance of any of the Akazawa children staying in this town or ever coming back, you know. Even me—if I go to col-lege, I'm thinking of moving to Tokyo."

I listened to her describe this to me in a slightly despondent tone of voice—and then I remembered something. Izumi had a brother who was much older than she was.

Come to think of it, he's also...

"Was it Germany, where your brother went? He's been there a long time, hasn't he?"

"Mm. Yeah." Izumi nodded, her expression becoming somewhat sullen this time. "He went to study abroad halfway through college and totally settled down there. He hardly ever comes back here. But despite how little he cares about us, Papa and Mama still think he's something special. I mean, just look at the name of these apartments."

"The apartments…you mean 'Freuden Tobii'?"

"It's German, 'Freuden.' It means 'happiness.'"

"Your brother named the building?"

"That's right."

"Ah, I see."

Just then, I remembered something and got up from the table. I went into the bathroom and retrieved the shampoo I had borrowed the night before.

"Thanks for this," I said. "I brought my own up today, so I won't need it again."

But at that moment, Izumi seemed preoccupied with something else.

"Oh, sure."

As she gave a half-hearted reply, she suddenly raised her right arm and pointed to the bookshelf along the wall.

"That's…" She was staring at the *thing* sitting on the center of one shelf. It was a photo in a simple wooden picture frame. "That picture…"

It was an old color photograph taken fourteen years ago, during the summer of 1987.

"The man pictured there, by any chance, would he be…Teruya Sakaki?"

"That's right," I answered, taking a deep breath. "He was my uncle on my mother's side. He died three years ago this spring, but…"

I wonder how much Izumi knows? I thought. *First of all, is she aware of why I had to leave the Hiratsukas and enter the care of the Akazawas three years ago? How much does she know about the series of incidents at Lakeshore Manor that caused all that…?*

"I've heard about Mr. Sakaki from Mama. That he was your mom's little brother and that you really looked up to him… She told me that he passed away three years ago, which really shocked you."

"Mm."

I slowly walked over to the bookshelf and picked up the picture in question.

The date in the corner of the photograph read: 8/3/1987.

Written on the frame was the caption: "The last summer of middle school!"

The image had probably been taken on the shore of Lake Minazuki. There were five boys and girls in the picture, and standing there smiling on the right side was Teruya, just fifteen at the time...

After what happened three years ago, I'd taken the picture from his library at Lakeshore Manor but hadn't wanted to keep it near me... So without warning, I sent it to her—to Mei Misaki. But before long, she returned it to me.

"You're really the one who should hang on to this," she'd insisted.

"This is Teruya," I remarked, pointing to the boy on the right as Izumi stared at the photograph. "The other four are his friends, and they were all in Grade 3 Class 3 at North Yomi that year."

"And that was...1987?"

I could tell that Izumi was surprised simply by the tone of voice in her response.

"1987 was an 'on year,' and they hadn't figured out an effective 'countermeasure' yet. So during summer break, they all escaped Yomiyama and went to the house in Hinami..."

I was pretty sure this was the first time I'd told this story to anyone other than Mei Misaki. I second-guessed myself but then concluded I was right—I hadn't even told Yagisawa in this much detail.

Realizing this, I observed Izumi's profile as she peered at the photo.

Her lips were drawn, frowning slightly. She was staring at the picture intensely, as though she were devouring it with her eyes. A faintly sweet-and-sour scent wafted from her soft hair, which was tied up in a ponytail. The same scent as the shampoo I'd borrowed.

"I've heard of the 'tragedy of '87,'" she told me, pulling her gaze away from the photo. "The Grade 3 Class 3 bus had an accident during their field trip, which resulted in a ton of casualties. Is that when Mr. Sakaki and his friends...?"

I nodded silently, then returned the frame to its place. Frankly, I just didn't want to talk about it anymore right now.

Izumi must have sensed how I was feeling, because she pulled away from my side without repeating her question. Placing both her hands on the table, she glanced around the small apartment.

Suddenly, she asked, "Isn't this place a little barren?"

"Ah? I guess it is."

"I think you should have at least a refrigerator and a TV."

"No, I don't need either."

Completely ignoring my response, she continued. "There's a mini fridge in my brother's room, so you can bring it down from upstairs. And I think there's an extra TV there, too."

"Wait, I said I don't—"

"You don't have to be shy, okay?"

"Hmm..."

"Also..."

The next thing Izumi laid her eyes on was the pile of books beside my PC on the table. I'd just borrowed all of them from the library that day.

"Mm-hmm. So you're a regular at the library in Daybreak Forest, huh?"

Sternly folding her arms across her chest, she brought her face close to the volumes and read their titles.

"If you like this type of book, there are a ton of them in my brother's room," she informed me, a slightly amused smile spreading across her lips. "Come look sometime. If there's anything you want to read, it'll be faster than getting it from the library."

"Oh, sure. But..."

"It's fine, it's fine. My brother almost never comes home anyway. It's totally cool for you to take whatever you want."

4

It was the morning of April 11, a Wednesday. Regular classes began that day.

I arrived at the standard start time, entered the classroom, and took my seat at the rearmost desk in the row closest to the hallway.

Yuika Hazumi, the other person assuming the role of "non-exister," was in the rearmost seat of the row closest to the window, which overlooked the school grounds.

The two positions had been assigned well in advance for the "non-existers." Moreover, there was something different about the desks and chairs in these two places—they were a different model than the others, both extremely old.

These pieces of furniture had been carried over from the Grade 3 Class 3 classroom on the second floor of the old school building, which was now referred to as "Building Zero." The desks and chairs for the "non-existers" needed to come from the old school building— this "rule" had been in effect ever since the implementation of the current "countermeasures." In accordance with this stipulation, the countermeasures officers had brought over two sets of furniture, one more than in a normal year.

The desks were all carved up. It was clear that they had been used by all sorts of students over dozens upon dozens of years. They were lined with traces of graffiti that had been scratched out and some that hadn't been fully erased... The desk's surface was also pitted here and there, which made it difficult to use without putting a desk pad under your paper first.

As a matter of course, I didn't say a single word to any of my classmates both before and after taking a seat, and I also tried not to make eye contact with them, either. Not with the students whose names I didn't quite know yet or Yagisawa, who I'd been close with ever since our first year, or even with Izumi, who I'd just seen earlier this morning in the entrance hall of our apartment building... I didn't look at anyone.

To completely transform into a "non-exister," I would have to conduct myself with a constant awareness that I was invisible to everyone around me.

I mulled over what I'd said to Hazumi the day before yesterday.

"To put it another way, you have to become sort of like a ghost yourself. Can you do that?"

I can do it, I thought. *It's something I can do, something I will do. But—*

A tinge of anxiety flashed across my mind.

What about her? How will Hazumi handle it?

Just before the teachers came in and the first-period Japanese language class started, I glanced over quickly at her window-side seat. She had an elbow on her desk and was looking up at the teacher's podium, but she must have sensed my gaze, for she suddenly turned toward me. Silently averting my eyes, I opened the textbook in my hands.

5

Morning classes ended without incident.

There was none of the usual "stand up, bow, sit down" routine. And when the teachers took attendance before the start of each class, they avoided calling role (so that they wouldn't speak the names of the "non-existers"). Likewise, they never called on the "non-existers" during class. All the teachers seemed to be fully cognizant of the situation.

During the breaks between classes, I passed the time reading a book I had brought with me.

Today I had John Dickson Carr's *The Hollow Man*, a very old mystery novel. I preferred books like this over the horror novels that Mei Misaki's friend Koichi Sakakibara had recommended to me.

Almost all novels in the horror genre tend to invoke supernatural fear and danger—the story focuses on some demon or monster, and ghosts are especially common. No matter how I tried to get into them, I seemed to have some kind of resistance against those themes.

That feeling extended to movies as well. When I was first starting middle school, I'd tried watching a few famous horror flicks, also at Koichi Sakakibara's recommendation. But they hadn't been a good match for me. It was very clear that I wasn't going to grow to love them like Koichi did. As with novels, I honestly just couldn't enjoy stories about demons and monsters and ghosts, no matter how often I reminded myself they were fictional.

I preferred mysteries. Especially classic detective tales, like those by John Carr, Agatha Christie, and Ellery Queen.

Because no matter how inexplicable or nightmarish the events that occurred between their pages, in the end, all those books' puzzles are solved through logic and reason. The world of the mystery novel is predicated on the principle that supernatural and unscientific beings like demons, monsters, and ghosts don't exist at all. I'm sure that my preference for these kinds of works came from some sort of rebellion or reaction against the strange world I'd confronted every day for years; they were like a coping mechanism.

Fourth period that day was science class with our homeroom teacher, Ms. Kanbayashi, and the atmosphere in the room during that hour seemed several degrees tenser than during any other course. I don't think it was my imagination. The teacher herself was a "member" of Grade 3 Class 3 and carried the risk of being struck by the "calamity" if the worst was to come to pass, so...

Ms. Kanbayashi was very thorough when it came to ignoring Hazumi and me, the "non-existers." From the time she entered the classroom until the time she left, she didn't even look our way once. When the bell rang, signaling the end of class, I saw a look of relief pass clearly across her face.

During lunch, I left the classroom alone and went up to the roof. I figured it was better to eat my lunch where none of my classmates was present. That had been my intention anyway, but as I settled down in a corner of the dreary rooftop and opened the lunch box that Auntie Sayuri had made for me...

"Ah, here you are!"

To my surprise, I heard a voice, and my hands came to a halt. The voice had come from none other than Hazumi.

"You're eating your lunch here, Sou? Can I join you?"

Whenever I had gotten anxious and looked over to check on her during morning classes, Hazumi had shot me a glance like she'd wanted to say something to me, so...that didn't seem like a good sign. I should have expected that she would approach me during our break.

Kaah...

Just then, a crow cawed somewhere.

I looked up at the sky, then brought my gaze back down but didn't direct it toward her. Instead, I silently shook my head right to left.

"Huh? Huh?"

She responded with surprise. Ignoring her, I stood up and hurriedly left the roof.

"Why...? Sou!"

Though I heard her words of confusion, I didn't turn around. I simply remarked, "Fifth period is PE, so I think I'll skip it and leave school."

I was speaking only to myself, but I think she overheard me.

6

"You could have mentioned that a little earlier!"

This time I met Hazumi's gaze straight on as I told her, "Even though we're both 'non-existers,' I don't think we can actually speak to each other normally at school."

It was the middle of fifth period—gym class. We were currently off campus, in a neighborhood of Yomiyama that was a several minutes' walk from the back gate.

Hazumi had followed me when I'd left school. Normally, leaving before classes were over was a violation of school rules, but as "non-existers," we got special treatment. Even if a teacher had discovered us, we wouldn't have been punished.

"Why is that?" Hazumi asked reluctantly. "It's fine, since we're both 'non-existers,' right? C'mon—we're a team. No one in class seems to mind, do they?"

"That's one way to look at it, but—" I narrowed my eyes and chose my next words slowly. "I can imagine an alternative."

"Which is?"

"I've got a hunch that we need to be strict about being 'non-existers,' okay? We don't know how it turned out three years ago when they tried adding another 'non-exister,' so…well, that's why I have my suspicions."

"……"

"Sure, both of us are on the same 'team' in the sense that we both bear the burden of the same duty, but does that mean we can acknowledge each other and act like we 'exist'? Don't you think that 'non-existers' should be invisible even to each other?"

"……"

Hazumi frowned and tilted her head.

"This is gonna get a little complicated, but think about it. 'Non-existers' shouldn't make their presence known to anyone, whether it's 'non-exister A' not existing to 'non-exister B' or the other way around. And they should act accordingly during school, right? At least that's what I think. So…"

I couldn't tell whether it was taking her a while to understand what I was saying or if it was taking her a while to react. Then, after several moments of silence: "No way…," she murmured. "But I came up there just to find you…"

Her voice was stiff, as was her expression.

She looks like she might burst into tears at any second… What am I supposed to do if she does? It's not like I said I hate her or something.

I knew I should have been clearer about this the other day.

Even as I lamented my oversight, I continued. "So you see, you shouldn't speak to me in school, and we should try to avoid doing things together while we're there. I think that's best—or at least, I think that's *safest*."

"……"

"So that means you need to act the part of the 'non-exister' on your own. I'm sure it will be difficult, but…you get it, right?"

Hazumi didn't answer me; she just rocked her head back and forth. It was an ambiguous movement, which didn't quite signify "yes" or "no."

I shifted my gaze to the flow of the Yomiyama River. Beneath the shade, the cherry blossoms on the trees lining the opposite bank looked sickly pale.

"Hey, Sou?" Hazumi opened her mouth to speak. "Listen, I—"

Interrupting whatever she was about to say, I announced, "I'm heading back to school," then turned on my heel. "The road ahead is long. And now that we've started down it, there's no going back."

Just as I was about to leave, I remembered something, stopped, then turned around. I suggested that we exchange cell phone numbers. That seemed to soften her expression a bit.

"If we have any problems or anything, we can contact each other," I told her, "but not during school."

This time, I didn't forget to add a warning.

7

"I spoke with Morishita yesterday," said Shunsuke Kouda as he took his glasses off and wiped dirt from the thick lenses. "I told him that we've missed him at biology club lately. It doesn't sound like he wants to quit. I didn't ask for specifics, but apparently, he's got something going on at home."

Morishita and I had been acquainted since our first year, as fellow members of the biology club. But come to think of it, I had never heard him speak about his family, what his parents did for work, or anything like that.

He doesn't talk about his home life—does he not want to? Well, that's the same for me, I guess.

"So that means that you don't have to worry about running into anyone from Class 3 there, you know. You can let loose about all the things you can't say during regular school hours."

"I don't really need a conversation buddy, though."

"Hold on now—don't say that!" Shunsuke put his glasses back on. "If you don't come, soon we'll be overrun with specimens."

He glanced around the room and grinned. Although he'd been joking, I forced my face into a sour expression and scowled back.

It was after school, and we were in the biology club room.

When sixth period ended, I'd gotten a text from him reading,

"Come to the clubroom." I'd understood that to mean that Morishita wasn't coming, at least for today—that's why Shunsuke was summoning me.

The North Yomi biology club used to borrow the cooking club's room, which was located in the specialty classrooms building (commonly referred to as Building T), once a week. It was a tiny group that barely kept up its activities. Several years ago, the biology club's new faculty adviser, Mr. Kuramochi, had pressured the school into securing it a new room. But considering that the group only had two or three members from each grade even now, nothing had changed about its "puny" status.

The new clubroom was on the first floor of Building Zero, the old school building. The second floor, which was lined with old classrooms, hadn't been used at all for a long time. Most of the structure was off-limits, but some sections of the first floor still saw use. There was the secondary library, where the aforementioned Mr. Chibiki worked, and the art room, plus some remaining percentage of rooms that had been allocated to various cultural clubs.

The current "master" of the biology club room was one Shunsuke Kouda.

Though he'd only become the head of the club this past April, in practice, he'd been its leader ever since the start of our second year. None of the upperclassmen had complained about that, and Mr. Kuramochi seemed to acknowledge his authority.

Shunsuke had a slender face and wore silver-rimmed glasses with thick lenses. He had a small build but was sturdier than you would expect.

On the other hand, his younger twin brother, Keisuke, who was in Class 3, didn't wear glasses and used contact lenses to correct his nearsightedness. And he was in the tennis club. I wondered why they were so different despite being twins, but when you examined their features, they really did resemble each other, so I was grateful to have the presence or absence of glasses to help me tell them apart.

"Is today your first time talking to someone at school, by any chance?" Shunsuke asked.

I nodded. *If you don't count my conversation with Hazumi during fifth period, that is,* I thought.

"Do you think you can keep it up day after day? Seems bad for your health."

"Nope, I'm fine in that respect," I replied.

"Even if it doesn't take a toll on your body, it can't be great for your mental well-being."

"I wonder..."

"I'm usually in here during lunch, so you can come hang out if you get lonely," Shunsuke insisted.

"Ah...okay."

"That said, I've heard the basics from Keisuke, but this problem with Class 3...just how serious is everyone about it?"

"One hundred percent serious."

"Keisuke seems about half convinced, though."

"We might not be able to change his feelings on it, but listen, it's real. This isn't some silly story like the Seven Mysteries or whatever. For the past twenty-eight years, a great number of 'related individuals' have actually died because of this thing. And unless our 'countermeasures' are effective, people will die every month this year, too."

"What an awful burden." He frowned. "And so you've taken on the responsibility of being the key to those 'countermeasures'?"

"Mm-hmm."

"Hmm. Well, if the worst happens to you, I'll scoop up your remains and put you with the rest of the specimens, okay, Sou?" joked Shunsuke as he gestured around the classroom.

The room was about half the usual size and was lined with all manner of tanks and cages. The adviser, Mr. Kuramochi, had limited North Yomiyama biology club activities to "breeding and observation." That translated to us keeping all sorts of creatures in these tanks and cages. From water fleas and flatworms to varieties of fish, amphibians, and reptiles. We also kept all sorts of bugs. As for mammals, we currently had two hamsters.

It was safe to say that Shunsuke was taking care of all of them basically on his own at the moment. There were ostensibly other students on duty for feeding and other tasks, but he would be alongside them without fail, helping out and giving instructions. He was this room's "master" in that sense, too.

"By the way, I've got some sad news. That's also why I called you down here," he remarked.

I cocked my head.

"The horrible truth is, little Woo has passed away."

"Huh, he did?"

"I think it happened this afternoon. He was still moving around during lunch."

"Woo" wasn't the name of a piglet or some giant monster from an old SFX drama. No, he was an axolotl (male, approximately four years old) that we had been keeping here. Axolotls were a variety of salamander that had been very popular for a while, which were also called wooper loopers in Japan. We hadn't been responsible for giving him such a basic name. Rather, one of the upperclassmen in the biology club who'd graduated last year had been keeping Woo at his house and left him with us as a "parting gift." At that point, the name had already stuck.

And today, Woo was dead. Though he didn't look any different than when we'd first come to take a peek at him during spring break.

"They say wooper loopers are supposed to live about five to eight years, so he passed a little early," Shunsuke remarked, staring at the tank by the window where we'd kept the axolotl. When I glanced over, I could see that it was already empty.

"What caused it?"

"Not sure. I don't think we made any mistakes in caring for him."

"Huh..."

"So then," Shunsuke continued, "I'm thinking of turning his remains into a transparent skeletal specimen. What do you think?"

You went out of your way to call me here and then ask that?

"I'm against it," I answered immediately.

"I knew you would say that. But it's rare to see a diaphanized wooper looper."

"Doesn't matter—I'm opposed."

"In that case, since I hear they're used for food in their original home, how about frying him up and letting everyone have a taste?"

"Absolutely not."

"Good grief!" Shunsuke grinned, throwing up his hands. "Guess I have no choice. I'll preserve the next one."

"I'll allow a fish."

I walked over to the empty tank, and Shunsuke pulled Woo's corpse out of the refrigerator. He was in a glass container, covered with plastic wrap.

Oh yeah. If you don't do this with animal corpses, they start to rot right away.

Woo was a beautiful golden specimen, about twenty centimeters long. Even in death, his round black eyes bore the same blank expression as always. Shunsuke held the container out to me wordlessly, and I accepted it with equal silence.

By no means were we on bad terms, but as members of the biology club, he and I had one major point of opposition: the question of what to do with animals that died in our care.

Shunsuke wanted to turn anything that expired into a transparent specimen, whether it was one of the hamsters, for example, or a rabbit or small bird, which we had none of at the moment. I was completely against the idea (though I didn't say anything about insects or fish) and wanted to bury the deceased in the ground.

I understood that his interests lay in furthering the study of biology, so it wasn't like I was constantly pushing my opinion on the matter, but...

For today, however, even if the deceased had been something like the Chinese red-headed centipede that we'd captured in this room last year, I probably wouldn't have felt like giving him the go-ahead. Rather than a matter of policy, this was mostly a question of mood. My opinion was colored by my current circumstances, since I was part of the class that was somehow "closer to death."

With Shunsuke accompanying me, I went out into the courtyard and walked around to the area beneath the window to the biology club classroom. There, with Mr. Kuramochi's permission, I had made a cemetery for certain creatures. Rows of modest wooden crosses marked the graves of the many tiny corpses we'd buried there so far.

I buried Woo's body in the ground and piled some small stones to mark the spot. I would have to make another grave marker and put it up soon.

I pressed my hands together lightly and prayed for his happiness in the next world.

Rest in peace. And—

Please don't get caught up in the "phenomenon" and return to this world, even if we mess up.

8

That day, I ended up walking home from school with Shunsuke Kouda.

I wanted to stop in at the secondary library and speak with Mr. Chibiki, but the door was locked and had a CLOSED sign hanging on it. Later, I would learn that he was on leave for the whole month of April, for "personal reasons," and that the secondary library was supposed to reopen in May.

As we headed for the school gate, we happened to run into Mr. Kuramochi, our club supervisor, and I greeted him right along with Shunsuke. We encountered Ms. Kanbayashi after that, but this time only Shunsuke gave a greeting. Since I "didn't exist" to my home-room teacher, I couldn't acknowledge her on school grounds.

As soon as we passed through the gate and were off campus, an unexpected person joined us.

"Sou! Good work today."

I'd known it was Izumi Akazawa as soon as I heard her voice. She seemed to have caught sight of us and run to catch up.

"Coming home from an activity?" I asked.

As she caught her breath, Izumi answered, "Yeah. We had a drama club meeting."

"Oh, you're in the drama club?"

"Yeah, though it feels like we're already giving way to the younger generation now that I'm a third-year."

Come to think of it, I feel like I also heard Hazumi mention that she was in the drama club last year.

"Um, and who's this with you?" Izumi asked, looking toward Shunsuke.

"Shunsuke Kouda. Member of Class 1 and head of the biology club. A real oddball."

I gave him a succinct introduction, then introduced Izumi to him as well.

"This is my cousin Izumi Akazawa. She's in Class 3 with me."

"Class 3?" Shunsuke rested a finger on the rim of his glasses. "But you're talking with her normally... Ah, is it okay because we're outside of school?"

I would have preferred not to have much contact with her on the way to and from school, but—on the other hand, I figured it was all right, because the person I was talking to was Izumi.

"Kouda...there's another boy named Kouda in Class 3, too, isn't there?" she asked.

This was the first time Izumi and Shunsuke had met, so she didn't know that he was a twin.

Once I explained the situation, her eyes went slightly wide. "Wow. It's really true—you do look alike when you take off your glasses."

"Yeah. My brother tells me all about the issues Class 3 is up against," Shunsuke admitted. "I've heard about the 'accidents' and the 'countermeasures' and all that. I actually know almost everything."

So when Shunsuke meets a girl for the first time, he gets weirdly uptight and awkward, huh?

Chuckling to myself about his change in demeanor, I turned to Izumi. "I called him an oddball, but he's really not a bad guy. You don't need to avoid him on the street or anything."

Izumi giggled, while Shunsuke turned a little red and glared at me.

Mm. I guess it's not bad to chitchat like this sometimes.

The three of us strolled down the road toward home while chatting about nothing in particular. It was a little past five o'clock, and the western sky was starting to turn faintly red.

And then, at the next intersection down, leading onto the main road, we stopped for a red light. When it changed to green, we began to step out into the pedestrian crosswalk. That's exactly when it happened.

A car came charging into the intersection—the driver had probably seen a yellow light and decided to speed up. A small truck that was entering the intersection from the left swerved to avoid it, its tires squealing, and dramatically spun out. The moment it did, there was a noise, a different sound than the engine and tires were making, a violent pop resembling an explosion.

The truck had been carrying a large stack of timber in its bed. The rope holding it in place must have snapped or come undone. That was the source of the noise.

I froze in surprise, and beside me, Izumi let out a sudden shriek.

"Whoa!" Shunsuke shouted.

The truck driver recognized the accident in progress and quickly applied the brakes, but it was already too late. He avoided tipping the truck over on its side, but dozens of heavy logs went tumbling out onto the road from the truck bed...

The lumber thundered and rolled through the crosswalk in front of us. If we'd stepped out into the street as soon as the light had changed, I don't know that we would have been able to safely avoid it. And if there had been any other cars in the intersection, it probably would have had much direr consequences.

"Damn! What a mess..."

The driver got down out of his cab and surveyed the disastrous scene in the intersection with a dumbstruck expression. Then he looked toward us. "Y'all okay?"

Of course, it was a complete coincidence that we'd happened to be there. For an instant, I felt a chill, but we hadn't really been involved, and no one had gotten hurt. Still...

Could this be...?

I couldn't have been the only one imagining the possibility. Izumi must have been as well, and Shunsuke probably was, too.

If we hadn't been taking the appropriate "countermeasures" at school, this incident surely would have ended in a terrible tragedy rather than a simple loss of cargo. Even the slightest change in the situation could have resulted in disaster. We might have been crushed by the falling logs or run over by the swerving truck—"death" would have probably "pulled" someone in.

That "someone" could have been Izumi or me, both members of Grade 3 Class 3. Although there's a good possibility it could have been Shunsuke, too. He had a "blood relation within two degrees" in his twin brother, Keisuke, who was in Class 3, so that meant the calamity could also affect him.

"We've got to be careful," Izumi stated, staring at my face as I sucked in deep breaths. "We have to make sure the 'accidents' don't start. We've got to be absolutely sure."

I met her look of concern with the steeliest expression I could muster and answered in a low voice, "Yes. This 'job' is certainly a heavy responsibility."

Chapter 4
April IV

1

Despite it still being early afternoon, the interior of "Blue Eyes Empty to All, in the Twilight of Yomi" was shrouded in its usual dusky gloom.

"Welcome."

Grandma Amane, waiting to greet customers as always, recognized my face. "Ah, Sou," she mumbled. "Mei's in the basement," she told me in her muffled voice. "You're a friend, so you don't need to pay."

The gallery was lined with lots of dolls, mainly the creations of Kirika, who had her studio on the second floor. Paintings dotted the walls, most of which Kirika had made as well.

Since my first visit to the gallery three years ago in autumn, some of the pieces on display had changed, but the overall spectacle was more or less the same. The standout pieces were ball-jointed dolls that looked like beautiful young girls, but there were also dolls that looked like androgynous young men and even some that weren't human—animals and half-beast people... The atmosphere was dark and slightly spooky. I'm sure that most people would hate it, but I'd always been attracted to spaces that seemed to sit in the "shadows" of the real world. I would have been drawn to this place even if Mei Misaki didn't live here.

The music flowing through the speakers never changed. It was usually classical pieces with a lot of strings, but sometimes I would catch a chanson or singing in Japanese. The underlying theme was quiet and dusky… It felt quite appropriate for a dolls' secret meeting place.

There were no visitors other than me.

MORE THIS WAY

A sign was posted on a wall in the back corner, small enough that it would be easy to overlook. The message was accompanied by an arrow symbol pointing diagonally downward, toward stairs leading to the basement level.

This space was narrower than the ground floor—it felt like a catacomb.

Plenty of dolls were *living* down here, too, but it was messier than upstairs. It was less of a display gallery and more of a storeroom. There were completed figures as well as what looked like works in progress, and all sorts of doll parts were sitting everywhere—heads, torsos, limbs, etc. And sitting in a chair beside the round black table that had been placed in the center of the room was—

Mei Misaki.

"It's been a while, Sou," she said, getting up from her chair. "Sorry about last time."

"How are you feeling?"

"Fine."

Though her voice was still a little hoarse, her fleeting smile seemed genuine.

She was wearing a simple ivory shirt and a black skirt. Vivid crimson embroidery decorated the shirt around the base of her neck.

Just then, the music playing throughout the gallery switched to a new song, Fauré's "Sicilienne." After a short piano prelude, the main tune came out on a cello.

As I stepped smoothly into the room, Mei also walked forward toward me. We stopped about a meter apart and stood facing each other for a moment.

Three summers ago, I had been shorter than she was, but now it was the opposite. Mei was as petite and dainty as she had been three years earlier, and I didn't think she'd gotten any taller, either.

Her black hair was cut in a shaggy, short bob. She had pale, bloodless skin like white wax. Recalling our previous encounters on the beach in the shadow of the Raimizaki Lighthouse years ago, it occurred to me that Mei didn't seem to have changed in the slightest. Somehow, it was as if she, and she alone, existed out of time—

That day, her left eye had been covered by a white eye patch. And today, she looked exactly like the image that was burned into my memory.

This took me by surprise; over the past two years or so, I'd hardly ever seen her with the eye patch that she used to wear.

"Why's your eye covered?" I asked.

"Just because," Mei answered, her smile quickly vanishing.

2

It was Sunday, April 15, 2:30 in the afternoon.

The day before, Mei had sent an e-mail suggesting that we meet here around this time.

"I'm worried about certain things," she wrote. "In situations like these, it's probably best to meet up and hear what I have to say in person."

"Of course, as long as you're feeling all right," was what I'd responded with. A lot was weighing on my mind, too, so I wanted to hear what she had to say…

"Sou, this place—this basement room, you don't mind it, do you?" Mei asked, lightly stroking her eye patch. When I answered in the negative, she smiled faintly, then pointed to an upholstered red armchair near the round table. "All right, you can sit there."

There was a single paperback book covered with a dark-blue book cover on the table. Mei must have been reading before my arrival. Next to it was a white cell phone, which seemed to my eyes like something strange and foreign in that moment, something that did not belong in this room.

According to Mei, the dolls were all "empty."

Their bodies and minds were hollow; they possessed the kind of emptiness that led to "death"... She told me that they were always trying to fill the cavities inside them with something.

That's why, she'd claimed, when you gather a bunch of dolls in a space like this, people who step into it often feel as though *something is being sucked out of them,* as if all sorts of things are being pulled from inside them.

That's why, in her words, *"Sakakibara always seemed bothered by this place, no matter how often he came here. He told me that he had gotten used to it, but I could always tell...you know?"*

She'd never once gotten that sense from me, however. On the contrary, I was at ease down here—or maybe it was more accurate to say that I'd been much less comfortable when Misaki had invited me to her residence on the third floor of the building. I hadn't been able to settle down the whole time I'd been up there.

I thought that was probably—probably because I had a lot in common with the dolls. There was nothing inside me to be sucked out. I was "empty" just like them. Because of that, we probably existed in a comfortable equilibrium...

"One week has passed since the start of first semester," Mei said abruptly from the chair across from the round table where she sat. "How is it? How's the class?"

"Um..." I didn't immediately answer as I tried to find the right words. "I think it's going pretty well for now? Everyone's kind of awkward and on edge, but...well, it's all calm so far."

"And how are you feeling, having accepted the duty of a 'non-exister'?"

"How am I feeling?"

"Are you lonely? Is it starting to get to you?"

"Ah, no, I'm totally fine."

There was no falsehood in my answer.

"But," I continued, "there is one issue that's worrying me a little. So, um, I wanted to ask you about something."

"Ask me?" Mei slowly narrowed her right eye. "About what?"

"About what happened three years ago...to the Class 3 of 1998. Actually, I wanted to ask you about it much earlier. But I couldn't find a good time. And I thought it would be best to meet and talk about it in person, not over e-mail."

Three years ago—

Mei Misaki had been a member of Grade 3 Class 3 at North Yomi. So had Koichi Sakakibara, who'd come to Yomiyama for just a single year, his third year of middle school. During that time, the two of them experienced the "phenomenon" firsthand and witnessed the "accidents" as they started. While on summer break, Mei had gone to visit Lakeshore Manor in Hinami where Uncle Teruya lived, thinking she could get some useful information out of him, since he'd experienced the same "phenomenon" in 1987's Grade 3 Class 3.

Mei had actually taken on the role of the "non-exister" as part of the "countermeasures" for 1998... That was the sliver of the story that I'd heard so far. But I didn't know anything beyond that.

Mei had never seemed inclined to reveal any more details to me than that. She didn't seem keen on talking about it, so I'd figured I shouldn't try to press her on it...

"...So you've got two 'non-existers' this year?" she asked.

As I explained how the "countermeasures" for this school year had turned out *like that*, Mei lowered her gaze to the table and mumbled, "We were in a similar situation three years ago; that's true. And come to think of it, I believe we also had a girl named Etou in our class."

"You were a 'non-exister,' right, Mei? But the 'calamity' started due to unforeseen circumstances, so you added additional 'countermeasures' in the emergency...is that correct?"

"That's right. The 'countermeasure' failed that year. So another 'non-exister' was added—Sakakibara."

"Sakakibara?"

"You didn't hear about it from him?"

"No."

Because he—Koichi Sakakibara—had, much like Mei, seemed very reluctant to talk about anything surrounding the "phenomenon" from three years back in any detail.

"I see." Mei slowly blinked her eye. "But you see, even that ultimately didn't work. The 'accidents' didn't let up, and just before summer vacation, our homeroom teacher died in an awful way, right there in the classroom…"

She let out a sigh and shook her head slowly. My heart ached a little. It obviously made sense that she wouldn't want to keep revisiting that affair.

"That's why," Mei continued, staring into my eyes, "I don't think there's much point to selecting two 'non-existers' as a 'countermeasure.'"

After she said that, she tilted her head slightly. "Hmm, but…well, there isn't any precedent for having two 'non-existers' from the start of first semester, so I guess we shouldn't make any assumptions."

"So why did the 'accidents' stop three years ago, then? I've heard that you all stayed together as a class during a trip in August and that some terrible incident took place while you were there, but…from September on, no one died, right?"

"Ah, about that—"

She bit her tongue and shook her head more forcefully than she had before.

Is she trying to indicate that she doesn't want to talk about it? How many times have I tried asking this question before? But whenever I do, she always acts the same way.

"Have you asked Mr. Chibiki? About his opinion on this year's 'countermeasures'?" Mei inquired.

This time, it was I who shook my head.

"He's away on leave for a while. The secondary library is apparently opening in May."

"Oh, really? I'm sure he's exhausted."

Mei sighed again, and then we heard a muffled voice from the stairwell. It was Grandma Amane.

"I made tea. Come on up here, the both of you."

3

The CD that was playing had looped, so the sound of "Sicilienne" was once again filling the shop. We were drinking hot green tea that Grandma Amane had set out for us after we relocated to the sofa on the first floor. The drink was tastier than I expected. Before I knew it, I found my surprisingly frigid body steadily warming up.

"So what are these 'things' you're worried about? You mentioned something earlier," Mei said abruptly. "Hazumi is the other one, the extra 'non-exister'?"

She was exactly right. Mei's insight was just as sharp as it had been three summers ago.

"She...how do I put this...she seems a little unreliable."

"How so?"

"Uhhh..."

I couldn't find a good way of putting it in the moment, so I briefly changed the subject.

"Mei, what was it like when you were a 'non-exister'?"

"Huh?"

"You asked me the same thing earlier, but...was it lonely? Did it get to you?"

She answered me flatly. "No, nothing like that. Just like you, I was fine. I accepted the role because I thought I would probably be okay with it."

"Ah...but—"

"I've always liked being alone, so it was pretty easy, actually."

"And did you only have to follow the guidelines for 'non-existers' during school?"

"That was the rule, apparently." Mei wrapped her cup in both hands and slurped up a mouthful of tea. "But I spent most of my time outside of class as a 'non-exister,' too. It was simpler like that and easier to keep straight. I didn't have any close friends in my class anyway," she said, smiling faintly. She really didn't seem bothered by it.

"What about Sakakibara?" I asked without thinking. "Weren't you friends with him?"

"He was… Yes. We had kind of a special situation."

Mei smiled faintly again. At the word *special*, I felt a momentary pang in my chest that I couldn't quite put my finger on, but I kept quiet and nodded.

"How about you, Sou?" Mei asked me. "Do you switch between school and the rest of your life without issue?"

"Switch…? Yeah, I guess so. I'm trying to do a good job one way or another, but it sure is a pain… I feel like there's a chance I might get confused and do something careless. So I'm trying not to have too much contact with my classmates, even outside of school."

"Do you have any good friends in your class?"

"I'm not like you," I answered deliberately. I meant it as a joke.

"Hmm. I see," she responded, staring me directly in the face as she folded her arms gently across her chest. "Sou, you've totally grown up, haven't you? In these two and a half years since coming to Yomiyama."

"Ah…no, I don't—"

Grown up? I guess I have, maybe?

Unlike before, I was doing okay going to school and interacting with other people while I was there. I even had a number of friends, and things were going pretty well with the people in the Akazawa household.

But can this really be called "growth"?

My sense was that my core personhood hadn't really changed much. That feeling was especially strong when I was chatting with Mei like this.

I had overtaken her in height these past three years, but that was only an outward difference, and internally I was the same as ever… When we'd met, Mei had been both taller and more mature than I was and had seemed more thoughtful about the future. That dynamic hadn't changed much now. So certainly, I was…

"I don't think you need to worry too much about Hazumi—about the 'second non-exister.'" Whether she knew what I was thinking or not, Mei finally spoke. "Not even if, for instance, she started to hate the idea of 'not existing' and eventually decided to abandon the role."

"Not even then?"

"I think it'll be all right."

"Will it?"

"As long as you at least maintain your role as a 'non-exister,' it will."

She pressed her lips together and stroked her eye patch in a diagonal motion with the middle finger of her left hand.

"By designating someone as the 'non-exister,' we can account for a 'casualty' appearing in the class and keep the roster at its original number. That way, balance is maintained. That's the original meaning of the 'countermeasures'—they're a *charm*. As long as you do your job, the class should still be protected from 'accidents.'"

"Right."

I nodded meekly.

As long as Mei thinks it's all right.

Yeah, if she says so, it will definitely be all right. On that summer day three years ago, she swooped in and rescued me from the chaotic situation I was stuck in. The things she says are always correct. She's been right before. So she must be this time, too...

"However," Mei continued, "once Hazumi abandons her role, she will revert to 'existing.' If that happens, you'll have to be diligent about playing the role of the 'non-exister' around her as well. You should be careful about that."

"Yes."

Although we were fellow "non-existers" at the moment, I'd still decided to make it a policy not to interact with her during school.

Seems like my hunch wasn't that far off the mark.

Just then, a tune that was in a totally different register than the music playing throughout the gallery rang out.

"Ah..." Mei let loose a yelp. Flustered in a way that I had rarely seen, she stretched a hand out toward the cell phone that was sitting atop her paperback on the edge of the table.

Her ringtone?

She glanced at the display.

"Sorry, just a second...," she told me, standing up from the sofa, putting the phone to her ear, and answering. "Yes?"

Without a moment's hesitation, she sped toward the door and stepped outside. I watched her go.

"Do you need some more tea?" Grandma Amane asked me.

"Oh, I'm fine. Thank you, it was delicious."

I wonder who called her?

A high school friend? Or maybe Kirika?

Now that I thought about it, I realized that I didn't really know anything that had happened in Mei's life after she'd graduated middle school and started at a public high school. Aside from the fact that she was still in the art club anyway. I didn't know what kind of friends she had or if she had a "special someone" like a boyfriend...nothing.

When she came back inside after two or three minutes, Mei apologized again, then sat back down on the sofa. I tried to catch a glimpse of her expression, but it looked to me like nothing had really changed from earlier.

"You're currently living alone, right, Sou?" she asked, placing the cell phone back on top of the book where it had been before.

"Uh, yes." I was a little flustered, but I explained, "I am, but the Akazawa house is right next door, and I'm relying on my aunt for meals and laundry just like I always have."

"And the place you're living also belongs to the Akazawas?"

"Natsuhiko...the second son owns the apartment building, and they just so happened to have a room open, so..."

"Hmm..." Mei mumbled quietly, "Akazawa, huh...?" She tapped her forehead with a fingertip and tilted her head, but soon she looked back at me and asked, "Could I come and visit sometime soon?"

"Huh?" I was getting increasingly anxious. "Ummm, well..."

"You have that doll that Sakaki used to have, don't you?"

"Uh, yeah."

"I want to see that, too. Okay?"

As I was struggling to give her a clear "yes" or "no" answer...

"We'd better be wrapping it up for today," Mei announced, standing. "If anything happens, I'll e-mail you. Or I'll call if it's urgent."

"Okay. Um, Mei?" Suddenly, I got the urge to confirm something.

"What?"

"Do you still hate cell phones, like you used to?"

"Mm…" I glanced down at the *thing* on the table as she answered, "Yes, I do still think they're awful devices."

After that, just as I was leaving—

The moment I opened the door and stepped outside alone…I turned to look behind me. In the dusky, gloomy gallery, Mei was standing beside the sofa where she had been seated, watching me leave. And what's more—

With her left hand, she slowly removed the eye patch covering her left eye. I tried to determine what color it was beneath the patch. But I couldn't make it out in the low light.

4

"Hey, Sou!"

A familiar greeting from the mouth of a familiar guy.

"I just couldn't seem to get a hold of you, so I decided to barge in."

It was Nobuyuki Yagisawa.

He was about a head taller than I was, with a lanky build. He was wearing bleached, distressed jeans and a red hoodie, and his hair was as disheveled as always. The whole getup made him look pretty shady, especially with his round, lightly tinted glasses. That was generally how I would describe him, actually—a very suspicious-looking middle schooler.

Apparently, he was obsessed with fashion, but I just didn't get it, even after he explained it to me. Personally, I thought that if he ditched the lenses, styled his hair normally, and maybe shaved the scraggly tuft growing out of his chin, he would be a pretty conventionally attractive guy.

After leaving the gallery in Misaki, I'd dropped by the bookstore for a little while before returning to the Freuden Tobii. I'd just put my bike back in storage and stepped into the building's entrance hall when Yagisawa had approached me.

"You came out here just to visit me?" I asked incredulously.

"Well, yeah."

It took twenty or thirty minutes on the bus to get here from where he lived. I wondered if he'd had something else to do if I wasn't home, seeing as he'd come late on a Sunday without prior notice.

"Okay, come on in!"

A voice crackled over the intercom set beside the auto-locking inner doors.

Hmm? That voice...

"I asked Akazawa to let me in," Yagisawa explained. "I called her and asked if you were here. And then she went and looked in your room... You seemed to be out, but she said that if you weren't back by the time I got here, you probably wouldn't be gone too much later and that I could wait for you. She said she could give me a place to wait."

"Give you a place to wait..."

I guess that means in Izumi's room?

I didn't know that she and Yagisawa were such close friends. Well, it's none of my business, is it?

"Sou just got home," he announced to the intercom.

Izumi responded, "Ah, okay then..."

"All right," I jumped in. "Since you came all the way out here, want to come up?"

"Yeah," Yagisawa answered, stroking his sparse goatee as he broke into an innocent smile.

5

"Must be nice, living in a room like this all by yourself," Yagisawa remarked, looking around at my empty one-bedroom after taking the seat I offered him at the table. "You said that Mr. Akazawa owns the whole apartment building?"

"Yeah. The family home where I've been staying is being renovated— they started this month. So they're letting me live here while that's happening."

"Must be nice," he repeated earnestly. "My place is a dump, and I've got tons of siblings. If I turn my music up a little, or put on a CD, or try to play my guitar, my mom or my sister comes to yell at me right away. On top of that, I can't find any quiet to read a book because my brothers are always stomping around making a ruckus, and if I want to rent a movie, the TV is never even free... There's nowhere comfortable, you know?"

"I think a lively home sounds nice, though."

I was halfway telling the truth with that answer. The thought of a normal environment, with parents and older sisters and little brothers all together under a single roof did inspire a bit of jealousy in me.

I opened the mini fridge I'd brought down from Izumi's older brother's room the day before and took out two cans of juice. I handed one to Yagisawa as I sat down in my own chair.

"So?" I fixed my eyes on his face. "What brings you here again so suddenly?"

"We haven't really had a proper chat since school started, have we? I understand your thinking, but things feel a little distant between us."

"Do they?"

"They do. We're supposed to be *comrades* here."

Of course, I understood exactly what Yagisawa meant by *comrades*. He was saying that we were more than simple Grade 3 classmates. Nevertheless—

"Well, that's true, but circumstances are what they are," I answered as calmly as possible. "I don't think that we can be friends, not like before, even when we're not at school.

"A year is a long time, you know. If we let our guards down and inadvertently say something to each other during class... I mean, I want to eliminate that risk."

"I heard all this earlier, about your policy."

"Well, don't call me *distant*, then," I appealed to him, my expression earnest. "Now that we know this is an 'on year,' we've all got to make our best efforts. Right?"

"Ah...I guess that's true—"

"By the way," I interjected, "why on earth did you volunteer as a candidate for class representative?"

"Will it be weird? If I'm a rep?"

"I honestly did a double take when I heard."

"Hmm, I can see that." Yagisawa raked his fingers through his long hair. "I was so optimistic that this year was going to be an 'off year,' but once we realized that it was going to be an 'on year,' you know, something about my frame of mind just changed."

"Meaning what?"

"I've never once been class rep, so I figured I'd give it a try now. Worse comes to worst, this could be the last year of my life, after all."

"So you've swung abruptly over to pessimism, huh?" I responded, filled with a complicated mix of feelings. "It's not set in stone that the 'countermeasures' will fail and the 'accidents' will start. And even if they do happen, that doesn't mean you're going to die."

"Well, yeah, that's true, but..."

Exactly at that moment, the sound of someone knocking on the door of <E-9> echoed through the room. I answered, "Yes?" as it swung open.

"Mind if I come in?" Stepping inside was none other than Izumi Akazawa. "Or are you in the middle of a boys-only secret meeting?"

"No, no, come on in."

This wasn't even his apartment, but Yagisawa stood up from his chair and invited her in.

"We had these upstairs, so I brought some over," Izumi told us, setting a white paper bag on the table. "Refreshments!"

Inside the bag were three large cream puffs.

"Whoa! Don't mind if I do!" Yagisawa immediately reached out to grab one. When he'd already snarfed down about half of it, he abruptly stopped, then mumbled, "Class representative...she was a rep in Class 3 fourteen years ago, too..."

Izumi, who hadn't been privy to our previous conversation, tilted her head in confusion.

"Fourteen years ago? I see." At the same time, I immediately understood. "A girl was class rep for Grade 3 Class 3 in 1987. *She was your aunt*, isn't that right, Yagisawa?"

"Yeah." He hung his head and nodded. "That's why I thought I'd volunteer. Though, logically, something like that shouldn't mean anything."

"What are you talking about?" Izumi asked, looking back and forth between the two of us. "Yagisawa's aunt was in Grade 3 Class 3 at North Yomi fourteen years ago? Then maybe she knew your...she knew Teruya Sakaki?"

"Right," I answered. "They were classmates in '87. My uncle Teruya and Yagisawa's aunt."

Not long after I'd met Yagisawa in our first year of middle school, I'd realized this *point in common* between us. Both of our relatives— my uncle, his aunt—were former members of the same Class 3 at our school. As "comrades," they'd witnessed the "phenomenon" and the "accidents" it caused firsthand.

Uncle Teruya, my mother's brother, had been seriously injured in the so-called "tragedy of '87" but managed to survive. Before the start of summer vacation, he had moved out of Yomiyama City and transferred schools. In doing so, he'd *escaped* from the "accidents." On the other hand, Yagisawa's aunt, his father's sister, who was class-mates with Teruya, had died of a sudden illness partway through the second semester.

Ever since we'd confirmed this, a *camaraderie* of sorts had developed between Yagisawa and me.

What if we end up in Class 3 when we're in third grade...? We'd always discussed the possibility, even way back in our first year of middle school, but we never thought it would actually turn out like this. Back then, I don't think even I'd really been able to fully comprehend the reality of the situation.

"She was pretty, you know. Risa," Yagisawa remarked.

Her full name was Risa Yagisawa.

"It happened fourteen years ago, so I'd just been born. Naturally, I don't have any memories of her to speak of. But when I look at old photos of her, I can see she was really pretty..."

Izumi shot a quick glance over at the bookshelf that stood against the wall. She seemed interested in the photo on top of it—

Following her gaze, Yagisawa also turned his head to look at the bookshelf. Naturally, his eyes also came to rest on the problem picture. I was already bracing myself.

Can I let him see it? Can I let him realize the truth?

"What's...?" He left his chair and looked closely at the photo. "Hey, Sou, what's this photo?"

The photograph was of the 1987 Class 3 students who'd temporarily "escaped" to Lakeshore Manor in Hinami over summer vacation. Aside from Teruya, there were four students in the picture. Among them was a girl standing to the far right and holding her long hair down so the wind wouldn't mess it up. Her surname was Yagisawa. I'd always been aware of that.

"I never found the right time to break this to you, but..."

Then I told Yagisawa what I knew.

Fourteen years earlier, summer break.

Teruya had invited his friends to Lakeshore Manor, which was outside of Yomiyama City and therefore "out of range" of the "calamity." There, they'd found a temporary reprieve from the horror of the "accidents." And the photograph they all took together during that trip was here with me...

"Why?" Yagisawa asked with a sulky frown. "Why didn't you tell me any of this until now?"

"Well, I...," I began, averting my eyes from him. "After their trip to the lake, Teruya ended up surviving because he ran away from Yomiyama. But everyone else went back after summer break was over, and your aunt lost her life. I think that Teruya probably felt awful, right up until when he died three years ago, about the fact that he was the *only one who escaped and lived*. I think he always blamed himself—so..."

"So it was hard to talk about?"

"Mm-hmm." I nodded slightly. "Sorry."

"You don't need to apologize, Sou." At that point, Izumi cut in decisively. "You have your own reasons, and it's sad for you to remember that your beloved uncle is gone... You don't want to bring the memories back too often, right? Of what happened three years ago. But you would have to remember no matter what if you explained the photo, right?"

I couldn't really say anything in response.

After a little while, Yagisawa remarked, "Yeah, I guess that's true." He smiled cheerfully. "Even if it was just during summer vacation, I'm glad they could find a chance to relax. Risa looks so happy in this photo—doesn't she, Sou?"

"Uh, yeah."

"I'd like to go sometime, too, to this Lakeshore Manor place."

"Uh..."

Despite his enthusiasm, I just couldn't bring myself to confirm Yagisawa's request.

6

"Yagisawa, I'm looking forward to working with you, okay?" Izumi said, trying to dispel the delicate silence that had filled the room. "I'm a countermeasures officer, and you're a class representative. Let's do our best to make sure that our 'countermeasures' go well this year so that everyone can graduate safely."

"Y-yeah." Yagisawa seemed quite overwhelmed. "Now that you bring it up, I don't really have any idea how I'm supposed to do that, though."

"Generally speaking, what we can do is pay very close attention to Sou and Hazumi, to make sure they keep acting invisible."

"I know what I'm supposed to do," I interjected. "I'm being very careful."

"I think you're probably fine, Sou. But if we're going to have a problem, it's definitely going to be with Hazumi."

"Yeah, she's right." Yagisawa nodded, placing a fingertip on the bridge of his glasses. "I'm also a little bit worried about Hazumi. Say, Sou?" He turned to me. "Don't you think you're a little cold toward her?"

"Am I?"

"You weren't aware of it?"

"I'm not really trying to be."

"No, no. But I mean, as far as I can tell, you're not being particularly friendly, either. But the two of you are fellow 'non-existers.' I wonder if it would be better to spend more time together during breaks and stuff, even at school."

After I reemphasized my policy of avoidance and the logic behind it, Yagisawa crossed his arms. "Mm-hmm... I understand your reasoning, but you know, I wonder if she'll be all right? The way I see it, Hazumi probably—"

"It's fine."

I spoke more decisively than necessary, in order to cut off the next thing Yagisawa was about to say. I recalled my conversation earlier in the day with Mei Misaki at the "Blue Eyes..." gallery.

"It'll be fine. I know she'll do great, no matter what happens. I'll make sure of it."

Chapter 5
April V

1

The third week of April—and the second week since the new semester began—passed without any incident. At least, that's how it felt to me.

With the cooperation of my classmates and teachers, I continued to solemnly play the part of a "non-exister." Yuika Hazumi was also diligent about following my wishes and ignoring me during school, even though we had the same position. Initially, I was relieved about this.

Hazumi also understood my line of thinking that it would be safer for "non-existers" to have as little contact with our classmates as possible outside of school. Or so I thought, but sometimes I would catch sight of her with other girls from Class 3 on the way to and from class, chatting like normal. Perhaps it was impractical for her to stick to "nonexistence" even outside of school.

She called my cell phone a lot. Whenever she rang, I would tell her something like, "Let's do our best to ensure the 'countermeasures' are successful," to encourage her, but no more than that. I had a feeling that, in the long term, trying to force more stipulations and pressures on her would just end up backfiring.

One Friday, at a slightly different time than when we'd met the day of the opening ceremony, I encountered Hazumi in the morning on the way to school—it was April 20. This time, we went down to the riverbank from the road that ran alongside the Yomiyama River, walking on the pedestrian path together for a while.

As we walked, she spoke about herself bit by bit.

Thanks to her parents' occupations, there was often no one in the house when she came home from school. She wasn't on particularly bad terms with them, but to make a long story short, they were pretty hands-off with their daughter.

"To put it bluntly, they're neglectful. But you know, I guess it's easier that way."

After she said that, Hazumi flashed me a carefree smile, but I wondered how she really felt about it. If Mei Misaki had given me the same line, for instance, I'm sure I wouldn't have doubted her at all.

Hazumi told me she had a brother five years older than her.

The year before, he'd graduated from high school and entered the law program at a university in Tokyo, so he was far from Yomiyama. His aspiration was to pass the bar exam and become a lawyer. He sounded like a hard worker. According to Hazumi, something about me reminded her of him, apparently...

"Do you have any siblings, Sou?"

I made a deliberate effort to answer indifferently.

"I have a younger sister in elementary school. She's at my mom's house in Hinami."

I didn't go out of my way to mention that she and I had different fathers or explain that she was the product of my mother's second marriage.

"What's her name?"

"Hmm?"

"Your sister's name?"

"Ah...Mirei."

"Is she cute?"

"...Not really."

Come to think of it...actually, I'd rather not dwell on that—I hadn't seen Mirei's face once since that summer three years ago. My mother, Tsukiho, had come to Yomiyama three times that I knew of during the two and a half years that I'd lived here, and she hadn't ever brought my sister with her.

"So you're living in the same apartment building as Izumi Akazawa now, right?" Hazumi asked abruptly that Friday morning.

"For the time being, I need to, yeah," I answered without hesitation. "I'm planning to go back to my uncle's place, where I was staying before."

"But you're in the same building for now. I heard you both are on the same floor—is that true?"

"Uh, yeah."

I wonder who she heard that from? Probably from someone she's kept up a close friendship with outside of school. *Or maybe... No, it doesn't matter. That's not really information I need to hide.*

"Does that mean you talk to her every day?"

"Uh...I guess? I wouldn't say it's *every* day, but..."

"Even though we're better off avoiding contact with classmates as much as possible, even outside of school?"

The moment she posed the question, I sensed a small prickle in her voice.

"Izumi Akazawa is my *cousin*."

After I replied, I looked over at Hazumi, walking beside me. She was keeping her eyes straight forward.

"Hmm," she reacted in a tone that sounded deliberately cool, then continued. "Do you have any special feelings about her?" she asked.

"Huh?" Surprised by her inquiry, I turned to her again. "What's that supposed to mean?"

"I mean...you know." Hazumi brushed back her chest-length hair with the hand that wasn't holding her bag. "Do you like her? Do you dislike her?"

"Ummm...if you're going to put it that way, then I think my answer is that I 'like' her, but..."

At that point, I'd caught on to why she was asking. To be honest, this was an area of weakness for me, in which I had a real dearth of experience. And my perspective at the moment was, I really thought that now wasn't the time, so I quickly pushed those thoughts out of my mind.

"But listen, I say I 'like' her, but Izumi is my cousin, okay? So I don't mean anything weird by it."

I added that comment in an attempt to end the conversation there. But Hazumi wouldn't let up.

"Cousins can get married, you know," she remarked. She continued looking straight ahead, just like before. And though it might have been my imagination, I thought I heard that small prickle in her voice again.

Ah, geez... I tried not to let my distress show on my face or in my voice.

I suck at this. Having this kind of conversation with a girl is a pretty big, no, enormous blind spot for me.

I wonder how a normal guy in his third year of middle school would handle this. Like Yagisawa, for example. Or like Shunsuke Kouda (though he doesn't seem like a great role model). Or like, yeah, like Koichi Sakakibara when he was in Grade 3...

Pondering this resulted in a several-seconds-long, unnatural silence.

Hazumi let out a slightly flustered "*ah, um...,*" stopped walking, and looked at me. Her cheeks were slightly red, and her eyes seemed a bit panicked. She had pretty, grown-up features, but her expression threw them out of balance, making her seem like a lost little girl.

All right. Let's keep going and transition away from this topic...

I thought for a moment.

"You know, Sou..." Hazumi gazed at me with dark eyes framed by long eyelashes. Her expression had completely transformed; now she was wearing an impish smile. Impish, but somehow more suited for her grown-up features. "When you volunteered to be the 'non-exister,' I—"

"Oh, a kingfisher!"

Just then, I shouted, interrupting Hazumi. Pointing, I took a step or two toward the bank.

"Look, right there. It's hovering."

It was just about in the middle of the river, slightly closer to our side. There, a bird was strenuously flapping its wings about three meters off the water's surface. It had vivid lapis-blue wings, an orange breast, and a fairly long bill for its small body.

Mm, that's a kingfisher, no doubt about it. This is how it hunts for its underwater prey.

This beautiful, nonmigratory bird, whose name was sometimes spelled with the Japanese character for *jade*, inhabited every region of the country, but this was my first time witnessing the spectacle of one hovering over this river in Yomiyama. Without thinking, I put together my thumbs and index fingers to form an imaginary viewfinder. Quietly pacing forward, I closed the imaginary shutter several times.

"Aw, come on…," I heard Hazumi say behind me.

The kingfisher plunged into the water for a moment, then emerged triumphant, having captured its fishy prey. I expressed secret feelings of gratitude to him (probably a "him," based on the color of the beak) as I clicked my imaginary shutter closed again and again.

2

The following day, Saturday, April 21, just before noon—

I submitted a notice of absence to the school and went to visit the "clinic" at the municipal hospital. I had ended up canceling last week's appointment and had been allowed to reschedule it for today, one week later.

The clinic was located on the spacious general hospital campus, which took up practically the entire face of Yumigaoka Mountain. The section housing medical offices was in the front and had been undergoing major remodeling work since the previous year. Together with the adjacent inpatient ward, they comprised the "main building." Behind it and a little separate stood a small, old structure, the "annex." The department that I went to was in there.

Currently, it was called the Psychoneurological Department, but I heard it had been simply known as the Psychiatric Ward until about ten years ago. I'm sure that the hospital had intended to place it somewhere where it wouldn't be too conspicuous, since most of society had a vague prejudice against people suffering from mental illness. That deep-seated bias persisted even to this day, which was why Tsukiho always wanted to call this place the "clinic." The words *mental health clinic* had a more acceptable connotation than *psychoneurological department*.

Long ago, Tsukiho had lost her first husband—my father, that is— to suicide. I'd heard it described as a "death resulting from mental illness." Additionally, there was the incident with Uncle Teruya three years ago. In that light, I imagined that she thought I was likely to do the same… Despite my blood relationship to both of them, however, I wasn't that worried, myself. And yet—

When I stood before the annex building, I did start feeling a little gloomy sometimes.

It was an unadorned four-story building made of reinforced concrete. Iron bars lined all the tiny windows of the rooms above the second story. Ivy climbed a few sections of the dingy walls. It was obviously a dreary place, and it had a slightly eerie air.

When I'd inquired about them, however, the staff told me that the rooms in the hospital annex weren't currently being used to house psychiatric patients. Apparently, the facility had fallen too far into disrepair. Patients with serious illnesses, the ones who required restraining measures, had already been transferred to a new specialty ward in a different area. This whole structure was slated to be demolished in the near future.

"Hello, Sou. You're a third-year already, right?" I entered the examination room to find Dr. Usui, my attending physician, addressing me from across the room in his usual polite way. "Our last meeting was in early February, huh?"

Looking over at my chart on the desk, he asked, "How are you doing? Has anything changed in the last two months or so?"

This was the psychiatrist who I'd been seeing ever since coming to Yomiyama.

He was probably a little under forty. He had the build of a judo athlete and a big, square face. Jet-black whiskers were growing around his mouth, on his cheeks, and on his chin. That made him look a little frightening at first glance, but his small eyes that were fixed on me always held a calm, gentle light.

"Nothing has really changed. I don't think I'm having any issues," I answered.

"Are you sleeping well at night?"

"Yes."

"Without needing sleeping medication?"

"Yes. I'm usually all right without taking any."

"And are you having nightmares?"

"I'm... Sometimes."

"But the frequency has decreased compared to before, correct?"

"Yes."

This doctor had examined me shortly before Tsukiho's husband—my stepfather, Shuuji Hiratsuka—wrote a referral placing me into the Akazawas' care. At that time, my mental condition had been unstable due to the shock from *that incident* three years ago.

Though I was doing fine intellectually, the reality was that I was suffering certain symptoms. Insomnia. Nightmares. The anxiety, fear, confusion, and sense of helplessness that sometimes rushed in on me even when I was awake. The heart palpitations, sweating, and stifled breathing that accompanied those feelings.

Post-traumatic stress disorder, PTSD.

I didn't really want to lump everything together under that title, but even though I'd voiced my objection, Dr. Usui had still handed down the diagnosis. However, since my condition wasn't as serious as it sounded, there was no need to be overly worried.

I remembered him telling me: *"The most important thing is that you're the one who will be responsible for your own recovery, Sou. I'm just here to help you out a little bit."*

Considering my stepfather had introduced me to him, I was initially wary of Dr. Usui. But gradually, we'd been able to develop a relationship that made me feel as if I could trust him...and as a result, my symptoms greatly improved after about a year. He'd prescribed me various medications in the beginning as well, but now I was mostly able to get by without them.

"Have you had any contact with your mother lately?" the doctor said. He asked this question whenever we met, but each time, I was fully aware that my response wasn't positive in the slightest.

"Not much. Once at the start of the month."

"By phone?"

"Yes."

"Did you have a proper conversation?"

"No. I just listened to the message she left."

"Have you called her?"

"I haven't."

"You don't want to speak to her?"

"Yeah…that's right. Not really…"

"You don't want to see her, either?"

"…………"

"Do you actually want to see her?"

"…………"

"You can say what you're really feeling here, Sou."

"I don't know."

"Is that so? Hmm." The doctor blinked his small eyes and gave another "mm-hmm."

Then he said, "I am also aware, generally, of the special circumstances of the Hiratsuka household. Considering your position, it's no wonder you have complicated feelings about your mother. Try not to worry too much over the presence of those feelings themselves. All right?"

I nodded obediently. "All right."

3

Apparently, I was Dr. Usui's last patient for the day. When I left the examination room, there was no one else in the waiting area.

"Here you go." Ms. Kikuchi, a nurse who I recognized, handed me some documents to submit at the cashier window. Just as she did, a small figure tried to slip past me, headed for the door of the examination room.

Startled, I took another glance and saw it was a very young child. An elementary schooler, probably in a lower grade. She had bobbed hair and was wearing a uniform and a backpack—from the color, I assumed she was a girl.

After spinning around to say "hello" to me in a small voice, she opened the exam room door without knocking, then disappeared inside.

"That's Dr. Usui's daughter," Ms. Kikuchi told me, seeing my confusion. She let out a low chuckle. "She always stops by here when she's on her way home from school on Saturday. They eat lunch together, and then she drags him home. Is this the first time you've met her, Sou?"

"Uh, yes," I answered, imagining Dr. Usui's hairy face *wrinkling* up in a huge smile the second his daughter entered the room. "They must be very close, huh?"

"Her mother passed away young," Ms. Kikuchi told me, lowering her voice a little. "He's been a single father ever since. It's just adorable to see the doctor with her. And she's actually quite clever and cute, too..."

Later, I would learn that the girl's name was Kiha. She attended the second grade at a nearby public elementary school.

4

It had been overcast since morning that day, and as I left the hospital annex, rain started pouring. Normally, I would have gone around to the front entrance from outside to get to the first-floor lobby in the medical offices building, where the cashier's window was located. This time, however, I walked down the connecting passage (that is to say, a walkway with a roof and walls) to avoid the rain and entered the main hospital building from the back. The primary building and the annex were connected by a similar sky bridge on the third floor as well.

As I walked slowly down the mazelike hallways, a result of the many piecemeal expansions made to the hospital over the years, a thought occurred to me.

Come to think of it, Koichi Sakakibara was hospitalized around this time three years ago, wasn't he?

I'd heard that it happened not long after he moved here from Tokyo. The night before he was supposed to start school at North Yomi as a transfer student, he'd had a sudden onset of spontaneous pneumothorax and had been hospitalized. What a miserable experience.

He seemed totally healthy by the time I got to know him, but it was crazy to think that a hole had once opened in one of his lungs and caused it to collapse. I could only imagine the fear and pain he'd felt at the time.

I wonder where in this hospital his sick room was...

I was idling down the corridor, glancing here and there at my surroundings. Just then—

With a low, reverberating *thud*, the world went pitch-black for a second. But it was really only a second.

Suddenly, a fact related to my previous thought surfaced from my memory.

Speaking of "hospitalization," there's a student who has been on leave from school since the start of the month due to illness. Come to think of it, they're in Class 3. I don't know all the details, but I heard that they needed to be hospitalized for a while, so coming to school would be difficult—now, when did I hear that? Oh yeah, I think it was from Izumi. That student—her name was something like Makino or Makise, maybe...

When I finally made it to the lobby of the medical offices building, the cell phone inside my jacket buzzed with a call.

The first face that appeared in my mind's eye was Hazumi's. *She's probably concerned about the conversation we had when we met up yesterday.* The second option, though I doubted it would be her, was Mei Misaki...

Or so I'd thought, but—

I looked at the display and gasped. The call was coming from Tsukiho.

Naturally, I remembered my earlier conversation with Dr. Usui, and despite some trepidation, I pressed the answer button this time around.

"Ah...Sou?"

This was the first time I'd heard my mother's voice in a long while. Before she could continue speaking, I said, "I'm doing just fine. And I'm going to the clinic regularly."

"—I'm sorry, Sou."

"Don't apologize. It's fine."

"But really, you know, I want to be there for you..."

"The Akazawas are doing a great job. I'm all right as is."

"Ah...but..."

"Don't worry."

"............"

"Bye, then. I'm hanging up."

I really was going to stop the conversation like this, but when I said so, Tsukiho blurted out, "I'm coming to see you next month," as if trying to keep me from stopping. Then she continued. "I haven't seen your face in so long, and I need to give my regards to Sayuri and her husband...so it's set, next month."

That's really okay—you don't need to come.

I was about to reject the idea right then and there, but I paused briefly and recalled Dr. Usui's words from earlier. *"It's no wonder you have complicated feelings about your mother."*

"Mm." After another short pause, I answered briefly, "Got it. See you."

I hung up, and after I had completed my payment at the cashier's window in the lobby, I left the hospital, still unable to shake my sense of gloom and uncertainty. Nevertheless, I passed through the automatic doors in the front entrance, stopping to look at the rain that was still coming down.

"Well then."

Suddenly, my eyes came to rest on the figure of a middle-aged woman, holding her semitransparent plastic umbrella closed as she entered the hospital with a sluggish gait. Taken aback, I tried to get another look at her face, but when I turned around, all I saw was her back. However—

She didn't seem to notice me, but was that...

...Kirika?

"Kirika" was the pseudonym that she used as a doll maker. Her real name was apparently Yukiyo—Yukiyo Misaki. Mei's mother.

She must have come here because she was feeling unwell. I'd been able to see her for only a moment, but somehow, I could tell that she wasn't in great shape...

I was curious, but we weren't on close-enough terms for me to run after her and confirm.

On Sunday, I'd gone to the "Blue Eyes..." gallery and seen Mei Misaki for the first time in two months. For some reason, the image of her with her left eye covered by an eye patch as it had been before came to my mind. A sense of vague apprehension, the true character of which I couldn't place, gradually spread through me...

I stepped out alone into the unceasing downpour.

5

It had been about two weeks since I started sleeping in unit <E-9> of the Freuden Tobii—

Before my move, we decided that I would stop by the Akazawa house for breakfast each morning and then continue to school. Auntie Sayuri was always fussing over me, just as she had from the start. She would ask things like, "Are you sure you're not lonely up there by yourself?" Each and every day, she also had a lunch box for me, ready to go. On my way back from school, I usually returned to my room in the apartment building first, then went to the Akazawas' in time for dinner. When I went over, I took my laundry with me. You could hardly call this lifestyle "independent living."

The renovation work on the house had begun. I heard it was progressing slower than they'd planned, but in spite of that, a section of the old wooden house had already been demolished and was now covered in blue tarps. The room I'd been using before moving into the apartment had been converted into a storage space for all the furniture and stuff that would be in the way during the project.

Most of the construction noise happens during the day on weekdays, so there isn't really a need for me to go to the trouble of "escaping" to the apartment, is there?

Or at least that's what I'd thought when I'd first heard about it. Now that construction was underway, however, I could see that it was actually making the whole place feel unsettled. Since I would be preparing for high school this year, I was grateful that my aunt and the rest of the family had been so considerate by insisting that I move out.

Once, when the end of the fourth week in April was drawing near, I encountered Izumi in the primary Akazawa house. She was there to visit our grandfather, Hiromune Akazawa, together with her mother, Mayuko. I just happened to be there at the same time.

Grandfather's health had been poor since the end of last year.

He was seventy-eight years old and had seemed healthy and energetic for his age, but one day he carelessly took a fall down the stairs. Though his injuries weren't life-threatening, he did break his right leg and hip. After being hospitalized for a little over a month, he'd stubbornly refused a transfer to a rehabilitation hospital, instead opting to recuperate at home. Apparently, he hated the hospital so much, he couldn't stand it any longer; just being there sapped his willpower to grapple with rehabilitation.

As a result of his obstinance, however, his broken bones were slow to recover, especially his hip... Since he still couldn't get up by himself and walk around, he spent most of his time sleeping. That held true even now. The doctor's verdict was that if things continued as they were, he would probably need to spend the rest of his life in a wheelchair. At that point—

The Akazawas had decided to take advantage of the situation to remodel their old home, which originally had many different levels, narrow doorways, and so on.

"Grandpa doesn't seem to be in a very good mood, of course," Izumi whispered in my ear.

She had come out alone from the tatami room in the back where he was staying, leaving Auntie Sayuri and her mother, Mayuko, behind, to find me alone in the front sitting room... That's what was going on.

"He sees his granddaughter's face for the first time in ages and just asks, 'What are you doing here?' Can you believe it? Don't you think that's awful?"

"Sure...yeah."

"He's never really liked me, has he?" Izumi frowned, revealing a somewhat lonely expression. "He was always worrying about my big brother, but he was cold toward me, or at least not very interested or whatever."

"I wonder if he didn't know how to handle girls?"

I made a timid attempt at backing up our grandfather, but Izumi kept frowning and didn't say anything in response. Sighing, she gulped down some tea from one of the bottles that had been set out on the table.

Our grandfather was certainly difficult to please. And it seemed like that quality had been intensifying ever since he'd broken those bones, to the point that it made me suspect he might be going a little senile. Auntie Sayuri had been taking care of him without complaint, but Mayuko rarely showed her face in the house, despite living close by. She was probably just as fed up with him as Izumi.

Personally, I'd never gotten that bad of an impression of our grandfather. I'd first met him when the Akazawas took me in two and a half years earlier. Back then, he'd fixed his gaze on me, then said softly, "*Sou...you're Fuyuhiko's boy?*"

The look in his eyes as he spoke to me had seemed both achingly sad and also kind.

I hadn't heard much from him since then, but I'm sure that his heart was still full of grief and longing for his third son, who'd passed away young, ahead of his own father. When he gazed at my face, those feelings had naturally begun to pour out... At least, that's what I imagined was going on. Anyway, as far as I knew, for as long as I could remember, that was a "look" that I couldn't recall experiencing much before.

The black cat, Kurosuke, padded into the sitting room and jumped right up onto Izumi's lap, even though he almost never did that for me. Not at all annoyed, Izumi stroked his back as she asked in a lowered voice, "Hey, Sou? There's something I want to talk to you about later, okay?"

"Something...about class?"

"Mm-hmm."

"Is there a...problem?"

"Kind of... Have you been talking to Hazumi lately?"

"Ah...a little," I answered vaguely.

"How's she doing? From your perspective."

"Ummm...well—"

As I was struggling to respond, Sayuri and Mayuko came into the sitting room, interrupting our conversation. Izumi leaned forward over the table.

"Anyway, we'll talk later," she whispered, bringing her face close to my ear.

It was April 27, a Friday. The following day would be the 28th, the fourth Saturday of the month. It was both a school holiday and the first day of a three-day break, which included the 29th and 30th. But the night before the break, something happened.

6

> WOULD YOU COME OVER HERE FOR A CHANGE?
> AROUND TEN O'CLOCK OR SO.

When I got back to the Freuden Tobii after dinner, I found a memo stuck to the door of my apartment. It was in Izumi's handwriting.

She had her own room, unit <E-1> on the fifth level, same floor as me. But as far as I could remember, I'd never come over to her place before, even though she'd done the opposite plenty of times. Despite the fact that she was my cousin, she was still a girl, so...I remained quite hesitant, but I figured it would probably be all right.

I waited until the designated time, then rang the doorbell of apartment <E-1>.

"Coming!" I heard Izumi answer. She must have just gotten out of the shower or bath, because her hair was still damp, and I caught a faint whiff of the shampoo I'd borrowed on my second night after moving up here. She had also changed out of her uniform into a sweatshirt and track pants.

"Come on in."

Her apartment was a one-bedroom, more spacious than my own.

Atop the built-in counter between the kitchen and living room sat a coffee maker, bubbling as it brewed. The scent of shampoo dissolved and disappeared into the fragrance of coffee that hung in the air.

She led me into the living room and offered me a seat on the sofa and, shortly after, a cup of coffee.

"Thanks, I appreciate it." I accepted sincerely, adding milk and sugar before taking a sip. Izumi left hers black and slurped up a mouthful.

"Mm-hmm." She nodded, looking pleased. "These seem like really good beans."

"You know about coffee?"

"A little, thanks to my brother's influence," she answered. Izumi looked toward the kitchen. "I used to have his favorite blend, but the bag got really old. This is a Hawaiian Kona coffee that I just got yesterday. It's really high-grade."

I'm generally pretty indifferent to the flavor of most drinks and food, not just coffee, so I responded with a noncommittal "Wow" and glanced around the room.

It was plainer than I'd imagined for a third-grade middle school girl's room and didn't feel very welcoming. I couldn't see many furnishings or decorations that looked particularly girlie.

The rugs spread on the floor were plain white, and the windows were covered with cream blinds instead of curtains. Next to one of them was a display case with a glass door, the contents of which caught my eye. There appeared to be quite a lot of dinosaur figurines lined up inside.

Hmm? I didn't know she was interested in that sort of thing.

"Through there is the piano room," Izumi told me. "It's been soundproofed, so I can play at night, no problem."

"Amazing. You're a real musician!"

"They've been making me take lessons since I was little, so I guess I'm pretty good… At least, that was my excuse so I could get them to build me a piano room and have my own space."

Hmm. How luxurious.

Izumi had lamented to me that her parents treated only her brother like "something special," but she seemed to do pretty well for herself otherwise. Once, she'd told me that *"Mama and Papa usually give in to my selfish whims."* Surprisingly, this seemed to be a source of stress, dissatisfaction, or some other negative emotion more than anything else for her. I had all these thoughts and more, of course, but I didn't let them out of my mouth.

"Are you trying to become a pianist or something in the future?" I asked.

"No, no," Izumi answered, forcing a smile, "I actually haven't done much with it lately. I went to play for the first time in a while the other day, and it was all out of tune."

"Huh…"

"I've ended up using that room more for practicing my lines for drama club, I think."

"Uh-huh."

Barely reacting, I drained my coffee cup. Izumi asked me if I wanted another, but I declined. She poured herself a second cup from the pot, then finally—

"To get back to our earlier conversation," she said, broaching the real issue at hand. "How has Hazumi been doing lately? From your perspective."

7

"That's…"

Unexpectedly, I found myself at a loss for words at the moment.

Since our encounter on the bank of the Yomiyama River the week before, Hazumi and I hadn't had any opportunity to get together again like that… No, it would be more honest to say that I'd been doing my best to avoid any more of those encounters. We'd spoken twice on the phone, but it had been nothing more than some harmless small talk.

"I'd say not much has changed. I guess she's probably doing all right," I answered, leaving out any detailed account of the situation.

When I saw her in class, at least, Hazumi continued to flawlessly play the role of the "non-exister" that she'd been assigned. And she didn't approach or address me during school, either...

"I don't think she's having any issues."

But Izumi mumbled, "Oh?" in a somewhat depressed-sounding voice, before sipping her second cup of coffee. Then she looked up sharply and remarked, "As countermeasures officer, I observe the state of the class every day...and I think that April has gone pretty well. There are three days left, but school is on break. I think you and Hazumi are behaving as you should, and all our classmates and teachers are handling it suitably."

She was right—the "countermeasures" did seem to be going smoothly. The proof of this was that the end of the month was now approaching without a single "accident."

"However—" Izumi continued. "Just today, I overheard something a little concerning. I thought I'd better let you in on it, too."

What could it be?

From the way our conversation was heading, I could surmise that it was something to do with Hazumi.

"I didn't really know Hazumi until we started our third year," Izumi said, "so I'm not too familiar with her personality, you know? Because of that, I haven't decided yet how worried I should be about this."

"About something to do with her?"

It sounded like some kind of problem had arisen in the one place I wasn't looking.

"It sounds like Hazumi has a number of good friends. She's diligently playing the part of a 'non-exister' during class, but outside of it...and on the way to and from school, she's been chatting normally with them."

"Ah, that...yeah. I did tell her to be careful, but I couldn't quite bring myself to say that it was absolutely off-limits."

"I thought as much." Izumi nodded. "But you know," she added, "that in and of itself isn't an issue. I'm sure that it's really difficult 'not existing' the whole time we're in class, so I'm glad she has friends to spend time with outside of school. I get that; normally I'd have no reason to blame her. But you know, I learned something from Tsugunaga just today."

Tsugunaga...that girl who's a class rep, right? What on earth does she know?

"First, you need to know that Shimamura apparently got injured this past Monday."

Shimamura was one of the girls in our class who Hazumi was friends with.

"Tsugunaga told me that on the way home from school, Shimamura was walking with Hazumi and another girl named Kusakabe. As the three of them headed down the sidewalk together, a bicycle charged into them from behind and collided with Shimamura."

"And she was injured? Was it very bad?"

"Her knees and arms got scraped, and she got an awful nosebleed from falling into the ground. The blood wouldn't stop for a while, which cause a ruckus."

"Who was riding the bicycle?"

"A middle-aged man, apparently. And he didn't apologize; he just kept riding off."

"So it was a malicious hit-and-run, huh?"

"That was the end of the incident with Shimamura, but—" After a short pause, Izumi started up again. "The next day, Kusakabe—"

"Did she get hurt, too, or something?" I asked, anticipating the next part of the story in spite of myself, but Izumi shook her head side to side.

"This time, it wasn't an injury..."

Tuesday—on the evening of the 14th, Hazumi had rang up Kusakabe. The two of them had a long chat about nothing, like usual. However—

In the middle of their conversation, an unexpected incident occurred. Kusakabe's great-grandmother, who was living with her and her parents, collapsed in a fit of poor health and had to receive emergency ambulance transport to the hospital.

"That means..." As I listened to Izumi's explanation, I frowned hard. "Did she, by any chance...die?" I asked fearfully. "Kusakabe's great-grandmother, I mean."

"She was fine, apparently," Izumi answered. "She recovered without difficulty and didn't even need to be hospitalized. But—"

Izumi leaned back against the sofa and listlessly brushed her bangs away, resting her hand on her forehead. She looked like she was checking herself for a fever.

"Tsugunaga told me that since those things happened in quick succession, Shimamura and Kusakabe are scared."

"Scared?"

"Because both incidents were connected to Hazumi. In Shimamura's case, she was with her, and in Kusakabe's, she was on the phone with her..."

...So what does it all mean?

When I thought about it, I vaguely clued in to the point Izumi was making.

In other words... Ah, but that would mean...

"In other words, Sou, *Hazumi is the object of their 'fear,'*" Izumi said, voicing the answer I'd been imagining. "They're thinking that it's a *bad idea* to have close contact with her even outside of school, as long as she's a 'non-exister.' That she might be the cause of Shimamura's injuries and Kusakabe's great-grandmother's collapse... They're convinced that *these incidents might be precursors to the 'calamity.'*"

8

"That's completely unfounded," I grumbled, feeling half irritated, half exasperated. "I've never heard anything about there being a 'precursor' or whatever to the 'accidents.'"

Shimamura had simply been unlucky to get hit by a bicycle. And in Kusakabe's case, she and her great-grandmother were related in the third degree. Only "blood relatives within two degrees" were in danger of suffering "accidents," so a great-grandmother was *out of range*. And even if she had died when she arrived at the hospital, it would have to be considered an unfortunate coincidence that was ultimately unconnected to the "calamity."

As a countermeasures officer, of course, Izumi had a good grasp on the rules governing the "accidents." There was no reason for me to explain them to her again.

"I said the very same thing. I told her neither incident had anything to do with the 'calamity.'" She put her hand on her forehead again and kept speaking. "That Tsugunaga, though, she's got her own ideas, and she's much more high-strung about all this than the others, so she gave me a hard time no matter what I tried to tell her. But she did seem to understand me somewhat. The ones I'm really worried about are Shimamura and Kusakabe."

"What do you mean?"

"According to Tsugunaga, both of them are going to avoid Hazumi from now on. Apparently, they feel that it would be best to avoid getting near her, even outside of school, and not to call her... They think it's dangerous to be friends with her. I don't know if Hazumi has realized it yet, but when she finds out, I think she'll be shocked."

"Ah..."

"So if this particular set of circumstances means that she ends up isolated, that would be bad, right? I don't think she's strong like you, Sou."

When she said that, I reflexively blurted out, "Strong? Me?"

The bewildered question just rushed out of my mouth. It was the first time anyone had ever called me *strong*.

"That's how you seem to me." Setting my objection aside as if it was nothing, Izumi sat up straight and fixed her gaze on me. "So," she continued, "somehow or other, I think I've got to stop the rumor from spreading that being friendly with Hazumi is dangerous. I've got to remind everyone that there are principles governing the 'accidents' and that as long as we follow the rules properly, we'll be fine. I'm getting help from the other countermeasures officers, Etou and Tajimi, as well as Yagisawa and his buddies for this."

"Mm."

"If Hazumi really does end up isolated, and if she says she's quitting being a 'non-exister,' all the countermeasures we've worked so hard to put in place will be for nothing—right?" Izumi's expression and way of speaking were serious from beginning to end.

I recalled Mei Misaki's contrasting take—that even if Hazumi was to give up her role, as long as I diligently continued to "not exist," then there shouldn't be a problem. But of course, there could be no better option than to continue with the "countermeasures" as originally planned, if possible. That seemed like the best bet.

"That's why, Sou," Izumi insisted, still staring into my face, "I think if you could have some sort of talk with Hazumi about this, make sure she's not suffering too much or getting desperate…"

"Calm her down carefully, is that it?"

"Yeah. That's what I mean."

"Got it."

I answered obediently, but at that moment, something was making me feel uneasy. Hazumi had called my cell phone the night before, but I hadn't called her back. I'd figured that I hadn't needed to, since she hadn't left a voice mail.

"Hey, can I ask you something?" After wavering over what to do for a minute, I went for it. "About Hazumi, um…I wonder what she thinks? About me?"

"Huh?" Izumi tilted her head in confusion but soon seemed to catch my meaning. "Ah, that?" She nodded, looking unconcerned. "Well, let's see, I've had my suspicions from the very beginning, of course."

"Suspicions?"

"And Yagisawa said something about it the other day, didn't he? I mean, anyone can see it. She likes you, Sou."

Well, when you just say it right out loud like that…

The only thing I could think was: *What am I gonna do? I don't really dislike her or think she's irritating or anything, but... How do I put this? Honestly, I think this isn't the time for that kind of stuff.*

"Did she happen to confess to you or something?" Izumi asked with a much more casual expression this time.

"Ah, no, nothing like that," I answered, unintentionally averting my gaze from her eyes, which were still locked on to me.

"Hmm." Izumi crossed her arms. "And what about you?"

"Uh—"

"Hazumi's pretty...right? She's not bad-looking at all, is she?"

"—I don't really think so," I answered truthfully.

"So do you dislike her, then?"

"—Not really."

"So you mean you don't really care either way?"

"Yeah, I guess so."

When it came to romantic feelings, to the question of liking or disliking the girls around me, I still didn't have any real interest one way or another. I think I probably also had less of a desire to have those emotions than the average person. Naturally, this meant I was a completely ignorant third-grade middle school boy about the finer points of this subject, so...

Narrowing her eyes at me as I awkwardly fumbled to explain as much, Izumi nodded. "Mm-hmm." Then she pulled both feet up on the sofa and sat cross-legged, tossing her long hair behind her back with both hands.

"In that case, it's best not to let it weigh on you too much, right?" she said plainly. "It's a special situation, but I don't think it would come to anything good if you were to, for example, try to force yourself to match your feelings to hers."

9

The remaining three days of April passed without incident. As far as I knew, at least.

During that time, I went over to the library in Daybreak Forest once; then I spent the rest of the days not really venturing out, except to go between the Freuden Tobii and the Akazawa house. With the exception of Izumi, who lived in the same apartment building as I did, I didn't meet up with any of my classmates.

I was nearly a shut-in, reading alone by myself. I was seized by the idea that I should just stay like this and skip the rest of the school year. My condition had improved greatly since coming to Yomiyama, but I still wasn't the kind of person who had much energy for dealing with other people. I knew that if I searched the depths of my heart, I would find hidden in there a very real desire to abandon everything and run away.

What if I use Golden Week as an opportunity to escape from this place?

Even that thought had flashed through my mind. Despite the fact that I would have nowhere to go and no place to stay after my breakout.

Though we didn't meet in person, I did talk to Yagisawa once on the phone.

"Hey, Sou! You feeling good? You must be, right?"

He spoke as carelessly as ever.

"April's almost over, but starting next month, man, we've really got to give it our all!"

"Yeah, guess so," I answered.

Without delay, Yagisawa continued. "If the loneliness of 'nonexistence' ever gets you down, you can come flying into my open arms anytime. As long as it's after school, there's no problem, right? If you want, we could even start a band together."

"Huh?"

"Can you play any instruments, Sou? If you can't, let's see…how about practicing percussion or something? You can start with a tambourine or castanets!"

"I'll pass, thanks."

"Oh, really? But I think it would be better for your mental health than just holing yourself up and reading books."

I knew that Yagisawa was, in his own way, expressing his concern for me and how I felt having to remain silent and invisible in class every day. And though I was grateful for his consideration on the

one hand, on the other, I felt like it was really none of his business...
I started to grow a little annoyed.

I didn't get a single call from Hazumi for the rest of the break.
What Izumi had told me was weighing on my mind, but in the end,
I didn't reach out to Hazumi, either.

And then, on the 30th, the night of the last day of April—

A little after ten o'clock, when I booted up my laptop on my living
room table, I found three new e-mails.

The first one was from Shunsuke Kouda. As usual, it was a report
on several things going on with the biology club.

The week before, three first-years had come by wanting to join the
club. Two boys and a girl. The e-mail said that these new members
were key personnel who would carry the club into the future, so if I
happened to meet them in the clubroom, I should treat them kindly
and politely...

Why is he going out of his way to give me instructions like that? I
wondered.

They had also started keeping a new axolotl in the clubroom, a
male, as a successor to Woo after his recent passing. One of the new
club members had brought him in, and against all odds, the new creature's name just happened to also be "Woo."

Shunsuke was planning to go to the clubroom every day, even during Golden Week. He closed his e-mail with an invitation: "Come
along with me if you feel up to it, Sou."

The second e-mail was from Mei Misaki.

It was the first e-mail I'd gotten from her since the opening ceremony. I recognized her sender name, "Mei M.," and opened the
e-mail, my heartbeat picking up as I did—

> LOOKS LIKE APRIL IS GOING TO END WITHOUT INCIDENT.
> HOPE IT GOES WELL NEXT MONTH, TOO.

Her message was short and to the point as usual, but it did give me
a sense of modest relief as well.

When I sighed and closed my eyes, the image of Mei wearing her eye patch, exactly as she had looked long ago, floated up before me. Come to think of it, when I had seen her two weeks ago at the "Blue Eyes…" gallery, she had asked me something: *"Someday soon, could I come visit your place?"*

I wonder if she was serious about that? Probably just one of those off-the-cuff things.

The third e-mail was another *Yomiyama Town News* e-mail newsletter. Those were normally sent out twice a month, and the second one for April had already come the previous week. The one today was garnished with a subheading that read, "GW Special Edition."

And yet, the content of the periodical was the same stuff as always.

A report on a minor "discovery" from a writer who had an interest in researching local history. A column offering miscellaneous tidbits about the "festival" part of the Boys' Day celebration coming up on the 5th of May. Plus, announcements about various events being held here and there around Yomiyama during the Golden Week holidays. There would be a charity bazaar in Daybreak Forest Park, a used-book fair in the plaza in front of town hall, a public goodwill concert being held somewhere or other, and so on…

I skimmed through it briefly, but none of the articles especially caught my interest.

Except—

At the end of the periodical, there was a section in small type titled, "News from the Editorial Department," which made an addendum. I read it, thinking nothing of it, and, without meaning to, let out an audible *"huh?"* But at the time, I didn't pay any further attention to it.

JUST PRIOR TO THE PUBLICATION OF THIS SPECIAL EDITION, WE RECEIVED A LAST-MINUTE OBITUARY NOTICE.

WE PRAY FOR THE PEACEFUL REPOSE OF MR. TAKAYUKI NAKAGAWA.

Interlude I

That girl—Hazumi—seems kind of dangerous to be around.

She does?

That's what they're saying. That it's risky, perilous to get near her.

Perilous? In what way?

Like **something bad will happen**. So I heard **it's better not to get too close**.

But listen, Hazumi is one of the "non-existers." No one ever talks to her at school anyway. That's the rule…

That's not what I mean. This isn't about being on campus; I'm talking outside of school.

We can't get near her? Even outside of school?

There were a couple of girls who walked home with Hazumi a lot, right?

Yeah, Shimamura and Kusakabe.

They say that Shimamura got injured on the way home the other day.

I heard she was hit by a bicycle. But she wasn't hurt that badly, was she?

Did you also hear that Kusakabe's great-grandma—or someone like that—collapsed and had to get taken away in an ambulance?

I didn't know about that.

And it happened just when she was talking to Hazumi on the phone, too. Do you think that was a coincidence?

If it was her great-grandma, she's probably already really old,
so...

But you know, Shimamura and Kusakabe seem to have gotten
spooked, and neither of them wants to walk home with Hazumi
anymore.

Hmm.

What do you think? This is pretty bad, right?

I wonder? I'm not really sure...

†

Hey, hey, we were right; she does seem dangerous. Hazumi, I
mean.

Did something else happen?

You haven't heard about the accident on the 30th?

Accident? No...

A student at First Yomi died in a motorcycle accident.

First Yomi—the high school?

Yeah, First Yomiyama High School, First Yomi. He was a
second-year...

†

...Apparently, the guy who croaked was a second-year in high
school named Nakagawa. He was driving without a license or something.

No, the story was that he was riding on the back of someone else's
motorcycle, and the car turning right blew through the intersection.
The driver survived, but Nakagawa got thrown when the bike overturned, and the next car ran him over, crushing him.

Oof, ouch. Are you sure he didn't join a motorcycle gang or
something?

No, no, I don't think those even exist anymore.

But wow, that's some bad luck.

Yikes.

And so? That Nakagawa guy, the high schooler, was he an acquaintance of Hazumi's?

Yeah, he was. So you see, I think she might really be unsafe...

†

...Did you hear? Hazumi went to the wake for the high schooler who died on the motorcycle.

So she really did know him?

They knew each other from way back. Someone said he was the younger brother of her older brother's best friend or something.

Her older brother...

He's a college student.

And it was his best friend's brother? Hmm.

Listen. There's no way this is a simple coincidence, right?

I wonder...

An injury, a family member collapsing, dying in an accident...and they all happened in quick succession, too.

Are you saying there's some connection because Hazumi is a "non-exister"?

I think there might be.

But the thing with "non-existers" is only a rule for this class. The dead guy isn't even related to anyone there.

That's exactly why I think it might be a possibility.

A possibility...of what?

I think it's possible that Hazumi might be the "casualty."

You mean the "extra person" who joined our class in April?

Yeah, exactly.

No way...

I really think she might be *it*. That's why *bad things* keep happening one after another to people around her.

Really?

I don't know if it's true or not. Akazawa's saying it isn't, but...

....

But apparently, there's no way to confirm whether someone is the "extra person" or not, no matter how we try. So she can't rule out Hazumi for certain.

....

At any rate, it's definitely best not to get too close to her. We'd better treat her like a "non-exister" at all times, even outside of school…

Chapter 6
May I

1

The name Takayuki Nakagawa, which had caught my eye when I saw it in the "News from the Editorial Department" section of the *Yomiyama Town News* e-mail, turned out to belong to an acquaintance of Yuika Hazumi... It was the evening of Wednesday, May 2 when I learned this. Izumi came to my room and told me that speculation was starting to fly in class.

"Apparently, the connection is that he was the younger brother of a close friend of Hazumi's older brother. No matter how you slice it, this has to have been an unrelated accident," Izumi said, crossing her arms indignantly. "But I am worried. I'm sure those unpleasant rumors are gaining momentum because of this. Has Hazumi come to you with any kind of information or consulted with you about this at all?"

"Not so far, no."

"I see..."

Someone told me later that the high schooler Nakagawa was also a journalist working for the publisher of the *Yomiyama Town News*. He sometimes helped gather information and even wrote articles on occasion.

"High School Student Dies in Motorcycle Accident"—the headline implied that the accident had been the result of a badly behaved teenager driving recklessly, but in reality, it was the exact opposite. Takayuki Nakagawa was a serious student and a popular guy. At the time of the accident, he'd been riding in the sidecar of the motorcycle, which someone connected to the *Town News* (age thirty-five, male) was driving. The majority of the blame for the accident fell to the car that had struck them while making a right turn.

There were a few days of school between the long weekend and the upcoming holidays, and when I'd seen Hazumi on Tuesday, there didn't seem to be anything unusual about her. But today, I'd noticed that she looked a little depressed. It was also obvious that she had something she wanted to tell me, so I thought we could talk a little on the way home, but—

The minute the bell rang to signal the end of class, she immediately fled the classroom, alone. Later on, I would discover that she'd hurried home so that she could attend Nakagawa's wake.

"And tomorrow starts another long holiday, huh?" Izumi grumbled, her arms folded across her chest. "It would be nice if those nasty rumors didn't spread too much over the break, but..."

The night grew late, and Izumi went back to her apartment.

After debating it for a little while, I settled on writing Mei Misaki an e-mail.

Takayuki Nakagawa, the deceased student, had attended First Yomiyama High School (abbreviated "First Yomi"), the same institution Mei went to. They were a grade apart, so I didn't think it was very likely that she'd known him, but I figured this was something I ought to report to her just in case. That was my reasoning.

I let her know that even though the "countermeasures" shielding us from the "accidents" seemed to be working for the time being, there had nevertheless been a series of unusual incidents surrounding Yuika Hazumi, which had caused a commotion to sweep through our class. I told her about my anxiety concerning this development and that I wanted to ask for her thoughts on it. And so...

A reply came the next afternoon.

> I WASN'T ACQUAINTED WITH A SECOND-YEAR
> NAMED NAKAGAWA, UNFORTUNATELY…
>   ARE YOU WORRIED ABOUT HAZUMI?
>   BUT AS I SAID BEFORE, EVEN IF SOMETHING
> HAPPENS TO HER,
>   I'M SURE EVERYTHING WILL BE FINE AS LONG AS
> YOU CONTINUE BEING A "NON-EXISTER."

2

"Um, Sou, I—"

Hazumi got that far before she cut herself off, revealing shades of indecision. I continued walking down the path parallel to the river at the same pace without doing anything to urge her on.

"Um, Sou?" she started again, coming to a halt. I stopped, too. The sky was full of dark-gray clouds, and a strong breeze from the river was forcing Hazumi to hold down her hair. "I—somehow, I feel like everyone is avoiding me," she continued.

I'd guessed she might be working up to *that topic.* About thirty minutes earlier, she'd called me, said she was close by, and asked to see me.

"They're avoiding you?" I responded in as calm a voice as possible. "When you say *everyone,* who do you mean? In what way?"

"I mean the kids in our class," she answered, casting her eyes downward. "I've been calling Shimamura and Kusakabe, but they never answer. Even outside of school, they act like they can't see me, like they don't know I'm there. When I asked them what was going on, they just turned away."

Ah, so they're being that blatant about it?

"And it's not just those two, either. The other girls, and the boys, too, they're all doing the same…"

"You're being treated like you 'don't exist' outside of class? That's how it feels?"

"Mm-hmm," Hazumi answered quietly. "Hey, Sou, why are the—?" She suddenly looked up, entreating me for answers. "Why are they all doing this...?"

It was May 6, a Sunday. The afternoon of the last day of Golden Week. It wasn't even five o'clock yet, but thanks to the cloudy weather, it had already started to get dark, as if the sun was just about to set.

On the 3rd, 4th, and 5th, I had done the same thing I had done for the first half of Golden Week—basically stayed cooped up and reading to pass the time. I'd gotten invitations from Yagisawa and Shunsuke Kouda to go out, but somehow, I hadn't felt like it, so I'd turned them down every time.

But I'd also been worried about Hazumi all break.

The e-mail I got from Mei Misaki said that as long as I played my part as a "non-exister," everything would be fine. Mei had been insisting that all along, and my confidence in her was unwavering. Nevertheless, that didn't mean I wasn't worried about Hazumi. I wanted our "countermeasures" to be a success, just as we'd originally planned. That was still how I felt.

"Last week, a high schooler named Nakagawa died in a motorcycle accident, as you know." Resolutely, I began to address the subject. "Did you mention he was an acquaintance of yours? The boy who passed."

"Uh, that's—" She cast her eyes downward again. "Mm. It was such sudden news. I was really shocked to hear it."

"He was the younger brother of a close friend of your brother or something?"

"That's right. He and the older Nakagawa brother have been close for a long time, so I've talked to Takayuki before, too, but I never thought he'd go out in an accident like that..."

She was wearing a light-pink top with a flowy beige skirt. This was my first time seeing Hazumi out of uniform, at least since we'd entered third year.

She bit her lip sadly and let out a deep sigh. Her grief was totally understandable.

"Everyone heard about the crash and lost their cool, I think."

I decided that there would be no point in trying to soothe her or sugarcoat things. I laid my thoughts out for her plainly. "I also heard about Shimamura's injury and the incident in Kusakabe's family. Both events have to be coincidences, with no connection to the 'calamity.' But then, the very next day, an acquaintance of yours passed away. Common sense dictates that this, too, was an unrelated incident, but the rest of our class wouldn't accept the rational explanation. Despite the facts, they blame it on the 'calamity'...that's why."

"............"

"Everyone's scared, you know?"

"Scared...you mean, scared of me?"

"Yeah. I think that's why they're avoiding you. They think that having contact with a 'non-exister' is dangerous, even outside of class."

"N-no way..."

"There's no grounds for it. I mean, I think it's a wild delusion that completely ignores what we know about the 'phenomenon' and the 'accidents.' Akazawa, the countermeasures officer, was worried that something like this might happen."

"It can't be... I didn't do anything wrong!" Hazumi's voice had turned shrill. Her expression was stiff, and her lips trembled slightly. "I did as I was told. I was always careful to act like I 'don't exist' at school! So why is this happening...?"

I couldn't come up with an answer right away, so I moved one or two steps toward the river. I took a deep breath, feeling the wind that blew across from the opposite bank, carrying the scent of the water with it, before turning back around to face Hazumi.

"It's all right," I reassured her. "No matter what everyone thinks, this year's 'countermeasures' are working for now, and there haven't been any 'accidents.' I'm sure that Akazawa and the others will put the gossip to rest for us. So don't get discouraged; keep doing what you've been doing...okay?"

Hazumi's expression didn't relax. But after a silence of several seconds, she wiped a few tears from the corners of her eyes, looked up at me imploringly, and...nodded, weakly but decisively.

"Because you're here," she said, mustering up a smile. "You're here with me, Sou. So I can do it...you know?"

"Uh...uh, yeah," I mumbled in answer. Her approach was leaving me totally bewildered.

Putting any further responses on hold, I started down the path again. Hazumi hurried to catch up with me.

After we'd been walking along like that for a short while, we arrived at the pedestrian-only Izana Bridge. I raised a hand, intending to signal that I would see her later, and kept walking over toward the other side of the bridge. Today, however, Hazumi followed along.

She must want to keep talking or something. Um, now what?

The bridge and its support columns were wooden. The handrail was made of iron, but the coating was wearing off, so it was getting rusty in places. When I was just about halfway across—

"Hey, Sou?" Hazumi called out, stopping me short. "Um..."

"What?"

"About when we held the meeting at the end of March and decided on this year's 'non-exister'... We'd discussed this a little before, right? You offered to take on the role of the 'non-exister,' but after that, someone asked if that was enough for the 'countermeasures.'"

"Yeah. We did go over that."

Everyone had agreed with the suggestion to try having two "non-existers" this year, and then...they ended up choosing the second one by drawing lots with playing cards.

"Why did you accept the role of the 'non-exister'? I certainly don't think it's going to be much fun."

I remembered asking Hazumi on the way home on the day of the opening ceremony.

"That's, um, because I drew the joker."

That's what she had answered back then.

"If you really didn't want to do it, I think you could have stubbornly refused during the meeting."

I think that's what I said to her. We'd made the decision so suddenly that I doubted anyone would have blamed her too harshly if she'd turned it down.

"You know, back then, when we picked the 'second' with the cards, I—" Hazumi had one hand on the railing, looking over at the flowing river. *"I pulled the joker on purpose."*

"Ah—!" Despite myself, I let out a short gasp of surprise.

She looked at me sidelong. "Do you remember? The cards we used?"

I was desperate for an answer.

"We chose the same number of cards as there were people, one of which was a joker... After that, several people shuffled them, but I happened to notice that the corner of the wild card was folded down just a little. When it was my turn to pick, I saw that the bent card was still in the deck, and I...I picked it on purpose."

"Why...?" I started to ask, then trailed off. I placed a hand on the railing like Hazumi and gazed down at the dark-green river.

"Because," she answered, "I figured that if you and I were the only 'non-existers' in the class, then that would be a very special situation."

"............"

"I've had my eye on you ever since we were in the same class in our first year of middle school, Sou. I don't think you ever realized it, though."

"Uh...n-no."

"Back then, you were even more—how do I put this—you had an air about you, like you had built up walls around yourself and didn't let anyone break them down. I never saw you act friendly with anyone other than Yagisawa. And when you were alone, you always sort of looked like your thoughts were off somewhere else."

"Did I? I don't really know what I looked like."

"But I was really curious about you... Somehow I sensed you had a similar aura to you as my big brother."

I had no idea how to respond.

Did I just receive a love confession?

I recalled what Izumi had said to me in half jest the night before the long holiday.

At the same time, I heard another voice, one that I recalled from many years earlier.

"What does 'falling in love' mean?"

It was my own voice, from when I was still an elementary schooler.

"Does it mean when you like someone?"

It was an innocent question that I'd lobbed at my uncle Teruya, whom I idolized, back at Lakeshore Manor during one of my frequent visits. I wondered how he'd responded.

"So you know..." As we looked down at the same river, Hazumi gently leaned her shoulder against mine. "...I'd like you to be friendlier with me. I understand that we can't hang out together as fellow 'non-existers' during school, so...come on—I want to spend more time together in other places. I went to all the trouble of 'not existing' with you, after all."

"Uh, ummm..."

"If we do, I'll be fine, no matter how much everyone else ignores me. I'll persevere."

"Um, when you say...*be friendlier*, I mean, right now, like, we're talking together like this, and I don't really, um..."

"That's not what I mean." Hazumi raised her voice a little. She stared straight at me, with that look that was both mature and childish at once, and said, "That's not it. I..."

I couldn't take it. I darted my eyes around helplessly. And today of all days, there was no kingfisher hovering above the water.

3

As I continued to puzzle over this unfamiliar situation, something suddenly flashed through my head.

"Sounds like there's a rumor that Hazumi might be the 'casualty.'"

"The 'casualty'...in other words, the 'extra person' who appeared in our class in April. They're saying that Hazumi is the one who's really dead, and that's why bad things *keep happening around her."*

This was information that Izumi had given me the night before, when she'd come to my apartment again. Apparently, those rumors had been building over the past several days.

But I'd thought it was ridiculous when she told me.

Sure, the "extra person" who blended into the class during an "on year" was called "the casualty," but the "accidents" weren't related to what they did. I'd never heard anything about misfortunes befalling people who'd come into close contact with the "casualty." And yet...

Generally speaking, yes, it was possible for Hazumi to be this year's "casualty." But it was hard to believe the girl standing right before my eyes had expired in an "accident" in the past.

Hazumi and I were in the same class in our first year. Since then, she'd developed a slight air of maturity and a reputation for being a "beauty" among the boys in our class. These were memories of mine. Concrete memories.

She was also definitely at the "strategy session" at the end of March. She'd really pulled the joker card when the class was deciding on the "second non-exister" and had made a declaration of intent to accept that result. I could recall how she had looked at the time. It was firmly in my memory.

April was when the "phenomenon" had started, bringing with it the "extra person" who appeared in our class. In March, *it* shouldn't have manifested in our world yet, so Hazumi, who'd been chosen as the "second" at the "strategy session," couldn't have been the "casualty." That was how it seemed to me, but...

Things weren't that simple.

Alteration of records.

Alteration of memories.

That was the most mysterious part of the "phenomenon," and it made certainty impossible.

Hazumi had been in the same class as I was in first grade. She'd been there at the "strategy session" in March. But what if these very recollections of mine were "false memories" that had already been altered?

What if, as the rumors went, the "extra person," aka "casualty," who had slipped into Grade 3 Class 3 this year was none other than Yuika Hazumi, and neither she herself nor any of the people close to her realized it...? If that was true, what then?

We knew that people didn't suffer "accidents" just from having contact with the "casualty." Even if we assumed Hazumi really was that person, that wouldn't necessarily mean anything would change. There was nothing we could do about it. Nothing we could do...supposedly.

Suddenly, the wind picked up force and blew down the river, rustling all the trees running alongside it and all the grasses along the banks. Little waves picked up on the river's surface below us.

Holding her skirt down with both hands so that it wouldn't go flying up in the wind, Hazumi lost her balance. I promptly extended both my hands to prop her up by the shoulders. I could feel her body heat through her shirt. Far from what I imagined "the casualty" would feel like, I sensed a warmth that seemed more "alive" than I was.

"Ah—!"

She yelped in surprise, so I pulled my hands away immediately.

"Th-thank you, Sou."

"Oh...don't mention it."

I turned my back on her and continued over the bridge. The wind kept blowing, and the scenery around us grew increasingly gloomy and dim.

"Ah...wait up," she said, following after. "There's a little more that I want to..."

I quickened my pace so that she couldn't catch up to me. Somehow, I got the feeling it wasn't a good idea to continue our conversation. Not for me, and probably not for her, either. However—

When I was just a few meters from the end of the bridge, it happened. I caught sight of that person on the path following along the opposite bank of the river.

It was an utterly unexpected coincidence, so for a second, I doubted my vision. But... *Ah, that's...the person over there, that's...*

...Mei Misaki.

There was no room for doubt.

There was quite a distance between us, and it was getting dark out, but...I was still certain despite that. She wasn't wearing her high school uniform but was instead dressed in an unreasonable amount of black from head to toe. It certainly wasn't her typical outfit. Nevertheless—

The short bob, tossed by the wind. The balance between her small-ish face and her slender body. One glance at the whole picture, and it was clear to me that this was indeed Mei.

She was walking to my right, slowly following along the path in the direction of the river's flow. Then she stopped in front of the Izana Bridge. Tilting her head a little, she stared at me.

"Mei..." I reflexively called her name. "Mei."

I completely forgot that Hazumi was at my side and jogged the remaining several meters of the bridge.

"Sou..." Mei Misaki smiled faintly and greeted me. The wind picked up considerably again, rustling the trees and grass. "What a coincidence, meeting you here."

Unlike when I'd seen her last month at "Blue Eyes Empty to All, in the Twilight of Yomi," Mei wasn't wearing her eye patch this time. She had an artificial eye in the left socket, where she'd lost her eye-ball due to a childhood illness. But it wasn't the blue "doll's eye" that had been there before—

It was a different "eye," black with some brown in it. A new sub-stitute that Mei had begun wearing about two years ago during her daily activities. Ever since getting it, she'd stopped wearing an eye patch as she'd done before.

"Mei..."

As I stood there face-to-face with her, my heart was pounding so fast, I could almost hear it throbbing. Sure, I'd run over here as fast as I could, but it wasn't that far of a distance. I had a feeling that wasn't the only cause.

"Is it all right?" Mei asked.

"Ah?" I tilted my head a little. She cast her eyes past me to the bridge.

"Weren't you talking with that girl?"

"Ah...but we already finished our conversation, so—"

"Did you?"

"Yeah."

"Hmm." Narrowing her right eye suspiciously, Mei continued. "I wonder if it's all right. She's glaring at us."

"Um…no, that's not really…"

I answered uncertainly, then slowly turned around. At that point, Hazumi had already turned her back to us and started going back to the opposite shore. I couldn't tell whether or not she had really been staring daggers at us.

"Ummm…uh, thanks for your message the other day," I said.

Mei smiled faintly again. "Seems like there's a lot going on. Do you think you'll be able to keep it up?"

"Yeah…yes, well—"

"The girl who was just here, would she happen to be the one who accepted being the 'second non-exister'?"

"Uh, yes. She is, but—"

"Hazumi, was it?"

"Yes."

"She's beautiful. Are you dating her, by any chance?"

"No way!" Her question came so suddenly that I made a mad rush to deny it. "I'm not. Nu-uh, nothing like that. We're fellow 'non-existers,' so, like, I give her advice on all sorts of stuff. But that's all."

"Hmm?" Mei narrowed her right eye again and stared into my face. "I think it should be all right so long as you do a good job, but…I can definitely see how she could be a cause for concern. I don't think you can neglect her."

"What do you mean?"

"How do I put this? It's like she's staggering along a narrow path above a precipice. But she hasn't noticed that there's a pit, and she's not about to notice, either…like that."

As I listened to Mei's words, I began to feel as though a cold, heavy mass were expanding in the pit of my stomach. I didn't know how to respond. All my attention was focused on Mei's mouth, waiting for her to speak again.

Then, mingling with the sound of the constant wind, I heard a faint electronic tune. It was her ringtone.

That's right—it's the same song I heard last month at the "Blue Eyes..." gallery.

Mei fished her phone out of her jacket pocket and turned to the side, as if hiding it from me.

"Yeah…ah, yes."

Her response was broken but audible.

"I'm… But…yes. All right…"

I wonder who she's talking to? I'd had the same thought last month, too.

"…Huh? Sure, okay… I haven't said anything, relax."

With that, she hung up the phone.

Who was that?

I was terribly curious, but in the end, I couldn't bring myself to ask her.

4

The next day was May 7. The morning of the Monday after Golden Week.

I went to school a little earlier than usual and headed straight for Building Zero to peek in on the biology club room. Just as I thought, Shunsuke Kouda was already there, checking on the various creatures he was raising.

"Oh, long time no see." When he noticed my arrival, Shunsuke pushed his silver-rimmed glasses up by the bridge and, with an earnest expression, said, "It's great that we were able to make it through April safely, right?"

"Yeah, somehow or other."

"Over the long holiday, we lost a striped loach and an Amano shrimp. I didn't bother reporting it, but they're both currently undergoing diaphanization."

Now he'd gone from serious to pouting. I responded with a pout of my own.

"I suppose it's okay for fish."

"And crustaceans?"

"I suppose it's okay for aquatic creatures…"

"By the way—" Shunsuke went back to his business. "I told you about this year's new members in my e-mail the other day, right?"

"Uh, yeah. Two boys and a girl?"

"Right, yes. So one of those boys is a guy named Takanashi."

As soon as I heard that, it piqued my interest. That was a name I had heard and seen before.

"This *Takanashi*, is his name written with the characters that mean *little birds playing*?"

Shunsuke nodded, serious. "I think he's probably the one you're picturing. Our new member, Takanashi, has a sister two years older than him named Jun. She's in Class 3."

Sure enough, there was a girl in Grade 3 Class 3 named Jun Takanashi.

Just my luck to have a "related individual" join the biology club!

"I was worried about it, so I did a little digging, but it doesn't seem like she's told him anything about the special circumstances of Class 3. She's upholding the rules about not telling other people unless it's absolutely necessary, this Jun Takanashi."

"Seems like it, yeah." I sighed, feeling somewhat heavier. I looked across the room, and my eyes landed on the tank housing the white axolotl, the second Woo.

"I happened to hear something from Keisuke," Shunsuke mentioned. "Something about a few unsettling incidents happening with your class?"

He must have heard that awful rumor about Hazumi.

"That's…" With mixed feelings, I recalled how she'd been acting the day before. "I don't know what you've heard, but most of it doesn't seem to be true. A student from First Yomi High did die in a traffic accident, but he wasn't a 'related individual.' The crash didn't happen due to one of our 'accidents,' so you don't need to worry. The 'calamity' hasn't started."

"Is that so?"

"Yeah."

"Hmm. Well, if you're sure, then I won't worry too much."

A few minutes before the first bell, I left Shunsuke behind in the clubroom. There was one more thing I wanted to check on before going to class.

I headed for the secondary library on the first floor of my current location, Building Zero.

A CLOSED sign had been hanging on the door all April, while the librarian, Mr. Chibiki, was on vacation. He was supposed to have been gone for the whole month, but the room had still been closed up during the first couple days of May. Now that we were back from the long holiday, I was curious to see if it would be open or not.

In the hallway of the old redbrick school building, the sun hardly shone, even in the middle of the day. Just as I finally arrived at my destination, someone called my name from somewhere behind me.

"Sou Hiratsuka." The voice sounded a little hoarse but low and melodious...

That's—

When I turned around, I saw a man in a black shirt, black jacket, and black pants; he was in black from top to bottom.

—Mr. Chibiki.

"Ah, good morning," I greeted him politely. "Have you started back at school today?"

"Yeah. Guess so," he answered. Compared to when I'd met him at the end of the previous year, his face, behind a pair of unfashionable blackish-green glasses, looked quite haggard. His hair had always been streaked with gray, but it seemed to me that it had gotten much whiter. He'd taken leave to deal with some "personal affairs," but now I wondered if he was having health problems.

"I heard about the situation from Ms. Kanbayashi," the black-clad librarian said, walking toward me where I stood. "She told me that this is an 'on year.' And that you accepted the role of the 'non-exister' so the 'countermeasures' would go smoothly—is that right?"

"Yes." I nodded obediently. "And also, um, there's one more person this year..."

"I heard that, too. That's the additional 'countermeasure' they decided on at the meeting in March, yeah? To try having two 'non-existers.'"

"Yes. That's right."

At that moment, the crackling sound of the warning bell started blaring through the old speakers of Building Zero, signaling that there were only five minutes left until the bell marking the beginning of class.

"Are you going to first period? You 'don't exist,' so you've got to be cutting sometimes, right?" Mr. Chibiki asked.

"No. I more or less try to go," I answered. First period on Mondays was math class. If I skipped too much, I wouldn't be able to follow the material at all. "If it was PE or music or something, I could miss it no problem, though."

"Hmm. All right then." Rubbing the tip of his pointed chin, he asked, "I wonder if you could stop by for a bit during lunch? This library will be open again, starting today."

"Ah, sure," I answered without hesitation, "I'll do that."

"Anything you wanted to discuss with me?"

"Yeah...sort of."

"Good, there are some things I want to ask you, too, plus some things I want to tell you," Mr. Chibiki said, roughly brushing back his conspicuously white mop of hair. "I'll be waiting."

5

First period math class. In hindsight, that was when I first noticed that Hazumi was behaving strangely.

By the time homeroom started, she still hadn't arrived. Our class had a tacit understanding that "non-existers" weren't required to attend either the daily short homeroom period or the weekly long homeroom, so this wasn't particularly unusual. After that, she ended up coming in about five minutes late to first period, but since the teacher was aware of the situation, there wasn't a word of censure.

Hazumi herself stayed quiet, of course, and took her seat at the last desk in the row closest to the windows overlooking the schoolyard…

During class, I tried glancing over at her several times from my seat at the last desk in the row closest to the hall. She had her textbook out, but she didn't have a notebook open, nor was she holding a pencil. On top of that, she spent the whole class period with one cheek in her hand, looking down. Maybe Hazumi was sleepy or wasn't feeling motivated. Or perhaps she was simply spaced out or was unwell.

Second period was Japanese language arts class. Hazumi's demeanor didn't change. Even during the break between first and second period, she remained seated with both elbows up on the desk, holding her face in both hands and staring straight down. She didn't so much as glance my way.

This struck me as strange and was definitely cause for concern, but we were in school, and in the room for Class 3 at that. *There's no way I can just go ask her what's wrong…*

When second period ended, Hazumi stood up from her desk and left the classroom alone before the next course began. As she left, I caught a quick glimpse of her face—she was pale. I still didn't feel I could say anything, but I stood up without really knowing why and walked over toward her desk by the window.

"What the…?" I heard a voice. It came from Izumi Akazawa, who'd gone over to the desk before I got there. Next to her was class representative Tsugunaga.

The two of them peered down at Hazumi's place, then looked at each other, and Izumi turned to me for just a second. Frowning pointedly and wearing a grim expression, she shook her head ever so slightly.

Oh, what's going on?

I waited for the two girls to leave, then walked over to the desk myself.

This piece of furniture had been brought over from the old Grade 3 Class 3 classroom in Building Zero for the "non-existers." Staring at its pitted, blackened surface, I found some graffiti.

*   *   *

"Non-existers," go away!

Nearby was more.

Unlucky Hazumi
You're cursed
Are you the "casualty"?

This was written in black (seemingly) permanent ink, with (seemingly) mixed penmanship. The awful words were freshly written, too.

"How cruel," I mumbled unconsciously. "Who would do this?"

What kind of person would take these rumors seriously and stoop to such cheap harassment?

I glanced around the classroom. Naturally, as a "non-exister," I had no one's eyes on me.

Amid the din, Izumi's voice reached my ears. "We have to do something."

"You're right; we do," answered Tsugunaga.

"If this keeps up..."

"It would be awful if it spread, wouldn't it?"

"I can't imagine... In any case, I've got to say something to Ms. Kanbayashi. And warn everyone after school, maybe..."

Perhaps her statement came from a sense of responsibility as a countermeasures officer. That and a sense of justice. From the way she was speaking, I could feel Izumi's irritation and anger at her classmates' failure to maintain their composure and follow the rules.

6

Thinking back on that day, the weather had been strange all morning.

It was unpleasantly chilly for early May. The wind was strong and cold, but about half the sky was cloudless and clear. The other half was full of thick clouds that were shifting from moment to moment.

When I looked outside just after the end of second period, the sky had changed once again. I couldn't make out even a sliver of blue, at least not from the classroom windows. All I could see were clouds. There was an enormous mass of them, a swirling mix of white and leaden gray, swelling up from the ground toward the sky. It almost seemed to writhe ominously on its way up.

The scenery outside, which had been bright until just a moment earlier, was now dark and gloomy. The inside of the classroom had also darkened to the point that we needed to turn on the lights to continue.

Third period was science class.

The bell rang, and Ms. Kanbayashi appeared wearing a white lab coat that she hadn't been wearing during homeroom, but there was still no trace of Hazumi.

Ms. Kanbayashi opened her attendance book on the lectern and checked the number and faces of the seated students. Of course, she must have noticed Hazumi's absence right away, but she carried on without the slightest change to her expression. She also made a deliberate effort not to look toward me at all. Of all the teachers, Ms. Kanbayashi was the most thorough about treating the "non-existers" as if we didn't exist.

What happened to Hazumi?

I assume the graffiti on her desk made her pretty upset.

I guess she spent first and second period looking down like that because of the shock of seeing it. If she doesn't come back to class, it's probably because she doesn't want to be in here anymore—because she can't stand it.

Outside, it was growing increasingly dark. Thunder rumbling in the distance accompanied the sound of fiercely blowing wind…

Ms. Kanbayashi started class without waiting for Hazumi to return.

We were in volume two of the second section of our textbook, a passage on "cells and development of organisms." I was as serious and focused in science as in any other course, but it wasn't very interesting. As someone who'd belonged to the biology club since my first year of middle school, this was all information I knew already. Frankly, it was rather boring.

A little over ten minutes had passed since the start of class. Just as I was stifling my second yawn—

The door in the back of the classroom slid open, and in came Hazumi.

A number of students turned to look as she entered but immediately averted their eyes and faced the front again. Even Ms. Kanbayashi, up at the podium, continued her lecture after only the briefest of pauses, as if nothing had even happened. She didn't acknowledge Hazumi at all.

Seized by a somewhat…no, a *very intense* negative premonition, I glanced sidelong at Hazumi to try to figure out how she was doing.

Once she reached her seat, she didn't make any attempt to take out her textbook or notebook. Instead, she slowly stared up at the ceiling before looking my way. I averted my gaze without watching her complete the movement. From her perspective, it probably looked like I had panicked and turned away. From my standpoint, however, that was the only thing I could have done.

Thunder rumbled in the air. Wind blew through some windows that had been left open, sending the thin curtains that had been halfway pulled back fluttering. And then—

"I can't."

A voice murmured quietly.

"I can't do it."

The second time was a little louder than the first. Then, in an even louder voice—

"I can't do it anymore… I'm sick of this."

The voice was coming from Hazumi.

Ah, this is bad news…

At that point, I think less than half of the class had caught on to what she was doing. Ms. Kanbayashi didn't seem to have noticed; she ignored Hazumi and continued with her lecture, writing several key words up on the blackboard.

"So basically, cell division occurs in this manner in multicellular organisms. After that, the divided cells mature and divide again. Through the repetition of this process…"

Just as Ms. Kanbayashi was getting into her explanation—

Thunder boomed through the air again. The lights, suspended from the ceiling in rows, flickered from instability.

With a clatter of her chair, Hazumi stood up. And then—

"I'm sick of it!"

This time, she raised her voice loud enough to be heard in every corner of the room.

"I can't do it anymore..."

From behind the lectern, Ms. Kanbayashi looked surprised, taken aback even. Most of the students had a similar reaction, and even I couldn't say I was perfect in this regard, either. However—

"All right, let's turn to page thirty-six in the textbook next."

Despite it all, the teacher continued to ignore Hazumi, ignored the complaint she'd surely heard in an attempt to carry on with the lesson. Some students followed her lead and turned the pages of their textbooks, while others glanced over or turned to look at Hazumi where she stood... Despite the fact that no one was saying anything, a strained sort of commotion was spreading through the classroom.

"Don't ignore me any longer!"

Hazumi made another plea, rattling on as though she couldn't maintain control over her agitated emotions.

"I can't be a 'non-exister' anymore!"

The commotion died down briefly. She continued her appeal in a tearful voice.

"I *exist*! I'm not the 'casualty' or anything like that. I'm really alive, and *I'm right here!*"

She may or may not have been done speaking, but at that moment, a strange, unfamiliar sound suddenly began reverberating through the air.

The noise was utterly bizarre. If one tried to express it in an onomatopoeia, it would come out to something like...*papapa, bap, ratatatat...*

It was echoing from the windows.

From all the windows facing the schoolyard. No, on second thought, it was originating from the entirety of the school building, windows included. From every exterior of the building.

For a moment, it wasn't clear what had happened.

Some people probably just assumed it had started to rain. But they were wrong. It wasn't rain. That wasn't the sound of droplets—it was rougher, harsher than that...

This is hail.

I remembered encountering hail several years ago at Lakeshore Manor in Hinami. Back then, the thunder had also sounded as it did now, and a similar sound had also enveloped the house out of nowhere... As I'd looked around restlessly, wondering what it was, Uncle Teruya, who had been with me at the time, explained.

"That's hail. Drops of ice that form inside cumulonimbus clouds collect and fall. Regular hail is five millimeters or more across, while its miniature counterpart is less than five millimeters. From the sound of it, what's falling now is the regular kind."

That's what he had told me.

I heard a girl shriek from the front of the row near the windows.

Surprised at the hail blowing in through the open windows, she leaped out of her seat. A number of people around her also got up in a panic.

I could clearly see bits—more like clusters, actually—of white ice scattered around the area, even from where I was sitting. They were huge. About the size of glass marbles or quail's eggs.

The classroom grew louder and louder. At that moment, thunder roared again, as if striking a routed enemy. It was much closer and much stronger than before. The ceiling lights flickered again. The commotion in the classroom swelled with yet more confusion and fear.

"I am—"

Even amid the chaos, Hazumi continued shouting her appeal.

"I am not the 'casualty'! I am *right here*! I..."

Oh...give it up already, I replied in my mind.

Give up. We get it. You can stop already. You can stop being a "nonexister." It's fine.

...Settle down.

At the same time, I was trying to appease myself.

Calm down. Calm down. It's fine. Even if she drops out now, we'll be okay, as long as I keep doing well at acting invisible.

"As long as you do your job properly, Sou..."

I ruminated over the situation, recalling Mei Misaki's words from yesterday.

Even if Hazumi's actions threatened this year's "countermeasures," the class still has me as a "non-exister." That means the "countermeasures" are still in effect, and we should be able to prevent any "accidents" from occurring. So now...

"Close the windows," Ms. Kanbayashi ordered, dashing toward them herself. "Shut all the open ones!"

In response, several students stood up from their seats and followed the teacher's instructions.

But for some time, all the windows on the schoolyard side of the room rattled in a crosswind, strong enough to be called a gust. Large chunks of hail battered them like bullets; ultimately, they shattered a pane of glass in the back of the classroom—right next to Hazumi's seat.

With a short yelp, she crouched down beside her desk. The gale blowing in tossed her long light-brown hair up in disarray. Fragments of glass rained down on her.

And not a single person moved to help her.

Her insistence that she *existed* had been all too sudden. No one had been able to accept it. So even now, she was still a "non-exister"... That's why no one responded. They wouldn't dare move.

I, on the other hand, was frozen in place for quite a different reason.

Even if Hazumi's given up her duties, I still have to carry on being a "non-exister."

So there's no way I can act like I'm really here right now.

I was only able to entertain that thought for one or two seconds.

The hail kept falling, and the wind kept gusting. Thunder rumbled again, closer this time, and almost simultaneously, all the lights went out.

A power outage from a lightning strike?

Seconds later, the classroom, already in an uproar, descended into even more confusion.

Suddenly, *something* flew in through the broken window beside Hazumi's seat...

Just like when the hail had started, for a second, I wasn't able to grasp what *it* was. I just knew that some big black object had flown in from outside.

But a moment later, I realized what it was.

Something big and black...a bird.

From its pitch-black wings, body, head, and beak, plus its deep, piercing cries, I could tell it was a crow.

One of the crows flying above the school grounds must have been surprised by the sudden hail and flown in to escape. No, it's still acting far too strangely for the circumstances. Its movements are too violent somehow, too random.

Flapping its pitch-black wings, the bird charged toward me. I instinctively covered my face with both arms.

It grazed my head, then crashed into the wall adjoining the corridor. Then it immediately changed course, this time flying toward the blackboard in the front of the room.

I felt something warm on the back of one of the hands I had used to cover my face. When I looked, I found it stained red.

Blood? But I don't think I'm injured, so is this from the bird? I wonder if it's hurt? Maybe it took a direct hit from a big chunk of hail. Which caused it to freak out and do all this...

The black shape darted around the inside of the dim classroom, releasing strange cries all the while. It was a jungle crow, with a full wingspan of about a meter. It seemed huge as it circled around and around, struggling violently inside the classroom.

Screams without respect to gender could be heard in every direction. Some students fled from the erratically flying creature. Some overturned desks and chairs in an attempt to ward off the bird. Others tripped over themselves as they ran around trying to escape...

One boy even pulled a broom out of the cleaning supplies closet and wielded it like a bamboo sword. That individual was Tajimi, one of the countermeasures officers.

Another 2 0 0 1   163

"Everyone, out of the classroom!" In the middle of the confusion, Ms. Kanbayashi shouted, "Calm down! Get into the hall."

The students near the door followed her instructions, but not everyone could escape right away. A number of people had fallen, crouched down on the floor, or were frozen stiff in their seats, unable to move.

Other students were trying to assist them. Tajimi abandoned his broom and joined the effort. Yagisawa too. But as a "non-exister," I obviously couldn't do anything but watch...

Even though it was letting up a bit, hail was still pouring outside.

Meanwhile, the crow continued swooping around haphazardly inside the classroom, colliding with walls and windows and the ceiling, letting out discouraged shrieks and scattering bloody black feathers... Finally, it crashed into one of the light fixtures. The two long fluorescent light bulbs made a loud noise as they shattered.

And right beneath where they'd landed was a girl, facedown on the floor, motionless. She didn't move a muscle when shards from the bulbs rained down on her. The back of her neck, laid bare by her disheveled hair, was wet and crimson...

...*It can't be.*

I felt like my heart had stopped.

There's no way—she can't be...

Dead? Is she dead? Did she maybe hit her head when she fell during the sudden uproar?

Forgetting my duties as the "non-exister," I started to dash over to her, but someone got to her quicker than I could. "Are you all right?" they asked, cradling her in their arms.

"Kusakabe? Come on—get it together!"

The person clutching her was Izumi Akazawa. She had scratches of her own on her forehead as well.

I stopped moving, and Izumi looked toward me for a split second, then nodded slightly.

"You're all right, aren't you? You can stand, right?"

Finally, with Izumi's help, the fallen student—Kusakabe—sat up slowly.

"Thank you," I could hear her say. "It surprised me. I was too scared to move."

"Are you hurt?"

"I'm all right. Just a little sore."

Deeply relieved, I retreated from the area. By then, the sounds of the crow's rampage had ceased.

I slowly retreated into a back corner and looked around the classroom that was still dark from the power outage.

Hazumi was nowhere to be found.

I spotted the battered crow in front of the cleaning supplies closet. Its blood-smeared black wings were bent and broken in places…and one of its eyes was crushed. Its beak hung half open; it had used up all its strength.

"Poor thing…," I mumbled, keeping my voice quiet.

How awful. I'm sure it didn't mean to fly in here and cause all this turmoil.

I've got to get in touch with Shunsuke Kouda later.

If it's going to be treated like garbage and thrown away, I'd like to bury it in the graveyard outside the biology club room. Or maybe I'll let Shunsuke turn it into a display specimen this time if he asks.

7

The hail that had fallen at a little past eleven o'clock in the morning that day varied wildly depending on where you were in Yomiyama City. It was particularly violent in an area with a radius of about two kilometers, which encompassed North Yomiyama Middle School. Outside that zone, it wasn't all that bad. The damage to buildings and fields was also pretty much limited to the places within that circle.

There were a number of other classrooms in Building C, besides the one for Grade 3 Class 3, where the windowpanes broke and caused damage. However, Class 3 was the only room where a crow had flown in and rampaged around the area. It also was the only one in which students sustained cuts from glass shards, got attacked by a bird, or injured themselves in the commotion to escape. Fortunately, however, all their injuries were minor. And needless to say, there'd been no casualties.

During the middle of third period, however—

Hazumi, who'd undertaken the role of the "second non-exister" as part of the year's "countermeasures," renounced her role, insisting on her presence to the entire class. And since the strange sequence of events occurred immediately after her declaration—

I'm not surprised that some people are seeing a connection...

On the one hand, that made a certain amount of sense to me, but on the other hand, I wanted to believe anything but.

If Hazumi's declaration had indeed invalidated the "counter-measures" and started the "calamity," then shouldn't someone have died in the panic that followed?

Moreover—

"As long as you do your job properly, Sou..."

There was also what Mei Misaki had said.

Even if Hazumi called it quits, I was still playing the part of a "non-exister." The "countermeasures" should still be in effect. I figured the "calamity" hadn't actually started yet.

Or so I'd thought, but—

I discovered something else later that evening.

Around the same time that Grade 3 Class 3 was panicking in the face of the hail and the crow, a "related individual" somewhere in Yomiyama City breathed their last. A man in his sixties whose cancer had advanced to the terminal stage, who'd been admitted to a hospice on the outskirts of town some time ago. His name was Jou-kichi Kanbayashi. He was Ms. Kanbayashi's much-older brother.

Part
2

· · · · · · ·

I.A.

Chapter 7
May II

1

"So your 'countermeasures' called for two 'non-existers' this time… I see…"

First floor, Building Zero. The school's old library, which had been demoted to "secondary" status after the completion of the "primary" library in the newer Building A.

"I can't decide if there's any point to that or not." Mr. Chibiki sighed, winding a lock of his unkempt graying hair around a finger.

The gloomy space was tightly packed with documents on local history, rare books donated by former students, and volumes that had been culled from the main collection in the "primary" library. On the other side of the long desk that occupied a back corner of the room sat the "master" of the secondary library, dressed in black from head to toe as always.

"If anyone had consulted me about it ahead of time, I doubt I would have actively supported the idea."

"Is that so? Um…" Shaking off the dread inside me, I asked, "Why do you say that?"

"Because I'm well aware of *how it all turned out three years ago*," he answered, scrutinizing me from behind his blackish-green glasses. "Ms. Kanbayashi had nothing to do with Grade 3 Class 3 that year. I'm sure she doesn't know all the details."

"But...ummm..."

"Three years ago—in 1998, Class 3 also tried making two people 'not exist.' That's indisputable. But it's impossible to judge whether that was a success in the end."

During our "strategy session" in March, the teachers had also told us that it was unclear whether the "additional countermeasure" had actually made a difference or not. But back then, nobody had put it quite so bluntly.

"That year, first of all, Misaki... But you know this already, right? She accepted the role of the 'non-exister,' but..."

"Yes. But despite that, there were some unforeseen complications, so the 'accidents' started happening. And then, in a last-ditch effort, they added the 'additional countermeasure.'"

"That's right. In May, a student transferred in from Tokyo... Actually, I believe you're acquainted with him, too?"

"You mean Sakakibara, right? Yes, Mei introduced me to him, kind of."

"When he came in, no one informed him of the special circumstances of Class 3. Ignorant of Misaki's role, he interacted with her during school, and...to make a long story short, that was the 'unexpected complication' that kicked everything off. Most people think it was probably because of their interaction that the 'countermeasures' were invalidated and the 'accidents' began." Mr. Chibiki placed his hand against his forehead, as though the explanation had exhausted him.

Up until now, I'd heard of this only in vague terms... *I see, so that's what happened?*

"Then the rest of the class had a meeting about whether there was anything they could do about the 'accidents' once they had started and decided to make Sakakibara into a second 'non-exister.' But despite that, the 'accidents' that year continued, so..."

Right, Mei told me the same thing. She also said there wasn't much of a point to adding a second "non-exister" to this year's "countermeasures."

"But didn't the 'calamity' *stop* halfway through the year three years ago?"

"Stop…mm. But the thing is, it stopped that year after we'd already given up on the 'countermeasures' that depended on the 'non-existers.' That was later on."

"Why?" I had to ask. "Why did it stop?"

"Well now. I wonder."

For some reason, Mr. Chibiki turned anxious and shook his head several times. I couldn't tell whether that meant he didn't know or that he knew but couldn't tell me.

"So…" I changed the question. "In your opinion, do this year's 'countermeasures' not make any sense?"

"I told you, it's impossible to tell." Mr. Chibiki wrapped another piece of hair around his finger. "That's how it worked out last time, but this time, the circumstances are different. As far as I know, there's no precedent for trying to have two 'non-existers' from the start of the first semester. As to whether it's completely meaningless or whether it has made any difference—I can't say just yet."

2

May 8, Tuesday.

I'd skipped fourth period music class and gone to visit the secondary library alone. I'd actually intended to go during lunch the day before, but there'd been that big uproar during third period, so it was out of the question.

This morning's homeroom hadn't been with Ms. Kanbayashi. Instead, we were supervised by Mr. Miyamoto, the PE teacher. Until her older brother's wake and funeral service were over, Ms. Kanbayashi would be on leave from school.

The news of her brother Joukichi Kanbayashi's passing had circulated the night before (according to Izumi), so most of the students knew by now. Those who didn't know all gasped at Mr. Miyamoto's announcement. And then an uncomfortable silence descended over us…

…In the quiet classroom, students glanced around at one another with uneasy eyes. Occasionally, someone's gaze would come my way, but as the "non-exister," I had to be thorough about ignoring them.

The windowpane that had been smashed open during yesterday's hailstorm was covered up with cardboard as a temporary measure. As for the fluorescent lights the crow had broken, they'd already been replaced with new ones. And—

Yuika Hazumi was absent from her seat in the back of the row closest to the windows looking out onto the schoolyard.

She hadn't returned since yesterday's commotion. I was concerned about her and had tried calling her cell phone several times the previous evening, but she hadn't answered once, so…I anticipated that she probably wouldn't be coming to school today. *She might not be back for a little while. Now that I think about the way she acted yesterday, today's absence was probably inevitable.*

3

I had become very well acquainted with Mr. Chibiki in the two years and change since I'd started at North Yomi. Mei had told me about him originally, calling him an *"observer of the 'phenomenon.'"* She'd also advised me to listen to what he had to say. And so—

Since my first year, I'd taken every opportunity to slip off to the secondary library. I hardly ever borrowed books or read anything there, but we would always exchange a few words whenever I dropped by. He'd been the head teacher for Grade 3 Class 3 twenty-nine years ago, when the aforementioned student, Misaki Yomiyama, had died. Mr. Chibiki had been working at the school as a social studies teacher at the time, another fact I eventually heard from the man himself. Generally, he would also answer whatever questions I had about the "phenomenon" and the "accidents," though he didn't volunteer much, and he certainly wasn't very talkative.

So actually, I wished I had been able to meet with Mr. Chibiki earlier than I did. Maybe in late March, when I found out I would be in Class 3, or after we had decided on this year's "countermeasures" at the "strategy session." It would have been nice if I could have seen him and gotten his opinion as an "observer." However—

The last time I saw his face was at the end of the previous school year, and he hadn't come to school at all since the start of the new year. It had been easy to look up his contact information in the faculty roster, but I had hesitated to phone him without warning...

I wonder what kind of "personal affairs" would make him absent for so long? I hesitated to ask that today as well. I was concerned about the fact that his face looked much more haggard than ever before and that his voice and affect seemed to lack any spirit. But it wasn't my place to say anything...

"...Mr. Chibiki, what do you think about the series of events yesterday?" I launched right into the issue at hand. At this hour, there was of course nobody but the two of us here in the library room. "There was such a big uproar in the classroom...and then Ms. Kanbayashi's brother passed away. Do you think the 'calamity' has started?"

On the other side of the counter, Mr. Chibiki made a low "*hmm...*" as he stroked his chin where he'd grown a sparse beard.

"It's hard to know how we should react to it all," he answered carefully, "but one of the two 'non-existers'...Hazumi was her name, right? She raised her voice in front of everyone during third period yesterday, didn't she? She announced that she *existed*. In other words, she abdicated her position."

"That's right."

"I can't be a 'non-exister' anymore!"

The sound of her ranting from the day before rang in my ears.

"I exist! I'm not the 'casualty' or anything like that. I..."

It had been like an explosion of built-up emotions. I could easily imagine the thought process that had gotten her to that point. When I imagined what was going through her mind, I felt responsible to some extent, and my chest began to hurt.

But even more important than that was the question of understanding the present situation and gaining insight into what was to come... *I wonder if thinking that makes me a coldhearted person? I bet it would seem like that to, say, Yagisawa.*

"Hazumi quit being a 'non-exister.' Immediately afterward, hail began to fall. The classroom descended into disarray when the windowpane broke, and a crow flew in and caused a scene. Multiple people were injured."

"Yes," I replied.

"And yet, no one lost their life during all that."

"Correct," I answered again.

"But in a separate location, on the same day, Ms. Kanbayashi's older brother Joukichi Kanbayashi—he died. I wonder how closely related the two events were in time?"

"I heard they happened at around the same time."

"What was the exact time? Did Joukichi's death come before Hazumi raised her voice in the classroom or after?"

"Oh, I'm not sure."

"*If it happened before she spoke*, then we can consider Joukichi's death to be unrelated to the 'phenomenon.'"

"And *if it happened after*, then it is connected in the end?"

"No," Mr. Chibiki replied, tilting his head slightly as a vertical crease formed on his forehead, "I don't think that's likely."

"What do you mean?"

"It means..."

He started to answer, then held his tongue for a moment and stood up out of nowhere. He came out from behind the counter, walked over to the large reading table, pulled out a chair, and sat down.

"Come sit," he bade me.

I did as I was told and sat in a chair across the table from him.

"During an 'on year,' a 'casualty' joins the class," he explained. "Because of that, the whole class gets closer to 'death.' That is the terrible 'phenomenon' that has plagued Grade 3 Class 3 of North Yomi for the past twenty-eight years. We have absolutely no idea why this event happens, and we certainly can't explain it scientifically. We've grasped the laws governing the 'phenomenon' to a certain extent, but really only in a limited capacity. The 'countermeasure' of making someone in the class 'not exist' seems to be effective in warding off the start of the 'calamity'—that much is clear, but what the definition of a 'non-exister' is is actually very vague. The truth is, we're still fumbling in the dark when it comes to the 'phenomenon' and the 'accidents.' All we can do is observe events as they happen, then make conjectures...but I'm not sure whether that's bringing us any closer to the heart of the matter. It's possible that everything we do is far off from the reality of the situation."

Wearing the most somber expression I had ever seen on his face, Mr. Chibiki sighed deeply. "That said, it's not as if we can stop fumbling around. We must observe, make conjectures, and set our powers of reason to work to confront the 'phenomenon.' If we can't do that, we should just abandon it all and run away from here."

The words *run away* sent dark ripples through my mind.

During the summer of fourteen years ago, Uncle Teruya had chosen that option. He'd fled from this school, from this town, taking his whole family with him. And then...

"In any case," Mr. Chibiki continued, "what we need to do now is to calmly consider the facts of each situation as it happens, make a judgment based on examples from the past, and then address it as best we can. Even someone like me, who's been observing the 'phenomenon' at this school for ages, can only make an obvious statement like that, I'm ashamed to say."

"..........."

"Well then." Mr. Chibiki put both his hands on the table, sat up straight, and looked me in the eye. "How to take the events of yesterday is the question."

"Uh, yes."

"Hazumi quit 'not existing,' but there's still one 'non-exister' left— you. And the technique you're trying this year is a kind of 'insurance,' right? Even if you lose Hazumi, your 'number two,' there's still you, 'number one.' It would be strange, then, for the 'calamity' to begin right away, despite this tactic. When you take a step back, that's the theory."

Even if Hazumi drops out, as long as I continue in the role, the "countermeasures" should be effective. That's right. Mei's been consistently saying that from the beginning, and I also feel like that's correct. And yet...

"*Nevertheless*, let's work from the hypothesis that the 'accidents' began yesterday during third period," Mr. Chibiki continued. "As we've just confirmed, there was a violent hailstorm, a crow that flew in through the window and raged around the room, and people who got injured. But no one died there. That strikes me as quite unusual."

"..........."

"When the 'calamity' starts, one or more 'related individuals' will die every month. The way they succumb varies, from getting caught up in an incredibly unlikely accident, to the sudden onset of a fatal disease, or even suicide or homicide... But in any event, I think we can say that once the 'calamity' begins, *it becomes easier* for 'related individuals' to get killed. The likelihood of them dying unexpectedly, or in a trivial accident, skyrockets. That tendency is obvious. Whereas—"

"Even though there was a huge disturbance in the classroom yesterday, nobody died at the scene," I added.

"Exactly." Mr. Chibiki nodded. "If the 'calamity' had actually begun, we would expect someone to have died during yesterday's confusion. It's far stranger that everyone made it out alive, really. So..."

"So the disturbance yesterday was simply a coincidence, and the 'calamity' hasn't started yet?"

"I think we can accept that explanation."

Mm, that's what I thought yesterday, too. Of course, I may have mostly been trying to reassure myself then. But—

"The question then becomes the matter of Joukichi Kanbayashi's death," Mr. Chibiki continued on in an unperturbed tone. "Let's leave aside the earlier discussion about whether the hour of his death came before or after Hazumi's desertion. He was an inpatient at a hospice outside the city, wasn't he?"

"That's what I've heard."

"As you know, hospices are facilities that house patients in serious condition who have no prospect of recovery. Their purpose is to ease the physical and emotional pain of their residents as they wait for death to claim them—end-of-life care, they call it. Joukichi was afflicted with terminal cancer, right? In short, it wouldn't have been strange for him to pass at any moment given the condition he was in. And his final hour just happened to arrive yesterday. What if we think of it like that?"

"Ah…" I unintentionally let out a little noise.

"He wasn't connected to the 'calamity'—*he just died because he was going to anyway.*" Mr. Chibiki ran a finger across his cheek. "I think there's plenty of room for that interpretation. That's my take on it anyway."

He said that and nodded, but his expression was still slightly uneasy. As though wondering whether he was being overly optimistic.

4

"I just remembered…," I spoke up, right as the bell signaling the end of fourth period began to ring.

"What is it?" Mr. Chibiki pushed his blackish-green glasses up, a sour look on his face.

After waiting for the bell to cease, I said, "Yesterday morning, when I met you in the hall, I think you said you had something you wanted to ask me, plus something you wanted to tell me about."

"Oh yeah. I did say that, didn't I?"

"So?" I didn't get the impression it was anything all that serious, but now that I had remembered, I was obviously curious. "What was it?"

"It's nothing important," he answered and pushed his glasses up again. "The thing I wanted to tell you about was, well, basically what I said when you first got here. About there probably being no point to the 'countermeasure' of having two 'non-existers' this year. Though like I said before, it probably helps as 'insurance.'"

"Ah, all right."

"And the thing I wanted to ask you was…" He stopped, got up from his chair, and moved his neck and shoulders around a little like he was trying to work out muscle stiffness. "Man, I'm thirsty. Want anything to drink?" he asked.

"Uh, no, please don't go to the trouble."

"Really? You don't need to be polite."

Mr. Chibiki left the table and ducked behind the counter for a moment, then came back holding two plastic bottles. *Has he got a fridge back there?*

The bottles were full of mineral water. He handed one to me, then opened the cap on the other right away and swallowed half the contents in a single gulp.

"Thank you," I said, taking the bottle.

"I heard that you put your hand up and volunteered to be this year's 'non-exister,'" Mr. Chibiki remarked as he set his bottle on the table.

I nodded. "A long time ago, I decided that I would if I ended up in Class 3."

"Hmm. So then…now that you've actually been 'not existing' for about a month, I'm curious how you're doing. What I mean is, how are you doing mentally?"

"I'm—"

Cutting me off, Mr. Chibiki continued. "But from what I've seen of you today, there doesn't seem to be anything to worry about."

"Oh, really?"

"No matter how well you understand it rationally, it's very emotionally trying for your whole class to treat you like you don't exist. People say they feel needlessly isolated and get depressed or start experiencing paranoia, things like that. I can think of dozens of examples from the past."

Isolation… If that's all, then I've been accustomed to that since I was young.

And feelings of paranoid delusion? I don't think that could ever happen to me.

"I'm just fine," I responded flatly.

Mr. Chibiki softened his expression somewhat and nodded. "You seem fine. But just in case, come and see me if you find yourself losing control of your emotions. I don't know how useful my advice will be, but it's sure to be better than trying to deal with everything yourself. Got it?"

"Thank you very much." I politely expressed my gratitude. "But I'm certain that I'll be all right on that front."

"Hmm. What a reliable young man you are." Mr. Chibiki's expression softened even further. "By the way," he added, "I wonder if you've seen or spoken to Ms. Misaki lately?"

His question took me a little by surprise. Letting my gaze wander around the tabletop, I answered, "Yes. Occasionally."

"She's in her third year of high school by now, eh?"

"That's right."

"Have you been discussing this year's developments with her, too?"

"Um, yes," I replied. "And naturally, she seems rather concerned about everything."

"Hmm. Is that so?" At that, Mr. Chibiki looked up diagonally at the ceiling of the dimly lit library room and abruptly narrowed his eyes. He looked like he was reminiscing about the past. "Mei Misaki. She was, how can I say, a student with a mysterious presence. And I thought it had to be more than a coincidence when I first learned that you were a child who had some kind of fateful connection to her, two years ago, when you entered this school just as she was graduating out of it."

I'd never told Mr. Chibiki about the events I had experienced at the Hinami lake house three summers ago or about everything that Mei had done for me back then. I didn't think I wanted to discuss it with him now, either.

"Misaki was..." Just as he was about to say something else, the door slid open with a clatter. I was well acquainted with the two students who entered—

"Good afternoon."

"Sorry to intrude!"

They were two of my classmates, Izumi Akazawa and Nobuyuki Yagisawa.

"Oh!" Mr. Chibiki reacted. "How unusual to have so many visitors."

The two of them must have immediately realized that I was also in the room. Needless to say, a tension of sorts ran through them. This library was part of North Yomi, so the two of them had to treat me as if I "didn't exist," after all.

But I was fully aware of that.

They must have come to consult with Mr. Chibiki about something of their own, I realized and stood up silently from my chair. I moved away from the table, toward a spot by the back window.

I'll stand over here without saying anything so they can pretend like I'm not even here.

That was my plan, and they seemed to grasp it. Mr. Chibiki too.

"Um, I'm Yagisawa, class representative for Grade 3 Class 3...," he said to Mr. Chibiki, who nodded, then looked at Izumi, who was standing beside him.

"And you?" His mouth formed the words, *You are...?*

"Countermeasures officer Akazawa," Izumi replied. Her line of sight was directed straight at Mr. Chibiki alone, nowhere near me.

"Akazawa, huh?"

This might have just been my imagination, but as he fixed his gaze on her, he seemed quite confused. Tilting his head to the side slightly and frowning, he asked, "Hmm, you are...?"

Thud. I felt a low reverberation.

It was outside my normal range of hearing. I could only feel it.

This...sensation...it's like, yes, it feels like someone looking in from outside the world has stealthily clicked a camera shutter closed. Followed by a black strobe light...

That's how I felt, but only for a moment.

After that instance passed, I completely forgot about the sensation. By the time that happened, the look of bewilderment had entirely disappeared from Mr. Chibiki's face.

"Izumi Akazawa, is it? I see—so you're the countermeasures officer?"

"Yes. There are two others besides me, too—Etou and Tajimi."

"Interesting... So? What's your business here?" he asked them. "I'm sure you didn't come to borrow books. I bet you're here to talk to me about the 'phenomenon' and the 'accidents.'"

5

After that, Mr. Chibiki consulted with Izumi and Yagisawa—and I ended up listening to their conversation from a corner of the room far away from the table they were all sitting around, dedicated to the utmost to my role as a "non-exister." My predictions had been just about right—they'd come to discuss the same things with Mr. Chibiki as I had. Namely, the question of whether or not they should take yesterday's series of events to mean that the "calamity" had begun. The opinion he expressed to them was also roughly the same as what I had heard from him earlier...

"...So you see, there's still a significant possibility that the 'calamity' has not, in fact, started, right? In that case, I think it would be rash to decide that the 'countermeasures' are ruined just because Hazumi alone deserted her duty," Mr. Chibiki concluded.

Yagisawa responded, "So the thing with Ms. Kanbayashi's older brother had nothing to do with the 'calamity,' right?" I expected to hear his sigh of relief any moment now.

"That's not a question I can answer with one hundred percent certainty, but from what I've heard, there's a good chance that's correct."

"That's not a reassuring way to put it...," Yagisawa replied. "But, well, I feel like I won't be able to keep going if I don't carry on that way."

"But I don't think there's anything wrong with that. So..." As she was speaking, Izumi's gaze flicked over to me briefly. Though, as a "non-exister," I couldn't nod or signal her with my eyes or anything in response...

...*So I'm* continuing on, *just as I expected.*

Silently, I directed my thoughts toward Izumi.

Today, after this, and from tomorrow morning on...I must continue to play the part of a "non-exister" as a "countermeasure" to prevent the "calamity." Not with Hazumi at my side but alone. All by myself. Of course—

As long as there's a purpose to it, that's no problem for me.

I'm not the least bit frightened of solitude. I don't have any paranoid delusions. I can keep it up just fine.

6

Hazumi didn't come to school again the next day. Or the day after that or the day after that, either.

Ms. Kanbayashi reappeared two days later, on Wednesday the 10th. She seemed like she'd probably also spoken to Mr. Chibiki and gotten a positive assessment of the situation.

During homeroom that day, she announced, "Let's continue with the 'countermeasures' with the assumption that the 'calamity' has not begun." She looked around the classroom with a face as expressionless as a Noh mask; it appeared as though she was suppressing her emotions. "My brother's death on Monday was unavoidable and came at the end of a protracted illness. It appears to be unrelated to the 'calamity.' And so…"

Her only comment about Hazumi's absence was, "It is what it is." In a tone of voice like she was keeping any unnecessary emotion in check, she explained, "If you consider Hazumi's feelings, it's perfectly reasonable that she might want to be absent from school for a little while. For the time being, it's probably best to give her some space."

The old desk and chair placed at the rear of the row closest to the windows on the schoolyard side for the "non-exister" were still there. Before long, these were sure to be replaced with the newer desk and chair that had originally been there.

On Tuesday night, Izumi sent me a report. "Hazumi may have dropped out, but we all agreed that you should continue being a 'non-exister' for the 'countermeasures' from now on, Sou."

She went on to tell me that the countermeasures officers and other key students had discussed the matter off campus after school; ultimately, they decided on this course of action, and they'd already told

Another 2001   183

the rest of the class. All that remained was to get Ms. Kanbayashi's seal of approval.

In this way—

The chaos that had threatened to overtake the class had, for the time being, given way to some sense of stability. Though it was a delicate balance, one that had not entirely dispelled the currents of anxiety and fear that came from deeming Hazumi a "deserter."

But it's all right; it'll be all right—I admonished myself strongly.

As long as I just continue "not existing" exactly as I've been doing until now, everything will turn out okay. The "calamity" hasn't started yet. Which means I can still prevent it. I have to.

Repeating this thought like a prayer, I solemnly devoted myself to my duty.

Another two days passed, then three, and then the week was over... Hazumi was still absent, but no misfortunes worth mentioning befell the class. The delicate balance had started to stabilize somewhat.

If only this equilibrium could continue on forever so the "calamity" doesn't start, I wished ardently.

7

Eventually, I got another opportunity to speak with Mei Misaki.

I'd tried visiting "Blue Eyes Empty to All, in the Twilight of Yomi" several times on my way home from school, but no matter what day I went, Mei wasn't around, so I hadn't gotten to see her. I summarized the events of Monday and the main points of my conversation with Mr. Chibiki the following day in an e-mail, but I wasn't sure whether she'd read it, as I never got a response.

But on Saturday, she called me at last.

"I think it's fine," Mei said. "I don't think Mr. Chibiki's judgment will let you down. I do feel bad for that girl Hazumi, though. But as long as you keep it together, you'll be all right."

"Okay."

Hearing Mei say, *You'll be all right*, was probably the best encouragement in the world for me. That was enough for me to believe. With a renewed feeling of confidence, I took a deep breath and held it, then once again answered her with an obedient, "Okay."

"Oh, and listen," she continued. "Next week, I've got my school trip."

"School trip...?"

"These days, it's popular for people to go on their high school trip in their second year, but at my school, we go during the third year, around this time."

"Ummm...where are you going?"

"Okinawa."

"Huh?"

"Honestly, I'm not that interested."

When I pictured Mei mixed in with a big crowd of students on a group trip to Okinawa—it didn't seem to fit at all. It made me kind of antsy. But it wasn't like I could tell her she didn't have to go if she didn't want to.

"My dad even told me I could pass on Okinawa and join him on a work trip to Europe instead; he was totally serious. But I don't exactly feel like doing that, either."

Mei's father, Kotaro Misaki, apparently flew from country to country year-round for his job in international trade. I was acquainted with him as well, so I could imagine him suggesting that like it was nothing.

"We're scheduled to return on the twentieth," Mei said with a short sigh. "Call me if anything comes up while I'm gone."

"Uh...sure."

There shouldn't be any emergencies, since everything's "all right," like you say. That was my first thought, but of course I obediently agreed.

A brief silence fell between us before Mei started talking again. "Oh, right, I mentioned something about this before, but I'm coming over to your place soon."

"Ah. Uh, ah...o-okay." My reaction in the moment was one of utter confusion. "But even if you come over, there's nothing to do."

"I'm curious to see what kind of apartment you're living in all by yourself. And I want to see the doll you have as a memento of Teruya, okay?"

"Uh...sure."

The doll was out of its box, displayed on top of a chest in the bedroom.

It was a beautiful figure of a girl in a black dress, probably the first- or second-most important object I owned... And as Mei had said, the doll was a memento of my uncle Teruya, who had passed away three years earlier. On top of that, it was a creation of Mei's mother, the doll artist Kirika.

"All right, see you later, Sou." Before she hung up, Mei muttered something partly to herself: "I'm sure everything will be fine."

8

"What's this one called?"

A bunch of dinosaur figurines were lined up in the display case. With their owner's permission, I picked up a creature that I wasn't too familiar with and asked about it.

"Velociraptor."

Izumi looked back from the counter where she had been preparing coffee and answered.

"Veloci...?"

"Raptor. You don't know about them? I thought you were in the biology club."

"I know about tyrannosaurus and triceratops and a bunch of others."

"Have you never seen *Jurassic Park*?" Yagisawa asked. He grabbed the figure from my hands and scrutinized it. "They showed it on TV the other day."

"...I've never seen it."

"But you must know the title?"

"I've heard of it, but I've never watched the movie. And I don't particularly want to."

I knew the basics, of course: It was a huge blockbuster directed by Steven Spielberg. I recalled the original novel by Michael Crichton being on the bookshelf at Lakeshore Manor, but I hadn't read that, either.

"Most boys love dinosaurs and monsters, you know. I'm not bragging, but I'm a fan."

"Well, it's not like I'm scared of monster media like Gamera and whatever."

"Then *Jurassic Park* should be fine!"

"Hmm."

Dinosaurs were creatures that actually used to exist in this world, so completely fictitious creatures didn't seem all that different to me, at least not while they were rampaging around on-screen. But I didn't feel like having that conversation now, so I kept quiet.

"You like them, huh, Akazawa? Dinosaurs and monsters and stuff?" Yagisawa asked, setting the figure down on the living room table.

"I don't really care about monsters," Izumi answered, "but I love dinosaurs. My favorites are the raptors."

"Oh? Why those in particular?"

"Partly because *Jurassic Park* was the first movie I ever saw in theaters."

"I like T. rex better, though. It's so big and strong."

"But the main characters in that movie are definitely the raptors, right? They're ruthless and clever... They're my favorite by a long shot. Plus, they're cute."

"How on earth are they cute?!" Yagisawa brushed his ruffled hair back. "But you said you saw it in theaters... It was shown a really long time ago."

"My older brother wanted to see it, so he took me along."

"The guy who's in Germany?"

"Yeah, him."

"He took his elementary-school sister to see a dinosaur flick, huh? I couldn't have handled it!"

"Let's see...what grade was I in when we went?"

"I think the sequel, *The Lost World*, came out three or four years ago now."

Izumi put our three coffees on a tray and brought it over. Then she reached out for the figurine on the table.

"My brother bought this for me after the film, you know." She narrowed her eyes nostalgically as she spoke. "I heard the third movie in the series is supposed to come out this summer. Do you want to go see it all together?"

"Sure, okay," Yagisawa answered.

"How about you, Sou?" Izumi looked at me.

I didn't feel like I could tell her I wasn't interested, so I nodded. "Yeah, okay."

It was the evening of May 17. We were in unit <E-1> at the Freuden Tobii—Izumi Akazawa's room.

A little after eight, Yagisawa had called up uninvited to my room, asking if I wanted company. Then Izumi came over and said she would treat us to coffee…

"Please have some," she offered, pouring cups for us. "You know the café by the river, Inoya? This is their blend. It's got a characteristic mellowness to it. It's really tasty."

"Thanks!" Yagisawa took a cup.

"Oh, wait," Izumi said before bringing in a paper bag from the kitchen. "I've got all sorts of doughnuts, too. They're from my mom."

"Wow, don't mind if I do! Thanks, Mom!"

Unexpectedly, we'd started a little nighttime tea party. Yagisawa and I gently toasted with the cups of Inoya-blend coffee Izumi had poured for us.

"I don't know how we managed to do it, but some congratulations are in order for warding off the start of the 'calamity' this past month and a half…I think," noted Yagisawa. "I wasn't sure how things were going after last Monday, but nothing has happened since then. Anyway, it's a relief that it hasn't begun yet."

"That's for sure." Izumi's lips curled into a smile. "It's all thanks to Sou."

"I don't really feel like I'm putting in that much effort, though," I answered as casually as I could manage. I sighed slightly as I added, "And the road ahead is still long…right?"

9

"By the way, about Hazumi...," Izumi started.

Yagisawa stopped chewing on his doughnut. "She hasn't shown up at all this week. Has she gotten in touch with you, Sou?"

"She hasn't," I answered quickly.

"Not even once after all that?"

"Nope."

"Aren't you worried?"

"Well, kind of."

"Geez, you're cold!"

"I said I was kind of worried! But what else can I do?"

"Look, man, first of all, you—"

"I'm the one responsible for failing to stop the rumors from spreading," Izumi interjected. She bit her lower lip in regret. "Anyone would be shocked to have graffiti like that scrawled on their desk. It's totally understandable that she couldn't take it anymore."

"I don't think you need to feel so responsible, Akazawa. The people who wrote that stuff are in the wrong." Yagisawa frowned decisively, then stuffed his half-eaten doughnut into his mouth. He turned to me again. "Sou, you must feel a little responsible, too."

"Uh...yeah, I guess."

"If only you'd been a little nicer to her... Well, too late to do anything now."

It was probably only natural that Yagisawa would want to say that. After all, when I thought back on my various interactions with Hazumi since the morning of the opening ceremony in April, I did feel a twinge of pain in my chest. However—

Was I supposed to put on an act and welcome her advances just because of that?

Though I posed the question to myself, I couldn't come up with a better solution.

There's no way that I would have been able to fake it convincingly. And even if I could have, I probably would have ended up hurting her even more in the end...

"Apparently, Shimamura and Kusakabe were worried, so they went to visit Hazumi's house last Sunday," Izumi said.

Yagisawa reacted immediately. "Oh, did they? So how is she?"

"They said no one would come out, no matter how much they called. She probably wasn't home. Or maybe she was pretending not to be there. She didn't answer when they called her cell phone, either."

"Hmm. What about her parents or extended family?"

"Her parents are both busy with work, so they aren't home very often. It's always been that way, apparently."

"They're basically hands-off. To put it bluntly, they're neglectful." I remembered Hazumi telling me that herself.

I had to assume that her parents probably weren't aware that their daughter hadn't been to school in a week, much less that they knew about the unique circumstances of Grade 3 Class 3. And even if they did know, they probably didn't take it seriously. That's how it seemed to me.

"So at this point, we have no idea whether she's shut up in her room or wandering around aimlessly outside?" Yagisawa stroked his scraggly chin hairs solemnly.

"But you know, after that," Izumi continued, "either the day before yesterday or the day before that, someone saw her."

"Oh? Who?"

"Tsugunaga."

"The class rep? How did she seem? Hazumi, I mean."

"Well…" Izumi brought her coffee cup up to her mouth and sighed deeply. "Tsugunaga just happened to catch sight of her sitting in the passenger seat of a car."

"A car?"

"She said the driver was a young man who looked like a college student. According to Tsugunaga, Hazumi looked like she was really enjoying herself."

"No way!"

"It was probably her big brother or something, right?" I interjected. But when I realized that Hazumi's brother was attending college in Tokyo, I added, "Or maybe her brother's friend?"

"Well, isn't that great?" Yagisawa grinned. "The heartbroken young lady, spurned by Sou, suddenly finds herself with an older college boy..."

"Yagisawa!" Izumi snapped and scowled at him.

He held his tongue and scratched his head.

Later on, I would learn that the young college student was the older brother of Takayuki Nakagawa, the high school boy who had died in a motorcycle accident at the end of April. He was a close friend of his, so Hazumi knew him as "Big Brother Nakagawa." I'd never met him, so I didn't have any idea about his character, but she'd once told me that, *"Big Brother Nakagawa has always been very kind to me..."*

In that case...

If spending time with him can help Hazumi deal with the stress she's been under since April, if it can soothe her hurt feelings in any way—in that case, there's no need to worry too much about her skipping school.

10

"I can't believe midterms are next week!" exclaimed Yagisawa after finishing off his own doughnuts and what was left of my portion, too. He gave a big yawn. "I wish they would waive exams for Class 3 out of respect for our unusual circumstances."

"And once the tests are over, we've got career guidance counseling, too," I added.

"And they're calling in my parents for a conference. How 'bout you, Akazawa? Are you going to a public high school like most people?"

"Who knows?" Izumi tilted her head a little to the side, a gloomy look on her face. She glanced at the door to the piano room in the back. "I don't have the option of going to conservatory anymore. My parents seem to want to send me to a prestigious private girls' school, but I don't know how I feel about that."

"Would the girls' school be in Yomiyama?"

"It's in another prefecture, a full-on boarding school."

"No way!" Yagisawa leaned back exaggeratedly. "Your family's really classy, Akazawa."

"Come on—don't say it like that."

"Heh-heh. What are you doing for high school, Sou?"

I wasn't sure how to answer, so I made some noncommittal noises. "Ah, well…"

The undeniable truth was that my own family had cast me out, so the Akazawas were now responsible for me. Both Uncle Haruhiko and Auntie Sayuri had told me I could go to high school, and even college, but I was torn over whether it was all right for me to presume that of them.

"Speaking of high school, it's going to be hard for you to keep 'not existing' as you study for entrance exams."

"I normally study alone, so I don't think it's going to be much trouble to do both," I said matter-of-factly. "But it doesn't feel like it's really happening yet. The entrance exams aren't until next year, and there are still seven months left in this one. And of course, there's the more pressing issue of the 'calamity' and the 'countermeasures'…"

"I still can't believe this place. How could they let a messed-up situation like this go on for years without doing anything about it?"

"Probably because there's no scientific explanation for it," Izumi responded. "Like, there's no way that a public institution responsible for our education could admit, however obliquely, to being the site of a mysterious supernatural 'phenomenon.' Right, Sou?"

"I think that's part of it. Also, how do I put this? The 'phenomenon' probably extends some sort of influence over the entire town of Yomiyama, up to and including altering the awareness and perception of every person who lives here."

"What do you mean?" Izumi asked.

I pressed a thumb against my temple. "I can't find the right way to put it, but…there's talk of the alteration and falsification of records and memories that happens along with the 'phenomenon,' right? Same with the true identity of the 'casualty' who slips into the class— I've heard people can identify them after graduation but that, as time passes, everyone's memories become clouded. So in other words, a similar thing might be happening to the whole town."

"Hmm..." Yagisawa frowned and stroked his chin. "The whole thing... Come on, man. I really don't see how that could be possible."

"I don't really get it, either."

"Hmm—"

"That reminds me," Izumi interjected, "did you hear that three years ago, when it was an 'on year,' someone in the class died on the last day of the first-semester midterm exams?"

Ah, that...

The memory was painful.

An unfortunate accident that had occurred at North Yomiyama Middle School in May, three years back. I remembered reading a newspaper article reporting on it when I was living in Hinami.

"Apparently, a girl who was class representative died at the time," Izumi continued, "so sounds like Tsugunaga is a little worried."

"She's worried because she's the female class rep?"

Izumi stared Yagisawa straight in the eye as she answered him with a nod. "Yep. Her hunch is totally groundless, though. I mean, think about it. A female class rep dying on the last day of exams this time, just because it happened three years ago? ...Give me a break."

"The 'calamity' hasn't started, so surely there's no reason to worry about that."

"You're right. That's...spot-on." Izumi sighed as she placed her hand listlessly against her cheek. "But even I sometimes have a tendency to think the worst, despite myself."

"Like when?"

"For example, when Mr. Chibiki gave us his opinion on the incident last week. What he said pretty much makes sense to me, but if you take the pessimistic angle, what he actually said was the possibility that the 'calamity' has started is low. But what if the most unlikely outcome is what's really happening...what then?"

"Hey now, it's bad luck to say that!"

"It is, isn't it? But it's also not entirely impossible."

It wasn't impossible that last Monday, when Hazumi abdicated her role as a "non-exister," the "countermeasures" had lost their effectiveness, kicking off the "calamity." It wasn't impossible that Joukichi Kanbayashi's death wasn't an inevitable outcome of his terminal illness and had instead been hastened by the "calamity." That interpretation was still on the table.

I thought there was certainly room for doubt.

Even Mr. Chibiki had been extremely cautious about choosing his words. The expression on his face had been somewhat uneasy as well. He hadn't been able to deny with 100 percent certainty the possibility that the "calamity" had begun.

"I hope our fear turns out to be groundless. Sou's doing such a good job, and theoretically, a single 'non-exister' should be enough. But—" Izumi stopped.

"But?" Yagisawa urged her on.

After a moment's hesitation, she quickly glanced over to the window and lowered her voice somewhat. "If this is the worst-case scenario, then as a countermeasures officer, I've got one last-ditch idea."

11

"I'm coming to see you next month. I've already decided on the days."

My mother, Tsukiho, called to tell me her plans on Wednesday the 24th—the same day that midterms started. But she had no idea about my situation, of course.

When my phone got the call, I'd glanced at the display and saw that it was coming from Tsukiho, so I was naturally indecisive over whether to answer it or ignore it. As Dr. Usui at the "clinic" had said, I was still harboring very complicated feelings toward her, after all.

It was true that she had thrown me out three years ago, but that didn't change the fact that she was also my mother. As much as I told myself that there was nothing I could do about this, I went through an emotional roller coaster every time she came up...

"…I've got midterms," I told her in a subdued tone. "I'm studying, so…"

So I want you to let me off the phone quickly, was what I wanted to say. *But if I blurted that out, it would have been better not to answer in the first place,* I thought, scolding myself.

"Ah…," Tsukiho answered in a fluster. "I'm sorry for interrupting your studies."

"It's fine, whatever."

"So you're graduating next year, aren't you?"

"Mm-hmm."

"What about high school, after graduation?"

"Auntie Sayuri and them said I can go."

"Ah…you've got to talk it over carefully with them, you know," she said wistfully, then apologized weakly again: "I'm sorry, Sou."

Despite her apology, there was nothing I could say in response.

"Are you coming? Next month." I got the conversation back on track. "You said you had decided when you're visiting?"

"Ah…yes. Yes I have," Tsukiho answered nervously. "The tenth of next month, Sunday."

"…I see."

"Mirei's coming with me."

"Oh. And Mr. Hiratsuka, too?"

I hadn't called Shuuji Hiratsuka, Tsukiho's second husband and Mirei's father, "Dad" for years now.

"He's busy, so…it'll just be Mirei and me. I thought we could have dinner together or something; it's been so long. And your little sister also wants to see you."

I hadn't seen her even once since leaving Hinami. And I was pretty sure the last time I'd seen Tsukiho was not long after I entered middle school, when she'd come to escort me to the "clinic."

"I…"

I don't really want to see either of you, is what I was about to say, but I changed my mind just before I responded.

"That's fine. Let me know when you're close."

12

May 25, Friday.

It was the second day of the midterm exams, and it had been raining since morning.

It was the kind of rain that wasn't too heavy but still required an umbrella. But the wind was quite strong, so even if you put one up, your clothes got a little wet.

Despite the weather, I got up earlier than usual that morning and walked down the path along the Yomiyama River for the first time in several days. The water level hadn't gone up, but the river was muddy, so there were hardly any of the wild birds that I usually spotted on the surface of the water or in the air above it.

The birds are around sometimes even on rainy days like this, though...

As I walked for a while, my thoughts drifted to Yuika Hazumi.

This was the place where she'd first spoken to me at the beginning of April. Only about a month and a half had passed since then, but somehow, it seemed like something that had happened a long time ago.

Hazumi still hadn't come back to class, and she'd been absent for the exams the day before, too.

Obviously, I was worried about whether she was all right. But I knew that no matter how much I worried, I couldn't do anything to help.

These days, student truancy was a nationwide issue, and the teachers and administrators at North Yomi were struggling to address it. When I reflected on my time in elementary school, I certainly had no right to scold Hazumi for ditching.

I stopped in at the Akazawa main house for breakfast as always, then headed to class alone.

13

We had tests in first period English and second period science.

I didn't consider myself much of a "high achiever," or whatever you want to call it, but since coming to Yomiyama especially, I'd be lying if I said I struggled with schoolwork or tests. I easily absorbed most of what I needed to know during lessons, so I could usually manage exams with a little last-minute cramming. This hadn't changed even after entering third year and volunteering to be a "non-exister." I'd always been confident in this area.

That being said, during this particular two-day exam period, my attention was entirely focused on something other than the tests. Namely—

> INCIDENT AT NORTH YOMIYAMA MIDDLE SCHOOL
> FEMALE STUDENT DEAD

I had happened to see that newspaper headline three years ago in Hinami. I even remembered the date—May 27. The incident it covered had happened on the 26th, the second day of midterm exams at North Yomi...

I was even able to pull some of the content from the article that I had read out of my memory.

The deceased was a female student in the third grade, Yukari Sakuragi. Immediately after she'd received notice of her mother getting caught in a traffic accident, she lost her life in an unfortunate fall. Her mother had also breathed her last that same day at the hospital. They were the first victims of the "calamity" that had occurred three years earlier—in 1998.

According to what Izumi had told me last week, Yukari Sakuragi had been the female class representative at the time for Grade 3 Class 3. So our female class representative, Tsugunaga, seemed a little worried...

But at the start of this week, I had visited the secondary library and gotten some more information from Mr. Chibiki, who told me, "Yes, I remember that day. It had been pouring nonstop since the night before. I think we can say that the rain helped cause the accident."

As he spoke, he set down on the counter a binder with a pitch-black cover and opened it. This was commonly referred to as the "Chibiki File." It contained three decades' worth of class rosters for Grade 3 Class 3, from the "year it all began" twenty-nine years ago up until this school year. The pages for "on years" were filled with notes about the names and causes of death for the "related individuals" who'd succumbed due to the "calamity," along with the names of the "casualties" who slipped into the class and what happened to them after it all ended—everything was there.

"Sakuragi was indeed the female class representative for that year. I even remember her face. She was a very serious-looking girl whose glasses suited her well."

It happened on the second testing day, right in the middle of the final exam. She'd heard the urgent news—that her mother had been in an accident and was going to the hospital—and rushed out of the classroom in great haste. Just as she started to run down the staircase, her foot gave out, and she went tumbling down. As she fell, she let go of her umbrella, and its pointed tip unfortunately tragically pierced through her throat as she came down...

"I saw it myself; what a gruesome scene. She was taken away in an ambulance, but the blood loss and trauma were extreme, so apparently, she didn't even make it to the hospital."

"Oh..."

As he told me, I pictured the graphic circumstances of her death and caught my breath, feeling grim. If Tsugunaga had heard the same story, it would be impossible for her not to worry, no matter how ridiculous it sounded. That's what I thought anyway.

Regardless, today was the second day of midterms. The first-period English exam had ended without incident, and the second-period science exam had begun...

When there were about ten minutes left until the end of the exam period, I turned in my answer sheet and left the classroom. The questions had covered an area I knew well, so I'd answered them all quickly.

The proctor for this exam was Ms. Kanbayashi, but she didn't object to my leaving early. Of course, that was because I "didn't exist."

I glanced quickly around the classroom as I left. Not a single person noticed me... No, actually, Izumi and Tsugunaga both looked back for a split second, then immediately returned their eyes to the front. That's how it seemed to me anyway.

Of the desks and chairs that lined the classroom, two were empty again today. One was Hazumi's seat. The other belonged to the girl who'd been hospitalized since April.

Her name was...yeah, I think it was Makise? No, Makino?

I stepped out into the hallway alone, opened the window a little, and gazed out. The rain was still falling, and the wind was strong.

When I turned to look at the state of the hallway floor, I noticed it was wet and dirty in places. *North Yomi doesn't use indoor slippers, so the water and mud on people's shoes and umbrellas get tracked into the school building... I bet it was like this three years ago, too. In the hallway, on the stairs. That's why Sakuragi slipped on the way down...*

"...It's fine." I shook my head and tried to talk myself out of getting worked up. "This year will be okay."

Finally, the bell signaling the end of the period began to ring, but right after it did, something happened. I heard the sound of hurried footsteps coming from the stairwell.

Before long, a male teacher whose face I recognized but whose name I didn't know showed up. He passed right in front of where I was standing by the window and bolted into the Class 3 classroom. From inside the room where the exam had just concluded came a low commotion.

Just as I was wondering what it could be, a single female student came rushing out of the door.

That's...Takanashi? Jun Takanashi. The girl whose first-year little brother just joined the biology club.

She was holding her bag in her right hand, and with her left, she snatched her umbrella from the stand. Her face was pale, and her movements were panicked...and just then—

"Don't run in the hallway!"

A high-pitched voice echoed down the corridor.

"And don't run down the stairs. Calm down, Takanashi. Be careful!"

The voice belonged to Tsugunaga. She'd chased Takanashi out of the classroom and had shouted at the other girl, who still seemed poised to run down the hall.

"Be careful, Takanashi. Okay? Understand?"

The other girl smiled awkwardly in response, her face still pale but otherwise grateful. She adjusted her grip on her bag and umbrella, took a big breath with her shoulders, and set off walking toward the stairs.

Since I couldn't say anything, I just watched over her as she went.

As she saw Takanashi go, Tsugunaga let out a deep, long sigh. Her face was just as pale as Takanashi's.

14

The teacher had run into our classroom with an urgent message— Jun Takanashi's mother had been in some sort of accident and sustained serious injuries. It was as if the incident three years ago—as if Yukari Sakuragi's case—was being copied to the letter.

After she left, however, Takanashi had met up with her little brother, who had received the same news, and they safely headed for the hospital where their mother had been transported.

After hearing Ms. Kanbayashi's explanation during homeroom following the end of exams—

I didn't immediately go home, so I stopped in to visit the biology club room instead. Shunsuke Kouda was there like usual, so I went over what had just happened with him.

"I wonder what condition Takanashi's mom is in," Shunsuke said, wiping his glasses. "Even if the two of them are safe, if something bad happened to their mom, do you think that might constitute the start of the 'calamity'?"

I didn't know how to answer, so I cast my eyes down. I couldn't guess what kind of accident she had been in, but all I could do was pray it wasn't life-threatening.

"It's been a while since you came to club, right?"

"Ah...I guess it has."

"As you can see, everyone here is looking healthy after Golden Week," Shunsuke remarked, gesturing around the room filled with aquarium tanks and cages. "Woo II is full of energy, too."

"None of them wants to become a specimen."

"That's right. The diaphanized Amano shrimp turned out nicely. Want to see?"

"Mm, maybe next time."

"That science test was a piece of cake, huh?"

"Yeah, I guess."

"How about the striped loach specimen?"

"I'll see that next time, too."

And so on... We kept chatting for a bit, then left school together.

"You're continuing to 'not exist' even after that Hazumi girl dropped out, right, Sou?"

"Ah, yeah."

"And that preserves the peace in your class?"

"For now, yeah. If Takanashi's mother is all right, that is."

"I really hope she's okay."

"No kidding."

With a heavy feeling that wouldn't clear up at all, we proceeded down the hallway of Building Zero. On the way, we passed in front of the secondary library, but the CLOSED sign was out on the door.

It must be shuttered during the exam period. Either that or Mr. Chibiki is taking more leave from school.

Outside, it was still raining. The wind was also blowing strongly; the old building was creaking here and there.

We went through the connecting passage from Building Zero to Building A, where the front entrance was located. From there, we stepped outside. We each put up our umbrellas and started walking down the paved path to the school gates, when—

We could make out the figures of several students walking in front of us. They were less than ten meters away.

"Are those girls from Class 3?" Shunsuke pointed and asked. "Look, Akazawa's up there."

There were three students ahead of us, all girls. Now that Shunsuke had mentioned it, one of them indeed resembled Izumi. I'd seen the light-crimson umbrella she was carrying before.

Of the other two, one was carrying a clear plastic umbrella. She was a little taller than Izumi and had a short haircut.

That must be Etou. And the other girl is—

The last student had a small build, and unlike the others, she wasn't carrying an umbrella. She wore a raincoat (which was actually more of a loose cream-colored poncho) with the hood up... She looked as though she hadn't brought an umbrella along in the first place.

Is that Tsugunaga? Could it be?

Just then, I guessed what had happened.

Out of an abundance of concern over the incident three years ago with Yukari Sakuragi, Tsugunaga had *intentionally avoided taking an umbrella with her,* despite the elements. That probably meant that she knew about the details of the accident three years ago. She knew that the *lethal weapon* that spurred Sakuragi's death had been the umbrella she'd been carrying...and so...

That was probably also why Tsugunaga was worried when Takanashi went tearing out of the classroom right after the science exam ended. If Takanashi had run down the stairs in a big hurry just like Sakuragi did three years ago, the same thing might have happened. Fearing that, she instinctively...

Suddenly, a fierce noise echoed through the air, startling us.

Gora-gora-gora...boom!

Was that the wind? It must be much stronger than what's been blowing all day.

Is it sweeping through the upper atmosphere? Or maybe along the ground?

As I glanced around restlessly, all the trees surrounding us rustled and shook in unison—*sh-sh-shh!* The gale reached us and sent our parasols blowing away.

"Wow, that came on really suddenly, huh?" Shunsuke remarked. "It's like a typhoon is coming or something." Just as he said that, the intensity of the pouring rain doubled.

We pulled ourselves together and made two or three steps of headway, but then came another violent *boom*, echoing far and wide.

Is it up in the air, or did it come from the ground?

I could see two out of the three girls ahead of us struggling to keep their umbrellas from flying away. Tsugunaga was fighting to hold her poncho in place as the wind buffeted it …

As I was watching her, she suddenly fell to her knees on the pavement. Her hood had already come off her head.

What happened?

Tsugunaga tried to stand back up, but she looked like she couldn't move very well. Maybe that was due to the storm… No, the hem of her poncho probably got caught on the fence separating the path and the row of trees planted alongside it. That's what it looked like to me anyway.

The wind howled, and the rain gushed down. In between gusts, another strange sound suddenly rang out—that's how it seemed, at least. A second later, *something* coming diagonally from above cut a path through the shining white streaks of rain. An unidentifiable gray shadow…

Someone let out a short shriek. It was probably Tsugunaga. Both Shunsuke and I could hear it from a distance.

"No!" That was Izumi's or Etou's voice.

"Oh no!"

"What? What is this?"

"Tsugunaga?!"

"Th-they need help!" Shunsuke shouted beside me. Tossing his umbrella aside, he took off running furiously through the downpour.

I chased after him in a panic, and by that point, I could see that an obvious change had come over Tsugunaga.

She had stopped moving, still kneeling on the path, and was looking up at the sky. *Something* gray was sticking diagonally down into the right side of her neck. And—

A vivid red was beginning to stain her cream-colored poncho.

No sooner was the red washed away by the rain than it flowed down anew…

Ah, that's blood. Frightfully bright scarlet blood, coming from her neck...

As I rushed over, I finally understood the situation.

The object buried deep in Tsugunaga's neck was a piece of gray-painted metal, probably a sheet of galvanized steel or something—long, thin, and quite large.

It had flown out of nowhere to pierce her throat like a blade.

"Tsugunaga...!" Izumi had thrown her parasol aside just like Shunsuke and I had, and I could see her lips were trembling with fear as she spoke. Etou had slumped to the ground in a daze, several meters back. "How could it end up like this...?"

The class rep remained locked in place, still looking up at the sky. An anguished groan escaped her mouth, along with bubbles of blood.

She's still breathing.

"An ambulance!" Shunsuke shouted, pulling out his own cell phone.

Izumi gasped in surprise. I turned and saw Tsugunaga lifting both hands unsteadily, trying to grab hold of the metal plate that was sticking out of her neck.

Ah, don't do that! I immediately thought, panicked. *You can't! If you pull it out now...*

But my panic was fruitless in the end.

I'm sure Tsugunaga couldn't even comprehend what on earth had happened to her—

Driven by the intense pain, the girl used the last bit of her remaining strength to dislodge the foreign object that had embedded itself in her flesh. The moment she did, fresh fluid spurted with alarming force from the open wound.

As her blood dyed the still-falling rain red, Tsugunaga collapsed limply and completely ceased moving.

15

By the time the ambulance arrived, Tomoko Tsugunaga had already died from blood loss. On the 25th of May, 1:30 in the afternoon.

The gymnasium stood several dozen meters from the scene of the accident. The story was that the unexpectedly strong winds had peeled off a section of its roof and sent it flying. The building was several decades old, and the whole thing had been steadily deteriorating. Moreover, it had incurred a bit of damage during the hailstorm on the 7th of the month. But even when you kept that in mind...

It was an unbelievably unlucky coincidence that a fragment of the roof would get blown off and tossed up in the air like that and then, of all things, come falling down to strike Tsugunaga at just the right angle while she was held up on the path.

Late at night on the same day, May 25, Jun Takanashi's mother, Shizu, breathed her last in the hospital.

Earlier that day, she'd been in a minor collision with a small automobile. She'd broken her hip, but her situation hadn't seemed life-threatening when at the hospital. And when her children rushed over after hearing about the emergency, she had apparently been fully conscious.

Overnight, however, her condition suddenly took a turn for the worse. During the accident, she had suffered a blow to the head that somehow went overlooked during her intake examination; the resulting brain hemorrhage caused her death.

Two people "related" to Grade 3 Class 3 met their irrational deaths in the span of a single day.

At last, the dreaded "calamity" has begun... No, it probably had already started when Joukichi Kanbayashi died, as we suspected.

Whether we liked it or not, reality had come knocking at the door.

Interlude II

There was an accident yesterday, right around here.

An accident… What happened?

You don't know? There was a big uproar about it… Oh, right, you were absent yesterday.

I was in bed with a cold then, plus the day before. I've got to take the midterms alone next week.

My condolences. Are you feeling better?

Yeah, more or less.

You should sit out of club activities on the second and fourth Saturdays, too. Practice will be hard on you.

I really would have liked to sleep in for another day. What about the accident?

A third-year girl died. Apparently, she was one of the Class 3 reps.

She croaked? Here?

The wind was intense yesterday afternoon, and it sent a shingle from the gymnasium roof flying. It flew over here and…

It hit her?

That's what I heard… Ah, look over there. See where the pavement is stained? I think that's from the blood.

Gah, it's fresh!

The shingle stabbed her in the neck. It was going very fast; they say she died instantly.

Ow, that sounds painful.

If it was instantaneous, it probably wasn't too bad.
But yeesh, talk about bad luck. Of all the things that could happen...
Yeah. But you know, **she was in Grade 3 Class 3.**
What's so special about that?
What, you don't know?
Know what?
I'm surprised there's anyone who isn't aware. According to the rumor, Grade 3 Class 3 has been cursed for a long time...

†

It's begun, **hasn't it?**
It has.
The "calamity" has begun.
Yes.
So the "countermeasures" failed after all?
That's what it comes down to. It's...unfortunate.
It must be because Hazumi, the "second non-exister," called it quits...
Probably, yeah.
Could it be anything else?
It's not clear. But we can't stop people blaming her now...
....
....
......So?
Hmm?
So what should we do now? There's no point in my keeping being a "non-exister" anymore.
That's... Well, listen, I'd like you to hold off on that for a bit.
Wait?
I told you before, didn't I? **If this is the worst-case scenario, I've got one last-ditch idea.**
Uh...yeah, sure.
I don't know whether my hunch is correct or if it will even accomplish anything, but—but I think it's better than doing nothing. So

please, don't give in just yet… At least keep acting invisible like you have been. I'll inform the teacher and the rest of the class.

Why…what's your idea?

Okay, here it is…

†

It's started. The "calamity" has begun.

Really? I heard it was the female class representative on exam day, just like three years ago. Though that could simply be a coincidence, of course.

If you include Ms. Kanbayashi's older brother, there have already been three casualties.

So it probably started on May 7, huh?

The day that Hazumi resigned. I knew it…

I thought that wouldn't do anything, though.

We were supposed to be all right as long as I took it seriously, weren't we?

Yes, that's how it was supposed to be.

But it didn't turn out that way.

It shouldn't have happened…so why?

…………

Something feels *off*… Ah, I'm sorry, Sou.

Oh no…

You trusted in what I said, didn't you? I'm sorry.

Oh. It's not like that; you don't have anything to apologize for, Mei…

…………

……And now that it's started, more people are going to die, aren't they?

…………

At least one "related individual" a month.

Yes.

And there's nothing we can do about it anymore, right? Once the "calamity" starts up, it's over.

Yes. Basically…

But there's still **one more "countermeasure"** we can discuss.

Wait, really?

Let's look into it for now. We won't know whether it'll do anything until we try, though.

Hmm. And just what kind of "countermeasure" is it?

It's…

Chapter 8
June I

1

We passed the remaining days of May in a state of confusion and despair, grief and trepidation...then June arrived.

In accordance with Izumi's request, I continued "not existing" at school, even after the deaths of Tsugunaga and Takanashi's mother.

Meanwhile, the countermeasures officers and other key students held a conference and presented their decision to the whole class for approval...and things progressed accordingly. Ms. Kanbayashi also had no strong objections. Izumi was selected as the new female class representative, and she began serving concurrently as representative and countermeasures officer.

Hazumi's string of consecutive absences continued as before. Assuming news of the "calamity" starting had finally reached her, she was probably even less inclined to come to school for a while. That was easy enough to guess.

2

"I heard there was a very unfortunate accident at North Yomi last week. A student in your class passed away?" asked Dr. Usui.

Reflexively, I glanced down to the side. I think I also bit my lower lip slightly.

"Were you close with the student who died, by any chance?" he asked.

"No." I shook my head side to side. "We'd talked a bit, but that's all."

"Still, I'm sure it must have been quite a shock."

"Yeah, I guess."

"Are you all right? What I'm trying to ask is, does it hurt that a graphic death happened close to you? Is it bringing back memories of the incident three years ago?"

"I'm fine," I answered, my eyes still on the floor. "...I think."

I'm not sleeping well, and I can't stop having nightmares.

I'd been experiencing the usual symptoms this past week, but it had nothing to do with the events of three years ago.

The visions in my nightmares weren't from that time; they were recent—especially incidents from the past month. *Her* voice shouting, *"I exist!"* and *"I'm right here!"* The pitch-black figure of the crow flapping about the room. The *boom!* of the wind and the disheveled cream-colored poncho...and then the fresh, spurting blood. *That girl* collapsing, covered in so much blood...

This hadn't been my first time seeing someone die. Three years ago, I'd witnessed Uncle Teruya's death at Lakeshore Manor. And yet—

Even though they were both "deaths," I felt like what happened then and what happened last week were completely different things.

One difference was the feeling of guilt that had settled into my gut, the frustration and sense of helplessness at having not been able to prevent the start of the "calamity." And if Hazumi's defection was actually the reason why our efforts had failed, then I bore the responsibility for my failure to keep her from quitting... In other words, I was carrying unbearable feelings of personal responsibility.

Dr. Usui was persistently calm and gentle as he asked his questions, but I didn't think I was honest with most of my answers. I wasn't sure whether or not he realized it.

It was Saturday, June 2, just before lunch. As usual, I'd submitted my notification of absence to the school and come to the "clinic" in the annex of the municipal hospital—

"I'd like to ask you about a strange rumor going around."

After an exchange that superficially resembled my usual monthly or bimonthly sessions, Dr. Usui abruptly changed the subject.

"I hear there's a strange legend concerning 'death' at the middle school you attend..."

He's aware of it, too, huh?

I suppose it's inevitable that rumors would spread.

I didn't dislike Dr. Usui; in fact, I trusted him, but I had never spoken a word to him about the peculiar circumstances of Grade 3 Class 3. Not about the "phenomenon," or the "accidents," or the "casualty" who joined the class, or about the falsification and alteration of records and memories... No matter how seriously I might try to discuss those things, I was sure there was no way that a doctor of psychiatry would take me seriously. Not so long as he himself wasn't a related party. That's what I'd assumed.

"I don't know what legend that would be." I decided to dodge his question this time. "I'm sure it's just some half-baked story. I'm not interested in that kind of thing."

3

Although it wasn't really raining, I left the same way I had the last time when my appointment was over, without really knowing why. I went through the passage on the first floor, from the annex to the main building. As I was moving slowly down the complex, twisting corridor exactly as I'd done last time—

My thoughts drifted back to the past of their own accord. To two days after the gruesome accident that was painful to even recall—to Sunday evening, when Izumi had come over to my apartment. The words we'd exchanged then were still fresh in my ears.

"If this is the worst-case scenario, then I've got one last-ditch idea."

That's what Izumi had said before.

I'd asked her what exactly that entailed.

"Well, it's—" Izumi broke off and stared directly into my face. After a short pause, she said, "You remember what happened at the 'strategy session' at the end of March, right? When we decided who would be the 'non-exister' if this turned out to be an 'on year'?"

"Yeah. Of course I remember that."

When the conversation had turned to the question of who among us would bear the burden of "nonexistence," I had raised my hand. But right after that, Etou had commented, *"Is that really all we need to do?"* leading to us choosing a "second." After that, we'd used playing cards to draw lots...

"They picked out the person with cards, right? That's when Hazumi pulled the joker and became the 'second,' but... Okay, so think back. To *before* that happened."

Izumi narrowed her almond-shaped eyes, as if she was looking at something far away. I narrowed mine in tandem. "Before that?"

As I asked the question, I searched my memory.

Izumi replied, "Before the lottery began, someone else tried to volunteer, right? In a small, quiet voice that everyone was a little surprised to hear. Why so suddenly? We all wondered..."

"...Ah!"

The scene on that day more than two months ago burst forth in my mind, as though revealing itself out from the darkness. *That's right. Now I remember—something like that did happen. There was someone other than me who volunteered to accept the role of the "non-exister," and I was a little surprised when they did...*

"...But ultimately, their offer wasn't recognized, so we went ahead with the lottery, right?"

"The cards had already been shuffled, and I think...yeah, Hazumi said in a weird, panicked way, 'You can't do that now,' then immediately started the lottery drawing."

"Ah...you're right. I guess that is how it went."

If that was true, then by that time, Hazumi must have already noticed the mark on the joker and made her decision to become the "second." So...

"And it was Makise who volunteered for the role back then, wasn't it?"

"Makise..."

...*Right. That's correct. Her name was Makise. I can't picture her face very well, but she had a small, quiet voice and was sort of a feeble, inconspicuous girl...*

"She had some pretty serious health problems and needed to be hospitalized for a while starting in April, right?" Izumi said, then blinked slowly. I felt as if my own vision blacked out for a second in time with the movement of her eyelids.

"That's why she volunteered at the meeting. She didn't tell everyone this, but since she wouldn't be able to come to school that much anyway, I bet she was thinking it might be best to take on the role of the 'non-exister' herself, don't you think?"

Now that Izumi had pointed it out, I could see how the proposal did make a certain amount of sense. Even if she was out of school and hospitalized, that wouldn't change the fact that she was a member of Grade 3 Class 3. Ignoring her as the "non-exister" would have been easy for everyone else, physically and psychologically. Much simpler than if anyone else did it. And yet—

—her proposal hadn't been accepted. Then Hazumi had pulled the joker, becoming the "second non-exister."

Izumi continued. "I've been thinking about talking to Makise again and getting her to replace Hazumi as the 'second non-exister.'"

"Ah..."

I see, so that's it. But I wonder how that will go? I wonder if that could really shut down the "calamity" now that it's already begun?

"So to solve this problem, I'm sure that finding a 'power balance' will be essential. That's how it seems to me, at least."

"What do you mean?"

"An 'extra person,' the 'casualty,' has appeared in our class and invited the 'calamity.' But by designating 'non-existers,' we prevented the 'calamity' from starting. The 'power' of the 'casualty' pulling us toward 'death' is offset by the 'power' of the 'non-existers,' maintaining a balance. That's how I see it."

"Hmm."

"This year, we established two 'non-existers,' just to be safe. In doing so, we kept the 'calamity' from starting in April, which means the equilibrium was correct, right? However, once Hazumi abandoned her duties in May, the 'calamity' started. That must mean we're working with a different power dynamic this year."

"Wait...you mean that we're out of alignment with only one 'non-exister'?"

"Out of whack, off balance...yes, that's the picture. If we don't increase the 'power' of the 'non-existers,' we won't be able to negate the 'power' of this year's 'casualty'...get it?"

So the theory is that by enlisting another "non-exister," we can restore the equilibrium that Hazumi upset when she abdicated her position? And if we do that, it should stop the "calamity"?

Izumi reemphasized that she didn't know if her line of thinking was correct, or if it would do anything at all, but that we couldn't know until we tried. She also insisted it was better than doing nothing.

I agreed with her. *I'm sure she's probably right. And it's certainly better than sitting on our hands...*

Three days after our conversation, on Wednesday, the countermeasures officers Izumi and Etou went as representatives of the class and visited Makise, who was hospitalized in the internal medicine ward of the same hospital that housed my clinic—this had been on May 30.

Apparently, Makise had been sympathetic and kindly accepted the request, telling Izumi, *"I'll be glad to help if I can."* She was likely to be hospitalized for quite some time, so being a "non-exister" was no big deal to her for now. And she'd promised that even when she could leave the hospital and return to school, she would be fine with continuing to be a "non-exister" if it would curtail the "calamity."

Today was the fourth day since this new and desperate "countermeasure" had been put into practice.

4

As I was walking down a hallway in the main hospital building, I was suddenly struck by the urge to go find Makise's room.

Although I hadn't had the chance to see her at school for some time now, starting this month, she and I were going to both be "non-existers"... That's as far as that thought went before I decided to give up on the idea for the day. I had a feeling that it would be insensitive for a boy from her class to suddenly show up for a visit. Plus, I couldn't say what would come of my having contact with her here...

But...

She was still my classmate. I'd met her only once at the "strategy session," and I could barely recall her face.

Now that she's in the middle of a long hospital stay, I wonder what's on her mind. How is she passing the time? When I imagined her anxiety and loneliness, another set of problems entirely from everything surrounding the "calamity," it felt unbearable. It made me want to visit her someday soon, maybe with Izumi.

It was about thirty minutes past noon when I finished paying at the hospital desk. I hadn't come by bicycle that day, so I waited at the bus stop in front of the building for a while, standing with several other people who, as far as I could tell, were all older than I was.

The bus finally arrived under a featureless cloudy sky, as though foreshadowing the start of the rainy season. Getting my coins ready, I was heading for the door in the center of the vehicle when—

The disembarking passengers exited from every door of the bus. When I looked up inadvertently, I saw a familiar face.

Is that...

...Kirika?

I'd seen her for only a moment, so it was possible that I had made a mistake. But on the other hand, I also remembered passing a woman who looked a lot like her in the entryway on my way home last time I came here.

In which case, I bet that really was her...

She must have some kind of physical condition that keeps her coming back to the hospital.

Thinking exactly the same thing I had last time, I boarded the bus.

5

After getting off at the Daybreak Forest stop in Romero, I visited the library, then ate at a nearby fast-food restaurant before setting out on foot toward Misaki. I was headed for the doll gallery "Blue Eyes Empty to All, in the Twilight of Yomi," and I needed to be there by 3:30.

I had plans to meet Mei Misaki.

We'd gotten confirmation that the "calamity" had started with the deaths of two people, Tsugunaga and Takanashi's mother, and I'd been able to speak with Mei only over the phone since then. As might be expected, I wanted to speak with her in person. I felt it was urgent, so here I was.

It was the first time I had come to see her at the "Blue Eyes..." gallery since mid-April.

More than a month and a half had passed since our last meeting. The situation had changed considerably, but the inside of the gallery was, as always, hushed and still, as if entirely detached from the outside world. As usual, a haunting string melody was playing, and as usual, Grandma Amane was the one to greet me.

"Welcome. You're a friend, so you don't need to pay. Mei is downstairs."

"Thank you."

Mei was sitting alone in a chair at the same round table I'd seen when I'd visited in April, with her chin resting on her hand. She was wearing a dark-blue, almost black blouse and seemed like she might dissolve right into the crouching shadows that filled the space. Something about her was quite gloomy.

"Hello, Sou." Mei took her chin off her hand and greeted me. "It's been a while since our last rendezvous."

"Yes. Well...hello."

"Sit."

"Okay." I sat down across from her.

Mei had her eye patch off again today. She wasn't wearing her "doll's eye" in her left socket but the artificial eye that was black flecked with brown.

"So..." After staring silently at me for several seconds, Mei opened her mouth. "Are you okay?"

"Okay...? Do you mean the class?" I answered her question with a question, and Mei shook her head side to side.

"I mean you, Sou."

"Me...?"

"How are you feeling; where's your head at? I'm wondering how you're holding up after everything that's happened."

"Ah...ummm, well..."

"You did your best, but the 'calamity' started anyway. You're not beating yourself up or feeling disheartened, are you?"

"Well, I would be lying to say that I'm not disheartened at all, but..."

Despite everything that was going on, Mei was worried about my feelings. I was ashamed of how happy that made me.

"But I'm all right." I tried to answer her as calmly as I could.

"The accident last week with that girl Tsugunaga happened right in front of your eyes, didn't it?"

"That was...yeah, of course, it was really shocking, but, well... yeah, I'm okay."

"Really?'

"At least, I'm not thinking that I'm ready to run away from *this place* or anything."

"I see."

The music flowing through the building changed to a familiar tune. It was Fauré's "Sicilienne."

If I recall correctly, this piece was playing when I visited in April, too...

The coincidence stuck out to me.

"By the way—" I started to say.

"By the way—" In the same moment, Mei uttered the same words. I panicked and held my tongue while she continued speaking.

"About the new 'countermeasure' I heard about on the phone the other day...you've started that already, right?"

"Uh, yes." I sat up straight and nodded. "A new 'second non-exister' has replaced Hazumi. We hope to bring the 'power' back into alignment that way; that's the 'countermeasure'..."

I told Mei again about the new "countermeasure" that I had explained quickly on the phone the other day.

"...And the girl who we approached about taking on the role of the new 'second' already agreed and accepted. Today's day four."

"...I see."

Mei answered me like that again, then looked away from me with her right eye. She had her chin in her hands just like last time I'd come down here. She seemed listless.

I heard the faint tinkling of the bell on the door upstairs.

I guess a customer showed up? Or maybe it's Kirika coming home...?

"But you know, Sou," Mei murmured, "I think you'd better not be too optimistic about whether this new 'countermeasure' is going to be effective. Though I doubt my saying so means very much."

"Why do you think I shouldn't be optimistic?"

"Well..." Mei hesitated. "Because that's what happened three years ago."

I was at a loss for words.

Mei continued. "I told you about this before, right? About how I took on the role of the 'non-exister' for Grade 3 Class 3 three years ago. Back then, our 'countermeasures' also failed, and the 'calamity' began, so at that point, we decided it would be a good idea to make Sakakibara into the 'second non-exister' to increase the number of people who 'didn't exist.' But in the end, this 'additional counter-measure' produced no results."

"But this time is totally different from what happened three years ago," I countered. "We had two 'non-existers' from the outset, and the 'calamity' started after one of them abandoned her duties. So now we're going back to two people to restore the balance...see?"

"I understand your reasoning. And your 'initial settings,' so to speak, were certainly different than ours three years ago." Mei tilted her head anxiously as she answered me. "But listen, no matter what type of 'countermeasures' you take at first, the 'calamity' that starts once those fail won't stop, can't stop, no matter what schemes you add *after the fact*—that's my perspective, at least."

I was once again speechless. She shook her head slowly and continued. "Ah...but you know, the very act of coming to this conclusion probably actually means nothing."

"What do you mean?"

"Since it's a natural phenomenon and all."

Hearing Mei's response automatically brought to mind the phrase that Mr. Chibiki liked to use, "a supernatural natural phenomenon."

"Thanks to Mr. Chibiki's observations, we understand some of the rules governing the 'phenomenon,'" Mei continued. "And we know that there are effective 'countermeasures' against it...but those things are probably just one part of the whole picture."

"............"

"Even now, with science as developed as it is, we still can't accurately predict and prevent the occurrence of all sorts of natural phenomena, right? Like typhoons or earthquakes. Even if you know it's going to rain today and carry an umbrella with you, it doesn't guarantee that you're going to make it through the day without getting wet. If there's a strong wind and the rain comes down sideways, your clothes are going to wind up soaked no matter how big your parasol. And if the rain turned to hail, your umbrella might get torn to shreds. Unforeseen things are happening constantly.

"To say nothing of the fact that this 'phenomenon' is a 'supernatural natural phenomenon' that defies scientific explanation...so from my modest experience and best guess, your plan probably won't amount to much. That's how it seems to me."

So what you're saying is that our new "countermeasures" might be pointless? Her wording made it seem like you could also interpret her assessment that way.

"But you can't say it will fail for sure, either, right?" I prodded.

She acknowledged the question with only a blink of her right eye. "The best we can hope for is that it goes well."

"Hey, Mei?" I couldn't help but ask at this point: "During the 'calamity' three years ago, neither the original 'countermeasures' nor the 'additional countermeasures' worked out, and a number of 'related individuals' died...but after that, it all *stopped*, right? Why was that? Why did it stop?"

It was a question I'd tried to bring up countless times before. But Mei never gave me a clear answer. I was sure there was *something* there she didn't really want to talk about. I had sensed that and tried not to pry too deeply, but...

"...It stopped because—"

After a short silence, Mei's lips parted. I laced my fingers together on top of the round table. Without meaning to, I pressed my fingertips tightly into my hands.

"Because..." She was trying to respond, but she anxiously shook her head a little. "*This* is one thing that I..."

Just then—

I heard something behind me. The sound of someone descending the stairs...and then a voice.

"Oh, here you are."

A familiar female voice, belonging to someone with whom I spoke nearly every day.

"Sou? Do you come here often?"

When I turned around in shock, I saw Izumi Akazawa standing there in her school uniform.

6

Come to think of it—actually, there was no reason to think too hard—I'd hardly ever spoken about Mei Misaki to any of my friends. Only to Yagisawa, who'd been my "comrade" ever since our first year. I do remember telling him a little bit about her, but regardless, the two of them had never met.

So yes, I figured that Izumi also knew nothing of Mei and that this would obviously be their first time meeting each other.

"Akazawa..." I got up out of my chair and turned to face Izumi, who'd come down the stairs. "Why are you here?"

"Just by chance. A total coincidence." After answering my inquiry with an earnest expression, Izumi laughed jokingly. "That's a lie, of course."

"Um..."

"I was on my way home from school when I just kind of had the urge to drop by the library at Daybreak Forest. And then I spotted you going into a nearby shop, Sou."

"Huh, you did?"

"We were close enough that you could have recognized me, but you didn't notice I was there...so that's pretty much what happened."

"You followed me?"

"I sort of got curious about where you were going...okay?" She broke into a grin and stuck her tongue out playfully. "But wow, Sou, you're surprisingly unobservant. I was following you pretty conspicuously, but you didn't notice me at all."

"Hmm."

I was obviously concerned about what Mei was thinking during this exchange of ours. I was worried she might be disappointed to have our conversation cut off by this sudden development.

"Is this a friend of yours, Sou?"

I turned around quickly at Mei's question.

"Not exactly a friend—um, she's my *cousin*. We're the same age and in the same class now."

"I'm Izumi Akazawa. Pleased to meet you," she said over my shoulder.

"Ah," Mei reacted. "Akazawa...same as the aunt and uncle who are taking care of Sou?"

"Uh, that's right," I answered. "She's a countermeasures officer this year and also the new female class representative..."

I went ahead with the explanation, but Izumi cautioned me while staring straight into my eyes, "Wait a second, Sou!" Her look seemed to be asking, *Who is this person?*

"Ah, um…" After glancing quickly at Mei, I answered Izumi's unspoken question. "This is Misaki. Mei Misaki."

"Misaki…hmm?"

Sure enough, Izumi reacted to the fact that Mei's last name sounded the same as the name of the student who'd famously died twenty-nine years ago—Misaki Yomiyama. She raised her eyebrows a little, as if putting her guard up.

I continued. "The Hiratsukas used to be good friends with the Misakis, which is how I got to know them. We've stayed close since I moved here. Misaki is a 1999 graduate of North Yomi, and she was in Class 3 in her third year. That was also an 'on year,' so she has experience with the 'phenomenon' and the 'accidents,' too…"

When I had explained as much, Izumi seemed to get it. She swung her backpack around in front of her and placed both hands on top of it. "I see…," she mumbled. "So you've come for an expert opinion, huh?"

"Well, yeah, something like that."

As for the fact that Mei had taken on the role of the "non-exister" three years earlier…I didn't think I needed to reveal that just then. I thought the same about mentioning her opinion on the new "counter-measures" we'd just implemented three days prior.

"Nice to meet you, Miss Akazawa." This time it was Mei who spoke to Izumi. "I'm Mei Misaki."

At this point, I was still standing in between both girls, blocking them from looking directly at each other.

Mei stood up out of her chair; Izumi took a step forward…and I moved from beside the round table toward the middle of the room. The result was that the two of them were facing each other at a distance of several meters. I think that was when they first got a good look at each other's faces, in the silence of the several-second gap between the songs playing in the background. Coincidentally, the next song that began to play was "Sicilienne" again…

"Mei…Misaki…"

I thought I could see surprise or maybe confusion surface in Izumi's eyes as she gazed at her face.

"You're..."

Izumi stopped whatever she'd been about to say, then shook her head slightly, right to left. She put one of the hands that had been resting on top of her bag to her forehead and sighed faintly.

Just as I was wondering what was going on with her, she took another step forward, further closing the gap between her and Mei. "Thanks for looking after Sou," she said in a strangely formal tone. "As his cousin, I'd like to express my gratitude—"

"Hang on, hang on!" I interjected despite myself. "That's not really something you need to thank her for."

Izumi glanced at me out of the corner of her eye. "I may be your cousin, Sou, but somehow you feel more like a little brother to me, so..."

"Come on—that's not..."

I gave up trying to object. Sure enough, Izumi had always felt kind of like an *older sister* to me, right from the start. But here—in front of Mei, a person she was meeting for the first time—she didn't have to play that up, in my opinion.

When I peeked over at Mei, she looked as indifferent as ever, quietly staring at Izumi, her expression blank.

"Izumi...Akazawa." I could hear her quietly mumbling. "Akazawa..."

What's up with her? Maybe it's my imagination, but she looks like she's trying to remember something important...

Thud.

A low reverberation materialized from outside my hearing range. At almost the exact same moment, I sensed the world go black for a split second, and my breathing stopped.

This is...

It's like someone outside the world just clicked a camera shutter closed. Like someone turned out the lights.

These strange images surfaced momentarily in my mind, then disappeared just as quickly.

Ah, what could it be?

The question itself vanished after a moment.

"Miss Akazawa," Mei said. Not in a quiet mumble like before but clearly, facing the person she was addressing. "I've heard from Sou about the situation of this year's Class 3. I've heard what kinds of 'countermeasures' you've enacted and the fact that, despite your efforts, the 'calamity' began last month. I also know that in the face of that setback, you've been trying out a new 'countermeasure.'"

"Uh, yes." Izumi accepted Mei's gaze and words without seeming overwhelmed.

Mei continued in the same tone. "Even though I experienced *it* three years ago, I'm not currently involved, so I'm not really in a position to form an opinion on this or that. Though I can give a certain amount of advice if you ask."

"We're doing our very best," Izumi stated. "We're trying to keep the situation from getting any worse, however we can."

"I know you both have it hard. Sou as a 'non-exister' and you as a countermeasures officer. And it's clear that you're trying your best. But—" Here, Mei turned to me. "If you feel you can't take it anymore, if you just can't stand it, Sou, you can run away."

"Run away...?" I shrank from her gaze, surprised. "By that, do you mean like Uncle Teruya did?"

As soon as I said that, my chest tightened. I recalled the many words I had once exchanged with Teruya at Lakeshore Manor in Hinami, and they threatened to break right through my flimsy rib cage and spill out into the void.

"I would absolutely never do anything like—"

"This place is incredible!" Just then, Izumi interjected, quite indifferent to what I was going through. It wasn't clear whether or not she meant to distract from my distress. Leaving the round table to walk deeper into the room, she slowly surveyed her surroundings. "There are so many of these spooky dolls. Do you like this sort of thing, Misaki?"

"Do I like them? Well, this is my house, so...," she answered.

Izumi looked surprised. "Oh, I didn't know."

"The second floor is the workshop," I added in explanation. "Mei's mother, Kirika, makes the dolls there."

"Come to think of it, wasn't there one in your room, Sou? A figure like the ones here?"

"Ah, yeah. That's also one of Kirika's..."

"Do you like them, Miss Akazawa? Dolls like these?" Mei asked, a smile rising on her pale cheeks.

"Hmm." Izumi thought for a little while. "Good question. To me, they're a little, how do I put it...?"

"Unpleasant?"

"Not unpleasant exactly..." Izumi pouted dramatically, then smiled like Mei as she answered. "I think they're incredible, but they don't really resonate with me. They're too pretty, and sort of scary, and I can't keep from staring at them somehow...yeah. Dinosaur figurines are more of my thing."

7

Rain started falling on Sunday afternoon. The next day, Monday, it was still raining. Tuesday was rainy, too. Then, on Wednesday, it was officially announced that the rainy season had begun, and the overcast, wet weather persisted for the rest of the week.

And every day that week, a kind of cold, damp tension hung in the air of the Grade 3 Class 3 classroom.

We were continuing with our "countermeasures" after establishing a new "second non-exister." No one knew whether it would work yet. It would be great if it was effective, but if it turned out to be nothing more than pointless resistance, then—

The "calamity" would continue its onslaught, and a "related individual" would die that month.

Back in March, when the "handover ceremony" and "strategy session" had taken place, I'm sure that some of the students had doubted whether the "phenomenon" and the "accidents" were real. I believed some students had been incredulous ever since the day of the opening ceremony, when it became clear that this was an "on year" and the class-wide "countermeasures" kicked off. But ever since our classmate Tsugunaga had died the previous month, even the skeptics had been forced to completely abandon their initial skepticism.

Anxiety. Panic. Fear. The tension choking the classroom was palpable. Everyone was wondering who the next "accident" would claim if our new "countermeasures" failed. Who was going to succumb?

We were only teenagers, but we were already facing down "death" at an age when we wouldn't normally be aware of the pull it had on us. Each and every one of us had already been forced to accept the twisted "reality" of our strange situation.

Thankfully, the week passed without incident.

Perhaps we two "non-existers," the hospitalized Makise and me, had restored the temporarily broken balance of "power"—I wanted to believe that was true. And it wasn't just me. The same went for Izumi and the other countermeasures officers, Yagisawa, Ms. Kanbayashi, and all the other students, too... I'm certain they all felt the same.

8

Saturday, June 9.

School was not in session, since it was the second Saturday of the month, but I woke up early in the morning as always. Typical of the season, it was pouring buckets outside, and I felt a little melancholy as I realized that it would be another rainy day. I didn't feel like getting up right away, but once I did, I felt no enthusiasm for venturing down to the Akazawa house for breakfast... Auntie Sayuri called to ask what was the matter, but I told her, "I'll come up with something on my own for breakfast and lunch." And so, even into the afternoon, I shut myself up in my room, idly passing the time.

Though I'd washed my face and changed my clothes, I laid back down in the bed right away, sighing weakly over and over. I was being undeniably pathetic, and I felt irritated with myself. It was all because—

I'd gotten a call from Tsukiho. Right after speaking with Auntie Sayuri this morning.

"I'm sorry, Sou," she had told me in the same tone as ever. "I was planning to visit you tomorrow, but Mirei came down with a sudden fever last night. She can't possibly come with me, but I can't go out and leave her here."

"We're coming to Yomiyama on June 10, so I thought we could eat a meal together or something; it's been so long"—I remembered exactly what she'd said during our last phone call. And there was probably some part of me, however tiny, that had been looking forward to that day, so...that's why.

"Oh, I see," I'd answered bluntly, while some part of my heart groaned dully. The groan eventually collected at a point deep in my chest and formed a heavy mass.

"I'm sorry," Tsukiho repeated. "But I can't go anywhere. I'll have to postpone my visit...to later this month or another time. I'm sorry."

"Don't apologize," I answered with deliberate detachment. "You can't help it, right?"

"I'm sorry. I'll call you again, okay?"

"Bye."

I gave a short good-bye and hung up, then hurled my cell phone onto the bed. I let out a sigh at the same time.

Tsukiho had told me she was coming to see me tomorrow, but she'd broken her promise. It was hard that that alone had upset me so much.

My thoughtless reaction perplexed me. It was pathetic to have reacted like that. I was angry with myself.

I shouldn't really care, but I do.

I don't even actually want to see her; I don't want her to come visit. And yet...

...Argh, I wish she would just give it up already. Stop contacting me whenever she feels like it and leave me alone completely. That would be better.

It's stupid to get all worked up over this—

It was about two in the afternoon when I finally managed to break out of my slump and leave bed. I hadn't dozed off or anything, but my eyes were bleary, and my mind was hazy. In fact, my whole body felt sort of sluggish. I decided the first thing to do was wash my face again and started to head for the sink.

That was when Mei Misaki showed up.

"Are you in your apartment now?"

Her call caught me off guard. I heard her voice on the other end—

"I'm in front of your building; what number is your apartment?"

9

"I was in the area, so I thought I might try and stop by."

A brown checkered skirt and a white blouse with a dark-red, thin necktie. When I opened the door, Mei was there, dressed in her First Yomi uniform. She wasn't wearing the eye patch today, so the blue "doll's eye" wasn't in her left socket.

"Did I bother you by showing up out of the blue?" Mei asked.

"No, not at all."

"Were you in the middle of an afternoon nap?"

"No..."

"Can I come in?"

"Sure...please do."

Does the uniform mean she's on the way home from school? But the high schools, at least the public ones, should be off on the second Saturday, just like the middle schools. I was a little curious about it, but I figured she had her reasons. It wasn't a big enough deal that I was going to make a point of asking about it.

More importantly—I glanced quickly around my apartment.

I certainly hadn't expected her to visit today, so even though I didn't have that many things, they were scattered all over. I would have cleaned the place if I'd known she was coming, or at least tidied up better.

But Mei didn't seem to mind. She proceeded into the living area and took a seat on one of the chairs at the table without waiting for me to offer.

"Hmm," she remarked. "It feels more lived-in than I expected."

"I-is that so? Um, uh..."

"I mean, Lakeshore Manor didn't have that feel to it at all."

"B-but..."

"Though that was only to be expected, of course." Mei looked at me and narrowed her right eye quickly. "I can see that you're living here all by yourself, Sou. That's a relief."

"A relief?"

"Mm." She nodded slightly. "Knowing how you were three years ago, I always worry about you a little bit."

There was nothing I could say in response to that. I pulled two of the few remaining cans of apple juice out of the refrigerator and set them on the table.

"Um, have a drink if you like."

"Thank you."

Mei took a can, opened it with the pull tab, and gulped down the juice. I tried to drink mine the same way, but even now, I was still feeling horribly nervous, so I could hardly taste it when I put it up to my mouth.

"You know how there's a café called Inoya nearby here?" Mei asked as I sat facing her from across the table.

"Uh, yeah."

"I was just drinking tea over there a little while ago."

"Oh? Do you go often?"

"I know the owner...but it's been a while since I went."

"Huh."

"And while I was there, she happened to come in—Miss Akazawa. The cousin you introduced me to last week. She came in to buy coffee beans."

Wow, that's a real chance encounter. They met while I was shut up in here, wallowing over something trivial.

"She told me where this apartment building was. That's how I found you...see?"

I felt sort of embarrassed or like I wanted to redo this whole day. Letting out a short sigh, I took a little sip of juice.

"Sounds like you've made it through the week all right," Mei said.

"Izumi told you that?"

"Mm." She nodded. "But she can't let her guard down yet."

"Is that what she told you?"

"It didn't come out of her mouth, but I could tell 'cause she was on edge. I think she's right to feel that way."

"It isn't over, is it?" I murmured. "Why would it be?"

At the very least, there were twenty-two days remaining in this month, today included. If we made it through "accident"-free, it would be proof that the current "countermeasures" were working as intended.

I put an elbow up on the table, rubbing my bleary eyes with the back of my hand. Due to Mei's sudden visit, I hadn't had time to wash my face again.

She gave me a once-over and asked, "You were in the middle of a nap, weren't you?"

"No, I definitely wasn't."

"You've got bedhead."

"Huh? ...Ah."

As I rushed to smooth down my hair, Mei smiled, then stared directly at me and asked, "Anyway, somehow you don't seem to have much energy today. Did something happen?"

I was about to answer that it was nothing, but I couldn't get the words out right away... Before I could say anything, Mei added, "Like, maybe you're missing your family in Hinami or something?"

"No way." The response rushed out of my mouth, almost reflexively. "Not at all, nothing like that."

"Hmm?"

With both palms resting on her forehead, Mei stared at my face with her eyes upturned slightly. After two or three seconds of silence...she mumbled, "All right."

It felt as though she had seen right through me and read my inner thoughts.

"Even after everything that's happened, the woman in Hinami is still your real mother, right?"

"That's not really..."

I frowned, shaking my head side to side, and Mei didn't seem inclined to touch on the subject any further. She got up from her chair and looked around the apartment.

"Where's that doll? The memento of Teruya?" she inquired, softening her voice somewhat.

"Over there... It's in the bedroom," I answered, rising from my chair as well. "I'll get it."

10

She was one of Kirika's girl dolls. Uncle Teruya had fallen for her and purchased her after he saw her at a doll exhibition in Soabi. After being expelled from the Hiratsuka household, I'd brought her with me from the study in Lakeshore Manor.

The figure had been sitting on top of a chest in my bedroom, so I moved her to the living room table, where I positioned her next to my PC, head turned toward Mei. She examined it with a bit of fondness in her eyes and mumbled, "This one's not so bad." I thought I saw a faint shadow flit across her face.

"Are there some you dislike?" I asked. "Even though your mom made them?"

"*Dislike* isn't the word I would use..." Mei blinked, hesitating slightly. "The thing about dolls is that they're 'empty.' They suck in all the thoughts of their creator and anybody who views them, but they're still vacant. So..."

So...?

"To me, Kirika's dolls are a little difficult... No, that's not it; they're, like, a little special. The long and short of it is that I don't particularly care for a lot of them."

This was the first time I'd ever heard Mei talk about Kirika's creations like this. As I fumbled around for my next statement—

"How does it seem to you, Sou?" Mei asked me. "My relationship with her—with my mother, I mean?"

"Ummm, well, that's..."

They didn't appear to be the normal sort of parent and child, who got along well. But that said, they didn't seem to be on bad terms, either. Mei always spoke to Kirika in strangely formal language, as if she was talking to a stranger, and she did the same toward her father, Mr. Misaki...

When I floundered for an answer, Mei nodded to herself. "Mm. This isn't something that I've talked to you about much, is it?"

She stretched her right hand out toward the doll on the table, softly stroking its forehead with the tip of her middle finger. Suddenly, she looked up and stared me in the face as she asked, "Shall I tell you the story of my life? Will you listen?"

11

"I had a sister who was born the same time as I was—a twin. We were fraternal, but we looked a lot alike..." Mei Misaki quietly started telling me her story.

She was right that I hadn't heard much about her birth and upbringing or about her family and relatives. Of course, that didn't mean I wasn't interested. She just never seemed to want to talk about it, so I hadn't felt like pushing the issue... That's why I was really taken by surprise when she said the word *twin* out of the blue.

"But she died before me, in April three years back. Of illness."

"...I didn't know."

"That's because the only person outside the family who knows is Sakakibara."

"Sakakibara... Uh, um, wait just a second!" I realized the significance of the timing of *April three years back* and gasped. "You can't possibly mean... Did that happen because of the 'calamity' in '98?"

Mei looked like she was hesitating to answer for a moment, then nodded. "It did. I think it probably was because of that."

"But if I remember, in 1998..."

"The 'calamity' started in May, is what everyone remembers, right? There's nothing written in Mr. Chibiki's file about the girl who died in April."

"Why?" I asked.

"I was conflicted about it," Mei admitted, "but in the end, I didn't say anything, not even to Mr. Chibiki. And I got Sakakibara to agree not to mention anything about it to anyone, either."

"Why did you do that?"

"Mm…my reason for that is…complicated."

It seemed like Mei was being terribly inarticulate. She saw me with my head tilted slightly to the side, and she tilted her own head in the same way. Then, confusion all over her face, she said, "Ah, sorry. I can't explain this very well. Whenever I try, the words get all mixed up somehow."

"Huh."

I nodded slowly, and Mei continued. "Anyway…" But for some reason, she hesitated to tell the next part of the story.

"So…" Another false start, and she failed to get going again.

Finally, after a minute, she opened her mouth. "Mitsuyo Fujioka."

It was a name I was hearing for the first time. I tilted my head slightly. After showing me the characters that spelled Mitsuyo, Mei at last picked up. "Mitsuyo Fujioka. That person is the woman who gave birth to us, our mother."

I was taken aback yet another time. Without thinking, I asked, "It wasn't Kirika?"

Kirika's real name wasn't Mitsuyo; it was Yukiyo. And her last name obviously wasn't Fujioka; it was Misaki.

"Kirika—so, Yukiyo and Mitsuyo were also fraternal twin sisters. Mitsuyo got married first, to a young office worker named Fujioka. A little while later, Yukiyo married my father—Kotaro Misaki."

"So…"

"We— The two of us were originally twins born to Mitsuyo, who married into the Fujioka family. In other words…"

"You were adopted?"

Mei was adopted out to the Misaki family—is that what she's saying?

"Right. Our family gave one of us to the Misakis. It happened when I was young, before I was really aware of what was going on, and they always kept it a secret from us. I was raised thinking of Mitsuyo as *Auntie Fujioka* and of my little sister as my *cousin*… I found out the truth in fifth grade of elementary school."

In a tone of voice that was detached and quiet to the end, Mei continued to reveal her personal history.

"Grandma Amane let the truth slip carelessly, which shook me to my core. I wondered why they hadn't told us all that time. My Misaki parents always doted on me and treated me like their own daughter, but still, you know...I had some mixed feelings, to say the least..."

She told me the next part of the story.

Kirika (Yukiyo) had gotten pregnant about a year after Mitsuyo had given birth. Unfortunately, however, it had ended in a stillbirth, and Yukiyo could not bear children after that. Her sorrow and grief had been unbearable.

A plan was hatched to save her from her grief by allowing her to adopt one of the Fujioka twins. Consequently, it had been implemented...

"...So that's the story. Before I was old enough to understand what was going on, I had gone from Mei Fujioka to Mei Misaki. I still remember very clearly how flustered Kirika was when she figured out that I knew the truth."

Mei sighed briefly and looked at me for my reaction. I wasn't able to respond at all, except to shake my head in an ambiguous way.

"Even though Kirika claimed that she was planning to tell me when the time was right, after that, she strictly prohibited me from seeing Mitsuyo, or calling her, or anything. Same went for my sister. Just around that time, the Fujiokas moved to a place farther away in the city. Up until then, my sister had gone to the elementary school in the next district over, but after that, she was farther away... We contacted each other in secret, always without Kirika's knowledge."

"Why was she like that?"

When I voiced this naive question, Mei gave another short sigh and answered, "She was anxious."

"Anxious...?"

"Probably, yeah. Worried that I would no longer be her little doll."

I was rather shocked by her blunt words. I let out a small noise of surprise. "Eh? Her...*doll*?"

What does she mean by that? Adopted or not, Mei's nothing less than Kirika's daughter. How could she consider her a "doll" despite that...?

"When I recall my emotions at the time," Mei continued, ignoring my response, "I had all sorts of feelings about Mitsuyo, my birth mother, as you would expect. I understood the circumstances, but... but I wondered why they'd chosen *me* over my sister to send to the Misakis. I wondered how my mother—how Mitsuyo saw me now that I was older."

"Ah...sure..."

I understand her feelings. At least I think I do. I nodded as an image of Tsukiho's face flashed across my mind.

"But I'm sure that Kirika was worried that I might have more contact with Mitsuyo because of those feelings. Anxious and probably afraid, too."

"How so?"

"Afraid that I might want to return to the Fujioka family. Afraid that Mitsuyo might start wanting to take 'her child' back."

"............"

"I mean, that was nothing more than an unfounded worry of hers. I never really thought that hard about it, and I'm sure the same went for Mitsuyo and Mr. Fujioka..."

Mei continued her story matter-of-factly. Her face was cool and composed, as though she was trying to keep her emotions in check. It might have been my imagination, but I thought I saw a faint shade of sorrow make it through, which saddened me as well.

"But regardless, I think Kirika felt more anxiety than necessary... and because of it, she gave me those strict orders. Forget visiting the Fujiokas—she told me I was absolutely prohibited from having any contact with Mitsuyo or seeing her on my own."

12

"And what about being a *doll*?" I asked, curious. "Kirika raised you, and she was afraid that her daughter might drift away from her, so she tried to keep that from happening—I think I get that. But where does the *doll* come in? She and Mr. Misaki saw you as their real

daughter and really doted on you, right? But you said you were a
doll... Is that all you are to her?"

When I asked this, Mei drew her lips in a little bit and looked
down. She extended her hand again toward the figure wearing the
black dress sitting on the table and stroked its cheek with the tip
of her finger, exactly as she'd done earlier. As she did, she mumbled, exactly as she had earlier, "I don't dislike this one. Because she
doesn't look like me."

"Huh?"

"She doesn't look like me, right? That's why."

When she said that, everything clicked.

I'd seen a lot of Kirika's creations, either at the "Blue Eyes..." gallery or the Misaki family's vacation house in Hinami before arriving
in Yomiyama. Sure enough, quite a few of them resembled Mei to
some degree...

"Do you hate them? The dolls that look like you?"

"Hate... Not exactly, but I don't like them much."

"Why not?"

"Because...they aren't me. I can tell."

"They're not you?" I asked, not grasping what she was implying.
"What, um, what do you mean?"

"Those dolls, they're not me; they're the child who was never
born—Kirika's child. Even as she makes imitations of me, *that* is
what she's always seeking in the 'emptiness' of her creations. As far
as she's concerned, I'm not the 'real thing'...I've always been a 'substitute,' a little figurine."

"But that means..."

I got that far and couldn't continue. I wasn't sure how well I had
understood Mei's tale so far, but I could at least say that *here* was the
source of the tension that I could sometimes sense between Mei and
Kirika and Mei and Mr. Misaki.

"What I've just told you is more or less the same thing that I confided to Sakakibara when we were third-years in middle school," Mei
continued. "I told him when we were at the boarding house during
summer vacation. I had never spoken about it to any of my friends

before then. And I hadn't wanted to talk about it, either, but back then..."

Mei's third year of middle school—the class trip during the summer of 1998. And what happened that summer after I encountered her at Lakeshore Manor...

"But listen, Sou." She stared me in the face. "It's been three years since that day. The circumstances have changed somewhat between then and now. And my feelings and my relationship with Kirika, I sense those have changed in due course, too."

"Is that...really true?"

"I'm not as much of a 'substitute' these days."

"Really?"

"I don't want to say that I 'grew up.' I think there's more nuance to it than that."

"Three years...huh?"

"It's the same for you, right, Sou?" I could sense what the question was insinuating.

Three years. That's right—that time passed for me as well as for Mei. And during that time, I've... I'm sure there have been some natural changes in me. Perhaps, like Mei, in my relationship with my mother, Tsukiho... Oh, no.

No. I'm wrong about that, I think.

"Also, this eye," Mei remarked, pointing at her left socket with her right pointer finger. "I think I talked to you about it before, but I was four years old when I lost it. Kirika said that normal prosthetic eyes weren't cute, so she made a 'doll's eye' for me instead."

That beautiful azure glass eye. The one that supposedly held a mysterious power...

"Have you noticed I hardly use it anymore?" she asked.

"Uh...yeah," I answered.

"Do you want to hear why not?"

"Uh, no." I shook my head left to right, flustered. "Somehow, that seems like the sort of thing I shouldn't be hearing."

"Oh? I guess most people would decline, huh," Mei answered with a candid smile. "My left socket is empty, and it can't see anything on its own. And yet, when I put in that 'doll's eye,' I can see a kind of 'color' that normal people can't perceive, don't want to perceive... You remember me telling you about this, don't you?"

What she told me three years ago, that summer... Of course I remember. I couldn't possibly forget it.

I nodded forcefully, and Mei's smile disappeared.

"That's why I used to wear an eye patch whenever I went outside. Because I didn't like what I could see. I didn't want to see that."

"............"

"But I did wonder if I should use a different prosthetic in place of the 'doll's eye,' rather than hide it behind the eye patch. But no matter how much I thought about it, I couldn't go through with it. I'm sure that was also part of Kirika's spell."

"Spell?"

"Or whatever. I'm exaggerating a bit, I think. She went to the trouble of making me that 'eye,' so...get it? It was like, if I switched to a different prosthetic, she would get mad, or it would make her sad, or something. I was convinced of that for so long, probably mostly unconsciously...but—"

"But you did switch it to the 'eye' you're wearing now," I stated, turning my gaze toward Mei's left eye. It wasn't blue but black with flecks of brown...

"When I started high school, I saved up my allowance and bought this one on my own. When I wear it, I can't see 'things that I shouldn't see,' so I don't need the eye patch."

"And Kirika?" I asked, slowly and quietly. "Was she angry and sad?"

"She didn't say anything," Mei answered, pouting ever so slightly. "Just that this one suited me pretty well, too."

"Ah..." I couldn't help but sigh with relief.

Though that probably didn't mean that Mei's fears had been groundless. I was sure that Kirika's feelings had also changed with the passage of time. So...

"I suddenly just started monologuing about myself... I'm sorry. I probably surprised you," Mei said.

"No!" I immediately shouted. "I'm sort of happy you did."

"Oh?"

I don't know whether it was purposeful or not, but Mei shrugged kind of rudely, then said, "As to the point of telling you that story now...well, you can interpret it however you like."

"Sure."

The melancholic mood weighing me down before Mei's arrival had mysteriously vanished. Though that didn't necessarily mean listening to her story had touched me so much that I was considering changing how I dealt with Tsukiho.

Mei is Mei, and I'm me. And the circumstances of the Misaki household and the Hiratsuka household are totally different...

Instead, I think I just was glad to hear her talk about herself. Since that summer three years earlier, Mei had always been "special" to me. It was an honor to have her open up to me about things she normally kept to herself.

"I'll go ahead and add that my Fujioka mother—Mitsuyo—has also gone through some changes in these past three years," Mei continued. But in contrast to how she'd sounded before, her voice was quite frail and thin this time.

"I don't really know if it was a consequence of my sister's death three years ago or not, but last year, she divorced my Fujioka father. My Misaki father was worried about her, so he took it upon himself to help her get remarried..."

".........."

".......Ah, sorry, Sou. You didn't need to know that."

"No, it's fine, I..."

"Aaah." Mei stretched, something I rarely saw her do. Still sitting in her chair, she interlaced her fingers and pushed her arms up straight above her head. "I'd rather just not deal with it—family, blood relations, none of that."

Now that I thought about it, this was the first time I'd heard her say that.

"But children can't escape. And while they're stuck, they inevitably become adults, too."

I never want to grow up. When I was in elementary school, at least until three summers ago, I had sincerely thought that. But now I wasn't so sure. I didn't know what to think.

"Oh, that's right." Her tone shifted again. As I was wondering what it could be, she opened up the bag she had set down beside her chair and dug through the inside, then finally—

"Here," she said, holding something out to me. A white paper bag about the size of a student notebook. "I completely forgot to give you this. It's a souvenir."

"A souvenir?"

"You know, from my school trip to Okinawa."

Out of everything that had happened that day, this was probably the biggest shock of all.

"Th-thank you," I replied shakily, accepting the bag and peeking into it. "Can I open it?"

"Go ahead."

Inside was a cell phone strap with a silver mascot charm on it. The character seemed to be designed after a legendary Okinawan beast, and it had a small green stone inlaid in its belly.

"It's a *shisa* lion, right?"

"There were a lot that were too cutesy, so I picked one that was the least like that I could find."

"It's really cool."

"It's supposed to be a charm that wards off evil spirits. Well, it's the thought that counts, right?"

I laid the *shisa* charm in my open palm. On closer inspection, it was actually a little cutesy; it certainly wasn't making a very dependable expression. I thanked her once more and closed my hand around it.

"Hey, Mei?" For some reason, I suddenly got anxious. "Can I ask you something?"

I didn't particularly have to inquire about it right then and there. But I saw her nod silently, so I asked *that question.*

"The younger twin who you talked about just now. What was her name?"

And then—

The world around us froze, suspended in time.

Both her eyes opened wide, the living right and the false left. She didn't blink once. She tried to move her lips slightly, then stopped. The upper half of her body was utterly motionless, so still that it seemed as though she wasn't even breathing.

Like some sort of strange stop-motion performance, the stillness persisted for three or four seconds. For some reason, I was acting the same way as I sat across from her...

Five, six, seven, eight seconds it continued, until finally, at last, "Her..." Mei's lips moved. "She was..."

I was right in front of her, but it was like I was hearing her from some unfathomable distance. And although my apartment was bright during the day, it seemed as though her words were leaking out from the depths of some deep, dark place. No one else was in the room with us. And yet, it was almost as if someone was threatening her, preventing her from saying the words.

With great difficulty, in a voice that was barely audible, Mei croaked out the girl's name in a series of disjointed syllables.

"Her name was......Mi...saki......Misaki."

And then she managed to tell me the characters used to spell it.

The world went black for a moment.

Just for an instant, accompanied by a deep, reverberating *thud*.

Chapter 9
June II

1

No "related individuals" suffered any "accidents" during the third and fourth weeks of June, either.

Three vacant sets of desks and chairs had become a fixture of the classroom—one belonged to Tsugunaga, the "casualty of May." Another to Hazumi, who had still not returned to school. And the third to Makise, whose hospitalization was ongoing. Day after day, a frigid tension filled the air, and with each new dawn, it somehow faded in some ways but grew stronger in others. Mentally, part of me wanted to believe that the new "countermeasures" we had employed at the end of the previous month had been successful, while another part of me was growing more anxious about whether it had worked or not. This turmoil had always been lurking deep in my heart.

Takanashi, who had lost her mother to an accident, came back to school after a little while. Even after her return, however, it was plain to see that she was in low spirits. That was only natural. I couldn't imagine going to class feeling so much grief. They hadn't really known Takanashi before everything that happened, but I did catch sight of Izumi and Etou and the rest trying indirectly to encourage her sometimes.

From the third week of June, three-person meetings for guidance on post-graduation options began. The homeroom teacher, the student themselves, and a parent or guardian would convene for a conference after school.

My turn came at the start of the fourth week. The person attending as my guardian was Auntie Sayuri. Ms. Kanbayashi had to treat me as if I "didn't exist" at school, so the Japanese language teacher, Mr. Wada, served as a substitute. My aunt probably thought it was strange that she wasn't speaking to my homeroom teacher, but Mr. Wada explained the situation away as a problem with Ms. Kanbayashi's health, which Sayuri seemed to accept.

I do want to go to high school, after all. To First Yomiyama Prefectural High School (the same as Mei) if possible.

After some hesitation, I expressed this desire to my Akazawa aunt and uncle. As always, they told me that they would support me in whatever I wanted to do. They added that Tsukiho should have no problem with it, either.

And since my teachers could attest that my academic credentials were solid, the discussion went quickly enough.

However—and this time I had to reason with myself—however, that all depends on whether we make it through this year. To be honest, it all depends on whether I can avoid losing my life in the "calamity"— that's the real question.

2

The renovation work at the Akazawa house was proceeding much more slowly than expected. It was supposed to be finished around the time I started my summer vacation. Grandfather, who was more or less confined to his bed in the back room, was moody as always and very displeased about the construction dragging on. Whenever I stopped by, however, he received me in fairly good spirits.

Kurosuke, the black cat, also hadn't changed much, and he would alternate among frolicking around, being annoyingly affectionate to the humans, and pretending not to know you when you called.

After the renovations were complete, I would have to vacate my room at the Freuden Tobii and return here. Or so I'd assumed, but it turned out that Mayuko and her husband said that I could stay there longer if I wanted.

"It's up to you, of course, but you can do whichever you please, Sou. I'm sure Izumi would be happiest if you stayed here. Despite how strong-willed she seems, she tends to get lonely..."

Why are my aunts, Sayuri and Mayuko both, treating me so kindly? Up until three years ago, I was just a nephew they scarcely ever interacted with, whose face they barely recognized.

Considering this question made my mind wander to Tsukiho, who I could never manage to have a decent conversation with on the rare occasions that we actually spoke. Then I was the one who felt a lump in my throat. I hated it.

During this period, the Akazawas invited me to the penthouse for dinner on two occasions.

Auntie Sayuri and Uncle Haruhiko joined me on one of them. As for how the conversation went, the topic of my real father, Fuyuhiko, who had died long ago, came up for a while, but I was able to stay composed to a degree that left even me surprised.

"If only such things wouldn't happen," Mayuko muttered.

By *such things*, she meant Fuyuhiko's death fourteen years earlier—death by suicide after a long period of depression—but even when she said it aloud, I was at a loss for how to respond.

I couldn't even remember the face of my biological father, much less make sense of any feelings I still had about him. I wouldn't say that I felt absolutely no sadness or loss. Yet, I also could not deny that my feelings were somewhat...subdued.

That was probably because I'd always thought of my maternal uncle Teruya as my real father figure. And I had said good-bye to him three years ago over the summer. That's why...

While at the penthouse, I once again peeked into the room belonging to Izumi's older brother, who was staying long-term in Germany (his name was Souta, and he was twenty-five years old).

At a glance, it was obvious that the room's "owner" had been absent for an extended period of time; every nook and cranny was far too tidy. As Izumi had said, the bookcase filling one of the walls had a shelf jam-packed with mystery novels, both domestic and foreign.

With Izumi's encouragement, I borrowed several of them.

One was Umberto Eco's *The Name of the Rose*, parts one and two. It seemed difficult to understand, but I had always wanted to read it and had somehow failed to ever borrow it from the library. The other was a title I had never seen before and that didn't seem much like a mystery, a book by Ágota Kristóf—*The Notebook*.

3

While all this was going on, June entered its final week.

We just need to get through this week without incident—I'm sure that's what everyone was desperately hoping. Me included, of course. If the week ended with no casualties, we could finally be certain that our new "countermeasures" were working.

June 25, Monday.

Thanks to a break in the rain, the weather had been fine all morning, without a cloud in the sky.

I woke up even earlier than usual and spent the time before school taking a walk alongside the Yomiyama River. While I was there, I happened to encounter a kingfisher hovering above the river's surface. I reflexively put my fingers together to form my imaginary viewfinder and recalled the last time I had sighted this bird by the same body of water. I had been with Yuika Hazumi, and our conversation had started to head in a direction I didn't like...

That was just past mid-April, yeah. Already two months ago...no, only two months ago.

Had two months *already* gone past since then, or had it been *only* two months? It felt like both were true. Suddenly, I found myself wondering about what Hazumi had been up to lately.

My feelings all out of order, I clicked my imaginary shutter to capture the kingfisher's hovering, then realized my cell phone was vibrating in my bag.

"Hey, morning!" As soon as I picked up, I heard Shunsuke Kouda's voice on the other end.

Without thinking, I asked, "What's up? Why are you calling so early?"

It was a few minutes past seven a.m. There was still plenty of time before homeroom started at 8:30.

"And from where?" I continued. "Are you at home?"

"No, I'm in the clubroom."

"Huh?"

If I recall correctly, the school gates are supposed to open every morning at seven. If he's in the biology club room already, he must have gotten in as soon as possible.

It wasn't unusual for Shunsuke to stop by the clubroom before school started, but this was ridiculous.

The sports clubs aren't even doing their morning training yet, geez...

"I figured you'd already left home and were walking along the river right about now."

We had known each other for a long time, so Shunsuke had a good grasp on my morning routine.

Still, why go to the trouble of contacting me now?

I was soon given the answer to my question.

"Do you think you could come to school now, too, and stop by the clubroom for a bit? I'm thinking about the Culture Festival. I figured it's about time we discussed the biology club's display..."

"The Culture Festival's in the fall, isn't it?"

"It's better to start getting ready early."

"But there's no reason why we need to have a meeting first thing in the morning like this."

"Come on—don't say that. There's no time like the present, right?"

"...I guess so, but why are you there so early today, Shunsuke?"

"Ah, that's because—" As he answered, I could hear the rustling sound of him moving around. "For the last few days, Woo has looked kind of strange, like he hasn't got any energy. I feed him, but he hardly eats, and his reactions are sluggish. I stopped in to check on him yesterday, too."

You mean the second wooper looper?

"And of course, we just lost the previous Woo early on in the new semester. I was pretty worried, so I came to see how he was doing first thing this morning."

"Is he sick or something?"

"No. When I fed him earlier, he gobbled it up, so he's probably fine for now."

"Thank goodness."

"But you know, if the worst does come to pass, I'll put all my heart into making a beautiful transparent specimen out of him…for sure this time."

Oh no, he's on about that again.

Just as I was about to voice my objection, Shunsuke let out a short yelp of surprise.

"Wah! Wh-what'd you do that for?!"

I heard static noise for a while, as if he was losing reception. Puzzled, I asked, "What happened?"

"Ah, nothing," Shunsuke answered evasively. "It's nothing…"

He got that far before letting out another short shriek. "Wah! Ah…owww!"

"What happened?! What is it?"

He didn't reply. Instead, it sounded like his cell phone was being tossed onto a desk or something. I strained my ears as best I could, but I couldn't tell what was happening on the other side. Then finally—

"Ah man, he really got me!" Shunsuke's voice came back to the phone.

"What happened?"

"Dude, for some reason the trapdoor on one of the plastic cages was open just a bit, and Toby escaped through the crack."

"What?"

"I just caught him and put him back, but he bit me as hard as he could. It really hurts…"

"Toby" was the name of the centipede we had captured and started raising last autumn. He was a Chinese red-headed centipede, fifteen centimeters long, with the characteristic reddish-brown cranium of his species (though his markings looked like more of a true red). Shunsuke had christened him.

Despite being a member of the biology club, I wasn't very good with things like cockroaches and stink bugs and maggots—"creepy-crawlies." To say nothing of centipedes! Because of that, I'd been opposed to raising Toby in our clubroom. Even if centipedes weren't technically insects.

"Are you all right?" I asked.

"Ugh." Shunsuke made a pained noise but answered, "I'm fine. It hurts, though."

"You should go to the infirmary."

"It's not open yet. I know how to treat this. He's already bitten me once since we captured him, after all. I've got the steroid cream and everything."

"Are you really okay?"

"Yeah, I'm all right."

"Well, at any rate, I'm headed to school now. It should take me about twenty minutes from here. Okay?"

"I'm fine... Ah, owww!"

I hung up the phone and put it back in my bag. The *shisa* lion phone strap I had gotten from Mei caught the morning light and sparkled dully.

4

I arrived at the south gate of the school about ten minutes later. I hadn't been worried at first, but as I got closer to school, the anxiety in my chest gradually ballooned... At one point, I'd tried to contact Shunsuke, but—

The call hadn't connected.

I don't mean that he didn't pick up. The ringtone never even sounded, and all I got was the standard message saying, "The number you have dialed is not available or may be outside the service area..."

How can that be?

Entering the school grounds, I crossed the side of the field to find people who belonged in sports clubs grouped up in twos and threes, engaged in their morning training. I headed for Building Zero. As I got closer, I picked up my pace, and by the time I could see the old school building I was aiming for, I was practically sprinting.

I wasn't in a rush to talk about the Culture Festival. No, my hurry was due to my increasing anxiety, an uneasy premonition that I couldn't suppress...

The shriek Shunsuke had given when the centipede bit him kept ringing in my ears.

Thankfully, I'd never experienced a centipede bite myself, but the noise he'd made had certainly sounded like he had been in great pain. I could only imagine his wounded flesh, filled with venom.

He said he's all right, but if that's circulating through his body... No, centipede venom shouldn't be strong enough to kill someone, and Shunsuke said he knows the treatment for a bite. So I'm sure he won't do anything rash. I'm sure he won't but, if by some chance, something was to...

Those were the thoughts racing around in my head.

Nothing's happened; I'm certain. At least, I want to be.

I want to believe... Ah, I'm begging here—don't let anything happen to Shunsuke!

By the time I got to the front entrance of Building Zero, I was basically praying.

"Hiratsuka?"

Someone called out to me, and I leaped back in surprise. The voice belonged to none other than the master of the secondary library, dressed in all black despite the season—it was Mr. Chibiki.

"What on earth is going on? Why are you rushing at this ungodly hour?"

Of course, at this time of day, Mr. Chibiki had also just arrived, and I could see that he was carrying his old box-style briefcase in his right hand.

"Going to clubroom. Biology club room."

Suppressing my impatience, I ground to a halt and answered him. Several beads of sweat trickled down my neck.

"Shunsuke…Kouda is in there. And I'm worried about him."

"Worried?" Mr. Chibiki walked over to me quickly. "Did something happen?"

"I got a phone call from his cell earlier, and…"

"Kouda, you mean the club president?"

"Yes. Shunsuke's in Class 1, but his twin brother, Keisuke, is in Class 3."

As soon as I said that, Mr. Chibiki frowned sternly. "What? He's a 'related individual'?"

"During our phone call, um…a centipede bit him, and he claimed he was all right. But, well…"

I was in such a hurry that I couldn't explain the situation very well. Mr. Chibiki urged me on sharply. "Let's go."

Together, we both rushed into the annex and finally arrived in front of the door to the clubroom.

Chu-chu, chu…

The first thing I noticed was a high-pitched sound emanating from the other side of the wooden sliding door.

What's that? The hamsters we're keeping in there?

The noises were small, but I couldn't help but feel uneasy when I heard them. The hamsters didn't usually cry out like this. My fear doubled instantly.

Ahhh, no way! Don't tell me something really happened in there?

Holding my breath, I pulled the door open resolutely. When I did and saw the scene inside the room—

For a moment, I lost the ability to move. My throat seized up, and all I could choke out was, "Ah, ah, ah…!"

"No!" Mr. Chibiki shouted, tossing his bag aside and darting in. "Hey! Are you all right?"

It took me a moment to follow him into the chaos of the biology club room.

The beige curtain over the main, south-facing window was still drawn. Under the pale light of the fluorescent bulbs overhead spread a disastrous scene.

When you entered the room, there were several open steel racks against the wall to your right. One of them had fallen over. It had crashed into the edge of a large desk nearby and come to rest at a sharp angle. All the miscellaneous stuff that had been on the shelves—instruments and containers, bottles, cans, cardboard boxes, books and notebooks, paper filers, and so on—had broken loose or been flung away to scatter across the room.

We'd set many of the tanks and cages that we used for raising creatures on the big desk that the rack had toppled onto; now they'd either been shattered by the items that had fallen off the shelves or had fallen off the desk and onto the floor. A number of the tanks had been filled with water, so the desk and floor were soaked. The fish, frogs, newts, and other creatures that had been kept in them had also spilled out... The fish couldn't breathe and were flailing about, gasping for air, while the frogs, newts, and other amphibians who had gained their freedom were all trying to escape.

The lids had come off the plastic cages used for raising insects when they had been thrown off the desk, so there were all sorts of bugs and spiders about as well. The tank where the grass lizards and skinks were being raised had broken, and they were already nowhere to be found. The hamster cage was on a separate table some distance away, so its occupants had escaped the danger, but two hamsters inside had been screaming noisily out of either excitement or fear ever since we'd arrived...

...and in the middle of this disastrous scene was Shunsuke Kouda.

I couldn't tell for sure just what had set this all off, but in any case, Shunsuke was currently slumped over on top of the desk with his face stuck in one of the shattered tanks.

Mr. Chibiki had already rushed over to him. "Hey! Kouda!" He put his hand on Shunsuke's shoulder. "Kouda... Oh, this is bad!"

"—Shunsuke!"

Finally, I found my voice.

Taking care not to tread on the fish or other creatures lying all over the flooded floor, I approached my friend.

"Ah...Shunsuke..."

He had collapsed into the tank where we'd been keeping Woo, the axolotl. Though destroyed, there was still some water left in it... which had been dyed a sickening crimson...*bloodred.*

I wondered whether he'd sliced his neck open on the broken glass when he fell on the tank.

"Shunsuke?" I called his name, but there was no answer.

My eyes, which had been darting around in a panic, landed on the bodies of one of the creatures lying on the ground. On a pitiful pink lump of flesh... *So this is Woo, huh? He must have been carried out of the tank along with the water before Shunsuke trampled him by accident...*

"Kouda!" Mr. Chibiki called out to the boy again, but there was no response. No sound and no movement... Actually, his right arm, which was dangling limply at his side, was twitching ever so slightly.

Mr. Chibiki put his arms around Shunsuke's torso from behind and tried to pull his top half upright.

"Give me a hand!" he barked at me, and the two of us pulled his body away from the desk to lie him down on the floor nearby. The wound in his neck looked deep. He was stained red with the blood flowing out of it, from his face, to his neck, to the collar of his shirt and down his chest. His glasses were also soiled with blood, and I couldn't tell whether his eyes were open or not behind them.

"Hand me that towel," Mr. Chibiki commanded.

"H-here," I said and handed it to him.

He pressed the towel against Shunsuke's neck. Before my eyes, a red stain spread out across it. For a second, Shunsuke's legs shook weakly as he lay stretched out on the floor.

"Hey, hang in there! Hey!"

As he was talking to him, Mr. Chibiki put his ear close to his mouth.

"Shunsuke..."

I squeezed Shunsuke's hand. He didn't have the strength to squeeze mine back. He felt incredibly cold, maybe because his hand was wet or maybe...

"Don't die!"

"He's still breathing. Call an ambulance," said Mr. Chibiki. "Dial 1-1-9. Can I trust you with that?"

"Yes!"

Still holding Shunsuke's hand, I searched for the whereabouts of my bag, which had my cell phone in it. I'd lost hold of it as soon as we'd entered the room.

"Don't die." I mumbled the same words again and let go of his hand. As I did, his legs trembled once more...

...Shunsuke.

I dashed toward my bag, nearly falling, and fished out my cell phone.

It can't be... Shunsuke, are you dying? Are you going to die like this?

The crimson staining his cheeks made me recall the sight of the blood gushing from Tsugunaga's neck in the rain one month earlier. That day, Shunsuke had happened to witness the accident with me and had called the ambulance himself. And now...

...Are you dying? Is it you this time?

You were talking to me so normally just thirty minutes ago.

I shook the thought out of my head and tightened my grip on the phone. But my fingers were shaking, so I struggled to dial the numbers.

Just then, something caught my eye.

Something small and black was crawling from Shunsuke's feet toward his belly, where he was laid out on the floor...

Is that a bug? One of the crickets he was keeping as live bait for the reptiles?

On closer inspection, I could see that there were several of them. Their cage had fallen off the desk, and the lid had come open, and now several of the escaped crickets were crawling over his body...

I think that sight was probably what triggered me. In that moment, the seal on a small box in a corner of my mind was broken. When it did, everything that had been stowed away in there came spilling out...

...Someone's corpse, lying on a filthy sofa.

Rotten skin. Rotten flesh. Rotten innards... Countless squirming, swarming insects.

The repulsive horde of vermin streamed out of my memories and into my current reality. From my mouth. From my nose. From my eyes. From my ears. From every pore in my skin. Then they crawled toward Shunsuke's body in droves, clambered up onto him, and dragged the boy who was on the border between this world and the next definitively down into "death."

"Ahhh, stop it!" I gasped weakly.

Though I hadn't accomplished my goal, all the strength left my hands, and I dropped my phone. My whole body began to tremble violently; then I lost my ability to stand and dropped to my knees on the floor. As my breathing became strained, a bout of dizziness assaulted me.

"Hiratsuka?" It was Mr. Chibiki. He had noticed the state I was in. "What is it, Hiratsuka...?"

That's as far as I remembered clearly.

I'm sorry...Shunsuke...

I fell facedown on the spot, swallowed by hopelessness. As I fell, my consciousness receded from the "present."

5

I would later find out that Shunsuke Kouda, who had been taken to the hospital by ambulance, was confirmed dead at about nine o'clock that morning. When the paramedics got to him, he was still barely breathing, but his heart and lungs had failed in transit. They tried everything they could to resuscitate him, but in the end, they were fruitless...

A little past noon, I was informed of the truth as I lay in a bed in the infirmary on the first floor of Building A.

Mr. Chibiki broke the news to me. Apparently, I had collapsed in the clubroom and been carried to the infirmary, where I had opened my eyes once or twice but never fully awakened. I'd been dozing there since. It had felt as though I'd been having the same bad dream over and over, but I couldn't remember anything about it now.

"I'm so sorry," I apologized as soon as I knew it was Mr. Chibiki sitting on the stool next to my bed. "It was such a critical moment, and I—"

"Don't worry about it." He shook his head slowly from side to side. "Sure, it was a serious situation, and I was surprised when you collapsed all of a sudden, but that's what shock does to people. No one is blaming you."

"............"

"After you passed out, another teacher noticed the commotion and came to help. I got him to look after you while I ended up riding along in the ambulance to the hospital. I spoke to the head physician while I was there..."

Shunsuke's immediate cause of death was blood loss. Just as I suspected, the wound in his neck had been as serious as it looked.

"But they think that something might have been wrong with Kouda even before the accident. That's what the doctor's examination said."

Another cause? Something wrong?

Without lifting the back of my head off the pillow, I tilted my head quizzically. I was still in a bit of a daze, but one thing suddenly came to mind.

Another cause...? Could it be...?

"Is it possible that...the centipede bite somehow...?"

"That's right." Mr. Chibiki frowned grimly. "I told the doctors what you'd said about the centipede. And they confirmed that there was a bite mark on his right hand. They said it was possible that Kouda went into anaphylactic shock."

"Anaphylactic..."

"It's when the whole body has a violent allergic reaction. The immune system runs wild in response to foreign matter entering the body and experiences symptoms akin to an infection."

"Ah, yeah, that's..."

I already knew the basic definition.

The first thing that came to my mind when I heard *anaphylactic shock* was what people said about beestings: that the second is always more dangerous than the first. People normally get away with just some pain and irritation the first time they're stung, but then they're sensitized to the bee venom, so the second time might produce a life-threatening allergic reaction. I'd read a short novel a year or two ago in which a killer used this trick to commit murder.

"But wait, can that happen with centipede venom?"

"Apparently, there's a slim probability it can, yes. They said it's a one percent chance."

"I know that Shunsuke was bitten by a centipede once last year. Was he sensitized because of it?"

"It's possible, yes." Mr. Chibiki sighed. "Bee venom is famous for causing anaphylactic shock, but it doesn't necessarily always happen on the second sting. Apparently, there are plenty of instances when someone dies from the accumulated effects of getting stung several times in the past. But with centipede venom, there are unfortunately too few cases, so a lot is still up in the air."

"Did they find something that made them doubt their findings?"

"They said they couldn't confirm without a more detailed investigation. But—" Mr. Chibiki got up from his stool. "It's undeniable that a centipede bit him right before he passed. Furthermore, there was visible swelling that they thought could be traces of hives all over his body. And here's what I told the doctor: If we put together the clues from the state of the room and the details of the incident we can deduce from that, then..."

"The details of the incident?"

"What happened during the half hour after you spoke to Mr. Kouda on the phone. It's practically impossible that he simply knocked over the shelf by accident and broke all the tanks, isn't it?"

"Uh...right," I answered frailly.

Mr. Chibiki put a finger against the frame of his glasses and stared at me. "Let's say that immediately after he hung up the phone with you, he started to show symptoms of anaphylactic shock from the centipede bite. When that happened, if it was a bad case, his blood pressure would have dropped drastically in a short time, and this would have caused difficulty breathing. Once that started, his symptoms would have progressed to full-body convulsions and loss of consciousness. Though it's impossible to know how severe his symptoms actually were or how well he understood what was going on... He probably felt suddenly unwell and couldn't stand, and maybe he tried to use his cell phone to call for help, but his fingers were shaking, so he couldn't work the buttons..."

"Where did they find Shunsuke's phone?"

"In the tank that he crashed into. He must have dropped it when he was fumbling with it. It was soaked and unusable."

As I was listening to Mr. Chibiki tell me this in a detached yet despondent tone—

The *scene from earlier* that I really would have preferred not to imagine was playing out in my mind in disturbingly vivid detail.

Images of Shunsuke after I hung up the phone, right after he said, *"I'm fine... Ah, owww!"* Pressing down on the wound where he'd been bitten by the centipede, starting to pull medication out of his bag. Then the symptoms of anaphylactic shock setting in.

I pictured him noticing the strange itchiness of the hives as they quickly spread across his body, after which his arms and legs starting to go numb. With his blood pressure dropping suddenly until he couldn't stand, he desperately clung to one of the open racks for support. I saw the rack falling and everything sliding off it, destroying the tanks and other stuff on the desk. Shunsuke had escaped being pinned between the rack and the desk but still couldn't get to safety. Even when he pulled out his cell phone to call for help, he dropped it in the water and panicked. And then—

Shunsuke unknowingly trampled Woo, who'd fallen onto the floor after pouring out of his broken tank. It was the worst thing that could have happened, for both boy and axolotl. Shunsuke slipped, making him lose his balance, and the momentum sent him plunging headfirst into the broken aquarium tank, where he collapsed...

A torrent of blood gushed from his throat where the glass had cut him. As this was happening, the physical symptoms of anaphylactic shock were also overtaking him. Breathing was difficult, his blood pressure was dropping further, he was losing consciousness...

"...Ohhh," I groaned, unable to stand the thought. It was getting hard to breathe. I felt like the air in my chest was being pumped out of me.

"Why that, of all things...? Is that something that would normally happen...?"

"It's apparently a highly improbable, unfortunate chain of events... yes. You're right," Mr. Chibiki answered me. He pushed his glasses up on his forehead and pressed on the inner corners of his eyes with his right thumb and forefinger, moving his fingers to massage them.

"But you know," he continued, steeling himself and speaking as if he were wringing the words out, "something that seemed like it would almost never happen *did* actually happen. And tragically, he was drawn in to 'death.' This is exactly the kind of 'accident' that the 'phenomenon' would bring about."

6

It was a decisive comment.

An "accident" produced by the "phenomenon."

That's right. That's what befell Shunsuke this morning—because he was "related" to Grade 3 Class 3...

"Mr. Chibiki." I lifted my head from the pillow and propped myself up. I was still having difficulty catching my breath. "Shunsuke—Kouda's really dead, isn't he? He's not coming back, right?"

Mr. Chibiki nodded silently.

"And was Keisuke also at the hospital?"

"His younger twin brother? Yeah. He got the call and made a mad dash over to the emergency room. Their parents showed up soon after him."

"............"

"The parents were heartbroken, of course, but his brother was especially distraught..."

Mr. Chibiki described how Keisuke had clung to the corpse and broken down crying. *"Why you?!"* he'd asked. Why Shunsuke, who'd been in a completely separate cohort from the "cursed Class 3"? It must have felt cosmically unjust to him.

"You guys," Mr. Chibiki said. He wasn't addressing me. There was a white curtain on the opposite side of the bed to where he was sitting on his stool—to the left from my perspective—drawn around the foot of the bed. I looked up at it.

Is there someone else here?

Just then, it dawned on me.

From the way he called them *you guys,* he wasn't speaking to the teachers who staffed the infirmary. It was probably students, several of them...

"It's all right already. Come on out here."

In answer to his request, the curtain swayed slightly. I could see someone's silhouette on the other side of the white fabric. Just as I noticed that, the curtain slid smoothly open.

Two people, with whom I was very well acquainted, entered—Izumi Akazawa and Nobuyuki Yagisawa.

They took a step or two toward the bed but didn't look me in the face. They didn't speak to me, either. Their expressions conveyed confusion and dismay as they cast their gazes toward Mr. Chibiki, who was standing at my bedside.

"It's all right now," he repeated with a faint sigh. "It's as you just heard. Kouda's sudden death this morning was the result of the 'calamity'—of that there is no doubt. So in other words—" Mr. Chibiki cut off and glanced at Izumi, Yagisawa, then me in turn. "In other words, the 'calamity' that began last month is still going on. We haven't ended it."

Upon hearing this news, Izumi looked him squarely in the face and asked, "Does that mean there's no point in keeping up with the current 'countermeasures' any longer?"

"Unfortunately, yes." Mr. Chibiki wore a severe expression. "I cannot help but arrive at that conclusion."

"Ah..." Izumi bit her lip in vexation. Standing next to her, Yagisawa had a similar reaction.

There was an even longer pause before the two of them at last fixed their gazes on me. In response, I finally opened my mouth and said, "Looks like it didn't work out, huh?"

I felt just as frustrated as Izumi... I was overwhelmed with an enormous sense of helplessness. These were the first words I'd spoken to either of them in school since we'd begun the initial "countermeasures" back in April.

"It didn't make any difference, no matter how well I kept 'not existing.'"

"I guess not," Yagisawa said in a dejected voice. "We don't need to do that anymore, huh? This year's 'countermeasures' are through, I guess. So this is what it means to exhaust all your options."

"...Seems that way."

Trying to get out of bed, I pushed aside the terry-cloth blanket that had been laid over me. My body felt unsteady again.

"So now that we know the new 'countermeasures' had no effect... at this point, it doesn't seem like there's much more we can do," Yagisawa remarked, addressing Mr. Chibiki this time.

The librarian couldn't really give him an answer. His severe expression remaining unchanged, he sighed deeply, then shook his head slightly.

I heard the sound of the infirmary door opening, and soon a new person appeared at my bedside. It was our homeroom teacher, Ms. Kanbayashi.

She looked at the four of us, three students plus Mr. Chibiki, in a way that told us she had realized herself that the "countermeasures" were now meaningless.

"You've had such a difficult time since April." She spoke to me, wearing a somewhat awkward smile. "I think you really made a very good effort, Hiratsuka. But starting today, you won't need to be a 'non-exister' anymore, okay? You can be like everyone else, even in the classroom..."

Despite what she was saying, in the moment, all I could hear was her blaming me.

Why on earth did it have to turn out like this?

The unanswerable question looped through my mind again and again, and all I could feel was darkness swallowing my heart.

7

Two days later. Wednesday, June 27.

Shunsuke's funeral was held at the funeral hall in a neighborhood called Furuchi. At Ms. Kanbayashi's behest, I was granted a half day's leave from school so I could attend. I wasn't a classmate of his, but I was there as a representative for the biology club, which he'd led. We'd known each other for only a little more than two years, but during that time, we had gotten fairly close, so I was there as a friend as well.

In a total contrast to the mild weather two days ago, it had been raining nonstop since morning on the day of the funeral.

Besides me, a number of other students in North Yomi uniforms also attended. They were probably all students from Shunsuke's class, Grade 3 Class 1. The Class 1 homeroom teacher was also there, and Mr. Kuramochi, the adviser for the biology club, came, too. So did Mr. Chibiki. Avoiding all of them, I sat in the very back corner of the funeral hall. It was like I was still pretending that I "didn't exist."

Once the priest started to chant, I intentionally shut my eyes and refused to open them again. When I did, almost as a matter of course, I recalled the last time I'd heard Shunsuke's voice on the phone. I recalled the disastrous scene in the clubroom...

...That day.

I had spoken with Mr. Chibiki in the infirmary, but I didn't remember much after that. No, it wasn't that I didn't remember; it was more like everything was distant, unreal, like I was somehow

separated from that reality. Like a degraded black-and-white recording, nothing was clear…

…That day. After it happened.

It was normal in circumstances like these for the police to come
and examine the scene. They'd questioned me about what had
occurred as a witness to the accident. Mr. Chibiki sat with me during the interview… I just answered everything truthfully, although
neither he nor I said a word about anything related to the "phenomenon" or the "accidents." If we had tried to tell them, the police
wouldn't have been able to do anything. Not to mention the fact that
they probably wouldn't have taken us seriously in the first place.

Ultimately, I didn't end up going back to class at all that day, opting
to head home early… Auntie Sayuri looked awfully surprised when
she heard about everything. She already knew about last month's
casualties—Tsugunaga and Takanashi's mother—so…so I suppose
it was only natural that in addition, she felt suspicion, anxiety, and
fear along with the shock.

That evening, Izumi came over to my apartment and talked to
me about a bunch of stuff, though I didn't feel like chatting. But all
her topics were completely unrelated to the "phenomenon" and the
"accidents"… I was sure she was trying to cheer me up. Despite her
efforts, I still didn't feel like saying a word… I was largely dissoci-
ated, hardly paying attention.

The following day—a Tuesday—I was in absolutely no mood to
go to school, so I spent almost the whole day shut up in my room.
The entire time, it felt as though I kept repeating an unanswerable
question, *Why?* while fully aware that there was no explanation to
be had.

Why on earth did it turn out like this?

Why? Just why, why, why…?

If only I'd been smarter when everything was going on in April.

My heart was full of regret, guilt over something that I could no
longer do anything about.

*If only I had done a better job… Couldn't I have done something
to keep Hazumi, the "second non-exister," from quitting like that? I*

mean, I didn't feel the same way about her that she felt about me, and I'm really bad at dealing with that kind of stuff...but maybe I should have just played along anyway, kept her from feeling so isolated, like there was no alternative...

I had these thoughts and many more, even though I knew that all this musing was utterly pointless.

But somehow, I spent the whole day doing nothing. I didn't feel like doing anything, and I passed the time alone and depressed. Izumi was worried and came over to my apartment to check on me, but I didn't open the door. I also got a phone call from Yagisawa, but I didn't pick up... When the night grew late, I finally booted up my PC and managed to send Mei an e-mail informing her of Shunsuke's death. That was all. I actually would have preferred to talk to her on the phone or go see her, but my heart felt so weak that this was totally out of the question, so I gave up on the idea...

...The funeral chanting came to an end.

The atmosphere in the funeral hall was dark and oppressive, and I could hear sobbing everywhere. Opening my eyes decisively, I squeezed both hands tightly into fists on my knees.

Our club adviser, Mr. Kuramochi, had informed me of the time and place for the funeral via a phone call that came late the night before.

—I thought I'd better let you know so you can attend if you want. I'm planning on going, too.

When I'd heard his message, I finally started to pull myself together a little bit; I felt myself coming back to the "present."

The undeniable truth was that Shunsuke Kouda was dead. And we had to mourn the dead properly. I needed to be present to mourn Shunsuke and give him a proper good-bye. And so...

My experience three years earlier at Lakeshore Manor, or the memory of it, was whispering to the recesses of my heart.

I went up to light the incense and bowed to Shunsuke's family, who were sitting in the seats reserved for the bereaved. His parents looked absolutely exhausted, and beside them, his brother, Keisuke, was wearing silver-rimmed glasses just like Shunsuke's, instead of his usual contact lenses. It was the first time I'd ever really noticed that their complexions looked exactly the same.

As I was facing the portrait of the deceased, I choked back the tears that threatened to overcome me. The death of a friend was devastating, but I didn't want to cry there.

After all, three years ago, when Uncle Teruya passed, I...

Shunsuke's joke from an earlier moment suddenly rang in my ears.

"If the worst happens to you, I'll scoop up your remains and put you with the rest of the specimens, okay, Sou?"

It felt as though he were actually speaking in my ear. Without meaning to, I looked at the portrait. Shunsuke smiled back bashfully from a photo in a lovely green frame.

Now that he was gone, the biology club would be all but defunct for a while. As club president, Shunsuke had planned most of the important club activities himself. However—

There was the question of what to do with the creatures we had been rearing in the clubroom, aside from the ones that had escaped, died, or gone missing during the incident two days earlier. That was a big problem.

What should I do?

Of course, there was no way I was getting an answer to this question.

Good-bye, Shunsuke.

Closing my eyes softly, I bid farewell to the eccentric head of the biology club.

8

I watched the row of black cars leave the funeral hall, headed for the crematory.

When I powered up my cell phone again, I found two voice mail notifications.

The first one was from Tsukiho.

Ugh...of all the times to call, it had to be today.

*   *   *

—Ah, Sou? It's me. I'm really sorry that I couldn't make it the other day.

She probably doesn't even know about Tsugunaga's death last month or Shunsuke's passing two days ago. Actually, it's possible that she heard about them from Auntie Sayuri, but even if she did, she probably doesn't care that much.

—Mirei's totally recovered already, so I thought we could come have lunch or dinner with you soon. Maybe next Sunday... It's already July, but I'm planning to come see you with your sister. I'll call you again with the details, okay?

Without meaning to, I let out a sigh.

At this point, what feelings does she actually hold for me? What's she thinking? What does she want? 'Cause I sure don't know. No, honestly, it's less that I don't know and more that I don't care.

The second message was from Mei Misaki. She'd left it a little before eleven in the morning.

She called me from school, during a class break?

—The head of the biology club, Mr. Kouda... Sou, you two were close, weren't you?

It was a small reassurance to hear her speaking to me the same way as ever...

—I'm sure it's a big shock and very painful, but hang in there.

...Ah, thank you. Thank you, Misaki... Thanks, Mei.

"Thank you," I said aloud without realizing, my voice cracking with emotion.

—It looks like all your "countermeasures" have failed in the end, but...you can't blame yourself, Sou. It's no use. Okay? No matter how much you torment yourself, nothing will come of it.

*　　*　　*

Just like that summer three years ago, Mei seemed to be peering straight into the contents of my heart.

—E-mail is fine, but call me anytime if you need to. You can come for a visit, too, or I could go see you again. Listen, Sou, even if the "countermeasures" *have failed, there's still…*

At that point, some awful static cut in, and the message broke off.

9

I was planning to attend classes in the afternoon, so once I'd listened to my messages, I left the funeral hall and headed for the school. I got off the bus from Furuchi and walked a short distance, but just as the North Yomi school gates came into view—

My phone rang.

I checked the display and saw it was coming from Mr. Chibiki, who I had just seen in front of the funeral hall. We had exchanged silent bows before parting.

"Where are you right now?" he asked the second I picked up.

"At…school? I'm just about to get there."

"I see."

I noticed that something was odd about the tone of his voice. It was slightly shrill, somewhat shaky…

"What's up?" I asked.

"Well…" Mr. Chibiki hesitated briefly but immediately checked himself and continued. "As a matter of fact, I just got an urgent call from Mr. Oohata, the teacher for Class 1. It's hard to believe his account, but it seems to be true. One of the cars that just headed for the crematory was involved in an accident on the way, on one of the mountain roads…"

Mr. Chibiki told me that at this point in time, the cause wasn't clear. Maybe the driver had simply made a mistake in operating the steering wheel or brakes. Perhaps the accident had resulted from a run-in with another car or something. Or maybe it was more of an act of God...

The car had broken through the guardrail on the mountain road, fallen several dozen meters down a cliff, and gone up in flames. There had been four people in the car: the driver and three passengers—Shunsuke's parents and twin brother, Keisuke. Of all the people it could have been, it was those three...

Several hours later, the blaze was finally extinguished, and the four occupants of the vehicle were all deceased. A subsequent investigation determined that the driver and Keisuke Kouda, who had been sitting in the front passenger seat, had died almost instantly on impact, from concussive force to the head and body. Tokuo and Satoko Kouda, who had been riding in the back, had burned to death in the fire after the fall.

Interlude III

That *thing* with Grade 3 Class 3 is no joke, seriously.

The head of the biology club died, right? Aren't you a member?

Yeah. Kouda was the head… On Monday morning, he collapsed in the clubroom, covered in blood. He was in Class 1, but his twin brother was in Class 3.

That's why he died?

I heard that anybody related to Class 3 can get dragged into it, even if they're in a different class or they aren't a student.

That's too awful to consider.

And the other brother, he also passed in a car wreck after Kouda's funeral…they say. Same for the parents—they were in the same vehicle.

The whole family? No way…

I didn't believe in curses, but…remember in May? One of the Class 3 students died, right?

Oh yeah.

I wonder if it's real, this curse.

The question is, what kind of curse is it?

I have no idea. They say just knowing too much about it is dangerous.

Ugh, brutal.

I wonder if I should quit the biology club. Two of the upperclassmen are in Class 3. One of them hardly ever attends, but the other was good friends with Kouda, and when he died, that guy just happened to...

Hmm? Sounds like you'd better not get too close if you can help it.

My thoughts exactly.

†

...Unfortunately, none of the many "countermeasures" we've attempted have been successful. This is terribly unfortunate, but...the "calamity" is here, so now all we can do is pray for the souls of the departed: Tsugunaga, Kouda and his family, and Takanashi's mother.

Everyone here has upheld the "countermeasures" since the beginning of April... I especially want to thank the countermeasures officers and Sou Hiratsuka, who took the initiative to become a "non-exister," for their efforts. From now on, Hiratsuka will be leading a normal school life with the rest of us...

....

....

......Ms.?

What is it?

So does this mean...does this really mean that there's nothing we can do?

What do you mean?

Are there any more, you know, "countermeasures"...?

...There are none. At least, not as far as I know.

....

....

The "calamity" has already begun. Our "non-exister" gambit failed to prevent it. I'm afraid there is nothing more that we can do...

...No way.

No way...

....

....

...I'm so sorry.

I apologize, everyone. Even I don't know another way.

But there is a class that stopped the "calamity" even after it started. Apparently, it happened three years ago.

But **why did it stop?** No one can say for sure. We don't really know; no one does. So...

....

......But—

But, everyone—

Don't give up... Don't give in, everyone; don't get careless, all right? Be vigilant about your surroundings. Take care when you're on your way to and from school. Whenever you leave home, avoid getting caught in any sudden accidents. Maintaining your health is part of that. Remain vigilant at all times, and do your best to avoid opportunities for the "calamity" to strike...

......I will, too.

As your homeroom teacher, I also have to be careful. No amount of caution is too great. Keep that in your mind, everyone, and please...

......**Be careful.**

Chapter 10
June III

1

"...Hello?"

It was *her* voice. I hadn't heard it for some time.

"Ah, ummm...it's been a while." I adjusted my grip on the phone, trying not to think about how awkward I felt.

After a brief pause, the girl on the other end replied a few words at a time. "Sou. I called you many times. But you finally answered."

"Ah...well, I..."

After another brief pause, Yuika Hazumi said, "I'm sorry."

"No, with everything that happened, it was bound to end up like this. And I think it's only natural that you'd feel like skipping school."

"Mm...ah, but listen, I'm fine. I feel all right." Hazumi's tone was surprisingly easygoing. "I just noticed that you called me. At that point, I didn't want to talk to anyone in our class. Not even you. But now, now I'm okay."

"You are?"

"Well, I still hate the idea of going to school. But I met up with Ms. Kanbayashi once, and we talked. She told me not to push myself."

"I see. So then..."

At this point, I wasn't particularly concerned with how many days she had attended school, or her graduating, or her going to university. The more important question was...

"Do you know about what happened to Tsugunaga and Takanashi's mom last month?" I asked, thinking there was no way that she wouldn't. "And at the start of this week, Shunsuke...the twin brother of Keisuke Kouda, who's in Class 3, he died. And afterward, Keisuke himself and his parents also passed..."

Hazumi was aware of the incidents from the month before. But she hadn't known about what had happened to Shunsuke and Keisuke.

That's the answer I got back. But the way she replied, it sounded just like she was dodging the question, as if it was somebody else's problem.

"So you see"—despite how uncomfortable I felt with her responses, I put some force into my voice—"in short, the 'calamity' has finally begun. The 'countermeasures' we used in April weren't successful."

"Because of me?" Hazumi asked. Just like me, she put more force behind her voice. "Because I couldn't bear to continue 'not existing,' is that it? It's all my fault, is what you're saying?"

"Uh, no. That's not what I was trying to say." I was at a loss for words. I certainly hadn't called to scold her or place blame.

"That day, I couldn't stand it any longer, so I ran away from the classroom, but...but after that, I didn't go to school at all. So it's like I became the perfect 'non-exister,' right? And you kept on 'not existing' after that, too, didn't you, Sou? And yet..."

Though sad- and anxious-sounding, Hazumi also seemed detached from what she was saying. I knew that even if I tried to explain the situation or went over what had happened after she left, she wouldn't be receptive to me at the moment.

"Um, uh...so on a different topic..." I took a breath, then said, "Be careful—that's what I wanted to say to you, Hazumi. That's all."

"............"

"After all, it doesn't matter if you're never at school; you're still a member of Grade 3 Class 3. And the 'accidents' can affect 'related individuals' as well."

I was calling because I wanted to encourage her to be cautious. It was something I thought I needed to do. When it came to the particulars of her renouncing her 'nonexistence' and running away, I certainly couldn't deny my own responsibility, however slight.

"You say *be careful*, but, hmm…" Her response betrayed my expectations. "The thing is, I don't really believe in it."

"Huh? In what…?"

"In that sort of stuff, like, in curses or divine punishment, unscientific stuff like that."

"What? But people have really died…"

"All of those were coincidences," she countered bluntly. "People are always going to die of something, right? Risk is a part of all our lives. So you see, once in a while, unlucky coincidences pile up, and lots of people die. The world is made up of coincidences like that, and they certainly don't happen because of a curse or divine punishment. That was true for Nakagawa—for Big Brother Nakagawa…"

Nakagawa?

She must mean Takayuki Nakagawa, the high school student at First Yomi who was killed in a motorcycle crash at the end of April. Maybe she heard that from his older brother? She told me he was a good friend of his.

"Ah…you said you were close with him, right? With, um, Nakagawa's older brother."

I remembered hearing that from someone who saw them together firsthand. When I said that, Hazumi didn't seem embarrassed. On the contrary, she answered somewhat boastfully, "Mm, that's right. Nakagawa's brother is incredibly intelligent, you know. He's majoring in physics at university. My big brother said so, too. He told me, 'He's really capable; he's a great guy.'"

So Einstein here has completely dismissed the "phenomenon" and "accidents" at North Yomi as "unscientific." And Hazumi's taking her lessons from him… Is that what's going on?

…Even though he knows nothing.

In my mind, I conjured up a silhouette to stand in the place of this older Nakagawa brother I'd never met and found myself with bitter words for him.

You don't know anything. Not one thing about our present reality!

"Listen, Hazumi," I said, tamping down my feelings of irritation. "I'm sure that what he…that what Nakagawa said was perfectly—how do I put this—was a perfectly sensible point of view, but don't you get it? The 'phenomenon' and 'accidents' of Grade 3 Class 3 at North Yomi are *different*. There's no point bringing science or common sense into this…"

"What Nakagawa said was correct." Hazumi's assertion was even more forceful. "If you really think about it, it's too strange, too bizarre. Who would believe that a 'casualty' joins the class and causes people to die?"

"That's exactly why—"

"And about those 'countermeasures' and the 'non-existers.' Well, Nakagawa says that's a form of *bullying*, and he got very angry about it. If the curse was real, the school and the board of education wouldn't just let it be, he told me."

"Th…" No more words would come out.

It's pointless, no matter what I say!

That was my impression. I pulled my ear away from the phone for a second to sigh quietly so that she wouldn't hear me.

She ran out of the classroom and into the arms of the older Naka-gawa… She did that, and now she's completely inside his field of influ-ence; that's what I'm hearing. I wonder how deeply infatuated she is? How much are her feelings clouding her judgment? I have no way to tell.

"At any rate…well, be careful," I said finally. "And if at all possible, you ought to get out of Yomiyama…"

She didn't say a word in response. Before I could hang up, she did it herself.

That was what happened the evening of Thursday, June 28.

2

The atmosphere in the classroom the next day was awful. Utterly depressing.

A bouquet of white lilies had been placed on the desk of Keisuke Kouda, who had died in a car accident the day before. Mean-while, the flowers for Tsugunaga, who had died earlier, were gone.

Including these two, there were four empty seats in total. The other two belonged to Hazumi, whose absence was ongoing, and to Makise, who was in the hospital—

Now that we'd ceased using "non-existers" as our "countermeasure," there was no need for the old desks and chairs that we'd brought over from the old classroom in Building Zero. The desk and chair I'd been using since April had already been cleared away that morning, replaced by a new set.

The teachers in charge of each subject class had also been notified of the end of the "countermeasures." During Japanese language class, I was called upon to read from the textbook for the first time this school year. We also did the usual "stand, bow, sit" at the start of classes and had a roll call to check attendance. It had become a standard classroom environment, free from "non-existers," just like I had experienced in previous school years.

But even as things seemed to go back to normal, an awful weight was bearing down on us.

The weight of the "calamity."

If you included Joukichi Kanbayashi's death from illness, a total of seven "related individuals" had lost their lives in May and June. Despite that, there was no way to avert it, so we weren't doing anything. We *couldn't* do anything. A sense of failure and helplessness. Anxiety and irritation. And fear and uneasiness that we couldn't shake no matter what.

During the breaks between classes, a succession of peers I hadn't spoken to even once since April (like Tajimi's childhood friend Aonuma, and Nakamura from the soccer club, and Tsugunaga's best friend Fukuchi from the girls, and so on…) came up and practically forced themselves to interact with me. It was all bland small talk, and answering them one by one somehow put me in a melancholy mood… It even seemed like things had been easier for me back when I "didn't exist."

During homeroom, Ms. Kanbayashi told us that the Kouda family was planning to hold a funeral the day after tomorrow but that it would be private, for relatives only.

"So, everyone, please say your good-byes to Kouda in your heart..."
She teared up a little as she addressed us, then leaned against the
podium when she finished and sobbed loudly for a while. Even from
my seat in the back row, I could see her shoulders and knees shaking
terribly as she wept.

3

"Want to come over for some coffee?"
I got the call from Izumi not long after I hung up the phone with
Hazumi. I was grappling with how to answer the sudden invitation
when she cleverly added, "Mama baked an apple pie, so I thought
you might like to enjoy it with me. Let's see, give me about ten minutes? Then come over."
About ten minutes later, I arrived at her apartment, <E-1>.
"Ever since Kouda passed, you've been down, so it's been hard to
approach you. I totally get it, since you were friends since first-year
biology club, and I know I need to leave you alone to deal with it...
but there was that accident on the day of his funeral, right?"
The fragrance of the Inoya-blend coffee that she had treated me to
once before was hanging in the air of the apartment. As she poured
coffee into cups from the pot, Izumi continued. "It's really horrible,
isn't it? I mean, the whole family?"
She kept going, sounding sad and a little angry. "Even if the 'calamity' is some kind of 'supernatural natural phenomenon,' even if it
doesn't have a will or intent, that's not how it seems to me anymore."
"You sense some kind of malice?"
"I don't know what it is, but there's something. How about you,
Sou?" she asked.
I shook my head side to side without saying anything. It wasn't a
question of whether I felt or didn't feel something. I didn't even want
to acknowledge that there could be some kind of ill will at work. So
I rejected the whole line of questioning outright.
Shortly after we brought the coffee over to the living room table,

the doorbell rang. Izumi answered, "Coming!" and headed for the door. The person at the entrance was Izumi's mother, Mayuko. She'd come down to bring us a freshly baked apple pie.

"...Seems like the elevator is acting up a little."

I could hear the entryway conversation between mother and daughter from the living room.

"I just called it from upstairs, but it didn't come. I went down the stairs, but my attention was focused on the pie tray, and I was afraid I might lose my footing... I've got goose bumps!"

"Geez! Be careful, Mama," insisted Izumi. Her voice cracked with tension and wariness. "You should never rush on the stairs. If the elevator's acting up, hurry and call a contractor."

"Yes, yes." After replying to her daughter, Mayuko turned toward me, standing in the living room. "Welcome, Sou."

"Thanks for having me. And, um, I'm looking forward to the pie."

"It came out very nicely, if I do say so myself. Make sure and eat plenty."

"Thank you."

"It sounds like there have been all sorts of difficulties at school, but try not to get too depressed, okay?"

"Uh...sure."

"See you later." She turned back to Izumi. "You've got one more friend coming, right? Don't keep them too late."

"I know. Thanks, Mama."

"Good night."

As soon as Mayuko had left the apartment, I turned to Izumi and asked, "Who's the other friend?"

"Huh? Didn't I tell you?"

"I didn't hear anything about it... Yagisawa?"

"Bingo," she answered readily, then smiled cheerfully. "But getting back on track, you've been wearing a brooding, scary face all day long, Sou. I'm worried, and so is Yagisawa. I got a call from him saying he wanted to come talk to you, so that's why."

"In that case, he should have gotten in touch with me directly."

"Like I said." Izumi glared at me playfully. "You really didn't seem approachable, yesterday or today. It was almost like you were more of a 'non-exister' than when you were actually a 'non-exister.' Your whole body was radiating with hostility, like you would say, *I really don't want to talk*, or *Leave me alone*, if we spoke to you."

"............"

"I completely understand how you feel. After all, I ended up being a total failure of a countermeasures officer... But look, there's certainly nothing good about staying down in the dumps. Here's your coffee. Let's have pie after Yagisawa gets here."

I wrapped both hands around the cup that Izumi had poured for me and took a sip. It was delicious, but as I drank it this time around, the faint bitterness passing over my tongue seemed to soak down all the way into my heart.

"Um...about your conversation with Auntie Mayuko just now...," I started, checking Izumi's expression, "nearly losing her footing on the stairs...that could have been an opportunity for the 'calamity' to strike, huh?"

That's why she'd cautioned her mother so intensely earlier.

"Apparently, there was an 'accident' involving an elevator in the past, so...," she answered, nodding meekly. "In fact, it happened three years ago, when your friend Misaki was in Grade 3 Class 3."

Mr. Chibiki had also told me about the elevator accident that had claimed the life of a "related individual" during the 1998 school year. In fact, it was supposed to have happened at Yumigaoka Municipal Hospital...

"So we have to keep our guard up. The 'calamity' doesn't affect just the Class 3 students; it can also befall our families."

Izumi was pensive as she reconfirmed this fact. I nodded wordlessly, my eyes still fixed on her face.

Now that the "countermeasures" of April had ended in utter failure, we were completely powerless. We had no choice but to pass the days in anxious terror of the unpredictable "calamity" that could strike anyone at any time...

"Let's go into the other room for a little while," Izumi suggested suddenly, setting her coffee cup down. By *the other room*, she must have meant the soundproofed piano studio. I'd only ever been in there once.

"Come on in." She left the table and held open the door to the other room in invitation. "For some reason, I've got the urge to play piano. Will you join me?"

4

The western-style room was about seventeen meters square, and in the center stood an elegant grand piano. But the lid was closed, with all sorts of things—magazines, notebooks, memo pads, pen cases, and so on—scattered about carelessly on top of it. It was obvious that Izumi didn't ordinarily play much.

"It's been a while, so I'm probably out of practice."

With that preface, she sat down at the bench and gently opened the keyboard cover. Gingerly, she spread out the fingers on both hands and lowered them onto the keys. Then she began to play a beautiful, haunting melody.

"Do you know this song?" Izumi asked me as she was playing.

"I do remember hearing it before. Um…"

"It's a very famous tune. Beethoven's 'Moonlight Sonata,' first movement."

"'Moonlight'…"

"I'm not in the mood for Chopin's 'Funeral March,' okay?"

I figured that the people who'd died were on her mind.

"Anyway, in a book that I read in my second year of middle school, there's a scene where they play this song to send off the deceased. It left quite an impression on me, so…"

She continued the performance.

As I watched and listened to her play, I let my eyes drift closed. Carelessly, I backed up against the window curtain. A foul odor suddenly filled the air, and my nose started itching…

Huh? Is that the smell of dust?

For just a second, I got the impression I was standing somewhere that had been uninhabited for a long, long time. When I squeezed my eyes shut as tight as I could, scenes of a dilapidated, deserted room seemed to float up in my mind's eye…

…*Thud.*

There came a low reverberation. Below my range of hearing.

This is—

What is this?

The question bubbled up in my mind, but a moment later, it completely vanished… I heard the sound of the keyboard cover close nearby. I saw Izumi, wearing a somewhat dejected expression after ending her performance partway through.

"What's up?" I asked. "Why did you stop?"

"You didn't notice?" Izumi asked me back. "One of the keys wasn't playing the right note."

"Really?"

"It's way out of tune. It's because I almost never play anymore… but I can't just play it like this, can I? Poor piano. I'll have to ask Mama about it."

Izumi let out a huge sigh and stood up, then returned to the living room. Just as I was about to follow her, a piece of the clutter sitting atop the instrument caught my eye.

"Hey, hang on," I called out to stop her. "This is—" I held *it* up to show her. "When was this photo taken?"

Izumi turned around and glanced at the picture I was showing her, then mumbled an answer, as if it was nothing. "Ah, we took that on the day of the entrance ceremony. In the classroom."

The school entrance ceremony—April 10. The day after the opening ceremony. By then, we'd already started the "countermeasures." Hazumi and I had taken on our roles as "non-existers," so we hadn't gone to school…

"During homeroom that day, Ms. Kanbayashi said we should take a commemorative photo as a unit. Apparently, she always takes these kinds of group photos of her new class at the start of every school year."

As she explained, Izumi folded her arms sternly.

"It sounds like she always takes them on the day of the opening ceremony, but since we knew that this year was an 'on year,' she couldn't very well take a photo with you two 'non-existers' in it. The next day—the day of the entrance ceremony—you and Hazumi didn't show up, so we took it then."

A group photo of Grade 3 Class 3 taken in the classroom. Certainly, that's what this was. Hazumi and I, who'd skipped that day, weren't in it. And neither was Makise, of course, who was already in the hospital by then. And since Ms. Kanbayashi wasn't in the picture, she must have taken it herself.

"We're supposed to make a graduation album, so we'll have to take another sometime. You can be in there with everyone when we do, Sou."

Izumi got that far before her expression stiffened abruptly. After that, she didn't say anything else. With a long sigh, she lowered her gaze to her feet and bit her lip. Brushing her bangs back with both hands, she pressed one of her palms against her forehead.

She was obviously dealing with many conflicting emotions, even if she didn't seem cognizant of herself.

Of course, I realized, *I'm not the only one suffering. I'm not the only one who feels trapped, who doesn't know what to do...*

5

Yagisawa arrived just as we were returning to the living room from the piano room.

Apparently, he'd biked over in the light drizzle that had been constantly falling since the night before. He removed his flashy orange raincoat in the entryway and came into the living room, blotting himself here and there with a towel that Izumi had handed him. When he saw me, he raised a hand. "Yo! You look a little better, huh?"

I showed him my best scowl.

"What happened to Keisuke and his family was a huge shock for me, too. I went to the same elementary school with the twins, you know. I totally get why you're sad, but nothing good'll come of you moping in here forever, you know. Right?"

"Uh…yeah, sure."

Even in this situation, Yagisawa maintained his characteristically optimistic demeanor.

"Man, I hate when it rains half-assed like this. I'd rather just resign myself to a downpour."

"How so?"

"Like, tearfully turn down an invitation for coffee and apple pie." He shrugged jokingly. "And it's already getting late. If I didn't come on my bike, there would be no bus to get me home."

"Be careful on your way back. Of accidents and stuff…," I warned him instinctively.

Yagisawa's smile disappeared immediately. "I know that," he answered. "That's why I'm wearing the flashiest-color raincoat I could find. I've got an extra light on my bike, too…"

Izumi prepared his coffee, and the three of us ate Mayuko's handmade apple pie. As we were eating, Yagisawa's eyes came to rest on the class photo I had brought out from the piano room and set on the corner of the table.

"Ah, that picture?" he mumbled. "We took that back in April, huh?"

"Anyone need more coffee?" Izumi interjected.

"Yeah, I'll have some," Yagisawa replied.

"Sou?"

"All right, me too."

"We should take one with you, too, Sou," Yagisawa suggested out of the blue, completely serious.

"Huh?" I looked back at him.

"A commemorative photo, I mean. Right? You're good at photography, aren't you?"

"Mm, kinda." I nodded.

Film and film development cost a lot of money, so I rarely had the chance to actually capture things with a camera. Typically, I just formed an imaginary viewfinder with my fingers and clicked away.

"Well, let's do it one of these days, then," he insisted.

"You want me to take a commemorative photo like this one?" I asked.

"Mm…ah, no, not like this." As he spoke, Yagisawa looked slightly confused. He shook his head gently right to left, then nodded to himself. "It doesn't have to have everyone in it. For example, we could take one with the three of us—you, Akazawa, and me. As a memento of this 'calamity' year or something."

He got that far; then he broke into a guileless smile. "Of course we're all going to live through this, so we'll have it to look at later when we get together to reminisce…right?"

"Set in your optimism to the very end, I see," I muttered.

"If I wasn't, I don't think I could go on."

"Well…"

"Hey, you guys, here." Izumi came back from the kitchen, holding something out to us.

"What is it?" Yagisawa first cocked his head a little and took *it* from her, then let out an excited, "Oh!"

I took mine next and gasped, "Ah!"

"My treat, okay?" Izumi said with a brilliant smile. "Let's go see it together over summer break, okay?"

They were advance tickets to *Jurassic Park III*, premiering at the start of August.

Come to think of it, I'm pretty sure we talked about this the last time the three of us were here together.

Just then, my cell phone began to vibrate in my jacket pocket. I took it out, examined the display, and let out a sigh too faint for the others to hear. Without answering it, I silently returned the phone to my pocket.

"Is it okay for you not to take that?" Yagisawa asked.

"Ah, yeah."

"By any chance was that her—was it from Misaki?" Izumi asked.

I shook my head. "No, it wasn't."

The phone call had been from Tsukiho. I knew what she wanted to say without answering. She was going to tell me about how she was coming here and bringing Mirei on Sunday.

I had no idea what I would have said if I had answered her phone call then and there, or even what I *wanted* to say. I really didn't know, so...so I didn't pick up. I couldn't. I *evaded*.

"Hey, Sou?" Izumi said. Her smile from earlier was long gone. Staring at me with a straight face, she asked, "Um, so, about what Ms. Kanbayashi said today at school...that there have been years when the 'calamity' started *but it stopped halfway through?*"

"Mm-hmm?"

"That happened three years ago, right?"

"Yeah." I nodded. "That was an instance when it happened."

"I know it's true that they stopped the 'calamity,' but I don't understand how they did it," Izumi said. "I asked Etou about it, too, to be sure. And her *cousin*, who was in Grade 3 Class 3 three years ago, also said that she didn't know the 'how,' that it wasn't clear. But..." Still staring at me, she continued. "I wonder if maybe Misaki would have an inkling."

She narrowed her almond-shaped eyes abruptly. "If it was just that she was in Class 3 three years ago, her recollection would probably be the same as Etou's cousin, but I don't know, there's something about her, like she's privy to things other people aren't..."

"Misaki—is that the North Yomi graduate who Sou's friends with?" Yagisawa asked. "When was it? You told me a little bit about her, right?"

"Mm, yeah." Nodding at Yagisawa and Izumi, I answered, "I'm on the same page as you two; I'm certain that something can be done... That's why I've asked her about it several times already. But Misaki always gives me these ambiguous responses. It seems like it's hard for her to answer my questions. Or maybe that she doesn't want to be straightforward. That's how it seems to me."

"Oh, really?" Izumi cocked her head.

Picturing Mei's face in my mind, I said, "I'm almost certain that there's some sort of complicated reason for it. It's like she's somehow unable to answer with more than a few words..."

"In that case, we need to find a way to get her to speak with us, despite what's holding her back," Izumi suggested, her voice sharp.

"Even just a little something would be all right, but if she can give us any kind of clue...you know? Right now, we can't do anything except sit here and cower before the 'calamity.'"

I knew as much, even without Izumi telling me. I'd thought the same thing myself.

But after seeing Shunsuke on Monday... How do I put this? My mind had completely frozen up, and I'd lost my ability to look forward... That's why I hadn't been able to contact Mei yet.

I thought back to the phone call I'd received from her on the day of Shunsuke's funeral. I hadn't been able to answer, but she had left me a voice mail. At the end of her message, I believe she said something like this:

—*Even if the "countermeasures" have failed, there's still...*

She said *there's still...which probably means there's some other way to stop it. I think that was what she was trying to get across.*

"I understand," I answered under Izumi's serious gaze. "I'll try reaching out to Mei tomorrow."

6

"It sounds like there's been more misfortune at school."

I was sitting in the exam room at the "clinic" in the annex of Yumigaoka Municipal Hospital.

"I heard that two more third-years passed away this week."

Nodding slightly in response to Dr. Usui's inquiry, I told him that one of the students who died had been the head of the biology club that I was part of and that the other had been a classmate of mine.

"The deceased were close friends of yours this time, right?"

"Yes."

After some hesitation, I confided in him that I'd been the first to arrive at the scene of the horrible accident that had claimed Shunsuke, the head of the biology club.

"Oh." Dr. Usui must not have expected that, because his eyes bulged in shock. But he maintained his polite, calm tone of voice, just like always, as he said, "That must have been very difficult for you…and I'm sure that what you've just told me isn't the full account. Did the shock of that moment make you flash back to the incident three years ago?"

"Uh…yes…when it happened, I couldn't do anything…at all…"

I confessed that a sudden, dizzying panic had overtaken me and that I had passed out on the spot.

"Mm-hmm. That's understandable." The doctor nodded, maintaining his usual demeanor. "Was that the only time you lost consciousness?"

"Yes."

"Have you been able to sleep properly at night since it happened?'

"No. Not much."

"When you wake up, are you experiencing vivid flashbacks?"

"…………"

When I wasn't able to answer, he scribbled something down in my chart, then said, "At any rate, I'm going to give you some sleeping medication. If you continue to sleep poorly and have frequent night-mares despite the pills…and also if you start suffering bad anxiety during normal day-to-day activities, then please don't hesitate to come see me. Even if you don't have an appointment, it's okay. Call this department directly, and we'll get you in."

"All right. Thank you."

Dr. Usui closed my chart and stroked the whiskers around his mouth. "Hmm." He lowered his voice somewhat. "And yet, the disturbing—no, tragic incidents continue to occur. Now, unexpected accidents can happen anywhere, of course, but still…"

He frowned keenly and muttered, "Let me see…"

"Is it that legend you mentioned?" I asked, anticipating what he was working up to. "What kind of stories have you heard, Doctor? You told me there were some strange legends related to 'death.'"

"I do hear some irresponsible rumors on occasion. Unscientific stories about places being cursed and so on."

Unscientific, *you say?*

I cast my eyes down, recalling my phone conversation with Hazumi the day before last with unpleasant feelings.

"Ah, well." Dr. Usui lowered his voice even more. "Actually, my daughter was a little worried about that, you know."

"Your daughter..."

That little girl I ran into after my April counseling appointment. If I remember correctly, her name was Kiha.

"Kiha?"

"Oh! Have I introduced you two before?"

"Uh, no. One time when I was here before, I bumped into her outside the examination room. She said hello to me."

"Did she? She's surprisingly friendly toward strangers." He grinned, nodding to himself. Then he stopped stroking his beard abruptly. "I don't really know where or how she heard it, but one time, she suddenly blurted out that more people were going to die at your middle school."

"She's still in the lower grades at elementary school, right?"

"She's a second-year now." Dr. Usui grimaced and blinked his small eyes. Then, for some reason, he continued in a wistful tone of voice. "You know, that girl's always had something a little strange about her. She... No, it's not worth worrying about. I've said too much."

After shaking his head slowly once, he looked back at my face. "Anyway, try not to worry about curses and the like, no matter what urban legends you hear. The most important thing for you, Sou, is to maintain a sense of emotional balance. You need to try and put some mental distance between yourself and the deaths that have happened around you..."

Saturday, June 30, late morning. Once again, I found myself unable to tell Dr. Usui about the "phenomenon" surrounding Grade 3 Class 3 at North Yomi.

7

Afterward, I caught sight of the woman who looked like Kirika at the hospital again.

After my counseling session ended, I moved from the annex into the main building through the connector as I'd done before. From there, I headed for the first-floor lobby of the clinic building, where the cashier's window was located. On my way, I saw someone.

She didn't seem to notice me, so I missed my chance to say hello, but I was certain it was Kirika. Compared to the last time I had talked to her in person (at the start of February at the "Blue Eyes..." gallery, I believe), she looked extremely haggard. My hunch that something was wrong with her must have been right, since she was here at the hospital.

Despite my curiosity, I passed her, finished paying as always, got my medicine from the pharmacy counter, and headed for the exit. And then, as I was on my way out—

"Sou?"

Someone unexpected called out from behind me, catching me by surprise. It was Mei. When I turned around, I saw her standing there in her First Yomi uniform.

"Oh, ah...um..."

Caught completely off guard, I faltered in my confusion.

Why is she here now?

Did she come with Kirika or something? Or maybe something's wrong with her and she's here for an exam?

"Um, ah, uh..."

My mind was just spinning fruitlessly, so I couldn't get any proper words out. Mei stared at me somewhat listlessly.

"I know you had plans to come by the gallery this evening, Sou, but—"

Mei Misaki was not wearing an eye patch. Squinting her left eye, which was a regular prosthetic instead of her "doll's eye," a little, she quickly closed the distance between us.

"But we just ran into each other. What should we do?" she asked. Her somewhat listless look remained. "Should we talk here?"

"Um...ahhh..."

I was still struggling to get any words out when the cell phone inside my trousers pocket rudely interrupted us.

"Ah, sorry... My phone..."

I couldn't ignore it, so I pulled it out. Just as I expected, the display showed Tsukiho's name, along with her phone number.

I sighed despite myself. I wondered how many times she'd called me in the past few days. I hesitated for a second and, out of the corner of my eye, saw Mei tilt her head in a question.

In the end, I didn't pick up. Without checking to see just then whether or not she had left a voice mail, I put the phone back in my pocket.

"You don't need to answer?" Mei asked. The way she said it told me that she could tell who the call had been from.

"It's all right."

Somehow suppressing my distress, I took a deep breath. Then I said, "Mei, do you have time to spare now?"

"What?"

"I mean, um, are you done with your business at the hospital...?"

I felt like it would be difficult to tell her that I had just seen Kirika, so I didn't mention it. Before I could ask whether she was unwell herself, she suggested, "All right, shall we go?"

"Ah...what?"

"There are lots of people here, and it's noisy. It'll be hard to talk unless there's no one else around, right? I'm sure somewhere like the roof would work..."

8

As I'd promised Izumi and Yagisawa the night before last, I had made up my mind and called Mei the previous night.

I'd told her everything, including that Shunsuke and the others had died, which indicated beyond a shadow of a doubt that the "calamity" had started, at which point we did away with the need for "non-existers." In addition, I had asked again about the possibility of stopping the "calamity" somehow, but as I had expected, Mei gave another ambiguous answer.

"Three years ago—how did you stop the 'calamity' of the 1998 school year?"

After repeating my question as if she were carefully digesting it, Mei had started to say something—"About that..."—before trailing off. I silently waited for her to continue, and she remained quiet for a long, long time before speaking again.

"I think it would be better to get together and talk in person, rather than over the phone," she'd suggested. "Would you come over tomorrow afternoon, say around four o'clock? I'll be waiting in the gallery basement. I'll tell you everything I know down there. Though I'm unsure how much I'll be able to reliably say..."

So that morning, I had left my apartment intending to go by her house later that evening. After my hospital visit, I was planning to spend some time at the library in Daybreak Forest until the hour arrived, then head for the gallery in Misaki. However, before that could happen, I unexpectedly ran into her here...

I had no doubt that she was also at least a little surprised by the coincidence.

When we stepped off the elevator onto the roof of the hospital, the rain that had been coming down continuously since that morning had cleared up. But the sky was covered in massive gray clouds, hanging heavy and low. It looked like the rainy season might continue on forever.

A strong wind was blowing. The wind was humid and awfully warm, so no matter how it buffeted me, it did nothing to remove the sweat welling up on my skin.

Mei walked along the outer wall of the rooftop structure that housed the elevators, and I followed after her.

Her short bob was disheveled by the wind. When she reached a particular spot, it suddenly died down. There, Mei stopped walking and looked back at me, then flattened her body a little against the wall. It was a spot right where the structure acted as a windbreak.

"Is it your first time here?" she asked.

I answered, "I've never been to this building. I've never been hospitalized."

"Three years ago, Sakakibara stayed here twice, you know."

The name "Sakakibara" came up suddenly, and I put myself on guard, feeling a little tense—that's how it felt.

"Sakakibara had, let me remember, um, a collapsed lung...a spontaneous pneumothorax?"

"Right." Mei nodded. "I came here to visit him the second time, and we came up to this rooftop together. When the weather's clear, you can see every corner of Yomiyama."

"Is that...so?"

I was acquainted with Koichi Sakakibara. I had met him several times and talked about all sorts of things in the several months between my arrival here in Yomiyama and when he and Mei had graduated from North Yomi. I mostly saw him when he was with Mei, but I had also talked one-on-one with him.

Koichi had heard about my history and my family's special circumstances from Mei beforehand and understood it perfectly well, so he was always nice to me. Not out of some kind of strange sympathy or pity but a very natural kindness. They were both a huge help to me back then, at a time when I was suffering considerable, profound heartbreak and was in a weakened state. I was still very grateful to him.

Once Koichi graduated from North Yomi, he returned to his home in Tokyo and entered a high school there. At the same time, I became a middle school student. At first, I would talk to him on the phone sometimes about how things were going, but before too long, we gradually fell out of contact...

Mei, on the other hand, had kept up a close friendship with Koichi even after they were separated after graduation. It was something I was acutely aware of whenever Koichi was mentioned. I worked to convince myself that to Mei, Koichi was like a special "comrade" who had survived the same "calamity," and that's why they were close.

And yet—sometimes, when I heard his name come out of Mei's mouth, I felt a twinge in my chest that I couldn't quite identify. *I wonder why? Why does that happen? Ah, I can't. I can't think about this too deeply.*

"Why did the 'calamity' stop partway through the year three years ago?" Mei questioned herself slowly, with her back against the gray wall. The roaring sound of the wind echoed across the roof.

"You said that summer vacation was the turning point, right?" I repeated the information I already had, looking for confirmation. "You all stayed somewhere together in August, and while you were there, the 'calamity' claimed many victims... But then, in September, the deaths suddenly stopped. Is there any chance that something special happened on that trip?"

"Ah, about that—" Mei started to say, then cut off. Just like she had on the phone the night before. "The reason the 'calamity' stopped was actually..."

After a short pause, she stammered out, "A-aside from three years ago, even earlier—during the 1983 school year, too, there was another case of it stopping halfway through. They stayed in the same place over summer vacation that year, too."

"So *something* really did happen on the trip?"

"*Something* did...yes, right. Something happened then. Something..."

As she spoke, the strength gradually left Mei's voice. She put her right hand to her forehead and stopped talking, then shook her head slowly, looking uneasy.

"Please tell me what happened." I took a step closer to her as I asked, "What was it? Why did the 'calamity' stop? Please, Mei, if you know, tell me..."

"*I used to.*" She took her hand off her forehead and said, "*I had to have known.*"

"Had to?" Unable to grasp what she'd just said, I stared at her pale face. Despite the afternoon sunlight, she reminded me of a doll draped in shadows. "What does that mean...?"

The wind roared loudly again.

Maybe because the direction of the wind had changed, the wall we were leaning against ceased to work as a windbreak, and a strong breeze blasted us from the side as we faced each other. My voice was completely drowned out in the wind, and Mei's hair and clothes were violently disheveled.

Almost as if the wind had chosen that very moment, just then—

From inside my pants pocket, I felt my cell phone vibrate.

That's definitely from Tsukiho again.

My attention was split. My emotions were a whirlwind.

Today is June 30. Tsukiho said she was coming to see me with Mirei in tow on July 1, so that's almost here—that's tomorrow. She wants to talk about when she's going to get here, where we should meet up, and what we should eat. I know that. I know, but I...

"Your phone."

I heard Mei's voice.

The powerful wind suddenly died, almost like it had chosen that moment in particular. Now that the noise was gone, she could hear my phone vibrating.

"It's probably from your mother," Mei said and smiled faintly. She was looking at me, and in her right eye, the one that was not a prosthetic, I saw a slight shade of sadness...

"Is it all right not to answer it?" she asked again. "You have to answer it, don't you?"

Ah, I thought, *Mei is always right.*

I have to take this call right now. That's right. I mustn't run away. I can't avoid this anymore.

I pulled my phone out and checked the display screen, then pushed the button to answer.

"Hello? It's Sou."

9

"Ah, Sou? This is Sou, right? I've been calling you, but you weren't picking up, so I was worried..." Tsukiho dutifully delivered her lines. She sounded almost exactly how I'd imagined she would. She was constantly trying to play up her affection for me, but she was way off the mark. That's how it sounded to me. "...Are you all right? Sou. You're not feeling unwell or anything?"

"I'm fine." For the time being, I suppressed my emotions the best I could and answered, "I'm feeling just fine."

"Ah, thank goodness." After repeating "thank goodness" with great relief, Tsukiho got to the question at hand. "As promised, I'm coming to see you tomorrow and bringing Mirei with me. Let's eat lunch somewhere together, okay? Okay? Is there anything you'd like to eat…?"

Tsukiho is coming tomorrow. She's bringing Mirei and coming to this city. To Yomiyama.

"…And then I'll need to say hello to Sayuri and everyone else, too."

When I had heard that much, I cast aside any doubts and opened my mouth. Sucking in a deep breath and letting it out bit by bit, I demanded clearly, *"Don't come."*

The moment I said it, I squeezed my eyes closed.

"Ah?" I heard Tsukiho voice her surprise. "What's wrong, Sou? What happened?"

"Don't come to Yomiyama."

"Huh? Huh? Why not?" I could tell from her tone that she was extremely dismayed. "Why would you say that…?"

"Because I don't want you to come."

I gripped the phone tightly and raised my voice slightly. Out of the corner of my eye, I could see Mei, observing silently. Her gaze was quiet and a little sad.

"I don't want to see you." I raised my voice again. "I don't want to see you or Mirei. So don't come here."

"What's wrong, Sou?" Tsukiho was totally flustered.

"What do you mean, what's wrong? Why visit all of a sudden?"

"It's not sudden!"

Then I cut her off. Raising my voice even more, I unleashed all my emotions at once, as if to strike her with my words.

"Have I ever once…at any point, have I said that I wanted to see you? That I want you to come to Yomiyama? Have you ever tried to imagine how I've been feeling since moving here, how I still feel?"

"B-but—"

Tsukiho's response was frail. She was surprised and confused by my unexpected "rejection." I'm sure this was a big shock to her. It was probably the first time since that summer three years ago that I'd spoken to her this way.

"Don't say that… Come on, Sou. I…I, you know, I really, I always… If we could, I'd like us to get back to how it used to be…"

"That's enough. Don't come here!" This time, I was practically shouting. It would be a lie to say that I didn't care about her feelings, about whether she had ever had any second thoughts, but in this current situation, those were secondary, maybe tertiary concerns. Because I—

I had already wrung this *answer* from inside my own heart…

"Don't ever show up here!" I shouted, squeezing my eyes shut again. "Not just tomorrow but forever!"

"Sou…"

"Listen to me. I never want to see your face again. I don't want to spend time with you, and I don't want to hear your voice."

"Sou, honey…you can't—you're lying."

"I hate you!"

"Sou…"

"Have you forgotten what happened three summers ago? I remember. I'll never forget it. I'll never forget how cruel you were after what happened to Teruya…"

"…………"

"I was in the way, so you kicked me out without a second thought. Mr. Hiratsuka and his household were more important than your own son. And the child you had with him—Mirei—took priority. Right? Do you think I still love you after going through all that? Do you think I didn't learn to resent you?"

She was speechless.

I imagined there was no way she could keep her cool, after being suddenly called out like that. Instead of a reply, I could hear quiet sobs.

Nevertheless, I continued pouring it on.

"Do you get it? Don't come for a visit. Don't ever come near me again. And definitely don't come here—to Yomiyama."

Speechless. The weeping continued. Twice I heard the word *sorry* in the gaps between sobs.

"All right, I'm hanging up."

A strong wind suddenly blew against me again. I let my hair get disheveled as the wind blew it up on end and went back to using a low voice with my emotions in check.

"Don't call me again."

10

I hung up the phone, and, still gripping it in my right hand, I gazed up at the dark sky. Gazed up so that the tears pooling in my eyes wouldn't spill down my cheeks. So that the tears wouldn't make me lose composure and burst out crying right there.

"Your mother—Tsukiho was planning to come and see you, right? Tomorrow was the day?" Mei took one step toward me. "You haven't seen her in a while? Tsukiho, I mean."

I lowered my gaze to answer her question. "It's been about two years since we last met."

"I see. Hmm." Mei nodded and stared straight at me. I didn't want her to notice that I was crying, so I turned away. The wind roared, somewhere much farther off than it had been until now.

I had just said exactly what I needed to say to Tsukiho. But still, my heart continued to ache…

Before long, Mei spoke. "…You love her, don't you? You love her all the same. But you got angry enough to tell her you loathe her."

Ah, of course, Mei can see right through me.

I guess…she's probably right; I don't hate Tsukiho as much as I just said I do.

It is true that I have a lot of resentment toward her…and I think it's horrible what happened three years ago and how she's treated me since. My sorrow and pain have never gone away. Neither has my anger. But while that may be true, I've never once been able to detest or "hate" her from the bottom of my heart.

"I don't really know whether or not I love her," I said. My mixed-up emotions were gradually settling down. "But I don't think it would have been a good idea for her to come to Yomiyama during this time, especially since Mirei would be with her. So I was being honest when I told her I didn't want her here."

"Because the 'calamity' is going on, right?" Mei asked.

I nodded deeply. "That's right."

"Because both Tsukiho and little Mirei are 'related individuals' within two degrees of you."

"…Yes."

"Tsukiho doesn't know about the 'calamity'?"

"…Probably not."

She might have known about it once. At the very least, she had probably been told a certain amount about the situation fourteen years ago, when the whole family left Yomiyama with Teruya. But I was certain that in the months and years since then, she'd let herself forget.

"How kind of you, Sou," Mei stated, taking another step toward me. "As long as they're in Hinami, they're 'out of range.' But if they come to Yomiyama, an 'accident' might befall the two of them, so…"

I cast my eyes down, trying to avoid Mei's gaze. Finally, the tears spilled out of my eyes and down my cheeks. My voice threatened to make a sound in spite of me, so I suppressed it with every ounce of my strength.

Mei silently left my side, put her back against the wall of the elevator housing, and stared up at the cloudy sky. The wind had stopped again. In the strange stillness that had suddenly arrived, I heard her sigh.

11

After several minutes passed, Mei spoke up.

"I'll tell you everything in order. This is a continuation of our earlier conversation, okay?"

"Ah, okay."

I had to switch my mind back over. For now, I wasn't worried about Tsukiho and Mirei coming to Yomiyama. So now I had to listen intently to what Mei had to say.

"I'm sure that *something* happened on the summer trip. And I think I *used to know what it was*. I've told you that much."

"...Yes."

"I say *I think* because I'm not entirely sure."

"You aren't?"

"Yeah. About my own memories. What I mean is—" Tilting her head slightly, with a look of distress on her face, Mei continued. "I can't remember clearly. Almost three years have passed since then, but *that part* of my memory is incredibly vague now."

"Is that...?" I remembered something and asked, "...Is it because of the 'phenomenon'?"

"Right." She nodded, looking uncharacteristically anxious. "It's one of the 'memory problems' that occur alongside the 'phenom- enon.' And I think that mine is a special case somehow."

"How so?"

"When the 'extra person'—the 'casualty'—slips into the class, memories and records that wouldn't otherwise be consistent get altered and falsified so that everything matches up. Once the 'phe- nomenon' ends and the 'casualty' disappears, all the evidence of that person goes back to how it was. After that, the memory of who was the 'casualty' for that year gradually fades away, sometimes quickly, sometimes slowly, depending on the person, and everyone forgets who it was. This is the basic pattern. But for something that breaks the mold, take that folder of Mr. Chibiki's."

"Ah, okay."

"There, he makes a note of the names of the 'casualties' in years when the 'phenomenon' occurs, and those names don't disappear; they remain on the page. That means that we can see who joined previous classes as 'casualties' in the past. You've gotten him to show it to you, too, right, Sou?"

"Yes."

I was also aware of the *peculiarity* of the "Chibiki File" kept in the secondary library room. While all sorts of other memories and records regarding the "casualty" who appeared during an "on year" would gradually "fade" and "dim" and "disappear" after the end of the "phenomenon," I'd heard that for some reason, only the memos in that file folder seemed to be *overlooked*.

"Still, there's one thing that isn't even recorded in his notes. That would be the names of the 'casualties' in the years when the 'calamity' stopped halfway through." That's where Mei stopped talking. She put her hand on her forehead and pondered something briefly.

"I'll tell you everything in order," she repeated, as if urging herself on. "It happened during summer break three years ago. Just after it began, through a strange sequence of events, the story of a *certain person* was handed down to us. Matsunaga, I think his name was. He was a graduate of the class of '83 at North Yomi, and when he was in his third year, he was in Class 3."

"1983...the other year when the 'calamity' stopped, right?"

"Right." Mei nodded slowly and started telling me the story in her usual quiet voice. But the way she was speaking, it was like she was carefully scrutinizing every word that came out of her own mouth.

"Three years ago, we were also wondering if there wasn't some way to stop the 'calamity' after it began, and just like you right now, we tried to look for some clues. What we found was Mr. Matsunaga's story..."

Three years earlier—in 1998—fourteen years had passed since the graduation of Katsumi Matsunaga from North Yomi. One time when he was in a drunken stupor and not in his right mind, he had claimed that *"I was the one who helped everyone in Grade 3 Class 3 back in '83."* However, once he sobered up and came back to himself, he had absolutely no recollection of what he had said. Basically, he had completely forgotten *his experience* during middle school, but—

According to Mr. Matsunaga's drunken complaint, he had somehow left something behind in an old classroom in order to pass some important information about the "calamity" on to his successors. Hoping against hope, the students had gone searching for that "something," and they had actually found it...

"We found a cassette tape, a recording in Mr. Matsunaga's own voice." Fixing her gaze on a single spot in midair in the space between us, Mei continued. "On the tape was the explanation of how he stopped the 'calamity'... I heard it, too, that tape. During the summer trip—"

"And so you learned how?" I hadn't meant to interject, but I was excited. "You learned how, didn't you? How to stop the 'calamity'?"

"*I must have*, but—"

At that point, Mei shook her head uneasily again.

But I could hardly hold my excitement in and asked, "But surely you implemented *it*, and that's why the 'calamity' stopped three years ago, right?"

"I think that's what happened. *That must have been it*, but..."

"You can't recall clearly? Or you don't remember?"

"............"

"Why did the 'calamity' stop? Who stopped it and how? Give me something, even just a little..."

"In Mr. Matsunaga's year, fifteen years before us, they also went on a class trip to the same place as we did during summer vacation. I know that for sure, but—"

"Is there any special meaning to the trip itself?"

"We went to visit Yomiyama Shrine together."

"Like, to do a cleansing ritual at the shrine?"

"But three years ago, we didn't end up visiting..."

"And Mr. Matsunaga's class did go, right? To visit the shrine."

"That's right. But in the end, their visit had no effect..."

"............"

"'*To you future underclassmen, who might be suffering the same things we did...*'"

"What's that?"

"It's from Mr. Matsunaga's message, the one that was on that tape. He probably figured he was going to *forget what happened* sooner or later, just like everybody else, and left it behind. That's why I'm certain that in some form or another, *it* must be a problem related to my year's 'casualty'... The fact that my own memory has gotten so vague in such a short time is further proof, I guess you could say."

Mei stopped talking and went back to thinking. She put her hand on her forehead again and shook her head slowly back and forth, then finally—

"How can I put this…? I feel like I can see a vague outline of what happened. And there are images of certain things in the fog… Ah, but in the end, I just can't get a clear picture. It's like I can't manage to make any sense of it. Fragmented words and images appear in my mind. But I can't say for certain how far I can trust them."

"Uh, Mei… Um, well, has this condition been going on for a long time? Not being able to recall things well even when you try, I mean?"

She nodded wordlessly, then continued. "That's why—that's why even when you ask me questions about it, I can only give you vague answers. I'm relying on ambiguous images to guess what happened, and I wouldn't want to say something careless."

"Ah…so that's why." As I answered, I was suddenly struck by an idea. "And what happened to the cassette tape that had Mr. Matsunaga's story? Is it still around somewhere?"

"It seems like…it's not around anymore." Mei shook her head weakly. "On that trip three years ago, a big fire broke out, and most of the building burned down. The tape probably burned, too."

"There must have been others besides you who heard the tape, right? What about them?"

"I tried reaching out to them, but no one remembered the contents." After answering, she added, "By the way, back then, I was keeping a sort of diary from time to time. I'm sure I would have written in the diary about whatever happened at that lodge on the trip. Thing is, I looked through it, and the passages I'm sure I wrote have disappeared or gotten stained by something that made them unreadable…"

When I heard that, I felt slightly dizzy.

The alteration of records… No, in this case, it's more like elimination? Or erasure?

Can the "phenomenon" of North Yomi's Grade 3 Class 3 really cause that to happen? It's almost like…yes, all I can think is that it's like some malicious spirit is at work here…

"Well," I said and let out a long sigh, "I guess that means there's nothing to be done about it. We're done for..."

I dropped my shoulders dejectedly. As she looked at me, Mei's gaze remained calm and a little sad, as before.

"Back then—" Mei abruptly opened her mouth. The wind roared in the distance. Mingling with that sound were the voices of a number of noisy crows somewhere. *"Back then, Sakakibara was at the heart of it all."*

I let out a gasp of surprise and looked Mei straight in the face. "What do you mean by that?"

"It's a hopelessly vague way of putting it, I know," she admitted. "But it's undeniable that three years ago, on that class trip, *something* was done to stop the 'calamity.' As for what that was, well, I can't picture anything clearly, but...but *when it happened, Sakakibara was there. He was in the center of whatever it was—he was at the heart of it...that much I remember."*

Koichi Sakakibara.

I recalled his face as he had appeared two years ago, before we'd fallen out of contact. All the words we'd exchanged in the handful of months we'd spent together came back to me as I pictured his face.

"So that's why," Mei continued, "maybe, if it was him—if you talk to Sakakibara, he may not have forgotten yet. That's the feeling I get. He was at the heart of the matter, and that means his memories ought to be stronger than mine. Also, Sakakibara left Yomiyama after graduation and has been in Tokyo this whole time."

"And if he's outside of Yomiyama—'out of range,' then the effect on his memories is weaker?"

"Probably, I think. So..."

Mei told me that for that reason, she had been trying to get in touch with Sakakibara in order to talk about this problem with him. Especially since last month, after Tsugunaga died in the way she did and we had conclusive proof that the 'calamity' was starting. She had tried many times. However—

"So far, I haven't made contact once." Mei frowned wearily.

"Why is that?" I asked. "Isn't he in Tokyo?"

"That's what I thought, but apparently, as of this spring, he's not in Japan."

"He went abroad? And he's still there? That's a long trip!"

"Apparently, it's not just a short vacation. Sakakibara's father is a researcher and flies around here and there for fieldwork, right? He's traveling along with him."

"Here and there...huh?"

"I tried calling his cell phone lots of times, but it never went through, so I called his house phone, and a house sitter answered and told me. She said that he would be coming back to Japan in the fall."

Mei frowned even harder and exhaled heavily. She seemed exhausted.

"What about e-mail?" I asked. "Did you try that?"

"I sent him one, but that didn't work, either. Maybe there's a problem with his computer."

"Hmm."

"I can think of all sorts of possibilities. But since I want to hear from him as quickly as possible, since I need to hear from him...I left a request with the house sitter as well. I asked her to call me immediately if Sakakibara or his father made any kind of contact..."

...*Koichi Sakakibara.*

Murmuring that name in my mind, I looked up at the sky above my head. The cloudy sky still stretched out, low and dark, just as it had when we'd first climbed up here.

I hope that we can get in touch with him—with Koichi—soon. I hope that he remembers what he did three years ago. At that point, all I could do was pray. It was incredibly frustrating.

Chapter II
July I

1

"All right, I'm taking it," said Izumi, readying her camera. "Mm… Sou, don't stand at attention—relax a little. Yeah, yeah, like that. Okay, say cheese!"

Next to me, Yagisawa shouted back, "Cheese!" as soon as he heard the standard phrase. He also raised his right hand and gave a thumbs-up. My lips curled into a smile of their own accord.

"Great. All right then, one more. Okay?"

The camera shutter clicked a second time, and I breathed a little sigh of relief. I liked cameras, but frankly, I wasn't a fan of being in pictures.

We were in the courtyard between Buildings B and C at school, standing in front of the lotus pond (which was actually a water lily pond). The pond was rumored to be one of the school's "Seven Mysteries." Rumor had it that sometimes, when the water's surface was disturbed by an overturned leaf, a bloody human hand would reach out.

It was the fourth day since the start of July, on a Wednesday after school.

The camera we were using was a compact model that Uncle Teruya had given me when I was in elementary school. Though small, it was an excellent machine, and it could take high-quality photos if you used it right.

"Okay, Sou and Akazawa, stand together next. I'll take the picture."

The camera passed from Izumi's hands to Yagisawa's as they took turns being the photographer. We had also planned to use the timer and take one with the three of us in it, but we couldn't find an appropriate place to set it up.

I should have gone to the trouble of bringing the tripod, I thought to myself.

Yagisawa was the one who had suggested taking a "commemorative photo" a few days earlier. He'd called me the night before, requesting that I bring my camera, *"because it looks like pretty good weather tomorrow..."* The long-haired class representative with his round glasses had also decided on this lotus pond for the location. Now he joked, "Well, somehow it works. But as long as the 'phenomenon' is happening, we might capture a hand in the pond, too."

"Stop it—don't joke about that." I scowled at him. Then I gave a forced smile, but frankly speaking, I didn't feel like it at all.

The weather was fair. The blue sky and vibrant sunlight were classic summer. But the rainy season wasn't quite over yet, and according to the forecast, another front was going to start moving in that evening.

"Okay, I'm taking it!"

Yagisawa readied the camera.

"Get closer, you two. Sou, your expression is too stiff again. Akazawa, you look great... Yeah, okay, say cheese!"

This time, as I was mouthing the word *cheese—*

Several scenes from other times played out in my mind, as though flashing back to the events of the past few days...

2

...I had accepted an invitation to the penthouse of the Freuden Tobii. Auntie Mayuko had requested I join the Akazawas for tea.

When I went, I returned one of the books I'd borrowed from Izumi's older brother's bookshelf. It was a book called *The Notebook*.

I had started reading it to distract myself, but once I got started, I ended up devouring it in no time flat. It was far more gripping than I had expected. The second volume was sitting on the same bookshelf, so with Izumi's permission, I borrowed that one to read next. After getting the book, I was served tea and cake in the living room.

"Wasn't Tsukiho supposed to come today?" Mayuko had asked me.

Without any particular agitation, I'd answered, "Seems like something suddenly came up."

"Oh, really?" said Izumi, who knew nothing about the situation. She had peered over at my expression with a look of anxiety on her face but hadn't made any further comments.

"Tsukiho must be worried, I'm sure," said Mayuko.

"Why is that?" I'd asked.

"Well, I mean, students from your class have been dying in accidents... There have been all sorts of unfortunate incidents since May. That's why."

"I don't think she knows about that."

"She doesn't? You haven't told her, Sou?"

My silence must have tipped her off, because Mayuko had narrowed her eyes with a kind smile and nodded. "Be that as it may, I feel so bad for all the people who passed away. I mean, what awful luck they had. You were good friends with the boy from the biology club, right?"

"Yeah, kind of."

Mayuko had never asked me anything before about the special circumstances of Grade 3 Class 3. And I hadn't even said anything about it to Auntie Sayuri or anyone else. I'd faithfully upheld that "rule." However—

"I wonder if there will be a summer trip this year?" Mayuko had said suddenly.

"Eh?" Izumi made a startled noise. "Mama, why would you say that?"

In 1998 and 1983, the two years when the "calamity" stopped partway through the school year, there had been a special class trip over summer break in both cases, where *something* had apparently happened—I had reported as much to Izumi. But why would Mayuko say something about that now?

"I mean." Mayuko had a slightly bemused expression. "When it comes to the Grade 3 summer vacation, um, well—"

She had gotten that far and then cut herself off, with a suspicious expression like even she didn't fully understand why. For a moment, I had wondered what was going on.

Thud, came a low reverberation from somewhere. For a split second, everything had gone dark.

"...You know, your big brother never took a class trip when he was in middle school. I'm sorry. I must have gotten mixed up." Smiling as if it was no big deal, Mayuko had asked, "Would anyone like more tea?"

That was one scene from the night of Sunday, July 1—three days ago.

3

...The biology club had held a meeting in the science room of Building T.

Since the incident the previous week, our clubroom in Building Zero had remained closed off. We had released many of the creatures we'd been raising, the ones that could go back into the wild. The rest we had divided among the club to be cared for at home.

The adviser, Mr. Kuramochi, and most of the club members were at the meeting. Even fellow Class 3 member, Morishita, came. I was no longer a "non-exister," so there had been no need for him to take that into consideration.

Our three new members had been reduced to two. Jun Takanashi's younger brother had submitted his intent to resign from the club after his mother had passed in May. I heard that one of the second-years had also been talking about quitting.

I guess that's no surprise, huh?

"What happened to Kouda was a truly...truly unfortunate accident," Mr. Kuramochi said, wearing a mournful expression. "As you all know, he was an irreplaceable part of the biology club. Now that he's no longer with us, we must decide how the club will proceed from here. We've got to come up with a proper course of action..."

Mr. Kuramochi continued, explaining that when it came to the question of how we should move forward, the first concrete step was to decide whether to continue the club at all or disband it then and there.

The room in Building Zero wasn't ready yet. There was also the question of how everyone felt about using it at all, knowing what had happened there.

"What do you think?" Mr. Kuramochi had asked us. "What do you all want to do? I want to hear your genuine opinions here."

He waited a while for our responses, but no one answered him. Everyone was nervously looking around at one another's expressions.

"Hmm." The teacher had crossed his arms, seeming as though he was about to say something else.

"I vote we continue," I'd declared boldly, unable to keep quiet any longer. "If we quit now, I think Shunsuke—I think Kouda would be sad. I'm sure we'll have to do things differently, but I think we should keep going."

I don't even mind becoming the leader, if no one else is willing to do it, I'd thought, riding the momentum of what I had said.

"So that's one vote for continuing." Mr. Kuramochi wasn't smiling, but there was a note of happiness in his voice. "Anyone else? What do you think?"

I didn't know how everyone there actually felt, but no one had raised any objections.

"You've got your final exams coming up soon this month, so let's talk again after those are over. Mm. If it seems like we have the required number of people who want to keep going, we can try to get things back up and running over the summer break."

No one had voiced any opposition to the teacher's suggestion...

Will this do, Shunsuke?

I addressed my dead friend in my mind.

It's okay, isn't it, Shunsuke?

That was one scene from the afternoon of Monday, July 2—two days ago.

4

...Mayuko and Izumi had come knocking at the Akazawa main house just after dinner. The renovations that had started in April were finally nearing completion. They'd said they wanted to see how it looked.

It had taken much longer than originally planned, but the old house had been boldly restructured and remodeled. Now it possessed a "newness" that made it scarcely recognizable. Overall, the interior was brighter than it had been before, and it had been made more functional in key places. Everything had been thoroughly redone to accommodate our grandfather's needs.

"What about your room, Sou?" Izumi asked, so I showed her. It had been used only as storage for a while, but now it was completely cleaned up, and even the wallpaper and flooring were shiny and new.

"Once the house is finished, you're coming back here, right? Soon after the start of summer vacation?" Izumi had asked as she looked around the empty room.

"I guess that's how it'll work out," I answered, letting out a small sigh. "After all, it's not like I can continue to be a burden over there forever, is it?"

"That's not how it is. I don't think so anyway." Izumi laced the fingers of both hands together and stretched toward the ceiling with a big sigh. "But I guess it's right next door. Come over and see me sometimes after you move back, okay?"

After that, the two of us went into the sitting room in the back of the house, where our grandfather was.

Our grandfather, Hiromune Akazawa, was as always sleeping

away most of the day. When he realized that his grandchildren had come in, he looked at me first. "Oh, Sou?"

He'd said my name the same way he always did, and a clumsy smile had appeared on his aged face. Then he'd shifted his gaze to Izumi, and when he did, that smile immediately disappeared.

"Are you Izumi?" His voice creaked. He sounded suspicious or maybe confused. "But you're..." He didn't seem able to focus on his granddaughter... It might have been my imagination, but his eyes had looked cloudy somehow. "How are you still...?"

Come to think of it, I recalled hearing from Izumi that he had said something like that to her before, too. It might have been a consequence of his poor health, and certainly, he had been growing more sullen and harder to please lately, but seeing him treat her like that in front of my own eyes, I realized why she'd complained about him before.

It was a strange way to act when your granddaughter came to visit—that was certain... It had seemed like an awfully unnatural reaction to me.

"Seems like the construction will be finished soon, huh?" Trying to dispel the awkward atmosphere, I cut in quickly. "Once that's done, it'll be easier for you to move around inside the house, won't it, Grandpa?"

"Well, I don't know about that," he answered glumly. "But, well, thank goodness the construction will be done. Even in this room, it's so loud, I can't stand it. Good grief..."

Grandpa had spat out the words, then sluggishly shifted around on his futon and looked toward the window.

Outside was a spacious rear garden lit by lamps. In the drizzling rain that continued to fall, the large hackberry tree that spread its limbs over the middle of the yard had looked like a dark shadow.

"Kyah!" Izumi had suddenly let out a short shriek. When I turned around in surprise, I'd seen that Kurosuke the cat had come into the room at some point and jumped up onto her lap. Kurosuke had been startled by the shriek, too, and started trying to leap down off her knees.

Izumi pressed on her right palm with her left hand and said, glaring at the cat, "Geez, what the...?"

Apparently, Kurosuke had confused her for something else and scratched her on the hand.

"What was that? Why?"

Lacking the ability to answer Izumi's questions, he simply meowed and padded out of the room.

She sighed and looked down at her right hand where he had scratched her. Small, bright drops of red blood welled up in the exact center of her white palm.

That was one scene from the evening of Tuesday, July 3—yesterday.

5

...Sayuri and Mayuko, the two aunts, had been deep in conversation in the living room, so Izumi and I left them there and went back to the Freuden Tobii ahead of them. The rain had stopped just as we were leaving, so we hadn't needed to put up our umbrellas.

"Is your hand okay?" I'd asked Izumi on the way.

"Mm. It's fine...but..." She raised her right hand, which was covered in medical tape. "But that was the first time Kurosuke's ever scratched me so hard. It shocked me. I wasn't even doing anything that would bother him."

"Hmm, well, cats are fickle creatures," I'd answered casually and then glanced over at her right hand. "You'd better disinfect it properly after you get home, you know. I mean, apparently, there's something called cat-scratch fever, so be careful."

"And if the scratch gives me a high fever and the symptoms get worse very quickly...if that happens, it'll be the 'calamity' causing it?"

"I'm worried it might be like that."

"I'm joking. I'll be fine. I'll disinfect it again once I'm home, and if I do start feeling bad, I'll go see a doctor right away."

"Mm."

"Did you hear anything from Misaki after the last time you talked?"

"Nothing yet."

She was referring to my meeting with Mei on the roof of the hospital last Saturday. I had relayed the basic summary of our conversation to Izumi that very same day...

"So she still hasn't gotten a hold of this Sakakibara guy, huh? Even if she does reach him, there's the question of whether he'll even remember anything that happened three years ago."

"That's right."

"If you learn anything, be sure and tell me."

"Ah, sure. Of course that's my intention, so..."

That was another scene from Tuesday evening—yesterday.

6

Yagisawa and me. Izumi and me. And while we were at it, we got solo shots of each of us, too. We were snapping pictures for some time, and our homeroom teacher, Ms. Kanbayashi, happened to pass by unexpectedly.

"Oh! Some kind of photo shoot?" she called out to us.

Yagisawa jokingly shouted back, "We're taking three-person commemorative photos!"

Ms. Kanbayashi nodded with a serious look on her face. "I see. Is that because Mr. Hiratsuka was a 'non-exister' when we took the group photo at the beginning of April?"

"That's our teacher, quick on the uptake," Yagisawa quipped again. "Because of that, we started talking about how we should take a commemorative photo with Sou in it before the end of first semester. Speaking of which, Ms. Kanbayashi, would you help us out and get one with all three of us in it?"

Cunningly pressing the camera into her hands, Yagisawa insisted, "Come on now, Sou, Akazawa, you get back where you were just standing. Akazawa can be in the middle, and Sou and I will be on each side... That should be good. Ms. Kanbayashi, if you please!"

"Okay, here we go."

Accepting the role of photographer with surprising willingness, she readied the camera.

"Please go ahead and use up the rest of the film," I said.

"Got it. Okay...you're standing in a good place. Hiratsuka, get a little closer to Akazawa. Yagisawa, you're too close. Okay, I'm taking it."

Ms. Kanbayashi seemed used to handling a camera. I heard the sound of the shutter several times in succession. The film ran out and started rewinding itself automatically.

"One of these days, let's take another one with everyone in the class, shall we?" Ms. Kanbayashi said in a deliberately cheerful voice. "There's the graduation album to think about, after all... When we put that together, we should take a picture with Hazumi and Makise in it, too."

The graduation album...graduation, huh?

That word had a hollow ring to it somehow, and I let out a quiet sigh.

There are still nine months to go before then. If the monthly "accidents" continue, just how many students are going to be left by the time graduation rolls around? I was sure I wasn't the only one thinking it, but no one said anything out loud.

"Next week is already the end-of-term exams, huh?" Ms. Kanbayashi said as she was leaving. "I know that focusing on your studies must be quite difficult, but there's no way Class 3 could skip out on testing. With that understanding, I hope you will do your best. If you have any trouble, please come and talk to me anytime..."

Having finished our "commemorative photo shoot," we briefly returned to our classroom on the third floor of Building C.

"Oh man, the clouds spread out really quickly!" Yagisawa noticed, staring out the window. "If we're going by the forecast, it's supposed to start raining again tonight. It'll be one of those flash floods that comes at the end of the rainy season."

"I hope the rainy season clears up soon," said Izumi. Knitting her eyebrows despondently, she continued. "It's always been my least favorite part of the year. Doesn't it seem like it's dragged on particularly long this time, too?"

"No. I think the average year is about like this," Yagisawa answered, running his hand through his long hair, which was crunchy with mousse.

Just then, I noticed that my cell phone was getting a call.

7

For a second, I thought it might be a call from Mei. Glancing at the display, however, I knew immediately that wasn't the case. It was showing an unregistered number that I had never seen before.

"Hello?" I answered.

"This is Sou Hiratsuka's cell phone, right?" came the voice on the other end. There was a lot of static or something, and it was hard to hear, but it was male. And then I realized it did belong to someone I knew...

"...Sakakibara?"

"Sou, right? It's been a while."

This sudden call from Koichi Sakakibara, it took me off guard.

How on earth did this happen?

He must have already talked to Mei. Or else...

I tightened the squeeze on my phone. Out of the corner of my eye, I saw the *shisa* charm on my Okinawa souvenir sway.

"Um...are you calling from overseas?"

"From Mexico. So I can't talk for that long."

Mexico, huh? There's probably about a half a day's time difference between there and Japan, isn't there? Which means it's the middle of the night for him now.

"I just got in touch with Misaki. She told me about your situation. I was hoping it wouldn't happen, but of all the classes, you ended up in Class 3, and it's an 'on year,' too. What luck."

"The 'countermeasures' didn't go well, so the 'calamity' started up."
I gripped my phone even harder. I didn't notice, but my voice got louder, too. Yagisawa and Izumi, naturally, must have been wondering what was going on.

"I heard that earlier from Misaki," said Koichi. *Ksh-ksh-ksh...* The rasp of static on the line made it hard to hear his voice. "So...memories of three years ago have already gotten fuzzy for her, huh? The question is what did we do, in order to stop the 'calamity' that year? She told me that she has no confidence at all in her own memories on that matter."

"And you, Sakakibara?" I asked almost prayerfully.

"I wonder? I wonder if I remember?"

There was a long silence, and then an answer came. "Ah! *I do remember.* I haven't forgotten yet. I remember our class trip during that summer break to the lodge. I remember what I did there."

"So...?"

"I talked to Misaki about this earlier, too. About what you need to do in order to stop the 'calamity' at this point and how to do it. When she heard what I had to say, I think it helped her dredge up some of her memories of that time. But..."

"But?"

"She was one of the people involved with the 'phenomenon' that year, and after it was over, she stayed in Yomiyama... So you see, I wonder whether she's going to be able to hold on to the information she heard from me earlier. Maybe the influence of Yomiyama as the 'site' of it all will make her memory go fuzzy again right away or alter it entirely."

"Can that happen?"

"...I don't know." He sighed. "I don't know, but she seems to be worried about it. That's why I figured I had better talk to you directly about this as well, Sou. She asked me to. She said she wanted me to call you and tell you *this* as well, just in case."

"Ah..."

"*Ksh-ksh-ksh...*ear me? Can you hear me? Sou?"

Another round of thick static accompanied his voice.

"Ah, yes," I answered him, but the noise continued to cut in. Koichi's words became garbled and unintelligible in places. Almost like something was blocking the signal.

"...Well...anyway, the main point...you ready?"

"Yes."

I adjusted my grip on my cell phone and pressed it firmly against my ear.

"Return the 'casualty' to 'death,'" Koichi told me.

"Huh?" Without meaning to, I repeated after him, "The 'casualty' to 'death'...?"

"Matsunaga, the guy who left us that tape, that's what he did. And three years ago, I did it, too."

"Um, so then...what does that...?"

Ssh-ssh-ksh-ksh-ksh... Again, the static interference cut in.

I wonder if it's this bad on his end? I wonder if everything I've said has made it through to him?

Before I could confirm, I heard Koichi again. "...Misaki's the only one...are you listening? If I can give you any advice..."

Ssh-ssh-ssh-ksh-ksh-ksh-ksh-ksh...

"—lieve it. Believe her...that 'eye' of hers...no matter what truths it might reveal, even if you can't accept them or don't want to—"

...That "eye" of hers?

Ah, could that mean...?

Ssh-ssh-ssh-ssh-ksh-ksh-ksh-ksh-ksh-ksh...

I managed to catch a few more words from him over the growing static. "Got it, Sou? Return the 'casualty' to 'death'... Don't hesitate, just act. Believe her, and..."

I didn't have time to ask what I was supposed to do. The static, which seemed like a manifestation of some malicious will, grew louder and louder, until I had to pull the phone away from my ear...

And then the connection finally severed.

Somehow, I knew in my gut that trying to call Koichi again was pointless, that the connection would never go through.

8

That evening, I spoke to Mei Misaki on the phone.

If I hadn't been with Izumi and Yagisawa, I probably would have left school and headed straight for the gallery in Misaki. But it seemed like Izumi and Yagisawa might have tried to follow me, after hearing my exchange with Koichi. I had no doubt that Izumi in particular had guessed the content of our conversation.

But I wanted to talk one-on-one with Mei first.

"That phone call was from the famous Mr. Sakakibara, right?" Izumi asked me on the way home. Yagisawa was walking with us, too.

"Yeah. He said he had something to tell me directly."

"And?"

I wasn't sure how to answer.

Before I tell Izumi, I have to get in touch with Mei. My first priority is to speak with her and compare the information we got from Koichi. In addition...

"What does *return the 'casualty' to 'death'* mean?"

Of course, if they had been listening to my side of the phone call, that phrase would have left an impression.

"Is that, by any chance—?"

"I don't know," I said, cutting Izumi off. "The static was awful, so I couldn't hear him very well."

"So..."

"Sakakibara said that he called Misaki and talked to her as well. The thing to do now is to go check with her."

I was able to get a hold of her that evening, a little past eight. I tried calling many times before then, but they didn't go through, so she called me back later on.

I informed her that I had received a direct call from Koichi, who was in Mexico. Then I revealed what he had told me—in minute detail. She kept silent and listened, then, after I was done talking, stayed quiet for a little while...

Finally, Mei spoke. "Return the 'casualty' to 'death.' That's what he said, right? Sakakibara."

"Yes."

"He told me the same thing. When I heard those words, it was like some sort of 'figure' took shape in my vague memories."

"Oh, really?" Without meaning to, I raised my voice. "So then, Mei, what should we do? Return the 'casualty' to 'death'... So in other words..."

"Calm down, Sou," she urged. In contrast to me in my haste, she spoke in a quiet voice, as if she was carefully checking her footing as she proceeded. "Return the 'casualty' to 'death.' You can guess what that means, right?" she asked in the same quiet voice.

"Yes," I answered with uncontrollable uneasiness. "In other words, kill the 'casualty,' right?"

"Well, they're already dead, so it's probably not right to use the word *kill*, but...in any case, you have to somehow return them to the grave. That is the only way to stop the 'calamity' once it's started."

"But wait, Misaki—" I'd wanted to ask her this since the phone call the night before. "Someone in the class is the 'extra person,' the 'casualty,' right? And we have no way of knowing who that is until after graduation for that school year... But then..."

But how, then?

When the question made it that far out of my mouth, I finally had a realization. The instant it struck me, I gasped. *Why didn't I realize this earlier? Why couldn't I see it?* I cursed myself for my own stupidity.

"I see. So that's why Sakakibara said to trust you?"

"..........."

"He told me to trust your 'eye.' Is it possible that your 'doll's eye' can...?"

Mei's "doll's eye" could see things that "shouldn't be seen." According to Mei, it was like the "color of death." And that "power" could be effective at distinguishing the "casualty" who'd slipped into the world of the living due to the "phenomenon"—that was my guess.

"Wait." Mei took over before I could say more. "What Sakakibara said was right. Three years ago during summer vacation, at that lodge...I did in fact identify the 'casualty,' and Sakakibara returned that 'casualty' to 'death.' And when that happened, I was there at the scene, too..."

Mei spoke matter-of-factly, but the look on her face was awfully troubled.

"But you know, even though I heard him tell me about it, and even though the 'figures' are coming back to me in fragments, I still barely feel like it was real... It's hard to be sure."

"............"

"I wonder what we'll do if we're wrong. And if that 'doll's eye' still has that 'power' in the first place."

"He told me to trust you." I raised my voice again. "He said... *'believe Misaki and don't hesitate.'*"

"Mm...he did. He said something similar to me, but..."

She let out another distressed sigh and, after a short pause, said, "Let me think a little—about whether this is really a good idea. And if it is, then how do we go about it?"

9

Just as Yagisawa's forecast predicted, it started raining around sunset. However, for some reason, it was a much more violent rain than expected. Along with the rain, the wind also began blowing very fiercely. I could occasionally hear claps of thunder in the distance. It looked like a storm was rolling in.

I spent the night tossing and turning.

Even after I took some of the medicine that I got from the "clinic," my sleep was shallow and unrestful. I woke up many times, and each time I did, I had to fight to repress the disturbing images that spread through my mind. Koichi Sakakibara's directive to *return the "casualty" to "death"* was probably what all the scenes had in common...

...*Uncle Teruya.*

For some reason, in my half-waking state, it felt like my heart was murmuring the name of the man who had passed away three years ago.

...Uncle Teruya.

I repeated his name, as if I wanted to ask him something. When I was a child, I had asked him all sorts of questions whenever I went to play at his home, Lakeshore Manor.

"What happens to people when they die?"

"What does it mean to grow up"

"What is falling in love?"

....

....

...If I had the chance, what would I have asked Teruya now? And what kind of answer would I have hoped to get from him?

10

The following day—the morning of Thursday, July 5.

When I stopped by the Akazawa house for breakfast, there was a message from the school. It said that since a heavy rain and flood warning had been issued for the whole Yomiyama area early that morning, classes would not be held that day.

Of course, I'd barely been able to sleep the night before; honestly, I still wasn't fully awake. So when I heard this, I felt inwardly relieved.

Now that the "calamity" was here, it was probably dangerous to go to and from class in stormy weather. I couldn't help but worry about things like that. And it seemed to me that most of my classmates were feeling the same way.

If this mentality escalated, and I started worrying about anything that could pose a risk, it would only be a matter of time before I stopped going to school at all. And after that, maybe I would become an agoraphobe. And if that happened, and my fear grew ever larger, then...

Quitting school, skipping town entirely—I wouldn't be surprised if other people are already considering the same thing, like they have to get out somehow.

But no one had taken such drastic measures yet.

I figured it was probably due to our immaturity and lack of freedom as middle school students. The taboo against freely discussing the special circumstances of Grade 3 Class 3 with family probably also had something to do with it...

In any case, after I returned to the Freuden Tobii, I spent my day without taking a single step outside of my apartment.

At least as long as I'm sitting shut up in here, I can get through it without being exposed to unnecessary risks. It's safe. I have peace of mind.

I felt a surge of strong fear like I never had before, and it stirred up many feelings and thoughts. It was as if my feelings were being stirred up by the intensity of the continuing rainstorm outside.

We had end-of-term exams the next week, but there was no way I was going to be able to bring myself to study. I tried to read the new book I had borrowed from Izumi's older brother's bookshelf, but even though I was turning the pages, none of the story was making it through to me.

As I was trying to read, a question came to me. As I recognized it, it coiled itself around my mind and wouldn't loosen its grasp on me no matter how I tried to squirm free...

...Who is it?

Who on earth is the "casualty" who slipped into our class?

I thought about the students of Grade 3 Class 3, with the exception of Tomoko Tsugunaga and Keisuke Kouda, who'd already passed. One of the remaining students was the "extra person," a "casualty" who shouldn't have existed in the first place.

But who the hell is it?

It was a question that I couldn't hope to answer, no matter how much I thought about it. But even knowing that, I couldn't help but wonder. And once I started ruminating on the problem, my mind turned to the names and faces of the students I had met only in third year (who I hadn't given much thought to before).

For example, Shimamura and Kusakabe, who had been close with Yuika Hazumi. And the countermeasures officers, Etou and Tajimi. Jun Takanashi was also new. As well as several others.

If that was the case, if the "extra person" turned out to be somebody I'd never known before this year, it probably would have been easier for me to accept. I could have just waved it off and been done with it... But in reality, *there was no reason it had to be one of those people.*

They weren't the only candidates. The people who I had known for a long time, whose names and faces I recognized—including Yagisawa and Izumi, as well as Hazumi and Morishita... Since all memories and records related to the "extra person" had been altered or falsified, they could be anyone. Nobody could be counted out for certain.

Not a single person... That's right, even as I sit here carefully thinking it out like this, I myself could be...

....

...I could be.

I could?

Could I actually be nothing more than the "extra person"? The "casualty"?

I suppose it's possible.

The more seriously I considered it, the less I was able to deny it with absolute certainty.

In any case, if my memories had been "altered," nothing was off the table. Everything that I *thought* I remembered was suspect; that's what it came down to. There was nothing I could believe in...

No, wait.

Koichi Sakakibara had said something to me the other day.

He'd told me to *"believe her."*

"Believe that 'eye' of hers"...

....

...By "her," he meant Mei Misaki, and her eye—the blue "doll's eye" that Kirika had made for her.

It had been a long time since I'd seen that false eye, which fit into Mei's left eye socket. Last month, Mei had confided in me the reason for that.

But…ah, that's right. I had seen her just once, earlier in the spring, wearing her eye patch like she used to…

When was that?

That was—

That's right—that was back in mid-April. It was the first time I saw Mei after we found out that it was going to be an "on year." I visited the "Blue Eyes…" gallery, and we talked in the basement, and she was wearing her eye patch on her left eye…

At the time, I remembered thinking it had been a long time since I had seen Mei with the eye patch on. The left eye patch…which probably meant that the "doll's eye" was concealed beneath it… If that was the case…

What would it mean?

Why would Mei have had in her "doll's eye" on that occasion?

Only one answer sprang to mind.

11

The rain kept pouring down furiously all day.

Finally, a little past six in the evening, around the time the sun was setting, the intensity of the storm started to weaken somewhat. The flood warning was also lifted around that time. Before long, I would probably get notice from Auntie Sayuri that dinner was ready.

That's when Mei called me.

I looked at her name on the display of my phone and reflexively stood up from the chair I was sitting in. Last night and now today. I had gotten phone calls from her two days in a row, which was a rarity in my experience.

"Hello? Mei?"

"Sou."

The moment I heard her voice, I knew that something was off.

How could I explain it? That instant, the first thing I felt was a deep sense of unease.

Mei definitely seemed off somehow. She had always been aloof, never one to let her feelings show. But as soon as I heard her voice, I could tell that her composure had been broken.

What's going on? Could she be dealing with some sort of crisis?

"Um...what's up?" I asked timidly.

After a very long pause, Mei answered, "It's about the 'casualty.'"

"Uh, okay?"

"I gave it some thought," she said before taking another very long, unnatural pause.

At that point, I felt certain that I had been seized by some sort of premonition. I couldn't tell just then what "shape" it would take, but it was obviously something dark and gloomy...

"What's going on?" I asked again. It had been only a few seconds, but I was already very nervous. My hand sweat as it gripped the phone.

"Sou." Mei said my name again, let out a sigh, then told me in a tormented voice, "We have to hurry. That's what I was thinking, and I—"

12

> BLUE EYES EMPTY TO ALL, IN THE TWILIGHT OF YOMI

The signboard for the gallery was a black board with cream-colored lettering. Looking up at the dripping wet sign, I tried to calm my labored breathing.

I had ridden my bike all the way from my apartment in Tobii to Misaki, in the ceaseless rain.

I was bitter over the fact that I had fallen once along the way, when a strong gust of wind blew against me from the side, causing my tires to slip and throwing off my balance. At that exact moment, I'd heard an ambulance siren like something shrieking in the night, which only startled me further.

Luckily, I wasn't really injured in the accident, but the chain of my bike did come off, and the handlebars were badly bent… I'd had to push my bike the rest of the way to the gallery.

I had hit my left knee on the ground when I fell, and it was still throbbing with pain. If I'd known that would happen, I would have given up on the idea of going out on my bike altogether.

I checked the time on my watch.

A little after seven. Not even an hour had passed since Mei's phone call earlier.

I parked my bike and headed toward the gallery entrance, struggling to remove my dripping wet poncho.

There was a sheet of paper posted on the door that read, CLOSED UNTIL JULY 8. I hadn't heard anything about the gallery taking off, so I was suspicious as I stretched my hand out toward the door—

I tried to push it open as usual, but it didn't budge. It was locked.

"All right, I'll be waiting on the first floor of the gallery, so come see me," Mei had told me on our earlier phone call. I had answered that I was heading over right away. So even if the gallery was closed, I had expected her to leave the door open for me. And yet…

I tried applying force to the door again. But as I expected, it didn't budge.

Maybe she went back upstairs because I took a while to get here? No, I don't think she would… As I was deliberating, I dug through my pants pocket under my poncho. I was hesitant to dial the interphone that connected directly to upstairs, so I thought I would try Mei's cell phone first. However—

"Hmm?"

I made a noise.

"What?"

My cell phone wasn't there.

In a panic, I searched all my pockets, as well as the inside of my backpack. But it was nowhere to be found.

Did I leave it somewhere or drop it? Maybe I lost it when I fell on the way over?

"Crap," I grumbled as I continued to rummage around in my bag for the missing phone.

Suddenly, the door before me opened, accompanied by the tin-kling of the doorbell.

"Ah!" I let out another cry.

On the other side of the door was Mei. Since she had her back to the lights in the gallery, her whole body was indistinguishable from a black shadow.

"Sou," she said. "Thank you for coming."

"Ah, sure."

"Come in."

As she bade me in, I saw that her left eye was covered with a white eye patch.

13

Once I got inside, I understood the meaning of the sign that read Closed until July 8.

The familiar first floor, which I had visited many times before, was practically unrecognizable. Calling it a mess would be underselling it.

The display cases had been moved from where they used to stand, and none of the dolls that had previously decorated them was present. Looking around, I could see a bulging pile in one of the corners of the gallery floor that was covered with white fabric. They must have been piled up together underneath that.

A tall stepladder sat in a different corner, and above it were several wires coming down from the ceiling. *Is that...for hanging something over there?* I wondered.

"Kirika suggested altering the layout of the first floor a little," Mei explained. "A contractor she knows started coming in yesterday, but he's kind of unreliable. Kirika seems anxious."

I see.

The long, narrow table where Grandma Amane always sat beside the door was also pushed up against the wall. On top of the table and in front of it on the floor were scattered tools that a contractor would use and bundles of wire...

There are only three days left until the 8th. I wonder if he'll be able to finish the remodeling properly by then? I was needlessly worried.

"Sorry about the entrance being locked," Mei said. "I left it open, but the wind was too strong, and the door seemed insecure."

"Ah, it's fine." I shook my head forcefully. "It took me a lot longer to get here than I expected."

"Are you hurt?" she asked. She must have seen me favoring my left knee. And noticed that my pants were very dirty.

"I fell off my bike and kind of… Ah, but I'm fine." I forced myself to gently pat my smarting knee and then folded up my poncho and set it at my feet.

"Are you really okay?"

"Totally fine."

"I was thinking maybe tomorrow would be okay, but…but—"

"You said we have to hurry?"

Instead of answering, she led me to the sofa in the back of the room.

Mei was dressed in an indigo-blue shirt and a short, pleated skirt. The piece of black clothing seemed to melt into the gloom of the twilight interior of the gallery. By contrast, the eye patch over her left eye was pure white, without the slightest hint of dirt—

"So why are you in such a hurry tonight?" I asked boldly, once we were seated on the sofa, facing each other at an angle. Mei swiftly shrank from my gaze.

"…I don't know why."

After a brief silence, that was her answer.

"You don't know why…you're in such a rush?" I asked. There was another brief silence. Then—

"I have a bad feeling…"

………

…Is she hiding something?

I felt like she might be.

Is she hiding something from me?

Something seemed off about the way Mei was speaking. But I didn't press her any further. I didn't want to force her to tell me something she didn't want to.

I looked at the patch that covered her left eye. Beneath it, she was probably wearing that "doll's eye." Her empty socket was filled with a "blue eye, empty to all."

Three summers ago, she'd told me that her prosthetic held a mysterious "power." That it could see things that shouldn't be seen—that it could glimpse the "color of death." But—

In what situations and in what way? Mei had never offered a more concrete description of the eye's abilities, so I had no idea what exactly it could do. It was clear that it could see some kind of special color surrounding people close to death—but that was as far as my understanding went.

That's why...

That's why, even when I heard those things from Koichi yesterday, I hadn't immediately made the connection between Mei's "power" and the fact that she could use it to recognize the "casualty" among my classmates. It took some time for me to connect the dots.

The first time I had visited the gallery, back in April, Mei had been wearing the eye patch over her left eye. Now, finally, I understood why.

I was certain that back then, once we had established that this school year was an "on year," she must have been using her "doll's eye" on me. To ensure that I, Sou Hiratsuka from Grade 3 Class 3, who'd come to deliver that information, was not the "extra person," the "casualty."

I told her my theory. And then I asked, "Doesn't that mean that back in April, you believed in the 'power' of your 'doll's eye'?"

Mei tilted her head uneasily and answered, "I wonder? That was probably it. Maybe I could still remember something about returning the 'casualty' to 'death' three years ago. Perhaps my memories hadn't been erased yet. After I spoke on the phone with Sakakibara, I felt more and more as if that was the case."

"And now? How do you feel?"

"…………"

Mei silently tilted her head again, then took one deep breath and straightened her shoulders. And then she slowly removed the eye patch.

"Last night, I put this 'doll's eye' in for the first time in a while…
then I tried it out."

"Tried it out?"

"I tested to see whether I could see the 'color of death' like I could
before."

"How?"

"On the Internet," she answered, knitting her eyebrows wearily.
"There are sites where they compile images of real dead bodies,
right? I searched for some of those."

"And?" I urged her on.

"I saw it." Mei sighed. "Just like before. That color, that seems like
it would be impossible to make no matter what paints you mixed,
which doesn't seem to exist in this world. The 'color of death.'"

"Ah…"

"Right now, when I look at you like this with my 'eye,' I don't see
the 'color of death' around you, Sou. I know that you're alive. Just
like you were when I witnessed you three years ago."

"Sure."

I am alive. I am not the "casualty."

The suspicion and self-doubt that had coiled around my heart and
refused to budge finally vanished, like a parting mist. As far as I was
concerned, Mei's words were still worth trusting above everything
else, after all.

Feeling a modest sense of relief, I looked again at her—at her left
eye, from which she had removed the eye patch. She blinked slowly,
then stared straight back at me.

"Yesterday, after I talked to you on the phone…" Mei took another
deep breath. "I thought. I thought about what I should do, what I
needed to do. Whether I should put in this 'doll's eye' and, for instance,
go to North Yomi, into your classroom, and look directly at everyone
in your class…or something. I felt like that might be the most defi-
nite way to do it. But…"

"You said we have to hurry?"

"Right." Mei nodded enthusiastically. "That's why…"

14

"...Hey, Sou?"

I thought back to my exchange with Mei on the phone an hour earlier.

"Do you have any kind of photograph?"

"A photo?"

"Like one that shows as many members of your class as possible. Something like a group picture would be best."

"The 'color of death' also shows up in photos?" I asked.

"I should be able to see it, but..." Mei had answered almost as if she was giving herself instructions. "If the picture is too small, it might not be as clear. But still, it will probably work—"

Suddenly, I recalled the class photo I had seen once in Izumi's room. The shot photo that Ms. Kanbayashi had taken on the day of the entrance ceremony.

"—to a certain extent." Mei had sounded like she was completely lost in thought.

I started to get worked up, too, and had found myself unconsciously raising my voice. "A class photo... Except for two or three people, I've got one that shows everyone."

"And I don't suppose you could come show it to me now?"

"Right now?"

"If you can...anyway, as soon as possible."

"Got it."

That's as much as she had told me. It wasn't a situation for wavering or hesitating. I'd made up my mind immediately.

As soon as I hung up the phone, I immediately dashed over to Izumi's apartment. I'd briefly explained the circumstances to her. She had been surprised by the sudden request, and I borrowed the aforementioned group photograph.

"You're going now?" Izumi had asked me.

"Immediately," I'd answered.

"I'll go with you, too," she offered.

"You can't," I'd insisted.
Then I had hurried off into the rain.

15

As Mei had said earlier, from time to time, the wind beat at the front door and set it rattling on its hinges. That was because we hadn't locked it after I came in.

If this is the noise it's making now that the wind has died down quite a bit, it must have been way louder before.

"Um...here you go."

Opening my backpack, I pulled out a light-green plastic folder. The group photo in question was about five by seven inches. I had stuck it in this folder before bringing it over to avoid bending it.

Mei nodded meekly and drew her lips together tightly. I also nodded, then handed her the photograph, folder and all. In the semidarkness of the gallery, I was bursting with tension that set my skin tingling.

"Okay..."

Mei took the folder. She gently pulled the picture out and set it on top of the table. Then she bent over it a little and peered down at it.

Then there was a brief period of silence.

Two seconds, three seconds... Mei silently examined the photo. I held my breath as I watched her. The front door kept rattling loudly, and in the intervals between rattling, I felt as if I could faintly hear the secret whispers exchanged by the dolls in the corner of the gallery floor.

At last, Mei lifted her eyes from the photograph. She let out a short sigh.

"Can you see it?" I asked timidly. "Are *they* there, in that photograph?"

She glanced briefly at me, but then without answering, she returned her gaze to the picture. After scrutinizing it, she put her right palm against her right eye to cover it, then stared again using only her left "doll's eye."

"Are they there?" I repeated my question.

A moment later, she nodded slowly. "Yes... I can see the 'color of death,'" she answered, her gaze still fixed in place.

I leaned forward off the sofa. Mei glanced my way again and gave another short sigh, shaking her head slightly.

"This is them."

She took her right hand off her right eye and extended her pointer finger, then brought it closer to the photo. As I leaned even farther forward in order to ascertain who she meant—

The clanging of the doorbell filled the gallery.

When I turned, I saw that the front door had just been opened, and a person had come flying in from outside.

"Sou!" *She* called my name in a loud voice. "Sou...ah, here you are! Thank goodness!"

Without even folding her wet umbrella, she threw it down and rushed over to me. I stood up from the sofa. I had no idea what was going on. She was gasping and panting for breath. It seemed like she had run here with all her might through the rain.

"Wh—?"

Why? I was about to ask, but I was cut off.

She said, "You dropped your cell phone in my apartment."

She pulled my phone, with its *shisa* lion strap, out of the pocket of her white raincoat and showed it to me.

"Ah..."

"We got a call after you ran off. It went to yours first, then mine."

"Huh?"

"...I knew that you were headed here, and I didn't know what else to do, so I followed you. Listen, Sou, something awful happened."

"Something awful?"

"The call was to let us know!"

Her face was extremely stiff, and her lips were strained and trembling, and she looked like she might burst into tears at any second.

"It's really awful! The hackberry tree in the garden fell down and crashed into Grandpa's room!"

"What?!"

That huge hackberry tree in the back garden of the Akazawa house.

The one that's visible from the window of the sitting room where Grandpa Hiromune lies. That tree fell...?

"Grandpa is badly injured; his life is in danger. That's what Auntie Sayuri called to tell us."

Perhaps... Those sirens I heard when I fell off my bike on the way here...maybe they were from an ambulance that was dispatched when the hospital got word of the accident at the Akazawa house?

"Sou." This time Mei was speaking. I turned around, flustered. Her face was pale and just as stiff as the face of the girl who had burst in.

"Sou, listen. Are you ready?"

"Ah...y-yes."

Mei had been pointing at the photograph on the table. As I watched, she raised her arm, keeping her finger extended, swinging her hand up to indicate the girl standing there...

"Are you ready, Sou?" Mei announced quietly. *"The 'casualty' is standing right there."*

I couldn't respond. It was suddenly very hard to breathe, like all the oxygen had been sucked out of the room.

"I can see the 'color of death' on her."

Still pointing to *her*—to Izumi Akazawa—Mei continued in the same tone of voice.

"I can see it on her in this photograph. And I can see it on her standing there."

16

Izumi?

She's this year's "extra person"? She's the "casualty"...?

I was utterly shocked, totally bewildered. The first thought that came to my mind was that no matter how confidently Mei identified her, I couldn't believe that right now; I didn't want to believe her.

But there was no hesitation on Mei's face as she looked at Izumi, and when she pointed, her finger didn't so much as quiver.

Izumi noticed Mei's finger pointed in her way and let out a small, "Eh?" She sounded like she had no idea what was going on.

"What...what's this about?"

Her face stiffened even more. Her lips tightened into a grimace. As if she understood what Mei was saying but couldn't possibly accept it.

"What do you...? N-no, it can't be..."

Her wide, almond-shaped eyes wavered. They darted back and forth unsteadily. As if it was all she could do to stand there perplexed, struggling to respond.

Izumi knew about the mysterious "power" that Mei's "doll's eye" possessed. I had told her about it when I'd borrowed the photograph in order to explain why I needed it.

So she... No, but she couldn't have expected this when she decided to follow me, even in her wildest dreams. That we would identify her as the "casualty."

Of course, the surprise and confusion that I was reeling from must have been nothing compared to what Izumi was going through.

"Miss Akazawa?" Mei opened her mouth. "I know that you don't actually feel this way at all, but listen—you are this year's 'extra person,'" she asserted, finally lowering her right hand.

"I don't know when it happened, but at some point in the past, you were one of the 'related individuals' who died because of the 'calamity.' The 'phenomenon' resurrected you, and you joined the class this past April...and you're here now. As the 'casualty,' appearing no different than when you were alive," Mei informed her, stiff voice free of emotion.

"You're kidding, right?" cried Izumi, almost laughing. But her expression didn't soften at all. "No way. I'm not the 'casualty.' Look here, I'm perfectly alive. I'm breathing. My heart is beating..."

"'Casualties' resurrected by the 'phenomenon' are indistinguishable from the 'living.' They breathe just like everyone else, and their bodies are warm. If you cut them, they bleed. But you've heard all that already, right?"

"I've got perfectly clear memories," Izumi insisted, "that extend well beyond March of this year."

"They were altered to make things consistent," Mei replied dispassionately. Her face, like her voice, was dispassionate. She looked cold.

Izumi held her tongue, then turned her bewildered eyes on me. "Hey, Sou. Say something..."

Just at that moment, the phone in my hand, which Izumi had handed to me earlier, began to vibrate. Flustered, I looked at the display and saw it showing the name "Sayuri."

"Ah, Sou!"

The moment I picked up, Auntie Sayuri's voice came bursting into my ear. "Izumi must have found you."

"Yes."

"Something awful's happened!" she cried without pausing. "Grandpa has...Sou, your grandfather has..."

"I heard," I answered while trying to keep my emotions in check as best I could. "I heard there was an accident and that he's badly injured."

"Actually...just now, he..."

"Did he die?"

"By the time they got him to the hospital, he was already beyond help."

I grasped my cell phone tightly, overcome by surprise and horror, and whispered, "It can't be..."

Sayuri broke down. "Why did that tree suddenly fall over...? And why did it have to fall on his room of all places? It broke through the window and struck him on the head while he was sleeping..."

Ksh-ksh. Static crackled on the line. As if something was jeering at us. *Ssh-ssh-ssh, ksh-ksh-ksh-ksh...* The noise drowned out Sayuri's voice, and then the signal cut out.

"That was from Auntie Sayuri," I told Izumi, still gripping my phone. "Grandpa's dead."

"............"

"This must be the 'calamity,' too, right?"

My grandfather, Hiromune Akazawa, and I were related within two degrees. Hiromune and Izumi were the same, two degrees. As a "related individual" to Grade 3 Class 3, he was of course *within reach* of the "calamity." And so...

But at that moment, another revelation passed through my mind of its own accord.

Now that our grandfather had passed away, a great number of relatives were likely to gather for his wake and funeral. More than a few people who lived outside of Yomiyama would attend. Should circumstances permit, Izumi's older brother, Souta, might even return home from Germany. Maybe even...that's right, the former wife of Hiromune's third son, Fuyuhiko, might even show up—Tsukiho.

If we didn't do something, all those people would come to Yomiyama in the near future and risk falling victim to the "calamity"...

...*I can't let that happen!*

My voice echoed through my head.

No more, this can't go on...

Shoving my cell phone into my pants pocket, I looked back and forth between Izumi and Mei.

Surprise, bewilderment, and extreme confusion—Izumi was surely feeling more than I could imagine. Panic flashed in her wide-open eyes. She pursed her lips and shook her head. Slightly but strongly.

Opposite to her, Mei's blank expression remained unbroken. Silently, coldly, she scrutinized Izumi with both eyes, her own and the "doll's eye." She took one, two steps forward until she was standing beside me.

"I can see the 'color of death,' so..." She threw out the same statement as before, this time in Izumi's direction. "Akazawa, you 'belong on the other side.'"

"Stop it!" Izumi shouted. "Am I supposed to believe that's true all of a sudden, just because you say so? Telling me that out of nowhere... get real, Misaki." She turned to look at me. "Come on...Sou?"

I was still entirely lost. "I...can't believe it...," I mumbled.

Mei's answer was different.

"The question isn't whether you believe it or not," she said, her

voice still calm and detached from any emotion. "You're the 'casualty.' That's the truth. Whether you believe it or not, the facts don't
change. And so..."

...And so?

I examined Mei's face.

*And so, in order to stop any further "accidents" from happening, we
need to return the "casualty," return Izumi to...*

"Sou!" Izumi shouted again. "Say something! I'm your cousin;
we've been close since way back, right? Since before you moved into
the apartment building in April..."

"...Aah..."

I certainly had those memories. But there was the undeniable possibility that they were false memories, planted by the "phenomenon."
That was the "world" we were in now.

...Thud.

I examined Izumi's face again.

On top of her increasing panic, there was now a shade of anger
permeating her expression as well. But that must have gone hand in
hand with "fear"... As I considered that, suddenly—

"Are you Izumi?"

I recalled a voice that was quietly suspicious or perhaps confused.
The voice of my grandfather, Hiromune.

"But you're..."

Indeed, this was a memory from the night before last. When Izumi
had come to visit the Akazawa house and the two of us had gone into
our grandfather's room.

It was almost like he hadn't been able to focus on his granddaughter. I'd chalked that up to my imagination then, but his eyes had
definitely looked cloudy.

"How are you still...?"

What an unusual way to react to a visit from a granddaughter.
Strange and unnatural. That's what I had thought at the time—and
now, even more so. The man hadn't seen his granddaughter in a
while, and the first thing he asked was, *"Why are you here?"* It had
struck me as awfully cold.

I remembered something similar had happened in late April, when Izumi was at the Akazawa house and went in to visit Grandpa.

"Why are you here?"

Our grandfather had asked her that. As for what he meant by it...

He'd been bedridden for some time and had started showing signs of cognitive degeneration. Because of that, perhaps the alteration of memory caused by the "phenomenon" hadn't taken sufficient hold of his mind. It was certainly possible.

"Why are you here?"

If those words had been a simple expression of disbelief at the fact that *Izumi, the granddaughter who he was sure had already died, was standing there before his eyes*, then...no...

But that alone didn't amount to proof that she was the "casualty." As long as we were in a world where we knew memories and records were being altered, then wasn't it actually impossible to find any kind of proof that would let us determine whether or not it was "true"...?

...Thud.

...Huh?

What?

What was that? Just now, suddenly...

...Thud.

"Hey! Sou!"

Izumi's voice. She sounded confused, angry, and scared. Like someone who was being ignored, treated as if she *didn't exist.*

"Sou." Mei called my name quietly. "You remember, right? You remember what you heard from Sakakibara on the phone. About what we have to do in order to stop the 'calamity'?"

Ah...of course. I remember. I do. But...

But nevertheless, I couldn't bring myself to answer right away.

I could feel the whole dusky, gloomy atmosphere icing over. My mind and body were frozen, too; I couldn't get a single word out, much less move... For some reason, the shrieking of unknown creatures sounded in my ears. Countless shrill screams. I knew I couldn't actually hear them—that would be impossible. And yet, they seemed to me like the voices of the dolls that inhabited this gallery...

Mei glanced at me sadly and took a faint breath… The next moment, she made a move of her own.

17

She moved swiftly.

Without a word, Mei headed for the table that was pushed up alongside the wall beside the door. Once there, she picked up one of the tools that had been dumped there.

It looks like a hammer—no, a nail puller.

Don't tell me…

She's going to use that? Right here, right now?

"Mei…"

By the time I had wrung my voice out of my parched, raspy throat, she had already raised the nail puller overhead and leaped at Izumi.

My cousin's scream echoed through the gallery, overlapping with the shrieks of the dolls. "Wh-what are you doing?! You can't!"

Mei swung her right hand downward. Izumi dodged, but not completely, and the pointed tip of the nail puller grazed her shoulder… The impact pushed her off balance, and she went down to the floor on a knee.

"Stop it…Mei!"

"Return the 'casualty' to 'death,'" Mei answered coolly. "There is no other way to stop the 'calamity.'"

"Stop!" Izumi pleaded fervently. "I haven't…I haven't done anything!"

"You're right. You haven't done anything. You are simply the 'casualty.' But many people have already died from this iteration of the 'calamity.' And if we don't do something, countless more will…"

"That's not my fault!"

"It's not your fault." Mei re-gripped the nail puller. "It's no one's fault. The 'phenomenon' has simply taken this form, that's all. And that's why…you see, Miss Akazawa?"

Mei swung her right hand down again. Still on one knee, Izumi crossed both arms above her head to block the blow.

"Stop!" This time, I was the one who shouted.

"Believe Mei's 'eye'"—that's what Koichi Sakakibara had told me—*"no matter what truths it might reveal, even if you can't accept them or don't want to..."*

That's what he'd said. But—

"Please stop. This is..."

In the end, I couldn't sit back and watch.

I didn't know what I believed, or what I should believe, in this situation. I didn't know what to do. It was clear in my head, but in my heart...

Mei stopped moving and looked back at me. Her eye was full of sadness, just like earlier.

Seizing the opportunity, Izumi leaped to her feet. By the time Mei turned back around, she had taken off in a mad dash, aiming for the front entrance.

The door opened, and Izumi darted out. Mei gave chase. I ran outside, following Mei.

18

The rain had slowed to a drizzle. The strong wind from earlier had also mostly settled down. Still, there wasn't a single person to be seen on the road. Although it wasn't that late in the evening yet, the town was weirdly quiet...

Izumi was sprinting, and Mei was pursuing her. And I was chasing after them both. Fighting through the pain in my left knee, I ran with all my effort. From time to time, a big raindrop would form suddenly and hit me in the face. Occasionally, the wind kicked up, bringing with it the low rumble of distant thunder.

The mayhem inside my mind continued.

Mei had moved on her own to solve the problem.

And I had prevented her from doing so.

What do I believe? What should I believe? What should I do? There's no way to know the right answer...

"Got it, Sou?"
Koichi's words from our phone call repeatedly rang in my ears.
"Return the 'casualty' to 'death'... Don't hesitate, just act.
"Believe her and..."
Does this mean I don't fully believe her? I don't trust Mei—or the *"power" of her "doll's eye"? Or maybe I...*

...Thud.

Meanwhile, I felt a strange sensation, one that I had felt somewhere before.

...Thud.

What could that be?
It was a low, faint reverberation, outside the range of my hearing.
I think I've experienced this sensation before. But when did I? And where?
I mulled it over, but my efforts were fruitless...
...As we emerged onto the path running along the bank of the Yomiyama River, I closed the distance between myself and Mei considerably. The path was dark, lined with sparse streetlamps.
The back of her indigo-blue shirt was just two or three meters ahead of me. A little farther ahead, I could make out the back of Izumi's white raincoat... I was keeping a steady eye on her when—
Something happened to Izumi. She let out a short shriek. Maybe she'd slipped or lost her footing. Either way, she fell.
Mei slowed to a walk. The nail puller from earlier was still in her right hand. There was no change in her determination. She was going to use the tool right here; she was going to...
"Mei!" I shouted. "Stop!"
But without so much as looking back, she raised her implement high above her head, then swung it back down.
I heard a hard *crunch*. Izumi must have scrambled to her feet and dodged the attack, leaving the nail puller to hit the surface of the road where it had whiffed its target.
At that point, I finally caught up with the two of them. The nail puller fell from Mei's hand as her attack hit the pavement. In a

split-second decision, I sent it flying with a kick so that Mei couldn't pick it up again.

"Sou?" She looked me in the face. As expected, there was a terrible sadness in her eyes.

"It's not my fault," Izumi reasoned in a trembling voice once she stood back up. "It's not my..."

At that moment, a gust of wind blew against us from the riverside, and at almost the same time, a bolt of lightning streaked across the night sky. When it did, as if in sync with the sudden flash of light—

...Thud.

—the strange sensation came over me again.

...Thud.

Along with the low, faint reverberation, a *certain scene* suddenly surfaced in my mind. It had absolutely no logical connection to the situation I was faced with now...

...A door.

I see a lone door.

It was the entrance to an apartment in the Freuden Tobii. The unit number on the plate beside the door was <E-1>. Like mine, this room was also on the fifth floor, on the opposite side of the elevator lobby.

Is this it? Is this the apartment? Hadn't that question flashed through my mind *back then*?

This is... Yes, I'm sure this is a fragment of my memory. Back then *means at the beginning of April, early morning on the day of the opening ceremony.*

...Thud.

...Desks and chairs.

I can see neat rows of desks and chairs. A blackboard with nothing written on it. One fluorescent light, flickering unstably. This is—

The Grade 3 Class 3 classroom on the third floor of Building C. This is... Yes, this is also from that day at the beginning of April, after the opening ceremony was over.

The students were present, but no one had made a move to take their seats. Not even to place a bag down on their desks.

"Let's take our seats for now, everyone."
One of the girls spoke up. In a sharp, crisp voice that was well articulated…and when I heard it—
Is that…? Who owns that voice?
Hadn't I felt a moment of doubt back then?
That doubt disappeared from my mind a moment later. That uncomfortable feeling just…

…Thud.

Ah…why?
Why is this scene coming up now?
Why are these memories playing back……?
Izumi was staring at me. Her hair had gotten completely soaked by the rain, and her raincoat was filthy with mud.
"It's not my fault."
Her pleading voice sounded weaker than before. When I stared at her face, I saw that some kind of change had come over her…
Maybe…
That's when a thought struck me.
It was a wild idea that bordered on delusion. But perhaps something had reached Izumi's heart just now, something akin to the strange sensation that I'd experienced when the sudden flash of lightning had dazzled me…
I took a step toward her. When I opened my mouth to speak, she slowly shook her head.
"It's not me," she insisted meekly in an even weaker voice than before. With that, she promptly turned on her heel and took off down the riverside path.
Mei was about to go chasing after Izumi again, but I steadied myself and addressed her. "I'm sorry that you weren't able to do what needed to be done. But, Mei, your job here is over…"
She tilted her head slightly, suspicious.
"Sou?"
"It's confirmed. You can see the 'color of death' on her—on Izumi Akazawa. There's no mistaking it, right? She is the 'casualty,' isn't she?"

"Yes. There's no mistaking it."

"All right." I nodded firmly. "I'll do the rest. I'll chase her down with everything I've got, and... I know what I have to do. You can go, Mei..."

19

Bolts of lightning crossed the sky several more times as I tore down the riverside path in pursuit of Izumi. With each flash, various scenes surfaced in my mind before they disappeared. They were all fragments of memories related to events I had experienced after April of this year. And the common thread among them was that they all had something to do with Izumi...

...For example—

That time, when I'd gone to the secondary library at the start of May to talk to Mr. Chibiki. While I was there, Yagisawa and Izumi appeared, and when the two of them greeted him, he'd reacted strangely to my cousin.

I recalled my momentary discomfort *that time*.

...For example—

Another time, when I'd stopped by the "Blue Eyes..." gallery on my way home from the hospital at the beginning of May and talked to Mei in the basement. Izumi had happened to catch sight of me outside. After that, she'd followed me in and encountered Mei for the first time. I remembered Mei's reaction *that time*, as well as my momentary discomfort again.

I had no idea what it all meant, why it was coming back to me now. These moments seemed to have no obvious connection.

But they filled my mind regardless.

It was as though a strong and supple shell of "lies" was wrapped around this "world." Here and there, microscopic holes were opening in the barrier, allowing the light of "truth" to shine in from outside. These beams were projecting scenes inside my brain.

If I had to put it in a different way, it would be like this:

I was living in a "world" that had been restructured by the

alterations and falsifications that accompany the "phenomenon" to maintain internal consistency. The scenes I was seeing were like small *tears* that had opened up in the fabric of that false reality.

The "casualty" for this school year was Izumi Akazawa—at this point, I was finally able to recognize that cruel reality.

Eventually, I caught up to her. She was just about to cross the bridge that spanned the Yomiyama River. The one for pedestrians—the Izana Bridge.

Izumi was standing in the middle of it with both hands on one of the handrails, bent over at the waist. Her shoulders and back were heaving violently up and down. She looked like she might collapse at any moment.

She noticed me standing there and straightened up slowly.

"Look over here," I said. "Show me your face…"

While we were running, the rain had started picking up. Atop the bridge, the wind was also blowing hard. And beneath it, the Yomiyama River was flowing fiercely, swollen with rainwater.

I wasn't sure that Izumi could hear me over the cacophony.

Lightning streaked across the sky, follow by a quick flash of bright white light.

…Thud.

Another scene came to mind.

…Thud.

…Unit <E-1> in the Freuden Tobii. The grand piano set up in the soundproofed room. I could see Izumi's figure, seated on the bench, her fingers splayed out across the keyboard.

This was *that time* at the end of June. That evening when she had played Beethoven's "Moonlight Sonata" to mourn those who had died.

As I was listening to her performance, I had backed into the window curtain and suddenly smelled something that was a little off… and for a moment, I had somehow gotten the feeling that I had stepped foot into a place that people had not inhabited for quite some time. I remembered my discomfort *back then*.

"You didn't notice? One of the keys wasn't playing the right note."

I recalled Izumi's words, after she'd stopped playing partway through the piece.

"It's way out of tune."

A key that wouldn't play. A piano out of tune. Which means...

Izumi lifted her face.

I beheld the expression she had on now and thought that maybe, by some chance, she was seeing the same vision in her mind. Which might have been why she was...

Rain and tears were streaking down Izumi's face. Confusion and anger and fear played out over it.

Ah, what is this...?

"Sou." Someone called my name from behind my back. It was Mei's voice. Despite the fact that I had pleaded with her to leave the rest to me, in the end, she must have followed me.

"Sou." She called my name again. "Sou...don't waver. Don't doubt yourself. Believe me, cast aside any hesitation, and act..."

Argh, I get it!

I already know that perfectly well.

I took a step toward Izumi. But even though she watched me do it, she didn't move from that spot. She just shook her head weakly, still looking at me.

I took another step. When I did—

With one hand still on the handrail, Izumi turned so that her back was to the railing—facing upstream. Then she let go.

As I got even closer to her, I raised my own hands up to about chest height. I think I had made up my mind about how I was going to move from there.

If I get right up beside her and push her off the bridge...

If I do that, no matter how strong a swimmer she is, there's no way she could survive the river's furious, muddy current. If she drops, her death is almost guaranteed...and so...

It wasn't clear whether Izumi could tell what I was planning. She stood in the same spot, not moving an inch, waiting for me to come to her. And then—

I decided to act.

Leaning against the handrail of the bridge, Izumi looked me in the face. There were tears in her eyes, but she was smiling. Her lips seemed to move as if to say something, but before I could make out the words—

I charged at her with all my might, aiming both hands at her shoulders.

However, *just before I made contact,* Izumi's body flopped backward, pivoting over the handrail, turning again and again as she flew through the air. She fell right under the bridge.

As shocked as I was, I rushed to the handrail and peered over into the river. Mei followed my lead. But by that time, Izumi's body had already been swallowed up by the violent, muddy water...

Thud.

Outside this world, someone clicked a shutter. For a moment, it felt like we were enveloped in absolute darkness.

†

The evening of Wednesday, July 5 was a turning point.

After that date, "Izumi Akazawa," who had existed as a "student in Grade 3 Class 3 at North Yomiyama Middle School" from April of that year, disappeared from the memories of everyone except for Mei Misaki and myself, the two people who'd participated in her "death."

Part
3

. . . .

M.M.

Interlude IV

It sounds like this year's "calamity" is already over.

Is that really true?

I heard a rumor that it was.

The "calamity" may be gone...but we can't say we really did anything to stop it, can we? I mean, didn't Hiratsuka's grandfather die in an accident just this month? That was probably the "calamity," too, wasn't it?

Ah. But that was the last one, and now it's done for the year—it's supposed to have stopped.

Really? I wonder why...?

According to one theory, it might be because **the "casualty" disappeared.**

The "casualty"? Is that the "extra person" who joins the class?

Yeah.

Why do people think that?

Because of the number of desks and chairs in the classroom.

Desks and chairs...

They say there's an extra set. Yeah, now that I think about it, there's definitely one too many.

Oh, really?

Counting Tsugunaga, who died in May, and Kouda, who died in June, plus Makise, who's in the hospital, and Hazumi, who hasn't come to school in a long time, that should make four empty seats, right?

Mm-hmm.

But now there's one more empty seat besides those four.

Whose seat is it?

Nobody knows. Nobody is absent besides Makise and Hazumi, but that seat's still empty. That didn't happen before. Weird, right?

....

So people figure that desk has to belong to the "extra person," to the "casualty." *They* went away, so the seat that was added at the beginning of April for them is now unoccupied.

....

The disappearance of the "casualty" must mean that the "phenomenon" is over, right? Which means the "accidents" are, too...

Really?

I hope so. The countermeasures officers and the teachers are discussing it as we speak.

†

......The "calamity" is over, so we don't need to worry about anything anymore.

Really?

Mm.

I heard that none of the "countermeasures" really worked...

It's all right now.

But how did that happen? I haven't heard anything from anyone in the class.

A report is coming soon.

....

So listen, you don't have to be afraid. Don't be so timid, okay?

But I...

This has dragged on for an awfully long time, so I think it's only natural to be a little hesitant, but...

You know, sometimes I have this thought. Well, it's less of a thought and more like, how do I say this...like something I've become aware of.

Aware of what?

It's like I've always been *here*, like time has been frozen *here* forever, so...you, me, our very existence, has also been on hold. Like we're stuck in time, trapped here for eternity...

No way. That could never...

Or, if time's not standing still, then we're circling around to the same places. Endlessly circling back on ourselves so that we're trapped *here* for the rest of time...

I understand you feel that way, but it's all right now. Time is moving forward like it should. You're not stuck here or anywhere.

But...but listen, maybe I already...

....

...Ah, sorry for whining like this again.

I don't mind listening to you complain a bit. You don't have to act brave all the time. But listen, I'm sure you're gonna be all right.

Thanks.

I'll come back again later, okay?

Ah, yeah. Thanks.

Chapter 12
July II

1

The rainy season ended, and summer truly began.

It was July 26.

The long first semester was over, and three days after the start of summer vacation, I completed my second move of the year. It was another small one, from unit <E-9> in the Freuden Tobii to the Akazawa main house, where I had lived previously.

I hadn't accumulated much in the way of personal possessions during my time in the apartment, just shy of four months since moving in in April, so as before, we didn't have to hire any movers, and I carried my own things over. Yagisawa generously helped with anything that was too heavy to move on my own.

We carried the last of the boxes into the room that had previously been my bedroom-cum-study. Everything was brand-new. Even the wallpaper and flooring had been replaced. Both of us sighed, glad to be done, and moved into the living room, where the air-conditioning was running, to rest. Auntie Sayuri brought out some ice-cold ciders to reward us for our hard work.

"You must be tired, boys. Thank you for helping out these past few days, Yagisawa dear. I'm sure it was hard work."

"No, no, I've got plenty left in the tank!" He gripped both ends of the towel that was hanging around his neck and puffed out his chest.

"Thanks for the cider," I said.

"I've got ice cream—would you like some?"

"Oh, sure!"

"Wait a minute, okay? You've been hard at work, so I'll make you my special parfaits."

When the month started, I had expected to be able to move back to the Akazawa house by the beginning of summer break, after the remodeling finished up. However, on the evening of the 5th, there was the incident with the tree in the garden and the death of my grandfather Hiromune. It had taken a long time to repair the ruined sitting room and torn-up garden, delaying my plans to move back.

Haruhiko and Sayuri had asked me to wait until that work was finished before moving back. Natsuhiko and Mayuko over at the Freuden Tobii had also said that as long as I was all right with it, I could remain there for several more months. But as grateful as I was, a feeling had been growing inside me that told me I shouldn't remain *there* any longer than I had to. So I'd pushed the issue with Uncle Haruhiko and Auntie Sayuri and gone ahead with the move.

As long as I was in the room in the Freuden Tobii, it didn't matter what I did; I kept remembering her—Izumi Akazawa, who no longer existed in the "present" in this world. And they weren't just memories. My mind kept producing visions of *things that shouldn't be there*. That was sad and scary...

After drinking my cider in one big gulp, I left Yagisawa behind in the living room for a moment. I soon returned, carrying a bag that I had tossed into my room along with the moving boxes.

"Hey, so here." I set the thing that I'd pulled out of the bag in front of Yagisawa. It was a miniature album that I had filled with the photos from a single roll of film.

"Hmm?" Yagisawa seemed slightly confused, but once he looked inside, he mumbled, "Ah, from that time," and stroked his scraggly beard.

They were the photos we had taken in front of the lotus pond in the courtyard after school, on the 4th of this month. The "commemorative photos" that Yagisawa had originally suggested. It had taken me a long time to send them out for developing, after everything that had happened, but I'd finally convinced myself to do it.

The album started with some two-person shots of Yagisawa and me, then Izumi and me, several of each in a row. Next came solo shots of each of us and then several group shots of Yagisawa, Izumi, and me from when I had gotten Ms. Kanbayashi to use up the rest of the roll. However—

"These are the commemorative photos *of the two of us* from that day, huh? Hmm. I guess we didn't capture any of the lotus pond hands?" Yagisawa spoke very naturally as he turned the pages of the album. "Just how many of these did we ask Ms. Kanbayashi to take?"

Ah...I thought so.

Although his response was what I'd expected, I shook my head, feeling like it was too much to handle.

As I suspected, Yagisawa couldn't see Izumi in the photos. The only people pictured were him and me. As far as he was aware, at the photo shoot that day, there hadn't been three people, only *the two of us*. When Izumi, the "extra person," disappeared, every memory of everything having to do with her had been rewritten, *for the sake of consistency.*

"What's up, Sou?" Yagisawa was looking at me quizzically. "Why do you look like...? Oh! Could that be it? Do these pictures actually show *that girl you mentioned—your cousin* Izumi Akazawa or something?"

"Yeah," I answered with a sigh, "good guess."

"I can sort of tell."

"You can tell, like, intellectually?"

"Sort of. Can you see her? In these photos, I mean."

"Yeah."

I sat down next to Yagisawa, picked up the album, and opened it again with my own hands.

"The first pictures of us weren't taken by Ms. Kanbayashi; Izumi took them for us. And the next ones were two-person shots of her and me that you took, but...you can't see her, right?"

"Right. I only see you by yourself, Sou."

Yagisawa blinked on the other side of his round glasses for a while, then hummed, "Hmm...now that you say it, the composition is kind of unnatural. When you think about it, there's too much open space to your left."

"That's where she's standing." I informed him of *what I could see with my very eyes.* "We only got our teacher to take the last few. They're pictures of the three of us lined up together. Izumi's in the middle, and you and I are standing on either side. You can't see that, either, can you?"

"You and I are the only ones in the picture...but there is an awful lot of space between us, isn't there? Unnaturally so. And the one before that, with no one in it, that one, too?"

"Mm."

"I see. Is that so...?" Even though he was nodding, Yagisawa had a confused look on his face. "So you can really see her, for real?"

Izumi was there in the center of the photograph, standing between Yagisawa and me, dressed for summer and smiling cheerfully. I didn't know how she had felt at heart, whether she had actually been happy or how happy she had been. She'd had no idea that the very next night, she would learn that she was the "casualty"...

"I can see her. *I can still see her,*" I answered and placed the album on the table. "It's because I was *at the scene* that night. I'm sure that's the reason why."

Right. I can still see her. But at some point, it'll happen to me, too— there will come a time when I won't be able to see Izumi, either.

"Hmm." Yagisawa hummed again. He looked confused. He took off his glasses and used his towel to scrub the area around his eyes dry. "But you know, no matter how you explain it, it doesn't feel real at all. I don't mean to say that I don't believe you, but, how can I put this, um, it sounds like you got bewitched by a fox or something, you know?"

I had disclosed more or less the whole "truth" about this whole affair to Yagisawa early on. I had told him about the "method for stopping the 'calamity'" that Koichi Sakakibara had told me about over the phone and about the extraordinary "power" that Mei

Misaki's "doll's eye" possessed. I had shared how Mei had used that "power" to determine that Izumi was the "casualty."

But as for the details of Izumi's "death" on the night of the 5th, how, after we'd told her that she was the "casualty," she, in her confusion, had fallen from the Izana Bridge into the Yomiyama River... that was the only thing I didn't tell him. Honestly, I didn't want to talk about it at length, and I didn't feel like it was something I should really tell anyone anyway.

Yagisawa hadn't asked for too many details. His memory had already been rewritten after the disappearance of the "extra person," so from his perspective, my story didn't fit with "reality" very well. It must have sounded ludicrous.

"Sorry to keep you waiting. Here you go—please eat up!"

Before long, Auntie Sayuri brought in some extravagant handmade parfaits that lived up to their reputation. Her eyes stopped on the album on the table.

"Oh, photographs?"

She peered over our shoulders at the last page of the album, which was sitting open where we had left it.

"You took them at school, I see. Recently?"

Auntie Sayuri was of course in the same situation as Yagisawa. She could see only the two of us in the photos. Izumi was invisible to her.

That's consistent, I thought.

Sayuri already knew "Izumi Akazawa" as her "poor niece who died three years ago" and nothing more.

2

The evening of July 5, after Izumi had been swallowed up by the muddy waters of the Yomiyama River—

The first confirmation I got that "Izumi Akazawa" had vanished from this world was on a phone call to Auntie Sayuri.

I'd called her almost immediately. She was with Uncle Haruhiko, at the hospital where they had taken my grandfather. When I had asked her what I should do, she'd answered anxiously, "For now, you should go back to your apartment. It's getting late, and the weather's bad."

She had sounded like she'd regained her composure considerably.

"Mayuko and her husband are also at the hospital now. Sou, you don't need to come here tonight. I think we'll be able to bring Grandpa home tomorrow."

When I had heard that much, I'd blurted out, "Um, listen, Auntie. Izumi just..."

I had stopped before saying anything more.

There was no way I could have said what I had been about to say. Even if I had said it, it probably wouldn't have made a bit of sense. I knew that was the case, but I was driven by the feeling that I had to say something about Izumi after what had just happened. However—

"Izumi...?" Auntie Sayuri had sounded slightly surprised or maybe bewildered. There had been a short silence. During the pause, I'd wondered how Sayuri was processing my words in her mind.

"When Izumi passed away, you were still in Hinami, Sou. Even though you were cousins, you never had a chance to meet except when you were babies."

The tone of Sayuri's voice had changed a little, and it wavered with a quiet sadness. That's how it had seemed to me.

"She passed away three years ago this summer, but after that, you came to stay with us... Grandpa seemed happy about that. I'm sure he was glad to have one of his grandchildren nearby..."

The following afternoon, on the 6th, the body of my grandfather had been returned to the Akazawa house. The corpse was temporarily installed in a large room that had just been converted from tatami mats to conventional flooring during the renovations, and it was there that I saw my grandfather's dead face. The moody expression he'd worn in life had been nowhere to be seen, and as the saying goes, he'd looked to be resting in some kind of peace. I remember feeling not so much sad as having a strange sensation like my head was going kind of numb.

At that point, Natsuhiko and Mayuko had also come over to the

Akazawa house, probably to discuss the dates for the wake and the funeral and whatnot. Haruhiko and Sayuri also had to think about the arrangements for the cleanup and repairs from the fallen tree. Among the four adults, not one had thought anything of Izumi's disappearance the night before. All of them remembered her as simply "a person who died three years ago." In other words, it was proof that returning the "casualty" to "death" had been a success, but—

I had caught sight of the black cat, Kurosuke, in the hall outside the big room. He must have sensed somehow that the atmosphere in the house was not normal, because he had been pacing restlessly up and down the hallway. Sometimes he would stop and give a long cry in a feeble voice.

As I sat there watching him, I'd suddenly remembered something.

I'd remembered what had happened on the evening of the 3rd, when Izumi and I had gone to visit Grandpa, just the two of us.

While we were there, Kurosuke had scratched Izumi's hand, deep enough to break the skin. At the time, I had wondered why he would suddenly do something like that, despite being normally quite attached to Izumi.

What was that...?

The moment was long past, but I remember thinking it over anyway. Kurosuke had been at the house for many years before I showed up. He had known Izumi, who lived just nearby, for a long time, since he was a kitten, and it was only natural that he would have gotten very close with her.

But three years earlier, Izumi had died. And then, that spring, she had reappeared. Kurosuke had remembered Izumi, even though there had been a three-year gap, so he'd cozied up to her as always.

However, perhaps Kurosuke had secretly sensed that something was off—that there was something wrong with *this Izumi*, that she was somehow different than before. Perhaps that's what had caused his sudden confusion that night.

I suppose that cats might have a special intuition that humans lack? No...maybe it's that the "memory alteration" caused by the "phenomenon" doesn't work on nonhuman creatures, so...

"Meow," Kurosuke had cried as he'd snuggled up against my leg. When I had leaned over and patted his back, he'd rolled over on the spot and looked up at me, as if to ask what was going on and what had happened.

3

"Miss Akazawa was a classmate of mine in Grade 3 Class 3 three years ago."

It was the day after my grandfather's return when I had heard that line from Mei Misaki—the afternoon of Saturday the 7th.

"She was a countermeasures officer three years ago, too. And she became the female class rep after Sakuragi died in May..."

Mei had invited me upstairs in her house in Misaki. The gallery had been undergoing an interior redesign at the time. I'd visited the third floor many times before; it was still the same spacious living and dining area that never really felt like a home.

Mei and I had sat facing each other across a low glass-top table.

"The night before last, after Miss Akazawa fell from the bridge, my real memories gradually came back to me. They were shrouded in a thick fog this whole time, but it was like I wasn't even aware of the fog itself... Then the fog began to thin, and I could see things that had been hidden—that's what it felt like."

Mei had been wearing a short-sleeve white blouse. Unlike the previous time I'd seen her, she hadn't been wearing her "doll's eye" in her left eye, so she hadn't had her eye patch on, either.

"I went to sleep that night, and when I woke up, I remembered pretty much everything. All my memories seemed absolutely normal, and I had no sense of unease. I think I felt like this three years ago, too, after the 'casualty' disappeared, though my memories of that time are a little fuzzy now." Mei had spoken quietly, staring at a point in space above the table. "How about you, Sou?"

"Same for me." I'd nodded slowly, looking toward the same point in space as Mei. "I remember how I had a *cousin*, who died the month before I was taken in by the Akazawas three years ago. She was three years older than I was, her name was Izumi, and she was in Grade 3 Class 3 at North Yomi. I told you this already, didn't I, Mei?"

"She died during the class trip in August, right? One of the victims of the 'calamity' that year."

"That's right. But starting in April, my memory of it completely…"

"Vanished. It was altered. It wasn't just the two of us—it happened to the memories of all the people connected to her."

"And the physical records were altered, too, right? Like the class roster and photographs. And Mr. Chibiki's file."

"All our original memories of Miss Akazawa were altered, yes. In their place, the 'fact' that 'Miss Akazawa exists as a member of this year's Grade 3 Class 3' was put into the record, to keep things consistent…"

"And into our memories."

"Right."

Several scenes had been restored in my mind, instances that had completely vanished from my memory until two days earlier, when they'd all come back to me completely.

For example—

On April 9. The morning of the opening ceremony.

I had left my apartment and headed for the elevator lobby, where I'd looked at the door of unit <E-1> across the hall.

Now, what was this room? The question had flicked through my mind as I'd stared at the door with some confusion… But almost immediately, it had occurred to me that the room belonged to my cousin, Izumi Akazawa; that she was the same age as I was; and that she'd been living alone for a while. My memories had been altered to conform to this new "false reality."

It must have been just that morning when Izumi made her "appearance" as the "extra person" in Grade 3 Class 3. Up until the night before, she hadn't existed in this world, and <E-1> had been an empty apartment with no one living in it.

And then, that same day, in the classroom after the opening ceremony—

"For now, everyone, let's take our seats," I had heard Izumi say, and of course I had wondered who the owner of that voice could be. But sure enough, almost immediately, I had somehow recognized her, even though that was the very first time I'd even met "Izumi Aka-zawa." In that very instant, I'd known her, known that she was one of the female students who had been selected to be a countermeasures officer during the "strategy session." Of course, Izumi hadn't actually existed back in March, so obviously she couldn't have partici-pated in the "strategy session," but the alterations to my memories stretched far back in time…

The same thing must have happened to the memories of everyone in that classroom that day.

"Thinking back on it now," I had said, talking to myself as much as Mei, "there were a number of things that felt kind of strange but otherwise seemed fine at the time."

"Like what?" Mei had asked.

"Ummm…" I'd faltered briefly, then said, "Izumi…Miss Akazawa, she was in the drama club, and she said something to me about quit-ting to make room for the younger generation once she started third grade. But that girl Hazumi…"

"The girl who took on the role of the 'second non-exister,' right?"

"Right. She was also in the drama club until last year and told me she had quit going. If they were in the same club, then the two of them should have been acquainted with each other, right? And yet…"

At the beginning of the semester, Izumi said that she'd never met Hazumi before the third grade, that it was her first time speaking to her. I wonder why I didn't find that suspicious at the time. Maybe something was keeping that from happening.

"There's something else I'd like to confirm with you, Mei. Do you remember when you first met Izumi in your basement here? I stopped by on my way home from the hospital, and she followed me in…"

Mei had closed her eyes softly and nodded. "Yes. It was around the start of June, right?"

"When she came in, you stared intently at her face and mumbled her name... It was like you were trying to remember something important. That's how it looked to me anyway. How did you actually feel at the time? Do you remember?"

"I do remember. *Now* I do." Mei had opened her eyes and answered, "When I saw Miss Akazawa's face, I think I must have realized I had met her somewhere before. But I only felt like that for a second. I immediately changed my mind and decided I was imagining it..."

"...I knew it."

That had brought back the low, reverberating *thud* in my head, but at the time, I had smoothly brushed it off.

If I remember right, when they first met, Izumi looked at Mei with surprise and confusion. Was that...was it because Izumi had the same sensation as Mei?

I wonder if the "casualty" can remember anything from when they were alive, even if it contradicts the alterations made to the "present"...?

I hadn't been able to shake that troubling thought.

"Three years ago"—I'd continued with my questions—"when you and Izumi were in the same class, what kind of...? Ummm, were you friends? What kind of person was she?"

Mei had tilted her head slightly, looking uncomfortable, and gone silent for a while. As I was starting to worry that I had asked a bad question, Mei had finally answered in her usual detached tone of voice.

"I didn't have any friends." A sad, lonely smile had spread fleetingly across her lips. "So I have no idea what kind of person she was."

"Ah...okay."

"But listen, Sou."

"Yes?"

"Even though she was resurrected by the 'phenomenon,' her basic personality and other traits shouldn't have changed that much, so..."

At that point, Mei had stared directly into my face and said, "So, you know, I'm sure that Miss Akazawa was exactly the sort of person you felt her to be, while you were interacting with her these past three months."

4

My grandfather Hiromune's wake was held on Sunday the 8th, and his funeral was Monday the 9th—that's what had been decided during the discussions on the 6th. I hadn't been privy to all the exact details. In any case, because of the scheduling, I'd had the whole day on the 7th free. Feeling very restless, I had reached out to Mei. As the only two people in the world who knew the "truth," I had wanted to get together to talk and confirm all the "facts." I had also wanted to ask her opinion on what I was supposed to do next.

Two days had gone by since the stormy night when "Izumi Akazawa" had disappeared, and the weather had fully recovered. The sky was clear and blue, without a single bit of cloud floating in it. But in my heart, I'd still felt as if the furious rain and wind continued to simmer and rage.

"What about Tsukiho?" Mei had asked. "Is she coming for your grandfather's wake and funeral?"

"Who knows?" That was the best answer I'd been able to come up with. "She hasn't said anything, and I haven't contacted her."

"Your aunt and uncle have probably told her."

"Probably. But I haven't said anything…"

"Don't come to Yomiyama."

"Don't ever come here!"

The last thing I'd said to Tsukiho on the phone, at the end of June.

"Listen to me. I never want to see your face again. I don't want to spend time with you, and I don't want to hear your voice.

"I hate you!"

I honestly had no regrets about saying those things. *Even if it means I never see her again, that's okay with me. That would be just fine.*

Rather than worrying about anything to do with Tsukiho, my thoughts at the time had been consumed by Izumi, who no longer existed in our world. I had only actually known her for three months, *my close cousin.* The "world" had returned to the way it was supposed to be after she was gone. But to me, it all felt like something was terribly wrong…

"So with this, the 'calamity' for this year has stopped, right?" I'd confirmed with Mei again. "My grandfather was the last to die, and after this, it's over…?"

"That's right." Mei had nodded slightly but decisively. "There's nothing more to worry about."

"My Akazawa aunts and uncles don't seem to remember anything about the 'Izumi Akazawa' who showed up this year, so their memories are totally back to normal. Same goes for Yagisawa and Ms. Kanbayashi, who called to check up on me yesterday."

"You and I are the only ones who remember both versions of Miss Akazawa, from three years ago and from this year, Sou."

"Seems that way."

"It's the cruel privilege granted to people involved with the disappearance of the 'casualty.'"

"*The cruel…?*"

"But you know, sooner or later, we're going to forget, too. No matter how much you try not to, it'll happen eventually."

Mei had leaned back against the sofa and let out a short sigh. She'd fixed her gaze on that spot in the air above the table again. To me, it seemed like she had discovered a tear in the fabric of time that would connect us to the past, right in that spot.

After that, there had been another brief silence.

"Um…so," I'd spoken up, "how do you think I should tell the rest of my class that the 'calamity' is over?"

It was a question I had been struggling with since the previous day. I hadn't even said anything to Yagisawa yet, even when he'd called me.

"Like, should I explain the situation during homeroom or something? But I wonder if everyone will understand if I do that?"

Of course, I had no intention of talking about the "power" of Mei's "doll's eye" or about the specifics of what had happened that night, even if I did tell them. So then, when it came to how I ought to explain the "circumstances," I just couldn't see a way forward.

"I don't think you need to go out of your way to do anything in particular," Mei had answered matter-of-factly, extending her right pointer finger and placing it against her temple. "If you leave it alone, the truth will become clear on its own. Once no 'related individuals' die in August, then it will be obvious."

"That's certainly true, but…but…"

"But?"

"I keep thinking about everyone's feelings, not knowing that the 'calamity' is over. And we're going into summer vacation, too. Surely it would be better if everyone could start their summer break with a little peace of mind."

"I see," Mei had mumbled, removing her finger from her temple. "Everyone, huh?" she'd mumbled again before blinking slowly several times and then looking me right in the eye.

"You're very thoughtful, Sou."

"No, not really…"

"At any rate, no new 'accidents' are going to happen, so it's up to you what you do. You don't have to do anything, but you can if you want."

Think for yourself and decide.

So that's what she's telling me?

That's what I had understood her to mean, and I'd nodded wordlessly.

Then a voice had come from the door of the room. "Oh, welcome, Sou."

Kirika's voice—I'd recognized it right away.

"It's terrible what happened at the Akazawa house. I heard about your grandfather's passing." When I stood up, Kirika had come closer to me, frowning with concern. "Is it all right for you to be over here today?"

"The wake is tomorrow. Even if I was at the house now, there would be nothing I could do."

"I see. I fixed the chain on your bicycle downstairs."

"Oh, thank you very much."

I had encountered Kirika several times in that house since coming to Yomiyama, and she gave off a very different impression there than when I had met her at the Misaki family's vacation house in Hinami. She was several years older than Tsukiho but had sharper features…

That hadn't changed, but at the vacation house, she had been "the wife of Kotaro Misaki" before anything else, while there in Misaki, she was more like "the doll artist Kirika."

During the day, she usually shut herself up in the studio on the second floor, immersing herself in her work. In her atelier, she exclusively dressed in casual clothing, plain shirts and jeans. She also often had a bandanna wound around her head, and that was the case when she came in that day.

"It's been several months since I've seen you, hasn't it, Sou? I hear things from Mei sometimes."

Kirika had always behaved very cheerfully and gently toward me whenever we'd met. I had often sensed a slight affection as well.

The Misaki family has been friendly with the Hiratsuka family for quite some time, so she must know all about my circumstances, the fact that I was driven out of that house... Actually, it's probably exactly because she knows that she's so kind to me.

"Sou, would you like to eat dinner here before you go home? We can get something delivered."

"Oh, no, that's..."

"Please, it wouldn't be any trouble."

"It's not, but that's..."

During this exchange, Mei had been sitting on the sofa with her knees pulled up, silent. She had idly looked at the ceiling, then turned her eyes toward the window, which had its white roller curtain drawn down... Watching her out of the corner of my eye, something had suddenly started to bother me.

"Um...Kirika?" I had asked. "Have you been having some kind of health troubles lately?"

"Huh?" Kirika had tilted her head quizzically. She'd looked me directly in the face and inquired curiously, "Why do you ask that?"

"Ah, ah, um...I saw you several times at the hospital."

"The hospital?"

"Um...s-so I thought..."

As I was stammering, Mei had stood up from the sofa. "Mother...," she had called out to Kirika—as if to interrupt our conversation.

Why'd she do that?

What's going on all of a sudden?

"It sounds like Sou has to get going soon," Mei had said, approaching Kirika. "But before he goes home, he wants to see the dolls, since he came all this way. Even if it's just the ones in the basement, you said earlier…right?" She'd thrown her gaze over to me.

In her expression, I had read the message, *Do as I say*, and nodded, trying not to look surprised.

"Oh, is that so?"

Kirika had raised both eyebrows, puzzled, but when I'd agreed without a moment's delay, her face had softened into a smile.

"You've always loved the dolls, haven't you, Sou? That makes me happy."

"May we go see them?"

"Of course! There are still construction workers on the first floor, so don't get in their way, all right?"

5

In the end, Tsukiho hadn't come to Grandpa's wake or funeral.

I didn't know how much of an effect it had had on her when I'd told her not to come to Yomiyama or to talk to me again. But after being left a widow by her first husband, Tsukiho had pulled away from the Akazawa family and remarried, becoming a part of the Hiratsuka family. Her relationship with my grandfather had never seemed especially close, so I wasn't surprised when she didn't show. And fortunately, if the Akazawas had any complaints about the situation, they never made it to my ears.

At the funeral hall, as the deceased's grandson, I had been seated in the corner of the relatives' section. I'd worn my school uniform, with a mourning band around my arm.

I had felt very sad throughout the mourning ceremony. I'd tried asking myself once again why I was feeling sad, and what I was most sad about, but hadn't really come up with an answer. After the funeral, everyone had traveled together to the crematory, and along the way, I'd thought about the tragedy that had befallen the Kouda family the month before, and the sadness in my chest had ached terribly.

Of Auntie Sayuri's two daughters, the younger one who lived in Okinawa (her name was Midori, and she'd changed her surname to Shukawa after marriage) had rushed to Yomiyama the day of the wake. Apparently, the older daughter, Hikari, who lived in New York, hadn't been able to find a way to get back to Japan in time.

The day after the funeral, Mayuko's son, Souta—Izumi's older brother—had arrived from Germany. Mayuko had introduced me to him. That night was the first time I'd met Souta face-to-face.

"I guess I was already out of the country by the time you came to Yomiyama, huh, Sou? I probably met you when you were a baby, but... Well anyway, nice to meet you, I suppose."

He was average height, with a slim build and brownish hair. He had a smooth, fair complexion and wore elegant rimless glasses. Souta gave off quite an intellectual air, and unlike Izumi, he wasn't a brisk talker. He strung his words together at a slow, deliberate tempo.

"I've heard a few things about you from my mom, Sou. It sounds like the situation at home is pretty complicated. I hope I'm not overstepping when I say that you have my sympathy."

"Not at all... Thank you very much."

"Come on—you don't need to be so stiff. We're cousins, after all."

Souta was twenty-five years old, Izumi's older brother by ten years... No, Izumi's original age was the same as Mei's, so if she had lived, she would have been eighteen this year. That meant that she and Souta were siblings separated by seven years. I'd been borrowing the refrigerator and some books from Souta's room. Mayuko was the one who had recommended it... That was the story now.

I had been invited up to the penthouse of the Freuden Tobii, into the living room. Mayuko had set out coffee and cake, and the coffee had tasted like that Inoya blend that Izumi had liked.

"What kind of books did you choose?" Souta had asked.

I had answered his question frankly.

"Ha-ha! Eco might be a little difficult for someone in middle school, huh?" he'd remarked. "Well, he's worth reading even if it's a lot of work. Agatha Christie might be good."

"Yes, very good. It's my first time reading a book like that."

"I've got tons more interesting books, too. You can help yourself, okay?

"I wonder if this is what it would feel like to have a little brother?" Souta had suddenly mumbled between sips of his coffee. His narrow eyes had seemed somewhat lonesome, or nostalgic maybe. "If Izumi were here, I'm sure she'd be all excited."

Souta's words had caught me off guard. "Ah...um..." Against my better judgment, I'd asked, "Were you also in Germany when Izumi passed away?"

Souta had bitten his lip slightly. "Ah, about that. When it happened...well, back then, I just barely missed the funeral. Just like now, it happened really suddenly, so..." He'd bitten his lip a little harder. "It's been three years since then, huh? I think you came here right after that, Sou."

"I came at the start of September."

"Right."

Souta had downed the rest of his coffee, then leaned back very deeply on the sofa. Running his fingers through his hair, he'd sighed. "I wonder what she thought. About me..." He'd sounded like he was talking mostly to himself.

"Ah, um..." For some reason, I hadn't been able to hold my tongue. "This is a strange question, but, um...did you go see *Jurassic Park* with Izumi a long time ago?"

"Hmm? Yeah, I think I did." Souta had narrowed his eyes again. "How do you know something like that, Sou?"

"Well, um, I heard about it from my aunt..."

There was no way I could have told him the truth.

The first *Jurassic Park* movie had opened to the public, as Yagisawa had said, "*a real long time ago.*" Specifically, in the summer of 1993. Eight years ago. I'd gone back and checked the dates.

Eight years prior, Souta had been in his second year of high school. Considering how old "Izumi Akazawa" was when she was resurrected, she would have been just starting elementary school when they'd gone to the theater together and he'd bought her that dinosaur figurine. Just six or seven years old—perhaps a little young to go along to see *Jurassic Park*.

If any of this had occurred to me back when Izumi had told me about it, I might have realized that something strange was going on. Or maybe there had been something *keeping me from realizing it*.

"I heard you've been staying in one of our apartments since this April, Sou."

"Yes. The main house was under renovation, so I've been here while that's going on."

"My mother and father were happy to have you. I heard all about it on the phone. I'm sure they've been lonely ever since Izumi passed. They've even left the room that she was using on the fifth floor just as it used to be. It's great that you came to stay..."

"No, don't thank me. I just accepted their hospitality."

"That's not true. Their oldest son hardly ever comes home, so I'm grateful to you, too, Sou."

"............"

"I'm heading back to Germany already in a few days, but if there's anything you want to talk about, you can get in touch with me. Do you use e-mail?"

"Yes."

"Okay, take this," Souta had said as he handed me a business card. Then he'd crossed his hands behind his head and slowly glanced around the room with a somewhat troubled look on his face. "Honestly, even though three years have gone by since Izumi died, it still doesn't feel real, man..."

Afterward, as I was stepping out of the elevator back down on the fifth floor, the door of <E-1> had caught my eye.

It was the apartment that Izumi had once actually used. The morning of the opening ceremony in April, "Izumi Akazawa" had appeared in that room. It had been left exactly as it was when she died three years ago...

Right. That night, she came out of this apartment carrying three big garbage bags. And...

"My room was a total mess. I had so many things I didn't need. I promised I would take care of keeping the place clean, but...man, it turned into a dump before I knew it."

That's what she said. Thinking back on it now, that was...

It was because no one had lived in the apartment for three years—it had been abandoned. So over the years, it must have been filled up with all sorts of things that the newly resurrected Izumi "didn't need." The room would have held all her school textbooks and notebooks and stuff, and maybe a photo of her set up as a portrait of the deceased, as well as probably all sorts of incense and incense holders. Izumi must have seen all this as insignificant clutter and thrown it away. And back then, without having the slightest clue, I'd helped her do it.

I had warily approached the door to <E-1> and, after a few moments standing there, suddenly heard something—the faint sound of a piano.

My breath had caught in my throat.

This sound...is it coming from the room on the other side of this door?

And this tune...this is Beethoven's "Moonlight Sonata," the one Izumi played?

It can't be... No, don't be stupid.

Squeezing my eyes shut, I'd tried shaking my head as hard as I could—and the sound of the piano had in fact vanished immediately.

Of course.

Obviously, I was just imagining things. Some kind of auditory hallucination perhaps?

But that was not the only time it happened. And every time, a scene that shouldn't have been possible had surfaced in my mind... of Izumi still in that room, playing that piano...and I had to fight to stave off the panic.

6

On my first day back at school after my bereavement leave, I had gone to the secondary library during lunch to see Mr. Chibiki. Mei had said that it was up to me to decide what to do next, and after some thought, that was what I'd chosen.

I had come right out and said it, straight to the point. "The 'casualty' who joined our class as part of this year's 'phenomenon' was 'Izumi Akazawa.'"

At first, Mr. Chibiki had clearly looked bewildered. "What's this, all of a sudden?"

By that time, the existence of that year's "Izumi Akazawa" should have already disappeared from Mr. Chibiki's memory.

"Akazawa…if I remember correctly, she was a student in Grade 3 Class 3 three years ago."

It was the response I had anticipated. His memory had once again completely reverted to *how things originally were.*

"She was one of the people who died in the 'calamity' three years ago, right? She was also my cousin, three years older than me. And 'Izumi Akazawa' was resurrected as a member of Grade 3 Class 3 this year. As my cousin still but the same age as me. She was one of the countermeasures officers, so you spoke to her many times as well…"

From Mr. Chibiki's current perspective, this must have all sounded quite impossible. On the other hand, he must have realized that I wouldn't have come to him like that without a good reason.

"Last Wednesday, on the night of that big storm, she fell into the swollen Yomiyama River. I was there; I witnessed it."

Mr. Chibiki hadn't said anything. A deep vertical wrinkle had carved its way across his forehead.

I'd held his gaze, unwavering, and continued. "When it happened, she was swallowed up by the river's muddy water… I think she *died.* And then that was the turning point, and this year's 'Izumi Akazawa' disappeared from the memories of everyone who had anything to do with her. From the class roster and all the records, too, instantly, from everything. Even her mother and father and everyone in our class, no one remembers *this year's version of her*. It's the same for you, right, Mr. Chibiki?"

"............"

"So that makes me certain that she must have been this year's 'casualty.' I only seem to remember because I witnessed her 'death' that night."

I had decided to try revealing the "truth," up to a point, to Mr. Chibiki at least. As he had been observing the "phenomenon" for many years, I'd thought that perhaps he would understand. That was what I'd decided.

Mei had told me that I didn't have to do anything, but of course there was no way I could let it go without trying something. If Mr. Chibiki wouldn't listen to me at all, then I would figure something else out. I could try a different plan, or I could give up and do nothing.

"So…," I'd continued. "So the 'extra person,' the 'casualty,' has disappeared from this world, and everyone's memories have gone back to how they were before the changes—which means that this year's 'calamity' is now over, right? That's what I think. Just like three years ago." That was probably the first time I'd ever spoken so directly and forcefully to a grown adult.

"Three years ago?" Mr. Chibiki had grumbled, then held his tongue. He'd placed a finger on the dark-green frame of his glasses and squeezed his eyes shut tight behind the lenses, keeping them closed for a little while…then finally—

"I remember hearing a similar story three years ago, too," Mr. Chibiki had said, opening his eyes abruptly.

"That year, over summer break…yes, that year, I heard something from Sakakibara, who I believe you know."

"Ah…"

"Back then, he also said that he thought the 'extra person' for that year had disappeared. You know about the incident that took place on the class trip that summer, right? About the murders, and the fire…and the theory that the 'extra person' also died in the uproar? We suspected that was why the 'calamity' stopped."

"What about the identity of the 'extra person'?"

"That's..." Mr. Chibiki had faltered, placed a hand on his forehead, and let out a troubled sigh. "I don't think I ever heard from Sakakibara, but...no, these memories are probably not reliable anymore. Regardless of whether he ever told me or not, I don't remember now. The 'phenomenon' can do that sort of thing, you see."

"Sure."

I knew all about that.

"Therefore, I think there's value in listening carefully to the story you just told me." Mr. Chibiki had taken his hand off his forehead and sat up straight. "As far as I can tell, you're very calm. I don't think you would be able to speak that way if you had merely had some delusion."

"Right."

"Three years ago, as Sakakibara said, the 'accidents' stopped after the disaster on the school trip. From September on, there wasn't a single victim... I hope that is the case this year as well."

"I'm sure that everything is okay now."

Mr. Chibiki had held his tongue again. Then, after a while, he'd finally nodded. "Hmm. All right."

"So..."

"For now, I'll take this to Ms. Kanbayashi and consult with her. We'll have to see what she says, but we might be able to tell your class that the 'calamity' is over..."

However, after that—

Before Ms. Kanbayashi could deliver her judgment, a rumor had started spreading among the students in the class that the "calamity" was already over. There were too many desks in the classroom (since Izumi Akazawa's disappearance). As soon as someone had noticed the discrepancy, people had started speculating that the "extra person" was no longer with us...

During the latter half of that week, we had finished the end-of-semester exams without any trouble (my scores were terrible, no surprise there...). Finally, after the weekend, during Monday morning's homeroom, Ms. Kanbayashi had made her announcement to the entire class.

It was possible, she'd said, that the "phenomenon" for the 2001 school year was already over in July. If that was the case, then we didn't need to worry about any new "accidents."

7

By the way...
A lot had happened over the past few weeks, but one thing in particular stuck out, and I couldn't get it out of my head. Again and again, I kept ruminating on my visit to Mei's house the night before my grandfather's wake, how she'd suddenly interrupted my conversation with Kirika, practically forcing us apart.

Afterward, at Mei's urging, the two of us had gone straight to the elevator at the back of the room and taken it down to the showroom in the basement.

"Thanks for playing along. I'm sorry to do something like that so suddenly," Mei had apologized. Then she'd lowered her voice to a whisper. "You saw her at the hospital?" she'd asked, referring to my exchange with Kirika upstairs. "My mother...Kirika. When did you see her?"

"Uh, it was..." I'd hastily searched my memory. "It was on my way home from counseling...I think around the middle of April. We crossed paths in the entry hall of the hospital. The next time was at the bus stop in front of the hospital. And then again at the end of last month, right before I ran into you and we went up to the roof of the hospital ward."

"You just saw her, right? You didn't speak to her?"

"Right. She didn't seem to notice me. But...that's why I thought she might be unwell, receiving treatment at the hospital."

"...I see."

Mei had moved quietly through the cellar-like basement, then stopped in front of the beautiful, conjoined twin dolls, the ones that had been there forever, and turned to look at me.

"Sou, *the person you saw was not Kirika.*"

"Huh? But I was certain..."

"I'm sure that she probably looked similar, but it was a different person." Mei had lowered her voice even more as she continued. "That person is..."

It had not occurred to me before that very moment that the woman I'd seen at the hospital might not have been Kirika but someone who looked a lot like her.

I'd recalled another day in the previous month—June 9.

That afternoon, Mei had suddenly shown up at my apartment in the Freuden Tobii. While she was there, I don't know how we got on the subject, but she had told me her "life story" for the first time...

She'd told me that Kirika, or Yukiyo Misaki, was not her real mother, and that Yukiyo had a fraternal twin sister, Mitsuyo Fujioka, who had been the one to give birth to Mei. Something had happened, and Mei had been taken into the Misaki family as an adopted daughter when she was still very young...

"So the person I saw wasn't Kirika; it was...Mitsuyo?"

Even though they were fraternal twins, their faces looked so alike that they were practically identical. Unusual, but not impossible.

Mei had nodded slightly and glanced at the conjoined twin dolls...then, almost in a whisper, she had said to me, "Mitsuyo got divorced two years ago, then remarried... That's what I was told. Then, around the end of last year, she moved here, even though she had always lived far outside the city. That's one of the reasons she's been contacting me directly since early this past spring..."

At that point, I had recalled the ringtone on Mei's cell phone. I'd never heard her phone ring before that spring, but since then, I'd heard it at least twice.

When I thought back on it, the first time had been when I'd gone to her house in April.

A tune different from the music flowing through the gallery had suddenly played...and when it did, Mei had acted uncharacteristically flustered. She had left the table and stepped outside the building. At the time, I had been a little surprised that Mei, who had never hesitated to call cell phones *"awful devices,"* had gone out of her way to set a ringtone on hers, but maybe that call had been from Mitsuyo?

The second time had been at the start of May, on the last day of Golden Week.

I'd encountered Hazumi near the Yomiyama River, and we had talked about various things. As we'd crossed the Izana Bridge, Mei had happened to be there, on the path on the opposite bank. She had gotten a call then, too, accompanied by the same melody, and when she'd answered it, I had overheard her disjointed responses. *"I'm... But...yes. All right... Huh? Sure, okay... I haven't said anything, relax."* I recalled being curious about who she was talking to.

That call was probably from Mitsuyo, too...

"...She calls me, so we've been talking, and soon we're going to start seeing each other sometimes. But it's an absolute secret from Kirika. If she knew, she would succumb to anxiety again and get very angry, and probably very sad."

After she had finished talking, Mei had sighed very deeply.

She obviously didn't want to upset Kirika or make her sad. But she couldn't refuse contact with her birth mother, and she didn't want to. Mei had been in this situation, pulled in two directions, for several months.

"So then your mother...Mitsuyo, she must be unwell in some way, and that's why she's going to the hospital?" It had felt like my heart was being pulled in two directions. "That day when we went up to the roof and talked, before I ran into you, were you there to see Mitsuyo?"

Mei hadn't answered any of my questions. For a second, her lips had moved as if she was going to talk, but she'd quickly stopped and sighed again.

"Listen, Sou," she had said, "don't say anything about this to anyone for now. I'm still figuring everything out, so...so..."

Mei had trailed off and stared down at the floor, as if she'd lost track of the words that were supposed to come next.

"It's all right," I had answered with a firm nod. "I won't tell anyone. I'll definitely keep it a secret."

Plenty of other questions weighed on my mind at the time, but I hadn't felt like asking them right then. I'd figured that we could talk about them when Mei wanted to. And if she didn't want to talk, I didn't want to hear, either. My feelings toward her in that regard had always been the same.

8

"What's wrong, Sou?"

Yagisawa's voice snapped me back to the present, out of my reminiscing. It couldn't have actually been that long, but to Yagisawa, I'm sure that I must have looked like my mind was elsewhere.

"Ah, sorry," I said, using my spoon to stir the totally melted ice cream in my uneaten "special parfait."

"I just sort of zoned out."

"Worn out from the move?"

"No… Well, yeah, probably."

I put the spoon down, let out a long sigh, and rested my chin in my hand, without really knowing why. Even though the air conditioner was running and the windows were closed, I could still hear the constant crying of cicadas in the garden.

"That reminds me." Yagisawa opened his fanny pack and pulled a folded wallet out from inside. "I've got this thing."

Then he showed me an advance ticket for *Jurassic Park III*, which was first going to open to the public in August—

"I don't remember buying this ticket."

"Ah, in that case…," I responded and searched through the same bag that I had stored the mini album in earlier.

I think it was in one of the inner pockets…

"…Got it!" I pulled *it* out and showed it to Yagisawa. "I've got the same thing!"

"Huh?" He stuck his lip out, looking puzzled or maybe a little disconcerted. "Did I promise to go see it with you or something?"

"You don't remember—do you, Yagisawa?"

Even though I was aware that this was the way it should be and that there was no need to be surprised or upset about it at this point,

I still felt a pain in my chest, as if my heart was being slowly but steadily crushed.

"You did make a promise," I said, looking down at the crumpled *Jurassic Park III* advance ticket sitting on my palm. "But it wasn't just you and me. We were all going to go together over summer break. That's what she said..."

9

I would go on to hear the piano playing "Moonlight Sonata" several more times after the night I spoke with Souta—two or three times in the elevator on the fifth floor, which was close to <E-1>, and even once in my own apartment, which was on the same floor. Every time, I would tell myself that it was only my imagination and shake my head, and the sound would quickly disappear.

No doubt it was all an illusion. First of all, the room in <E-1> where the piano sat was soundproofed, so the music shouldn't have been able to escape.

So why do I keep hearing that song, even though I know it's not possible? I had wondered. *Is it because, on some unconscious level, my mind is trying to reject the fact that Izumi is gone from this world? Is it because I wish that she still existed?*

I'd been reminded of my bizarre experience during summer three years prior at Lakeshore Manor, and it had filled me with anxiety and fear, as well as a great sadness. It had felt like there was a possibility that I was becoming obsessed with *someone who was no longer around...*

So I had begun to think that I shouldn't stay *there* any longer. Like I'd better get out of that apartment building as quickly as possible, or else...

I had pushed the issue with Auntie Sayuri and the others, and a week prior, we had settled on my moving back as soon as the summer break began. And then, one night, I'd been on my way back to my apartment from the Akazawa main house when—

I saw it just as I entered the building lobby. Standing on the other side of the open elevator doors—a pale figure.

It was someone wearing a white raincoat (even though it wasn't raining outside). Their head was deep in the hood, and I couldn't make out their face, but I promptly murmured, "Izumi?"

She had also been wearing a white raincoat on the night of the 5th, and my memory of her seemed to overlay onto the figure before me.

Astonished, I ran up to the elevator, but the doors closed immediately, and the elevator began to move...then it finally stopped. It stopped on the fifth floor.

As I pressed the call button, I closed my eyes and shook my head.

I mumbled Izumi's name without thinking, but of course there was no way that it could have been her. What I had seen just then had to be someone else wearing a white raincoat—that, or a complete figment of my imagination...a type of hallucination perhaps.

There's no such thing as ghosts. They can't exist.

That had been my unshakable conviction ever since that bizarre experience three years ago. To say nothing of the fact that the "Izumi Akazawa" who had *died* the night of the 5th had already been *dead* to begin with. The idea that she could appear as a ghost after we had returned the "casualty" to "death"...there was just no way.

It can't be; it can't be..., I repeated to myself, breathing hard. *I've got to get a hold of myself.*

I waited for the elevator cage to come back, then rode up to the fifth floor. When I stepped out into the elevator lobby, I nervously looked around. The pale figure from before was nowhere to be seen, and I felt a moment of relief. However, just then—

The sound of a piano.

I heard it coming faintly from unit <E-1>, where no one was living.

Ah, again?

I sighed.

I can't take it anymore. I can't do this...

Growing steadily more anxious, I shook my head hard. That had always made the sound go away before.

But it didn't go away, not that time.

I kept shaking my head, again and again, but the sound didn't disappear. I could still hear it, coming from <E-1>.

The tune the piano was playing was a different one than the times before. It wasn't the "Moonlight Sonata." Instead, it was some other dreary melody that I didn't recognize...

Though I was very confused, I approached the door of unit <E-1>. Without a doubt, the sound of the piano was audible from inside that apartment. I held my breath and put my hand on the doorknob.

The knob turned, and the door opened.

It's not locked. Someone is inside this apartment right now. They're in the piano room, actually playing the piano.

"Izumi...," I mumbled unconsciously, "...no way."

It can't be—going against my better judgment, I slowly and quietly stepped into the room.

Contrary to whatever vague expectations I held, it was bright inside. The lights in the living room were on.

Which means...?

At a glance, the room looked just as it had on the evening of the 5th, when I'd come to borrow the class photo. But there was something in the air, an indescribable sense of desolation.

Everything was neatly put away, so the place wasn't a wreck or anything, but something about it was definitely different. Despite the season, the air felt chilly and stagnant, like the bottom of a well. It might have been my imagination, but the color of everything in the apartment—from the rug spread on the floor, to the blinds on the windows, to the display shelf with the glass door—everything seemed more faded than before. This could also have been my imagination, but for some reason, I thought I detected a faint moldy smell, too...

...The piano performance continued.

I noticed that the door to the piano room was standing ajar. That explained how the sound was getting out.

Then, suddenly, the music ceased, and a voice came from the other side of the door.

"Who's there?"

It was a voice I knew.

"Is someone in here?"

Though I had boldly made it as far as the living room, I'd suddenly found myself paralyzed, frozen on the spot. The person at the piano had clearly noticed me.

Before I was able to manage a response, the piano room door had opened. Auntie Mayuko had looked at me with wide-eyed surprise.

"Well! What's wrong, Sou?"

"Ah, um...I..." As bewildered as I was by this unexpected development, I had answered with the approximate truth. "I was curious about the sound of the piano...so, and the door was open, so I just came on in... Um, I'm sorry."

"Ah...of course, I understand your concern. I think I told you that this is the room Izumi used to use, didn't I, Sou?"

I actually had never heard that from Mayuko, but I had stayed quiet and nodded. I'd understood immediately that this was one of her memories that had been overwritten with the disappearance of "Izumi Akazawa."

10

"Your grandfather died in that accident, and then Souta came home for the first time in three years. I just couldn't stop thinking about Izumi..."

After I'd discovered her, Mayuko had come out into the living area, pulled out a chair at the dining table, and sat down wearily.

"...I came in here for the first time in so long, and when I saw the piano in that room, I suddenly wanted to play it. Three years have already gone by, but somehow it feels like she was in here just yesterday..."

"Does it?" I'd answered as I sat in the chair facing Mayuko. I had just realized that she was holding a handkerchief in her left hand. I'd also noticed what looked like tear streaks running from her eyes down her cheeks.

"That piano is horribly out of tune; it must have sounded awful," Mayuko had said. "And there's one key that doesn't even play. It's been neglected all this time, so... It's such a waste, isn't it? Poor piano."

"Poor piano."

I'd heard the same words from Izumi the previous month.

"I'll have to ask Mama about it."

But in the end, she'd never gotten to make that request...

Mayuko sat for some time with her mouth closed and her eyes cast downward. Eventually, I'd asked her, "...Um, Izumi...she passed away on a school trip during summer break three years ago—is that right?"

Mayuko had nodded slightly but with no hesitation. I'd been able to tell that her memory of the "summer trip," which had previously been obscured by the "phenomenon," had completely come back to her.

"You know, at school that year, there was nothing but trouble. It seemed like there was something going on with her class, but no matter how I asked, she always told me it was nothing..."

So three years ago, Izumi obeyed the "rules" to the very end. She didn't even confide in her own mother about the "phenomenon" and the "accidents," huh?

"There have been a series of disastrous incidents at school this year, too, haven't there? A friend of yours passed away, too, right, Sou?"

"Yes."

"Is everything all right? Maybe something is going on, like three years ago...?"

Under Mayuko's concerned gaze, I'd answered flatly, "Everything's fine."

Everything is fine now anyway—I'd added in my mind. But I hadn't said it out loud.

"I certainly hope so." Mayuko had put on a stiff smile and used her fingers as a comb to tidy her slightly disheveled hair (the gray hairs were conspicuous for her age).

Slowly, she'd looked around the room. "It was a shock when she died so suddenly. We kept her apartment like this, but...but you know, I think it's time to stop."

"Huh?"

"I had the thought earlier when I was playing the piano by myself. It's not healthy. No matter how long I drag it out like this, she's not coming back to life."

I hadn't been able to find the appropriate words, so I had also looked around the room. The velociraptor that Izumi had said she liked had been sitting among the dinosaur figurines in the display case, and for some reason, it had looked just like it was scowling at me.

"You can come and visit anytime, Sou, even after you move back to the house," Mayuko had said, suddenly changing her tone of voice.

"As long as I won't be a nuisance," I'd answered.

Then Mayuko had smiled more naturally and pushed away from the table. "Souta also told me to loan his books out to you, as many as you like."

"Ah, all right."

"You two just met for the first time the other day, but he really seems to have taken a liking to you, Sou. So that's why."

"Well, okay, I won't hold back…"

After that, I had followed Mayuko as she moved to leave <E-1>, but as we were going—

I'd spotted something on the built-in counter between the kitchen and the living room—something that had been casually dropped beside the coffee.

An advance ticket for *Jurassic Park III*—one of the ones Izumi had purchased after saying we should all go see it over summer break. Her ticket had been sitting there…

Without thinking, I had picked it up and stealthily stuffed it into my pants pocket.

11

I placed my wrinkled ticket on the table and started digging through the same bag again, mumbling, "And I think…"

"What is it? You've got something else?" Yagisawa leaned forward.

"Yeah. I think I put it in here yesterday, but... There it is. I've got this."

I pulled out something from in between the various notebooks stuffed haphazardly into my bag. It was the third advance ticket, which I had put into a clear folder.

"I found it left behind in her room. I took it with me."

I removed the ticket and lined it up next to the one I had just put down.

"Whoa." Yagisawa nodded and set his ticket down in front of the other two.

"We really did make that promise, huh? I don't remember it at all... Geez." He made a fist with his right hand and rapped it against his own forehead. "We were pretty good friends, huh?"

"Pretty good, yeah," I answered as smoothly as possible. "You and her were, yeah, you seemed to get along really well."

"You don't say. Hmm, but I don't remember her. It's so irritating!"

"There's no helping it. That's what the 'phenomenon' does."

"Mm, but still..."

After Tsugunaga had died in May, Izumi had served as the female class representative. The male rep was Yagisawa, so the two of them had that in common, too.

By the way, in the present, where "Izumi Akazawa" didn't exist, a different girl had been chosen to be the class rep after Tsugunaga's death (a girl named Fukuchi, who had been a friend of Tsugunaga's)... That was a "fact" that had been overwritten. The same thing had happened with the countermeasures officers—an overwrite had occurred so that this year's officers had been Etou and Tajimi from the start.

"The premiere is August fourth, huh?" Yagisawa said, gazing at the three tickets lined up on the table. "Want to go see it together?"

"Yeah, let's do it."

"We've got three tickets, so should we invite a third person?"

"Mm, that would be all right, too, but..."

Who would we invite?

No sooner had I thought of the question than Mei popped into my mind. *But even if I explained the situation to her, would she be interested in this kind of movie? And even if she did show interest, would she want to accompany two middle school boys? Who knows?*

"Well then." Yagisawa glanced at his watch and stood up from his chair. "I'd better get going."

"Isn't it a little early yet?"

"Well actually, it's my youngest brother's birthday today, and we're all having cake together, so my mom insisted that I come home early."

I almost burst into laughter when I saw Yagisawa's extremely serious face as he told me that. *No matter what he might say, this guy loves his family*—I thought, feeling both jealous and heartsick.

"Anyway, it's summer vacation," Yagisawa said as he stood up and stretched with a groan. "I am concerned about high school entrance exams, but that's way down the road. It's our last summer vacation in middle school, and I plan to live it up."

There's the self-proclaimed "optimist" we all know...

"Have you got anything planned for the summer, Sou?"

"Like what?"

"I dunno, travel or something."

"Not really. I'll probably spend it cleaning my room and reading books."

"You never change." Yagisawa scratched his head with its long, stiff hair. "Well, let me know if you suddenly decide you want to form a band or something. You can start out on the triangle or the handbells, so..."

...And so on.

We kept chatting about nothing important for a little while after that, but when the talking stopped, a strange silence suddenly settled over us. I was sure Yagisawa had said that he had to get going, but he stopped short of moving to pick up his ticket from the table. When I noticed the way he was acting, it made me a little nervous.

I think the silence lasted three or four seconds. Then Yagisawa broke it. "Hey, Sou?" The tone of his voice was different than before. "I know I shouldn't be asking you something like this here, but do you suppose this year's 'calamity' is really, truly over?"

"Are you worried?" I asked him back.

"No." Yagisawa frowned. "It's not…worry; it's like it doesn't feel like reality."

"Reality, huh?"

"You have it, don't you, some sense that it's all real?"

"I do."

"That's why I asked—to check. The 'accidents' have really stopped, right? Everything's okay now?"

When he repeated his question, I threw the same question at myself again…and then I nodded. "Yes. It's okay. In theory."

"This whole 'phenomenon' and 'calamity' thing is completely absurd to begin with, but…does that pass muster, your 'theory'?"

It wasn't like Yagisawa to be so insistent. He wasn't giving me any room to maneuver.

I summoned all my strength and answered him. "It passes."

This year's "phenomenon" is over, and the "accidents" have stopped. Everything's all right now. We don't need to fear anything anymore. That's a fact. If not, then returning Izumi to "death" that night didn't mean anything.

Chapter 13
August

1

The remaining days of July passed without incident.

Although, for me personally, it wasn't entirely *without incident*. Two days after I finished moving, I suddenly came down with a high fever and sadly ended up confined to my bed.

Auntie Sayuri was concerned enough to take me to the neighborhood clinic, but the diagnosis was an ordinary summer cold. I was told to take in plenty of fluids and to rest quietly, and I would soon recover. If this had happened before the end of the "calamity," I'm sure I would have been terrified, no matter how confident the doctor seemed.

One way or another, it was August before I had completely recovered my health. After I got better, the rest of my summer vacation days were rather tranquil.

There had been two messages from Mei while I was laid up.

The first was a call to my cell phone. I had been knocked out by fever, so I didn't notice her call and didn't pick up. She hadn't left a message.

Once I was finally able to get up, I looked at my call history, and I thought about calling her back. While I was debating it, I booted up my PC and saw that there was an e-mail waiting for me. It was dated July 30. It had been sent after the call to my cell phone.

> Sou,
> I heard you're in bed with a cold?
> Don't push yourself—take your time and rest.

That was what the e-mail said.

When she couldn't get through on my cell phone, she had probably called the house phone and heard about my condition from Auntie Sayuri.

There was another e-mail, with the following report.

> Just like every year, i'm going to the vacation house in Hinami for a while. I'm leaving tomorrow.
> I don't really feel like going, but it would probably cause a lot of trouble if i tried to back out now...
> I might see Tsukiho while i'm there.
> But i won't tell her anything she doesn't need to know, so it's all right. Don't worry.

2

By early August, I had moved back into my normal room and mostly finished sorting my things. Then I started leading the life I had told Yagisawa I would, a life of reading.

Whenever I ran out of books, I would, as was my habit, make my way to the public library at Daybreak Forest. I thought I would wait awhile before taking advantage of Souta's offer to borrow books from his room at the Freuden Tobii.

It was around this time that I fell into a regular schedule, something that hadn't been possible through July. I woke up early, and after finishing breakfast, I went to the bank of the Yomiyama River and spent several hours there. I resumed this habit, which I hadn't really enjoyed since the incident with Shunsuke in June.

It was the height of summer.

Even in the early morning, the sunlight was strong and hot, but when I went out by the river, the breeze was somewhat cool. The row of cherry trees standing on the opposite bank was thickly covered in deep-green leaves, and the weeds underfoot were growing wild and tall. The cicadas and other bugs were chirping with enough energy to drown out the sound of the flowing river.

I sat down for a moment on a bench by the river and noticed a kingfisher hovering there.

I haven't seen one of those since the time I was here with Hazumi in mid-April... No, that's not right. I'm pretty sure I caught sight of one on the morning Shunsuke died, too.

Instinctively, I formed my imaginary viewfinder with my fingers and captured the bird's lovely movements. The fact that I was able to take such a spontaneous action made me realize that I might be working my way back to some sense of normalcy.

There was no longer any need to fear the "accidents" or to think about the "countermeasures." And of course, there was also no need for me to run away from this town, like Teruya did before me. I knew that I was supposed to be safe now, but something still felt strange somehow. What's more, from time to time, sudden pangs of loneliness would grip me whenever I remembered the face, the voice, the little gestures of the "Izumi Akazawa" who was no more. My heart would throb with a dull pain every time I thought of her.

Since leaving the Freuden Tobii, I hadn't heard the piano playing or seen any phantoms. So I figured I was fine. Something like what happened three years ago wasn't going to happen now. However, sometimes I did think back on it, of course, even though it was almost unbearable to remember.

I wonder how long it will be before these memories disappear? How long before I forget, like everyone else, the truth that she existed in this world for three months, starting in April? I wonder if I'm allowed to forget...

I also had moments when I thought about Mei being in Hinami.

I mentally overlaid the deadly still lake surface of Lake Minazuki onto the surface of the gently flowing Yomiyama River and imagined I could hear a low, distant rumbling out over the water.

"It probably can't happen for a little while yet, but..."

As I gazed at the river, these words that Mei had said to me at some point came back to me.

"How about we go to Lakeshore Manor together again sometime? Of course, we'd keep it a secret from everybody—it would just be the two of us. How about it?"

As Mei said, something like that would be impossible for a while yet. But if we were going *sometime*, then I could believe that the time would come, eventually, even if I couldn't imagine when that might be...

If it was like a normal year, Mei would be coming back from the vacation home before Obon—probably around August 10. I decided to find a good time to get in touch with her then. And to boldly invite her to go see *Jurassic Park III*.

3

It was just before noon on Wednesday, August 8.

For the first time in a while, I went to the "clinic" in the annex building of the municipal hospital and met with Dr. Usui.

"Ah, Sou, you look well."

It meant a lot to hear him say that today, as I sat across from him in the examination room. As far as I could remember, this was the first time he'd greeted me that way.

"I was worried about you when I heard that your grandfather passed away last month; have you been all right? You weren't terribly agitated again by the death of someone close to you?"

"Ah, right, it was a shock, but...but yeah, I'm all right."

I didn't hesitate to answer that way. I had been sleeping without trouble at night and having fewer nightmares. My health had also been good, once I'd recovered from that summer cold.

"And you still haven't seen your mother—is that right?"

"That's… Yes."

"Do you speak on the phone?"

"Well, sometimes," I answered in a deliberately quiet voice. It was unclear whether the doctor saw through my falsehood, but he nodded approvingly and blinked his small eyes.

"I'm glad to see you looking well. But don't push yourself too hard—don't try to force yourself to put on a good face. Tough times are tough. Sad times are sad. Scary times are scary. You maintain a healthy mental balance by feeling these things honestly and recognizing and accepting them for what they are. Do you understand?"

"Yes."

The weather this morning had been clear and summery, but as I arrived at the hospital, some suspicious clouds had been quickly spreading across the sky. By the time I was finished with my counseling and left the exam room, it had started to rain. The rain was strong enough that I winced and let out a reflexive, "Whoa!"

I moved through the connecting passage into the main building and headed for the hospital lobby. In the time it took me to get there, the rain grew more and more intense, and the sound of it could be heard reverberating through the building. I looked outside every time I passed a window, and the view was dark like dusk even though it was the middle of the day.

I didn't have an umbrella with me. Thinking I would stay put until it slowed to a light rain, I joined the line of people waiting at the cashier's window.

Just then, something caught my attention.

A pale figure, loitering inconspicuously in a section of the spacious lobby.

It was someone wearing a girls' summer uniform for North Yomi… *But who?*

She was quite far away, and there were many people coming and going between us. But I strained my eyes to look at "her" face.

"Ah!" I unconsciously made a noise.

It's her—it's Izumi's face.

That's impossible!

I shut my eyes in a panic, denying what I had seen. After keeping them closed for a moment, I warily took another look. But the pale figure was still there. I could see her face. It really was her—it was Izumi's face. A very white, blank face.

Impossible. Of course, this is just my imagination. It's some kind of hallucination or illusion.

I tried very hard to convince myself that that was true, but even so, she did not disappear from that spot. I couldn't pull my eyes away; it was like I was entranced.

Finally, her lips moved slightly. I felt like I could hear her voice right by my ear, despite the distance between us. I thought I heard her call my name, *So-ouu...*

It was definitely her voice—Izumi's.

I felt like I was losing my mind. Like I'd been pulled into some alternate dimension.

All other sounds around me were drowned out by static, like a radio that has gone out of tune. The figures of the other people in the lobby and their movements lost their sense of reality, as if they had fallen back behind a kind of translucent wall.

As this was happening—

Her silhouette moved nimbly. Without a moment's delay, I made to follow her.

After that, I can remember only scattered fragments, bits and pieces of what happened. Like trying to think back on the events of a dream after waking.

I remember leaving the lobby and jumping into the elevator. I saw her get in it, and I followed, slipping between the closing doors. However, when I got inside, there was no one there but me.

So-ouu...

Even so, the button for the destination was illuminated.

<B-2>.

The elevator cage arrived at the second basement level, and I hesitantly stepped out.

Long corridors stretched off in three directions...

So-ouu...

I thought I heard my name being called and set off down the corridor on my left. Several meters ahead of me, her hazy white figure appeared. When it did, all the lights lining the ceiling abruptly began to flicker. I followed her. But shortly thereafter, burnout followed the flickering, and the figure melted away in the descending darkness. I lost sight of her whereabouts, and as I was puzzling over which direction to go, the figure reappeared, several meters ahead of me. I followed again. But I lost sight of her a second time... It seemed like the cycle would keep repeating forever.

I think I climbed several flights of stairs as I was walking around, and I remember the corridor making many twists and turns along the way. I'm pretty sure I also went down some stairs and that the corridor had sections that sloped gently up or down.

It was like I had wandered into a huge, eerie labyrinth in the spirit world.

Following the figure had gotten me completely lost. I had no idea where in the hospital I might be. Honestly, I was gradually losing confidence that *this place* I was wandering around was even still inside Yumigaoka Hospital...

....

....

I suddenly came back to my senses when my eyes were dazzled by an unexpected flash of bright light.

Out the window—the true identity of the flash was a bolt of lightning, streaking across the dark sky. I correctly recognized that the noise made by the driving rain was not meaningless static but just the normal sound of rain. I also realized that I was standing in a gloomy hallway somewhere inside the hospital.

There was a pale figure, several meters ahead of me.

So-ouu...

Sure enough, there she was, wearing a girls' summer uniform for North Yomi.

Izumi...

"Huh?" She sounded surprised as she turned to face me. "Hiratsuka...?"

Huh? ...Ah, I was wrong. That's not Izumi.

She's not Izumi. She's taller than Izumi, and her hair is cut short. And she's holding a little bouquet. This is...

"Etou...?"

She's Etou, one of the countermeasures officers for Grade 3 Class 3. The girl who originally suggested having two "non-existers" for our "countermeasures" this year...

"Ah...um, hello?" I greeted her idiotically.

"Ah, um, uh..."

Why is Etou here?

I tilted my head to the side in confusion, and I felt as if I had just been released by whatever spirit had been haunting me. I looked around at my surroundings again, trying to get a grip on the situation.

I was somewhere inside Yumigaoka Municipal Hospital. Probably rather far from the lobby of the hospital's office building. From what it looked like outside the window, I was probably on the third or fourth floor above ground level.

"Nnh...," I groaned, and Etou tilted her head, too. And then, blinking her eyes with their large pupils, she asked, "*You too*, Sou?"

I didn't understand the meaning of her question. "Huh?" I tilted my head again. "I had a checkup scheduled with my doctor today."

"Oh, is that so? But..."

"What about you, Etou? Why are you in the hospital?" I asked her in return.

She indicated the bouquet she was holding. "I'm here to visit someone."

"A visit..."

"She was in the hospital ward in the main building before, but they told me she switched rooms. The layout of this place is kind of confusing, so I got pretty lost before I finally found it."

I see—it was at this point that I finally realized something. If Etou the countermeasures officer was going to visit someone, it would have to be...

Etou was currently standing in front of an unassuming cream-colored door. The room on the other side must have been her destination. I approached the door and checked the name on the nameplate beside it.

"Makise... So she's still in the hospital, huh?"

"Makise and I have been friends since she transferred to our school around the end of last year," Etou told me, lowering her voice somewhat. "Her body has always been weak, but she's a really nice girl. I mean, just look at how she accepted 'not existing,' since she was going to be hospitalized anyway. You must have thought so back then, too."

Back then, huh? Back at the "strategy session" in March...

"Since you took the trouble to come here, do you want to visit her with me, Hiratsuka?"

"Ah...would that be all right? Out of the blue."

"She said she's been feeling good lately. I'll go ask real quick, okay?"

Etou said that, knocked on the door to the hospital room and announced herself, then went in alone first.

A minute passed.

"Come on in." I heard a voice from inside the room. A girl's voice, but not Etou's.

Right. I'm sure I've heard this voice before; it belongs to that girl I met at the "strategy session" in March...

"Hiratsuka...Sou? I'm so glad you came."

Drawn in by that voice, which had a carefree sense about it, despite its frailty, I entered the room after Etou.

Thud. As I did, the low reverberation came out of nowhere. Simultaneously, the world went black, then went back to normal after just a moment...

....

And then...

And then *I realized, I remembered, I registered...*

I found an answer to a question I didn't know I'd been asking.

4

"Just seeing the dinosaurs move around so freely like that was totally amazing! The Spinosaurus was huge and brutal, and the Pteranodon was flying all over the place... Incredible!"

The look of excitement on Yagisawa's face never faded as he went on about how amazing the movie was.

"It felt a little plain compared to the first two, but...I mean, even so, it was really entertaining. Right, Sou?"

He threw the question to me, and I answered obediently, "Sure was."

"You said you haven't seen the first two?"

"Yeah."

"And that you don't have much interest in dinosaurs?"

"Uh, yeah. Yeah, but, like, the movie was entertaining."

Watching it on the theater's big screen with the surround sound, the dinosaurs were very impressive and looked incredibly realistic, so that I found myself drawn in to the movie despite the simple story. There were even scenes where I found myself literally on the edge of my seat.

It was the afternoon of Monday, August 13.

We had just seen *Jurassic Park III* at the movie theater in Akatsuki. The three of us—Yagisawa and me, plus Mei Misaki, who, contrary to my expectations, had readily accepted my invitation. After the movie, we two middle school boys had taken Mei up on her offer to treat us, and the three of us were in a juice bar near the movie theater.

Outside, the midsummer sun was blazing. It was time for the Obon holidays, and the town was bustling with quite a crowd. Yet, the inside of the shop was strangely empty, offering a moment of calm quiet.

"How about you, Misaki?" Yagisawa asked. He glanced up at Mei's face across the round glass table but then looked away, as if he had panicked when their eyes met. "Um, what I mean is, did you see the first and second movies in the series?"

When he asked this, Mei took her mouth off the straw in her orange juice and answered, "This was my first time seeing a monster movie."

If Yagisawa had been talking to me, he definitely would have come back with something like, *It wasn't a monster movie; it was a dinosaur movie.*

But all he said was, "O-oh, is that so?" and scratched his head.

Mei stoically put her mouth back on her straw.

Watching their exchange, I held back a smile.

"But it really was incredible, right, Sou?" Undeterred, Yagisawa turned to face me. "Those dinosaurs are mostly done with CG now. But in the movie, they look like they're right there in front of you, alive. The current CG technology is amazing. If O'Brien or Eiji Tsuburaya were alive to see it, it would knock 'em off their feet."

"Who's O'Brien?"

"Willis O'Brien. He handled the special effects for the 1933 version of *King Kong*. He was one of the pioneers of stop-motion animation. You know who Eiji Tsuburaya was, right?"

"The *Ultraman* guy?"

"Yeah, him. Before he did *Ultraman*, he worked on the first *Godzilla* in 1954…," Yagisawa told me gleefully. I knew from spending time with him that he liked those sorts of movies and TV shows, but I hadn't realized he was so much of an enthusiast.

"…And while we're on the topic, O'Brien had a real pride in his work and took only a single apprentice, who was the one and only Ray Harryhausen. You probably know his work from *Clash of the Titans*."

"I don't, but—"

"Hmm?"

"But he's pretty famous, right?"

Yagisawa nodded approvingly, then sighed. Pursing his lips as if to say there was no point in talking to me about it any further, he reached for his cream soda.

"I like Švankmajer," Mei said quietly.

Yagisawa abruptly tilted his head to the side, looking worn out. "Mm, who's that?"

"A Czech animator. Jan Švankmajer. You don't know him?"

"No, I mean, just the name."

"How about you, Sou?"

"Uh…"

"I think you might like his work, Sou," she said with a composed smile. "I've got some videos, so I'll loan them to you soon."

Today was Yagisawa and Mei's first time meeting. They had been aware of each other for a while through hearing me talk, and when they met in person like this, each of their reactions was basically what I had expected.

Mei was acting entirely normal. In contrast, Yagisawa had clearly been quite nervous from the moment I introduced him to Mei and he said hello.

While we were waiting in the theater lobby for the previous showing to end, he had occasionally made a bold attempt to talk to Mei, but even though she hadn't looked particularly displeased or anything, she also hadn't smiled. I didn't think she was being particularly unsociable, but to a young man who wasn't used to her, she probably seemed difficult to approach. And yet, how do I put this, that only enhanced the illusion that Mei was one of the "Blue Eyes…" dolls come to life, a fair-skinned beauty far surpassing two middle school chumps.

Yep, just as I expected—inwardly, on the one hand, I felt a little bit of satisfaction, while on the other hand, some part of me wanted to sympathize with Yagisawa.

Mei was dressed that day in a black blouse with a ribbon at the neck and a deep-blue skirt. She had an even more mature aura about her than usual, and even in the bright afternoon sunlight, she somehow gave off the sense of being clad in twilight. To tell the truth, I was also a little bit nervous in her presence.

"You've had a hard time since April, haven't you, Yagisawa?" Mei said after drinking about half of her juice. This was the first time she had brought up the topic that the three of us hadn't touched on yet—hadn't been able to touch on.

"I heard about it from Sou. About how your aunt was in Grade 3 Class 3 at North Yomi a long time ago…"

Yagisawa looked up with a start and replied, "You were, too, three years ago, right? I've also heard everything from Sou."

No, no, not everything—I thought, but I didn't interrupt. Yagisawa continued. "Looks like the 'calamity' stopped this year, just like it did three years ago, so…"

"That's wonderful," Mei said softly, narrowing both eyes. In her left eye, she was wearing the black eyeball with brown flecks. Naturally, since she didn't have the "doll's eye" in today, she wasn't wearing her eye patch, either.

"That's really great."

I could hear the unqualified relief in Mei's voice. I felt the same way she did.

"The two of you are graduating next spring, right? What are you doing for high school?" Mei asked.

Yagisawa answered, "I'm planning to take the exam for First Yomi, the prefectural high school. You too, right, Sou?"

"Ah…yeah. Probably."

Mei said, "I see. So we'll just miss each other, then."

That's right. She's graduating high school next spring, too. I had been curious about her plans after graduation, but I had yet to ask her about it even once.

"There aren't any troubling 'phenomena' at First Yomi, so you can relax about that," Mei added.

Yagisawa pushed his round glasses up as he straightened his posture in his seat and threw out his chest. "Consider me relaxed!" But he immediately dropped his shoulders again. "Though before that, we've got exams, huh? I'm pretty scared," he muttered to himself with a sigh.

"I thought you were living it up over summer break?" I quipped.

Yagisawa threw his head back in an exaggerated gesture and looked up at the ceiling. "Only half of my much-anticipated summer break remains. Oh, the cruel passage of time!"

Mei let a quiet laugh slip out. Yagisawa's cheeks reddened, and he cleared his throat awkwardly.

I gazed out the window.

The figures of the people walking down the street naturally caught my eye. I felt like there were more young people than usual. I also noticed a lot of happy, smiling faces. However—

Before I knew it, I realized I was scanning the crowd of unknown men and women for the phantom of "Izumi Akazawa."

I quickly caught myself. *It's over now—you can forget about her,* I thought. And then—

I shifted my eyes and looked at Mei.

I don't know how she interpreted my behavior, but when she saw me looking at her, she drew her lips in and gave me a small nod.

5

That day's dinosaur film festival broke up before evening set in. However—

"Well, see you later. That was fun," Mei said as she stood to leave.

"Ah, Mei?" I ran next to her and called out to stop her.

"What's up, Sou?"

"Um…there's just something small I'd like to discuss with you…"

I had spoken with Mei once on the phone since she'd returned from her Hinami vacation home—when I'd gotten her to agree to come with us to the movie. But ever since she came back, there had been something I'd wanted to tell her but was hesitant to say over the phone… It was a matter I wanted to discuss not by e-mail or phone but when we were together in person.

"Hmm?" Mei stared at me with eyes that seemed to ask, *Why are you being so formal?* But there was no need to repeat myself. She seemed to understand what I was feeling and quickly nodded. "All right. Will you come to the gallery?"

"Would that be okay?"

"It's fine. All right, see you later, Yagisawa."

"A-ah…sure."

So in that way, we ended up leaving Yagisawa behind. I would have to ask forgiveness from the class representative another day. He gave me a suspicious look as we were splitting up, and I resigned myself to the eventual interrogation about my relationship with Mei.

And then—

In the familiar basement space of the gallery in Misaki, I talked to Mei about *that thing*.

Until then, my stance had been that I wouldn't pry about things that she didn't volunteer, or that she didn't want to talk about, and that I wouldn't want to hear them anyway—I abandoned that now.

But I think that it was the correct decision in the end. We talked, I listened, we compared information…and in doing so, I felt the distance between Mei and me narrowing more than it ever had before. Of course, this should have been a welcome change for me. I mean, honestly, I was very happy that we were growing closer, so…

…………

…………

"…That reminds me," Mei had suddenly said as we were parting with Yagisawa that day. "Yesterday, I got a call from Sakakibara. From America—LA."

"Oh, you did?"

"Apparently, they had all kinds of problems in Mexico. He said he's coming back to Tokyo at the end of this month."

Mei's expression looked somewhat relieved as she told me this—

"Sakakibara was very worried about how this year's 'calamity' turned out, so I explained everything to him."

"Oh, okay."

"He said he would try to give you a call soon."

Koichi Sakakibara. Hmm.

Reminding myself how much I owed him, I gave a small nod.

6

I spent my 2001 summer vacation mostly peacefully.

After Obon, a big typhoon made landfall on Japan for the first time in a long while, but our region didn't suffer any real damage.

For several days, the news made a big deal about a record heat wave, and thanks to the forewarning, nobody got hurt...

From April until "Izumi Akazawa" disappeared at the start of July, it had felt like there was a threatening black cloud hanging over-head, and now it was like it had blown off somewhere. The town of Yomiyama in midsummer was quiet and peaceful. At least, that's how it seemed to me.

After the incident at the municipal hospital, I never saw Izumi's phantom again. And I didn't think I would see it anymore in the future, either.

7

When there were only a few days of vacation remaining in August, the biology club held a meeting at school. All the members were con-vened after a call from our adviser, Mr. Kuramochi. The meeting was not held in the science room in Building T but in *that* clubroom in Building Zero.

The inside of the room had been thoroughly cleaned, and there wasn't a single visible trace of the tragedy that had taken place there two months earlier. Even so, it took all my effort to shake off visions of the scene from that day, which my mind threatened to replay again and again.

"Well then, everyone, let me start with an announcement. Mr. Mori-shita will be assuming the role of the new head of the biology club."

I was a little surprised to hear the first thing that Mr. Kuramochi said. *The guy who could hardly ever come to club meetings because of some situation at home? I think I'm remembering that correctly. That Morishita will be the club head?*

"Um, the thing is, I've had a bit of a change of heart recently."

As if he had anticipated it, Morishita answered my unspoken question.

"Since this is the biology club that Kouda worked so hard for and all, I'd like to try and do everything I can to keep it going."

Morishita was tall and lanky but obviously had sluggish reflexes, and he was smart but not eloquent. He was the kind of guy whose existence you would be liable to forget in a class. But apparently, he and Shunsuke had been close, though their relationship was different than ours had been.

There weren't any particular voices of opposition from the assembled first- and second-years.

"Are you sure about this?" I asked Morishita.

"Yes," he answered. "But I'm anxious about doing it alone, so help me out, okay, Hiratsuka?" He seemed to be trying to convince himself. "Okay, okay."

He turned to the rest of the club. "So then today, I want to ask everyone for their thoughts. I was thinking that as the biology club, surely we need to start by putting the creatures we've been raising back into this room, but…"

Later, I learned that the "situation at home" that had been bothering Morishita involved the breakup of his parents' marriage due to his father's abuse. The divorce had finally been finalized that summer, and Morishita, who despised his father, had gone to live with his mother. He was finally able to put a lot of bad things behind him and had even made plans to change his surname to his mother's maiden name.

Then, when the meeting of the biology club came to a close, I headed for the secondary library alone. Before the meeting, I'd happened to catch sight of Mr. Chibiki going into Building Zero, so I figured he was still there.

There was a CLOSED sign out on the library door, but when I knocked, I got an immediate answer: "Come in." Then, before I could even open the door, there came a question. "Is that Hiratsuka?" Apparently, Mr. Chibiki had also noticed me coming to the school. "Up to something with the biology club?" Even in this season, Mr. Chibiki wore a black shirt and black trousers.

I nodded in response to his question. "Yes. Kind of a kickoff meeting to keep the club going."

"Ah. That's very courageous of you all."

"No, it didn't really feel that way."

"Hmm. Well, you did have an awful time of it back in June. Are you doing all right now? Did you feel unwell or anything when you went into that room?"

"I was fine."

"I see. Very good."

Mr. Chibiki pulled a bottle of mineral water out of the refrigerator behind the counter and handed it to me. "Stay hydrated. There's only a little bit of August left, and thankfully, no 'related individuals' have died. Looks like your theory that the 'calamity' ended in July was correct."

As he spoke, several vertical wrinkles etched across Mr. Chibiki's forehead. He placed one hand on the large reading table and continued. "As a matter of fact, I never doubted your story back in July, but I was also a little hesitant to believe it one hundred percent. This 'phenomenon' has caused me terrible hardship for many years, you know. So I couldn't really allow myself to relax. That was my thinking as I cautiously waited to see, but—"

Mr. Chibiki cut himself off, quietly cleared his throat, then told me, "Now I'm thinking we probably don't need to worry anymore. I'm sure of it."

"Right. I'm sure that's the case."

"If we make it into September like this, it will be proof that the claim you made in July was the truth. Then it will truly be over for this year."

8

After I left the secondary library and exited Building Zero, I walked alone down the path through the courtyard and before long came to a stop in *a certain spot*. The humble grave markers, made by tying scraps of wood into cross shapes, stood in little rows in the weed-choked ground. I paused in front of them.

Time had passed more quickly than I thought, and it was already nearing dusk. The wind was blowing vigorously, keeping things somewhat cooler than in the middle of the day. The evening cicadas were starting to make their shrill cries. Not to be outdone, the summer cicadas were calling, too.

I could hear students' voices from the sports grounds. The sports club members were going about their normal practices, but for some reason, they seemed to belong to a far-off world or some tenuous alternate reality. Their voices overlapped with the cicadas' calls, and suddenly I heard the cries of several crows high up in the sky. These, too, seemed somehow distant and diluted...

...I wonder when was the last time I put up a grave marker in this plot?

Was it when the first-generation Woo passed away in April? Shunsuke immediately diaphanized the striped loach and the Amano shrimp that died during Golden Week.

As for the animals that died in the incident in June, I hadn't had the time or the presence of mind to count them, much less collect and bury their bodies. I decided I would make new crosses for them once the second semester began. Even if we didn't have their remains, at least I could mark their graves here.

And next to their grave markers, I could secretly erect one more cross, much larger than the others. For Shunsuke. And for his twin brother, Keisuke.

As I was turning these ideas over in my head, even more time passed, and the evening glow began to spread across the western sky. It wasn't quite red, more of a vivid scarlet. No sooner had I decided it was scarlet than it morphed into a more concentrated, deeper hue, like dark-red clay... As the shade of the sky changed moment by moment, the sunset was breathtaking. Strangely, not one of the many shades of red reminded me of blood.

Somehow, I felt oddly at ease, and for a short while, I stood there looking up at the illuminated horizon.

Thinking back on it, these past few months have seen a lot of sad events. And lots of frightening events. And also plenty of events that have made me painfully aware, over and over again, of my own power-lessness in the face of the absurdities and unknowable evil of this world. But now it's as if all of that has been swallowed up by the beauty of the sunset coloring the sky...

I stared up at the glowing sky for a little while longer.

I felt somewhat at ease.

But lurking deep in the far reaches of my mind was something like a sense of overwhelming dread. Summer vacation would be over soon.

Chapter 14
September I

1

"The second semester starts today."

Saturday, September 1. After the opening ceremony, our homeroom teacher, Ms. Kanbayashi, stood at the teacher's podium in front of our class.

"This year's 'phenomenon' ended in July, and the 'accidents' have stopped—our predictions seem to have been correct. We made it through summer vacation without a single incident. Not one 'related individual' has died, and a new month has started. This means that we can put all our lingering worries behind us.

"Everyone," she continued, slowly looking around the classroom. Her expression was sunny, and she was even wearing a smile, something we'd rarely seen before. But the emotion behind that smile wasn't exactly happiness. Rather, it seemed to be relief, deep relief from the bottom of her heart. "I hope that the remaining seven months until your graduation can be a meaningful time for all of you and that you can still make many fun memories. As we grieve those we have lost to the 'calamity,' let's all do our best... Let's do it for those who are no longer with us as well."

At present, there were five empty seats in the Grade 3 Class 3 classroom: the seats belonging to Tsugunaga and Keisuke Kouda, who had died; the seat belonging to Makise, who was still in the hospital; the seat belonging to Izumi, who had disappeared when she "returned to death"; and the seat belonging to Hazumi, who was absent even today. The same number as before the break.

"Classes will begin on Monday, following the schedule for second semester, and—" Ms. Kanbayashi looked around the classroom again, then said very deliberately, "And Hazumi, who has taken a long absence since the middle of the first semester, will be coming back to school next week. I met and talked with her the other day and confirmed her intentions."

The air went faintly astir with murmuring.

Several students looked at one another silently. Yagisawa and I did, too.

"You all know what caused Hazumi to stop coming to school, yes? It was that disturbance in our classroom at the beginning of May. But the 'calamity' is over, and things are different now. Once I convinced her to forget about what happened before and return to school, she finally came around."

Listening to our teacher talk, I was honestly glad to hear it. After all, a part of me had been concerned about her this whole time.

"So, everyone, I have a favor to ask you. When Hazumi comes to school, please be decent and treat her as a normal member of your class, just like you did before all this. Okay?"

I exchanged another quick look with Yagisawa, then nodded obediently. After that, I just sort of let my eyes drift out the window on the schoolyard side. The late-summer blue sky stretched out with nary a hint of a cloud.

2

I got a call from Koichi Sakakibara the next day, on the afternoon of Sunday the 2nd.

I knew it was him right away when I looked down at my phone; his name showed up on my display, since I already had his number.

"Sou? It's me. Sakakibara."

And that was definitely his voice. It was clearer, plainer, and easier to understand than when he'd called me from Mexico at the start of July.

"Yes, it's me. Um, are you in Japan already?"

"I just got back last week."

"Um, ah…Mei said that she got a call from you from LA earlier."

"Ah, yeah, yeah," Koichi answered readily. "When I spoke with her, I heard all the details about what happened after our conversation. I heard who the 'extra person' was for this year and what happened to *her*. It must have been hard on you. But, well, it's good."

"Yeah."

"I guess the second semester started yesterday."

"That's right."

"And you made it through August okay?"

"Yes."

"Mm. So there's really no reason to worry anymore. It was the same way three years ago, too."

On the other end of the phone, I heard a sigh. Koichi must have been worried about our situation here all along, even as he dealt with his own problems in a faraway foreign country.

"Must have been hard on you, Sou," he repeated after a while. "Are you doing all right, emotionally?"

I found myself at a loss for words when he asked me this.

"I heard everything from Misaki. I heard you were the one who returned her—returned Izumi Akazawa to 'death.' She was your cousin, right? And you did it with your own hands."

That night, on the bridge, I had tried to push Izumi into the river, but actually, she had gone over right before my hands touched her…

But to Mei, it had certainly looked like I'd done it "with my own hands." And I hadn't made any attempt to clarify anything since it happened.

"Sakakibara?" I replied to him decisively. "Three years ago, you returned the 'casualty' to 'death'—is that right?"

"Yeah, that's right." Koichi's voice lowered slightly.

I continued by asking, "Who was it? And how did you return them to 'death'? You still remember, even now, don't you?"

"Yes, I remember."

"But at some point, those memories will fade and disappear, right?"

"They're supposed to."

"And when will that happen…?"

When will they go away, these memories of mine?

"Who knows?" Koichi mumbled. After a moment, he said, "We don't have any previous examples except for Matsunaga, the guy who left behind that cassette tape. They should fade sooner or later, after a few years…or so I'd thought, but it's probably different for everyone. The events might be gone by next year, or they might stick around. Do you want to forget quickly, Sou?"

"Well…"

"If you do, you won't be able to remember your time with *her*, either. But you'd rather just lose it all in spite of that?"

"How do you feel about it, Sakakibara?" I answered his question with a question.

Koichi mumbled again, "How do I feel…?" Then he answered me with a sigh. "I still don't really know what to make of it."

After that, the two of us were quiet for a while. Just as I was getting a little impatient for one of us to start speaking again—

"Oh, that reminds me," he added abruptly. "There's something that's been kind of weighing on my mind. I've been wondering about it; it's a little strange."

"What's that?"

"It's about my memories of Akazawa, this year's 'extra person.'"

His memories of Izumi? What could that mean?

"So back at the beginning of July, I heard from Misaki about the situation this year, and after that I called you, right? Back then, I told you everything as I remembered it from three years ago, but…there's something mysterious going on."

"Meaning what?"

"I know that 'my memories from three years ago' include some 'memories of Izumi Akazawa, who was in the same class with me that year.' Her name, face, voice, and what happened to her when she died on our class trip—*when you and I spoke, I was able to recall those things normally.* Which would mean, in other words, that up until that point, my recollections hadn't been altered by the 'phenomenon,' right?"

"Ummm, so then..."

"There's a possibility that these very memories that I'm recounting now have been changed, too. But somehow, I don't think that's the case. Because if you had mentioned 'this year's Izumi Akazawa' to me back when we talked, in that moment, my mind would have been altered, and I would have forgotten about the 'Izumi Akazawa of three years ago.'"

"That's...um, and why would you be able to keep your memories?"

"Nobody knows for sure. That's why it's 'mysterious,' but you know, I can think of a few reasons why this happened."

"Like what?" I asked.

Koichi answered, "For example, distance. There's the question of geographic distance from Yomiyama. As you know, the 'accidents' that befall 'related individuals' due to the 'phenomenon' only happen inside Yomiyama city limits. Once you get out of town, you're 'out of range.' The falsification of records and the memory changes also have a 'limit,' so to speak, so if you're in a place as distant as Mexico, for example, that 'power' ought to be weaker, don't you think? Depending on the circumstances, the changes could be incomplete or take longer, right?"

"Uh, sure. But..."

"And if that alone isn't enough to fully explain it, then maybe there's something different about me."

"You're special?"

"In the sense that I'm the person who returned the 'casualty' to 'death' three years ago, yeah. Also, I'm the only one who has the special privilege of remembering that year's 'extra person,' while everyone else immediately forgot about her."

I recalled how Mei had described it at some point, a *"cruel privilege,"* and nodded enthusiastically to the voice on the other end of the line.

"So maybe, when it comes to the whole 'phenomenon' and

'calamity' thing from three years ago, the fact that I still remember who the 'extra person' was means I've been able to hold on to more of my memories than expected."

"I can see the logic in it, more or less."

"But there's no point in discussing what it means or what to do about it anymore, is there? This year's 'calamity' has stopped already..."

"Ah, yeah. That's true."

"At any rate, I'm glad it's over. It's a relief. I'm sure you faced many difficult situations... Mm, you did really well, Sou."

He was thinking of coming to visit Yomiyama for the first time in a while before next spring. When he did, he wanted to get together with Mei and me. That's what Koichi said, and then he hung up.

Still gripping the phone, I let out a series of sighs. I wasn't really sure why. The *shisa* charm I had received from Mei swayed in time with my breaths.

3

Monday, September 3.

As Ms. Kanbayashi had announced, Yuika Hazumi came back to school. However, she didn't appear in the classroom until our first-period math class was about to start—

"Sorry to be late on my first day back," she apologized humbly.

The math teacher, Ms. Inagaki (female, approximate age mid-thirties), answered gently, "It's all right. There's no need to rush; go on and take your seat. Your absence has gone on for a while, so I'm sure there are many things you won't know. Please don't hesitate to ask, either during class or afterward."

Word of her situation must have been carefully shared among the teachers.

"Yes. Thank you," Hazumi answered, as politely as before.

Something's a little different about her, I realized.

Her hair was cut shorter than before. She looked like she had lost some weight. She was acting like she was walking on eggshells.

That's how it seemed to me. I was unsure whether I ought to go and say something, even just a few words, to her after class...

First period ended, and during the break between first and second periods, Hazumi spoke with Shimamura and Kusakabe, her friends from before. Same with the break between second and third periods and the next break as well. The girls seemed to be chatting naturally, with no hard feelings. I even saw her wearing a happy smile, which filled me with a great sense of relief and assuaged my concerns over her behavior. I figured there was no need for me to go talk to her right now, in that case.

With Hazumi's return, the number of empty seats in the classroom decreased by one, leaving four: those belonging to the two deceased students, the one for the hospitalized Makise, and Izumi's seat. I thought it would probably be a good idea to remove the desk and chair that had been Izumi's and decided to suggest it to the two countermeasures officers soon.

Etou, one of those countermeasures officers, came up to talk to me during lunch.

"Makise seemed to be very happy that you went to visit her the other day."

I didn't know what to feel when she told me that—

"Have you been to see her again since then?" I asked.

"The following week and once the week after that," Etou answered. "There was talk that she might be able to leave the hospital in the fall, but...well, apparently she took another turn for the worse."

"Is that so?"

"As things are, she's going to end up repeating the year... She's going to be held back, but she said there's no helping it. She really has become quite weak... She looked so pitiful."

Etou narrowed her big, dark eyes sadly and hung her head.

I couldn't stand it. "It'll be all right," I declared, without any solid basis for it. "Makise is definitely going to get better."

"I wonder... She will, right?"

"I'll go with you again to see her."

"Okay... Thanks."

*   *   *

The "phenomenon" was over, the "accidents" had stopped, and Hazumi, who had gotten hurt because she had taken on the role of a "non-exister" for the sake of the original "countermeasures," had even returned to school without incident...

Everything in the Grade 3 Class 3 classroom on September 3 seemed perfectly ordinary, probably for the first time since class had started in April. There was a tranquility hanging in the air, a peaceful, cheerful atmosphere that had never been there before. But in the midst of it—

Like a blot of pitch-black paint spreading over the corner of a fresh new sheet of paper, one thing threatened to ruin the pleasant scene.

Ms. Kanbayashi had not come to school that day.

In her place, the social studies teacher, Mr. Tsubouchi (male, approximate age late forties), had led the morning's homeroom. And he had informed us of the following in a businesslike tone:

"Ms. Kanbayashi is absent today. Apparently, she's feeling unwell... She's probably caught a cold or something. I think your fourth-period science class is going to be a study hall, but I'll get back to you with specific instructions later."

4

Tuesday, September 4.

Ms. Kanbayashi was absent again.

When Mr. Tsubouchi appeared during morning homeroom just like he had the day before, I was a little surprised, and I started to feel kind of uncomfortable. However, at that point, I think it was nothing more than a distant feeling of vague anxiety.

"Ms. Kanbayashi seems to still be unwell..." Mr. Tsubouchi gave us the same businesslike report as the day before, along with instructions for the day.

As I listened to him drone on, I tried to reassure myself.

I'm sure that Ms. Kanbayashi has been under a great deal of stress since the spring, being the homeroom teacher for Grade 3 Class 3 and

all. Couple that with the fact that her brother died in May, and most
likely, when summer vacation wrapped up and the ending of the "phe-
nomenon" was certain, all the tension that had been building sud-
denly caught up to her. I'm sure that's why she's been unwell...

Yagisawa had mentioned a similar line of thinking. "She seems like the kind of teacher who values hard work above all. Once she stopped for a moment, the fatigue must have set in."

Even so, there was one other thing going on that day that had me worried.

The day before, all the students in our class—except for Makise, who was still in the hospital—had come to school. But on the 4th, one person was missing from the classroom.

It was Shimamura.

One of the girls who was friends with Hazumi. The one who had gotten injured when she was hit by a bicycle in April.

I hadn't seen her all day. There had been no special mention of her absence by the teachers, so I figured she was probably out sick, and that turned out to be correct. Apparently, Kusakabe had been worried and had called Shimamura's house after second period to confirm that fact.

"She caught a cold."

Kusakabe's voice made it to my ear as she informed a group of girls that included Hazumi.

"She's been a little feverish since last night, and she's unsteady on her feet, so she's resting."

"Now that you mention it, I think Shimamura had a mask on yesterday?"

"And she was coughing a little."

"Yeah, she was."

"It's just a normal cold?"

"Probably. She said not to worry, and she sounded pretty good on the phone. She said she'll come back once her fever goes down."

"I hope she doesn't have the flu."

"Isn't it a little early in the year for that?"

"I guess it is."

Listening to the girls' conversation, part of me was relieved, but at the same time, I still felt a little uncomfortable. But at that point, the anxiety that accompanied that uncomfortable feeling was still very vague.

This year's "phenomenon" is over, and the "accidents" have stopped. I was certain of that. The image of Izumi after she threw herself into the muddy waters of the Yomiyama River that night in July was still burned vividly into my mind.

The "accidents" had stopped because of the death of "Izumi Akazawa." That was for certain. There was no way I was wrong about it. So…

"…It's all right," I reassured myself as I returned to the book I had borrowed from the Daybreak Forest library the other day—Ellery Queen's *The Siamese Twin Mystery*.

5

Wednesday, September 5.

A thick fog rolled in that morning.

It wasn't that bad in Tobii, where I lived, but even so, I probably would have been somewhat hesitant if someone had suggested I ride my bike in the fog.

The fog occurred across the whole area encompassing the city of Yomiyama and, in many places, was remarkably dense. The area around North Yomi Middle School was no exception. The whole area around the school grounds was completely enveloped in the bluish-white fog. Even if you came right up to the gate, all you could see of the school inside were vague gray silhouettes. Inside the classroom, people were excitedly telling stories about almost getting lost on the way to school, or of traffic signals being basically useless, or of encountering scared, crying elementary school kids.

"Wonder how many years it's been since we had fog like this?" Yagisawa said when I saw him. "There was one really bad fog day back in second or third grade of elementary school, and if I remember correctly, I think they canceled school. You wouldn't have been here for that, right, Sou?"

"So you're saying compared to that, today's fog is no big deal?" I asked.

Yagisawa grumbled, "I don't think that," and looked out the windows to the school grounds. "Man, we're up on the third floor, but I can't see anything but fog."

"It's incredible. Or rather, bizarre."

"Definitely. But you know, the forecast says it'll clear up this afternoon, so…"

Ms. Kanbayashi was absent that day as well, and the moment we were informed, an unnatural hush fell over the classroom. Followed by a small commotion. I could hear voices asking, "What happened to her?" and "I wonder if she's okay?"

Shimamura, who had been absent yesterday, was out again as well. *I guess she hasn't gotten over her cold yet?*

And another student was absent, too.

A number of people were late to first period, largely because of the fog. However, there was one student who never showed up, even as second period came and went…

A boy named Kuroi.

I had hardly ever spoken to him, so I didn't know much about him. He was small and quiet, not the type of person who stands out too much…that was about all the impression I had of him.

Kuroi didn't show up at all, but even though they were both absent, his absence seemed somehow different from Shimamura's sick leave.

Second period ended and then third period… Whenever we finished a class, some other teacher, like the head teacher for our grade or the guidance counselor, would peek into the classroom, confirming my suspicions.

"Mr. Kuroi hasn't shown up, has he?"

What on earth is going on? What's happening?

We learned the answers during lunch. Yagisawa went to the staff room for some other matter, and while he was there, he heard about the situation.

"Apparently, there was an inquiry made to the school by Kuroi's mother," Yagisawa reported.

"An inquiry?"

Isn't that the opposite of usual? A student hasn't come to school, so I would expect the school to make an inquiry to the kid's home.

Yagisawa saw me tilting my head in puzzlement and immediately continued. "She needed something and called her son's cell phone, but there was no response at all. So she called here to ask if he had come to school like he's supposed to."

I let out an involuntary gasp of surprise. "So that means that this morning, Kuroi left home headed for school? He didn't take the day off?"

"Seems that way."

"He headed for school, but he didn't get here."

"Yeah. Apparently, he left home much later than usual. He must have overslept or something. After he flew out the door in a mad rush, his mother found something he had forgotten, and that's why she called his cell phone... Anyway, that's apparently what happened."

"So he didn't come to school and went off somewhere else, maybe?"

"That's right." Yagisawa nodded stiffly, scratching his long, scrunchy hair. "Maybe he got lost in the fog and couldn't make it here? I doubt it."

"He could have had a fight with his parents and run away or something?"

"I don't know what things are like at the Kuroi house."

"Maybe he hates school and suddenly wanted to go somewhere far away?"

"I'm not sure he's the type to do something like that."

"But is he the type who would never do it?"

"Oh, I don't know. I hardly ever talked to the guy."

"Hmm," I responded, suppressing the unsettling thoughts that threatened to rise up in my mind.

Yagisawa said, "It seemed like the teachers were going to wait and see for now. His parents are probably trying to get in touch with any relatives' or acquaintances' houses he might have gone to, right?"

"I hope they find him easily."

"If Kuroi isn't back home by nightfall, then there'll probably be a big fuss."

"Probably, yeah."

The two of us were taking our lunch on the roof of Building C.

The fog had thinned considerably, and the dark, cloudy sky was visible when we looked up. The concrete underfoot was wet with moisture thanks to the fog… We hadn't been able to find a place to sit down, so both of us were leaning gently against the iron railing that surrounded the rooftop, eating our lunch standing up. I had a sandwich that Auntie Sayuri had made for me. Yagisawa had two rice balls that he'd bought at a convenience store.

"By the way, about Ms. Kanbayashi…," Yagisawa started. "Obviously, she's been out since Monday, but apparently, no one knows exactly why."

When I heard that, I let out another gasp of surprise. "Huh? How do you know that?"

"Oh, I just happened to overhear the teachers talking about it, so…"

"You were eavesdropping?"

"I just heard them, that's all. I wasn't standing around on purpose or hiding in a dark corner or anything."

"Well, it doesn't matter to me."

The discomfort I had been feeling since the previous day was back. Along with the vague anxiety. Deliberately shutting out both feelings, I urged Yagisawa to continue. "So?"

"It sounds like they haven't been able to get in touch with her since Monday. She doesn't answer when they call. They left messages, but there hasn't been any response." Yagisawa let out a short sigh. "At first, the other teachers figured that she was probably laid up sick, but then she didn't come in the next day, either. On top of that, they haven't been able to contact her."

"That goes for today, too?"

"Yeah. It's definitely strange, so now they're saying someone ought to go to her house and check on her. I heard them discussing it…"

"When you were eavesdropping, right."

This time, Yagisawa didn't contradict me. He turned around and put his chest up against the railing. A tepid breeze blew through, ruffling his long hair and making it stand on end.

"Hey, Sou?" Yagisawa turned toward me, not bothering to fix his ruffled hair. "What do you think about all this...?"

But when he asked me that, I wanted to leave immediately. I didn't know how to answer, even if he asked. And I didn't want to answer, either. However—

This series of events since Monday...

Ms. Kanbayashi. Shimamura. And now Kuroi. Each day, one person has stopped coming to school. Each day, one person has disappeared from our classroom.

What is going on? What does it mean? Is it just a coincidence? Or is there some meaning behind it? And if there is, then what on earth could it be...?

...Ah, no. There's no need for alarm. I don't have to worry.

This year's "phenomenon" is over. The "accidents" have stopped.

My conviction on this point was unwavering. I knew I couldn't afford to let it waver.

I went to bed early that night, but I couldn't get to sleep. That hadn't happened for a long time. As I was puzzling over whether or not I should take the medicine that Dr. Usui had prescribed for me, I fell into a shallow slumber.

As I was dozing, I had a dream.

The fog...

A bluish-white fog hung over everything. The fog was cold, and whenever I took a breath, it penetrated deep into my lungs. It was icy, freezing; I was shivering... I suddenly realized that something was approaching me through the fog. A mysterious gray figure.

I could just barely tell that it was in the shape of a human, but not whether it was actually a person. It multiplied, from one figure to two, from two to three...increasing in number as I watched. Growing frightened, I tried to run away. But by then, the multiplied figures had already completely surrounded me. I was cold, freezing, and shivering from fear on top of that. As I stood there trembling, I found myself unable to take even one step away from that spot.

That was my nightmare.

6

Thursday, September 6.

Ms. Kanbayashi didn't come in again.

As usual, Mr. Tsubouchi showed up and announced her absence during the morning homeroom, but his voice was lower and heavier than it had been before, and he seemed to enunciate his words poorly.

After what Yagisawa had told me the day before, I assumed there might be some information forthcoming, but there was nothing. I was concerned to see Mr. Tsubouchi wearing a puzzled expression for some reason as he looked around the classroom…

Shimamura is absent again today. This is the third day, huh?

I hadn't seen Kuroi, either.

I wonder if they figured out where he went yesterday? Did he go back home? Like Yagisawa, I don't know what the situation is like at the Kuroi house, but if he's still missing, any normal family would be in an uproar. I'm sure they're probably freaking out.

"Shimamura's still feeling bad, huh?"

"Her cold must have gotten worse."

"I hope she's okay."

During lunchtime, I overheard the conversation between Kusakabe and the other girls. Hazumi was with them, too, but I didn't hear her voice.

"I don't think Shimamura has a cell phone, does she?"

"I called her house last night. Her mom answered and said, 'Sorry for worrying you.' But her mom's voice didn't sound very good, either."

"Hmm. I wonder if she's really all right?"

"Should we go visit her?"

"Mm, but…"

…A feeling of discomfort came over me. Along with a vague anxiety.

These sensations that had been plaguing me for the past two days were now spreading through the whole classroom. That's how it seemed to me.

None of the other students was talking about Kuroi, but during lunch, Yagisawa had gone to find out some new information. He had probably been eavesdropping by the staff room again.

"So about Kuroi, they still don't know where he is."

"He didn't go home?"

"Looks that way."

"Has the family notified the police?"

"I don't know. I'm sure they've reported him missing. Unless he ran away, there's a chance it might be kidnapping or something."

"Kidnapping...no way."

"At any rate, the teachers were kind of, like, rushing around. They're definitely more worked up than they were yesterday."

Just like yesterday's lunch, the two of us were up on the roof of Building C. I was eating a boxed lunch that Auntie Sayuri had made for me, and Yagisawa had a sandwich that he said he bought at a convenience store... This, too, was like the day before.

"What about Ms. Kanbayashi?" I asked. "You said the teachers were going to check on her, right? I wonder how that went?"

"Ah, about that." Yagisawa frowned pointedly. "I didn't hear exactly, but it seems like something definitely wasn't right."

"Meaning what?"

"I don't know the specifics."

"You didn't try asking someone?"

"No, I tried very hard to ask. I cornered Mr. Wada, the Japanese teacher. But he got all flustered and wouldn't answer me... He looked troubled. It was obvious that he wasn't going to say anything then."

"...How strange."

"It was totally weird. With him acting like that, I can't help but imagine the worst."

"The worst..."

"Yeah."

"Which would be...?"

Neither of us could say the next part out loud. I'm sure that neither of us wanted to say it at all.

There was no fog like there had been the day before, and we could look out over the whole neighborhood from the roof. We could even see the flow of the Yomiyama River, but the sky wasn't a nice, clear autumn vista. Light-gray clouds covered the whole sky in a gloomy overcast, even obscuring the position of the sun. The breeze that occasionally blew past was unpleasantly tepid, hot and humid with the long, lingering heat of summer.

Suddenly, crows called out overhead.

Kaaah, kaaah!

I glanced up toward the sound of their cries, and then Yagisawa and I instinctively looked at each other, but neither of us said a thing. It was probably more accurate to say that we couldn't say a thing.

7

Extended homeroom in sixth period on Thursday.

We're probably going to get a substitute teacher soon. Mr. Tsubouchi or someone else... Just as I was thinking that, someone unexpected entered the classroom, a little bit after the bell rang.

Dressed in a black shirt and black pants with a black jacket...in full black despite the season, it was the librarian for the secondary library, Mr. Chibiki.

There was no doubt that all the students were perplexed about why he was subbing. I was the same, but my bewilderment soon transformed into nervousness. I stared straight at the teacher's podium and braced myself.

"My name is Chibiki. I've seen most of your faces before, so I'm sure that most of you also know who I am."

He stood with both hands on the lectern and looked around the classroom, seeming to deliberately take his time. As he was doing that, Mr. Chibiki himself looked like he was working to keep his emotions in check. That was the sense I got.

"First," he said, putting a finger to his glasses frame. He stayed that way, silent, for two or three more seconds, then abruptly informed us, "I have to make an unfortunate announcement. Yesterday, we learned that your homeroom teacher, Ms. Kanbayashi, who has been absent since Monday, passed away in her home."

It was shocking to hear, but strangely, in the moment, it was not a big surprise. It was probably because...yes, because I had been nursing premonitions of a situation like this for days, even before Yagisawa had said that he couldn't *"help but imagine the worst."*

The other students in the classroom had different reactions. There were several who let out cries of grief as soon as they heard the news and some who covered their faces with both hands. Other students stayed looking straight ahead, overcome with surprise, or silently shook their heads left to right...

"How?" someone asked. "What does that mean?"

"Let me explain," Mr. Chibiki answered in a calm voice. "By rights, I probably should have told you first thing this morning, but...this is hard on us teachers, too. We needed time to discuss certain things, like how to deal with the situation and how to tell you students. And so I'm here, telling you now. I think it's best to share with you all the facts. I don't want any half-baked rumors spreading around."

It turned out that they hadn't been able to reach Ms. Kanbayashi since the start of the week. And then the previous night, some teachers had volunteered to go and check in on her...that much was as I had heard from Yagisawa a day ago.

Ms. Kanbayashi's house was in a place called Asamidai, where she lived alone in an old stand-alone home. The visiting teachers had rung the bell at the front door, but no one came out. They tried calling, and there was no answer. But they could see a bit of light in the windows, which they couldn't help but conclude was strange.

"They consulted with the police and got an officer to come out to the house as a witness, then searched inside. Shortly after entering, they discovered Ms. Kanbayashi's body. In the washroom. Sitting in the bath..."

No one moved a muscle, and the classroom was deadly silent. Without letting any unnecessary emotion show on his face, Mr. Chibiki continued his explanation.

"The police investigation concluded that the cause of death was drowning. She probably died on Sunday night. An empty wine bottle and glass had been left behind on the living room table, so they think she took a bath after drinking the wine and fell asleep. Then, tragically, she drowned."

The circumstances corresponded to a so-called "accidental death," and the police didn't find anything criminal about it. No kind of note or will was discovered, suggesting that it hadn't been suicide.

An unexpected accident, caused by bathing after drinking. Not a rare story at all, broadly speaking.

"It's a fact that Ms. Kanbayashi hadn't been in very good health lately, so when she was absent from school without calling in at the start of this week, everyone thought that was the reason. The 'accidents' had stopped, and you'd safely started the second semester... We figured the exhaustion that had accumulated in her mind and body had caught up to her all at once. I don't know how much of a taste for alcohol she had normally, but I think it's possible that this was an unfortunate accident, a result of an understandable mistake. With that thought, all we can do is pray for her soul's repose."

Mr. Chibiki finished speaking and sighed deeply. As if prompted by this, other sighs escaped here and there throughout the classroom. I heard several of the girls start to sob.

We sat like that for some time, no one saying anything.

"Can I ask a question?" Finally, a student raised her hand. It was Etou. "Um…did Ms. Kanbayashi die because of the 'calamity'?"

"A very reasonable question," Mr. Chibiki replied. He paused for a while with a finger on his glasses frame again, but he didn't seem flustered. He looked to me like he was reviewing in his head an answer that he had prepared.

"If I was to express my thoughts at present…" He paused here again, then said, "I think *this is different*. This is not the 'calamity.'"

"Really?" Etou followed up. "Is that true?"

"The 'extra person' disappeared at some point in July, and this year's 'phenomenon' ended. The 'accidents' stopped, too. There wasn't a single victim in August, which is the best proof of all. Based on those facts, Ms. Kanbayashi's misfortune was most likely *a simple accidental death*, with no relation to the 'calamity.' If not, it doesn't make sense."

Mr. Chibiki spoke without hesitation, but his line of sight was not directed toward Etou, who had asked the question. Instead, he was staring at a point in midair in the middle of the classroom. It seemed to me that his assertion, *If not, it doesn't make sense,* was probably more of an attempt to convince himself than us students.

However, at that moment, honestly, I agreed with Mr. Chibiki.

The "phenomenon" was over, and the "accidents" had stopped. So Ms. Kanbayashi's death was something *different.* That didn't change the fact that it was a sad turn of events, but in the end, it was nothing more than an "ordinary death," the type that could happen anywhere in the world. That was all I could think. So…

8

"For the time being, I will be acting as your homeroom teacher in place of Ms. Kanbayashi. I thought maybe I should tell you that first, but when I considered the order of information, that didn't seem right…"

After his announcement, Mr. Chibiki changed the tone of his voice and introduced himself to us, a little late.

"My name is Tatsuji Chibiki. My main job is working as the head of the secondary library, but I do hold a middle school teacher's license, so I accepted an emergency request from the principal to cover this class. I'm sure that some of you are also aware that twenty-nine years ago—*the year it all started*—I was a social studies teacher here, as well as the homeroom teacher for Grade 3 Class 3. Considering all that, I couldn't possibly turn down the request."

Mr. Chibiki was speaking a little less formally than he had been before, but his demeanor seemed quite different compared to when he'd been in the library room in Building Zero. It was difficult to explain, but I could tell that he was very nervous standing at the podium during homeroom for Grade 3 Class 3. I recalled that he hadn't taught for many years.

"In the end, I'm just a temporary 'substitute' responding to an emergency situation, so I'm sure I'll be imperfect in many ways. In that regard, well, I'd like you to go easy on me. But if there's anything troubling you, don't hesitate to come and talk to me. You've already got a social studies teacher, so I have no plans to take over that class. As for your science course, which Ms. Kanbayashi was teaching, the administration is supposed to bring someone in to help with that soon..."

When he had more or less finished going through all the procedural stuff required after assuming his role as "substitute homeroom teacher," Mr. Chibiki left the lectern and leaned up against the wall beside the blackboard. "Well then." He was holding the attendance book in his hands. He opened it and looked at each seated student's face in turn.

"This girl Shimamura is out sick, huh?" he muttered, furrowing his brow. "Today's the third day...hmm."

What about Kuroi? I wondered. Surely, Mr. Chibiki should have some grasp on that situation.

"As for Kuroi, who has been absent since yesterday," he started, almost as if my thoughts had been transmitted directly to him. "You've probably already heard, but it sounds like he did not go home last night. His parents have submitted a notice to the police and are very worried, but...yes, I'm sure he's all right. He'll probably come back suddenly tonight or something. The 'accidents' have already stopped. So I don't think we need to be that alarmed."

But—

I almost spoke up, despite my better judgment, but I restrained myself. I could understand Mr. Chibiki's way of thinking and the attitude he was effecting here and now perfectly well, and I, too, wanted to think the same thing. I should have been on the same page as him.

However, no matter how much I tried to repudiate the idea with logic, anxiety welled up from somewhere inside me. No matter how strongly I tried to deny the idea and go around the wall of fear in my heart, or climb over that wall, or open a hole in it to escape, there was *something* closing in on me...

I suddenly recalled the gray figures in the mist from my nightmare the previous night, and before I knew it, I was trembling with *rage*.

"Hmm? Are you all right, Hiratsuka?" Mr. Chibiki looked at me with a concerned expression, maybe because he had realized the state I was in.

"...Yes."

I deliberately recalled the image of Izumi falling into the muddy flow of the Yomiyama River. Desperately warding off the shadowy figures squirming around in my mind by doing so, I just barely managed to answer:

"I'm fine, *sir*."

9

There was a lone child coming toward me.

From the looks of him, he was in his third or fourth year of elementary school, a petite little boy. He wore a yellow polo shirt, jeans, and a white baseball cap. There was quite a distance between us, and he was looking down as he walked, so I couldn't make out his face. He didn't look to be wearing a backpack, so he had probably gone home after school and then come out again.

The time was about 4:30 in the afternoon.

Since it was early September, sunset was still a long way off. But the clouds had been growing thicker all afternoon, making everything look dreary.

I had left school a little while ago and was on my way home. With me was Yagisawa, as well as the countermeasures officers, Etou and Tajimi. All four of us had left the classroom together.

"I know that's what Mr. Chibiki said, but I wonder if it's really true? Ms. Kanbayashi dying now is just kind of, it's a little, you know...," Tajimi said with a long face.

Tajimi was much taller and more solidly built than I was. At first glance, he looked tough. But in fact, he was a good-humored, sociable guy, if perhaps a little flaky. As far as "countermeasures officers" were concerned, the girls—Etou, and of course Izumi, who had formerly been one of them—seemed more dependable than he was.

"I think we can trust what Mr. Chibiki said," Etou replied. "He's the person at school who's been observing the 'phenomenon' for the longest. If there was still any risk, he would have refused to be our homeroom teacher, even if they ordered him to, don't you think? He wouldn't go out of his way to become a 'member of Grade 3 Class 3'...right?" Etou looked at me.

"Well...yeah. I'm sure that's true."

I nodded, but I was aware that I hadn't given a very clear answer. Somehow or other, I felt it would be out of character for Mr. Chibiki to make that kind of calculation—to accept the job only because it was safe, because there was no risk.

Be that as it may, it wasn't like I particularly wanted to consider the possibility that there was still a risk from the "calamity" facing Grade 3 Class 3 now, either. I didn't want to dwell on that at all.

"It's okay," I remarked. "Ms. Kanbayashi's death was the result of an unfortunate accident, a coincidence. Shimamura's absence is from her cold getting worse. It's not very unusual that someone would be out sick for three days."

In fact, I, too, had been laid up for several days with a summer cold at the end of July, and that had been totally disconnected with the "calamity."

"If we're concerned about her being ill, then we ought to be even more worried about Makise, who's been hospitalized this whole time," said Etou.

I nodded. "Yeah, for sure."

"I'd like to agree with Sou, too," Yagisawa said frankly, "but the thing with Kuroi is still bugging me. But you know, I guess we can't help getting worked up at this point."

"Yeah."

"Like Mr. Chibiki said, there's no problem so long as he shows up at his house tonight, but I wonder if that'll happen. By the way, Tajimi?"

"What?"

"My term of office as class rep only lasts until the end of this month. I feel like I've done my duty, so do you wanna take over for the rest of the semester?"

We started for home, continuing this kind of back-and-forth as we did. I went out through the main gate and walked over to a different bus lane than I would have used if I'd left school at the usual time, accompanied by my three classmates. The four of us were walking in a line down the sidewalk on the right side of the two-lane road that had sidewalks provided on both sides...and that's where it happened.

A lone child walked toward us from up ahead on that same sidewalk. Absorbed in conversation, he didn't catch my attention at first.

Before long, the distance between us closed, and the boy stopped walking and looked up at us. I glanced down at his face, and then—

I was suddenly seized by a peculiar sensation.

The brownish hair. The fair, docile-looking features. The vaguely lonesome expression. ...*Ah, what the heck is this?*

This child, his face... He looks like me? *He does. Wait, in fact—*

It was me; that was how I'd looked when I was in elementary school several years ago. From the time when I was in Hinami, going back and forth to Lakeshore Manor. *That version of me* had, for some reason, suddenly appeared before my eyes. I was captivated by the strange phantom...

...It can't be.

This—this feeling...

It was like my foothold on "reality" suddenly started to warp and weaken. Like the contours of the "world" started to slowly dissolve. In the midst of all that, "my" consciousness stretched and split in two, and one part seemed to leave my physical body...

It can't be!

I shook my head.

The sensation made me feel as if I was losing myself. The self of three years ago, of that summer... *Ah, I see, this is probably some sort of aftereffect of the strange experience I had back then, isn't it?*

This kid's face doesn't actually resemble me that closely. To say nothing of how ridiculous it would be for my past self to appear before my eyes...

On the other hand...

When the child looked at us, he tilted his head slightly, as if he had something to say. But in the end, he turned away without saying a word. And then—

I don't know what he was thinking, but he continued to turn, then abruptly jumped out into the road.

We all gasped, surprised by his sudden movement. Just then, a single black compact car sped toward us. The boy was facing the other direction, and he didn't seem to notice the vehicle at all.

"Watch out!"

"Look out!"

Etou and Yagisawa shouted at him simultaneously. The car blew a long warning on its horn. Luckily, it missed hitting the boy by a hairbreadth, and he finished crossing the street. It drove off without stopping.

"Whew, that was close!" Yagisawa sighed again, then shouted at the kid on the other side, "Hey! Watch where you're going!"

"Four middle schoolers were walking toward him, filling up the entire width of the sidewalk, so he probably decided to cross over to the other side on the spur of the moment," Tajimi opined.

"Sure, but still..." Yagisawa frowned.

Etou looked seriously relieved.

As for me, I was still watching the kid, unable to shake the strange feeling from earlier. When Yagisawa had shouted at him to watch where he was going, the boy had glanced back briefly but hadn't reacted beyond that before starting off down the opposite sidewalk.

However, right at that very moment—

Something unthinkable happened.

I don't believe there was any kind of forewarning. At least, not that I picked up on.

What I did sense was a sudden, strange, violent "noise" that gave me no time to react. I didn't even have time to wonder what it was before—

A second sound, even more violent. It was literally ear-splitting. And the child's figure disappeared instantly. At least, that's how it appeared. Actually, rather than "disappearing," he was erased. Snuffed out from view by the huge object that came crashing down at that exact moment.

What on earth was that? What just happened?

I couldn't comprehend it right away. All I knew was that some big, heavy object had fallen onto the opposite sidewalk and that the boy who had been walking down it was now underneath.

Yagisawa and Tajimi had covered their ears with both hands against the sound, so loud that its reverberations could be felt through the ground. Etou was hiding her eyes. I wasn't able to react in either way; I just stood there, stock-still, overcome with surprise.

The fallen object looked like some sort of concrete mass—I could see through the awful swirling dust that it had steel rods and metal plates embedded in it. Its structure had crumbled with the impact of the fall, and a forest of twisted reddish-brown stalks of rebar was sticking out of it.

This is...

I looked up and realized that the sidewalk ran right in front of some kind of construction site. It was either a remodeling job or the demolition of a building many stories tall. The whole outside of the building was covered with protective sheets and panels, but in the end, they hadn't done their job.

It wasn't clear what had caused the concrete to come loose. Some kind of accident had probably occurred near the upper floors of the building. An outer wall, or perhaps a part like a veranda, must have completely crumbled and plummeted to the ground, dragging the construction scaffolding that was wrapped around the edifice with it as it went. And that boy just happened to be standing in the exact spot where it landed...

The kid wasn't "erased" so much as crushed before he could realize that something was wrong and get out of the way. He didn't even have time to cry out.

"What happened to that kid?" Etou asked, on the verge of tears. "Hey, what happened to him? What was that?"

"He must be a goner under all that," Yagisawa answered her in a trembling voice. Tajimi still had his hands over his ears and was shaking his head left to right.

"A goner? He died?"

"We don't know yet, but…probably."

"We've got to help him!"

"Ah…no, it would be dangerous to approach now. Something else might fall."

"But—"

"More importantly, someone call the police and an ambulance!"

"Oh, uh, right."

The debris had spread out into the roadway, so it was starting to obstruct traffic. I heard the sound of sudden braking. The blaring of car horns. People stopped their vehicles to get out. There were others who noticed an accident had occurred and gathered nearby.

Amid all the commotion, I separated from the other three and crossed the road by myself to approach the scene. I think I was pulled into action by that part of my consciousness that had split off and separated from my physical body… No, actually, I don't know why I did it. All I know for sure is that in that moment, I was not in my right mind. I'm not even sure whether I was thinking about what I should do or what I wanted to do. It felt almost like the movement of a sleepwalker.

"Hey, Sou, don't!"

"It's dangerous!"

I kept on walking, shooting a backward glance at Yagisawa and the others as they shouted after me, and approached the tragic scene. The child had looked to be completely buried under the concrete, but actually, his head and right hand had escaped being crushed. His baseball cap had fallen off and was lying nearby. He was facedown on the pavement, his right hand stretched out in front of him.

"Uuuh…u, unnn…"

There came a faint, almost inaudible, groan.

He's still breathing. He's alive!

As soon as I realized, I dashed over to him. However, the moment I got in close, something terrible happened right before my eyes—it could only be described as an act of the devil.

A piece of iron pipe came tumbling down from above.

Of all the places it could have fallen, it struck the boy, who was still just barely breathing. In a flash, it pierced the back of his head and went all the way through… A spray of blood doused the sidewalk.

"Aaaah!"

A sudden wave of raw terror swelled up inside me, and I let out a tremendous scream.

"Aaaahhhhhh!"

I yelled so loud, it felt like my throat would split open. All coherent thoughts vanished from my mind. I was absolutely terrified and repulsed… I lost control and kept howling.

10

Yuuji Tanaka.

That evening, I learned the name of the dead boy. He was nine years old. A student at Third Yomiyama Elementary School. The accident was reported on TV, during the local news.

Auntie Sayuri was with me in the living room, where the TV sat, when the news aired. When she saw the report on the tragic incident, my aunt turned to me with surprise and grief in her voice. "Isn't that close to your school?"

I couldn't bring myself to answer her. I stood up quietly from my chair and left the room.

That evening, after witnessing the accident, I had returned home alone. I practically fled from the scene.

The shock had been too much, and I couldn't think clearly—or more like I had fallen into a state where I was refusing to think. It was as though the brain functions that I needed to produce thought had frozen in place.

I persisted in that stupor even after getting home. It wasn't just my thoughts; it felt like my emotions were paralyzed as well. I couldn't feel anything, not even sympathy for the poor child who had died.

Sensing something was off with me, Auntie Sayuri asked with concern, "Did something happen?"

But the only answer I could give was, "No, nothing." I couldn't work up the energy to answer a phone call to my cell from Yagisawa, either.

When I learned the boy's name from the news, I finally began to recover a little bit of brain function. As the feeling was coming back—

Yuuji Tanaka.

I tried murmuring his name in my mind.

Yuuji Tanaka. Yuuji…

Something about it made me bristle, but my brain was still refusing to work.

To be sure, "Tanaka" was a common surname, but—

Late that night, Yagisawa called me for the umpteenth time. I really couldn't ignore him any longer, so I gingerly pressed the answer button.

"Oh, you finally picked up. Are you okay?"

"Ah…yeah."

"You hardly ever go home without saying anything. I was worried."

"Sorry."

"Did you watch the news? That elementary schooler, his name was Yuuji Tanaka…"

"I saw that."

"There's a guy named Tanaka *in our class*, right?"

"…………"

"Tanaka" is a really common surname, so I'm sure that…

"Shinichi Tanaka, he's in the table tennis club. I haven't spent much time with the guy, but I was worried, so I called him up. And…"

Yagisawa paused. He seemed to be waiting for my response, but I didn't say anything. In my mind, I was repeating, *No way, no way,* but I couldn't get the words out.

"And I found out that *Yuuji Tanaka is Shinichi Tanaka's younger brother,*" he told me. "I'm not clear on the exact details, but apparently, Yuuji was headed toward North Yomi at the time to meet up with his big brother, who was still at school doing club activities."

"No way." Finally, my voice came out. It was a frail, hoarse sound. "It can't be."

"That boy was *a 'related individual' to someone in Grade 3 Class 3.*"

"It can't be...but—"

"But the 'calamity' stopped, right?"

"Yeah."

"So what the hell was *that*? Was it just an *ordinary accident*, like in Ms. Kanbayashi's case?" Yagisawa asked pointedly. His voice trembled.

I was stumped for an answer. My brain wasn't working yet, and my emotions were still leaden... After a silence of several seconds, I finally managed to choke out a simple response: "I don't know."

11

"First, I have to make an unfortunate announcement."

Friday, September 7.

During morning homeroom, Mr. Chibiki hit us with the same words he had used the day before. I steeled myself, certain that he was going to inform us that Shinichi Tanaka's little brother had expired in an accident, but contrary to my expectation, he revealed something different.

"A call just came to the school a little while ago. It only happened a few hours ago, so I don't think you all know yet."

Something that happened a few hours ago? What on earth could that be?

Mr. Chibiki was wearing a particularly grim expression. I had a very bad feeling about what he was going to say. My breath caught in my throat. For a moment, a shudder went through the air inside the classroom like a wave, but then the room fell silent.

With an even grimmer expression, in a strained tone, Mr. Chibiki made the following announcement. "It seems that Miss Shimamura, who has been out sick for a while, passed away early this morning."

In a sudden reversal from the silence, a terrific uproar spread through the class. There were even more screams than there had been when we'd learned of Ms. Kanbayashi's death yesterday. Even I let out a shocked, "Huh?"

"No way!" The girl shouting in a tearful voice was Kusakabe. "Shimamura? Shimamura's dead?"

Besides her outburst, I could hear a bewildered voice questioning, "Why? Why?" It was Hazumi. From her seat in the very back of the row closest to the window, she was staring straight forward, her head pressed between both hands and her eyes fixed on nothing. The hollowness in her gaze suddenly hit me.

As he observed his students' reactions, Mr. Chibiki put both elbows down on the podium, then put his forehead in his hands.

"Her condition probably took a sudden turn for the worse, but... ah, but we just don't know all the specifics yet." After shaking his head slowly side to side, he straightened himself up and continued. "It's hard for me to tell you not to be too shaken up. Everyone, I'd like you to try to remain as calm as possible. That's all I can say at the moment."

12

Apparently, something strange had happened the night before.

Shimamura had been sick for some time and hadn't been to school since Tuesday, but it hadn't seemed like much more than an ordinary flu, so her family hadn't been especially worried. Everyone had expected that she would quickly recover with a little over-the-counter cold medicine and some bedrest.

On the contrary, though her condition hadn't seemed to get any worse, she hadn't taken an easy turn for the better, either. She still had a high fever three days later, on Thursday, and was suffering from headaches and fatigue.

Then that night—

Shimamura's mother had gone to her bedroom to check in on her daughter and noticed that she was sitting up in bed, repeating something to herself in a daze. When her mother had asked what was wrong, Shimamura, still out of it, hadn't been able to answer coherently. Fearing that her daughter was delirious from fever, her mother lulled her to sleep, watched over her for a while, then left the room.

A little after two in the morning, Shimamura's mother had heard a strange noise from her daughter's bedroom. When she had gone in to investigate, she'd found that Shimamura had gotten out of bed and was standing in front of the built-in closet, beating on the doors with both hands. She struck them several times, then opened them, immediately closed them, then struck them again... She had repeated this nonsensical sequence of actions over and over in the same dazed state as before.

Shimamura's mother had found the behavior concerning, but once she had guided her daughter back to bed, the girl had fallen into a tranquil slumber. She hadn't even looked particularly ill. Even so, her mother once again watched over her daughter for a little while, then left the room, but—

About two hours after that, a little past four in the morning, just before dawn, her parents heard a terrible shriek, followed by some strange noises.

Shimamura's bedroom was on the second floor of a stand-alone family home. The room led onto a veranda. Shimamura had gone out onto it, climbed over the railing, and leaped into the air—she'd jumped off. A wall topped with sharp steel spikes surrounded the family's property. After landing on the wall, one of the spikes on it pierced her throat as she came down.

By the time Shimamura's parents had gotten to her, she'd already been bleeding out. Ultimately, she had drawn her last breath in the ambulance on the way to the emergency room.

All this I learned from Mr. Chibiki later on, during lunch break. Apparently, the school had only been informed of her passing during a call this morning.

"If she jumped off herself...does that mean it was a suicide?"

He shook his head slightly at my naive question. "No. The ongoing theory is that it was not a suicide. They haven't found any sort of note. And she hadn't shown any indication whatsoever that would make her parents worry she was at risk...so..."

As he spoke, he alternated between glancing at *our* faces. We were in the secondary library. Yagisawa was beside me. As soon as lunch had started, the two of us sought out the librarian, and eventually we arrived at his room on the first floor of Building Zero.

"It wasn't suicide. And of course, she didn't die of disease. It was probably some kind of accident," he suggested.

"An accident?" Yagisawa grumbled. "Even if it was..."

"A possible cause is delirium resulting from virus-induced acute encephalopathy, which led to a fall. It could be something like that."

Virus-induced acute encephalopathy.

Mr. Chibiki laid it out to Yagisawa and me. The unfamiliar words had left us bewildered.

"It seems like encephalopathy has been making the news lately, but its effects aren't limited to influenza. Infections from all sorts of other viruses can also produce acute encephalopathy. There are still lots of things we aren't sure about it, but we do know that it can manifest a wide range of symptoms, including strange behaviors, like speaking in a different voice or doing things that don't make sense. They believe that Shimamura's case may fit the bill."

All I could do was nod along silently. Yagisawa was the same. After saying that much, Mr. Chibiki stopped talking, letting out a long sigh as he ruffled his unkempt, graying hair.

"Um..." I spoke up after a short silence. "Mr. Chibiki...sir—"

"You don't need to start with the formality."

"Ah, okay."

"So, what is it?"

"Um, well, during homeroom this morning, you only made an announcement about Shimamura, but you must know about what happened with Tanaka, who's also out today, right?"

"Mm," Mr. Chibiki responded, wearily running his hand through his hair again. "You mean about how his younger brother died in an accident yesterday, right? Tanaka contacted the school about taking bereavement leave."

"Why didn't you mention it this morning?"

"That's something that will get around no matter what I do, so I wanted to make the news easier to handle, even just a little. Do you think it would have been better to break everything to them at once?"

"Ah...I guess I do."

The scenes from the accident the evening before threatened to fill my mind again, so I squeezed my eyes tightly shut to keep them from coming back. The last thing I needed was to remember *that* all over again. I was already just barely hanging on by a thread.

"So," I then asked Mr. Chibiki, "what's your take on this? Tanaka's little brother and Shimamura, two 'related individuals' in a row have... Wait, if we include Ms. Kanbayashi, that makes three. Is this...?"

"Is it the 'calamity,' you're wondering?" He stared pointedly at me, a deep vertical crease dividing his brow.

"I'm not sure," I responded. "This year's 'casualty' ended in July, so the 'accidents' should have already stopped. So...ah, but..."

Just then, a telephone that was sitting on the corner of the counter began to ring. Mr. Chibiki turned his back on us, faced the counter, and picked up the receiver.

"Secondary library... Yes. This is Chibiki."

It seemed to be an internal call. I couldn't tell who was calling, but they sounded like another teacher.

"...Is that so?" His voice was low as he answered. I thought I could hear a slight tremor in it. "...Understood. Thank you. I'll come right away...yes. Bye."

He hung up and took a deep breath, heaving his shoulders while he was still looking away from us. Then he turned back around to face us and said, "I have to go to the staff room, so I'm closing the library."

He took another big breath. He looked like he was trying his hardest to get his emotions under control.

"Um, did something—?"

Cutting off the question I was starting to ask, Mr. Chibiki told us the news.

"That was a notice that Kuroi's corpse was discovered. Apparently, someone found it this morning at the city waste processing plant."

Chapter 15
September II

1

"There was that day with the terrible fog, remember? Wednesday. Kuroi went missing then, and yesterday..."

"They found his body, yeah. At the waste processing plant?"

"Apparently, a worker discovered it yesterday morning, buried in that day's trash. They could tell he was a middle school student from his uniform and other things, and they pulled his bag from the same garbage pile. The police had already been notified that he was missing, so the call came to the school right away. His parents confirmed his identity, so there's no question it was Kuroi. I heard that he had a broken cell phone in his hand."

Mei Misaki raised an eyebrow slightly as she listened carefully to my exposition. That was practically the only motion she made. Her blank face was like a doll's.

"All the bones in his body were broken, and his internal organs were ruptured. From the state of the body, they say he had been dead for about two days. So almost certainly, on that Wednesday morning, he was..."

"............"

"Wednesday is household garbage collection day here, and it should be the same where he lived. So, um, I don't really want to imagine it, but..."

But there was no way to avoid picturing it.

On the morning of Wednesday, September 5, when a thick fog covered the town…Kuroi had left his house in a rush, much later than usual. While on his way to school, he had encountered a garbage truck making its rounds. That must have been when the unfortunate incident occurred.

I let myself imagine the scene.

A garbage truck stopped with its rear hatch open. Kuroi, accidentally running into the back of the vehicle. His momentum causing him to drop his cell phone into the trash chute. A surprised and flustered Kuroi hitting a switch on the control panel with his body, setting the rotating plates and pressing plates inside the drum into motion and then, whether he realized he had done that or not, hastily reaching his hand in to pick up his phone. But maybe his aim was off or his foot slipped, so he lost his balance, then fell into the truck. And then, just like that, he got caught in the mechanism…

Under normal circumstances, it would be a highly improbable turn of events. But that day, there had been that dense mist. Kuroi sprinting into the garbage truck, making a mistake in his assessment of the situation, getting swallowed up by the machinery, the workers not noticing such a major accident…all this was the fault of that fog. It hadn't just affected people's vision but had also dulled their other senses; somehow, it even seemed to alter people's awareness and judgment.

The truck swallowed Kuroi up, and no matter how much he struggled, he couldn't escape. He was crushed to death. Without so much as being able to cry out for help. Nevertheless, he'd held on tightly to his cell phone and didn't let it go…

None of the workers was aware of any of this as they finished their rounds with the truck and headed for the waste processing plant with his body packed in the back. It seemed like someone would have noticed when they dumped the accumulated garbage out of the vehicle, but again, either because of the thick fog that day or for some other reason, an unbelievable oversight occurred. Before anyone realized what had happened, Thursday had gone by, and then on Friday morning, they finally…

How on earth can that just happen? It seems awfully suspicious. But still...Kuroi's dead body was discovered at the waste processing plant. Because of that bizarre mist and the unlikely series of accidents. This actually happened. All we can do is accept it.

"What an awful accident," Mei mumbled, then slowly closed her eyes one time. "Something that would normally never happen, just dreadful..."

It was afternoon on Saturday, September 9. I was visiting "Blue Eyes Empty to All, in the Twilight of Yomi" in the usual basement space, sitting across from Mei Misaki.

Ms. Kanbayashi's death in the bath at home. Shinichi Tanaka's little brother Yuuji's death—that accident I'd witnessed on the way home from school. Shimamura's delirium and death while she was home sick. And Kuroi's death, which had been disclosed to us yesterday.

I had given Mei an outline of this sequence of events last night on the phone. Then the next day, we had decided to meet up. I'd wanted to tell her all the details in person and hear her thoughts...

"How did everyone in your class act yesterday?" she asked.

I was a little stumped for an answer. "As you would expect, everyone was pretty disoriented."

First thing in the morning, they had been informed of Shimamura's death; then in the afternoon, they were informed of Kuroi's passing, and in between, news spread that the boy who had succumbed in the accident the day before was Tanaka's little brother... The classroom had been in chaos. More than a few students were crying or having breakdowns, and for a while, it had devolved into what you could call pure hysteria.

"What did Mr. Chibiki say?" Mei asked.

I replied, "He...he also seemed to be at a total loss. He was like, *What's going on? This doesn't make sense.*"

"............"

"Sixth period yesterday was science class, and we had study hall, since Ms. Kanbayashi isn't there anymore, but during that hour, Mr. Chibiki came to our classroom to address the situation and explain things. I think he wanted to keep the rumors from getting out of hand. But that didn't really make anybody feel better, so things got pretty chaotic again..."

"............"

"People started saying that this was the 'calamity.' And no matter how you think about it, it is bizarre that in the first week of September, four people connected to the class have died one after the other. Why wouldn't that strike you as strange? So..."

"You think so, too, Sou?"

"What about you?"

When I asked her back, Mei raised her eyebrow slightly again. Just as before, hardly anything else about her face moved. But unlike last time, she no longer resembled "an expressionless doll."

2

The day before, I'd been just as shocked as everyone else, had felt agitated and confused... Until then, I'd been able to maintain a critical and analytical mindset, but now I didn't even have that luxury anymore.

Learning of so many deaths in such a short span of time was overwhelming. It was like my whole body was beset by vertigo; the inside of my head kept on swirling round and round in emotional cacophony. It was so bad that I couldn't recall my thoughts clearly, nor who I might have spoken to and what about.

Though I had gone home, resolved to get in touch with Mei, and arranged to meet her the next day, I hadn't been able to fall asleep as the night wore on. Even after taking some of the sleeping medication I'd been prescribed, I still couldn't really sleep. Instead, I had drifted in and out of a drowsy wakefulness until morning arrived.

Am I alive right now or dead?

This thought had filled my mind as I awoke, seizing me with a fierce anxiety... Not sure what to do, I'd tried calling the "clinic" at the municipal hospital that morning. However, Dr. Usui's outpatient care schedule was already booked up for the day. I had been told that he would be able to see me if I came late in the afternoon.

"It's fine," I'd answered right away, doing my best to repress the anxiety inside me.

I'm fine, I had simultaneously tried to persuade myself. *I have plans to see Mei this afternoon. Meeting with her is more important than Dr. Usui's counseling.* I didn't have to consider it twice.

It would be my first time back to the doll gallery in Misaki since I had stopped by after our "dinosaur film festival" in August. *Three weeks since then…no, almost four, I think?*

Grandma Amane was there as always, by the long, thin table that sat next to the entrance. She greeted me. "Welcome, Sou. Mei's in the basement."

The first floor looked rather different, thanks to the remodeling that had taken place during July.

There were fewer display cases, and their positions had been altered; the whole area felt more relaxed overall, including the space where the sofa set had once stood. Thanks to the renovations, the upper space of the room, which hadn't been used for anything before, was now full of eccentric fixtures. There was a balcony-like shelf made of transparent materials jutting out high up on the wall, and another transparent display case like a huge egg that hung down from the ceiling… The dolls were placed on their shelves and in their cases with the assumption that they would be viewed from below, and the lighting had been devised to match.

Nevertheless, the atmosphere of the place was still unchanged, dusky and gloomy despite it being the middle of the day. The music was also the same as ever. The tune currently playing was quiet and dark, perfect for the dolls' secret meeting place…

"…It's strange, huh?" Mei asked.

"How so?" I asked back.

After a moment, she answered, "It's definitely unusual for four 'related individuals' to die in quick succession like that. I don't think that's normal."

She moved her head slowly left to right, with the same expression on her face, one eyebrow still slightly inclined. It wasn't a blank look from a lack of emotion but rather was the look of someone being overwhelmed with *too much* feeling.

"It's no wonder that your class started to freak out. No amount of reassuring could have calmed them down."

"So then, you do think...?"

My voice sounded unnaturally flat—like I was being overwhelmed by a particular emotion.

"What do you think about the 'calamity'?" I asked.

Mei sighed quietly as I did. "I don't want to believe it, but..."

"But, Mei..."

"It doesn't make sense!"

"That's what Mr. Chibiki..."

"What about you, Sou?"

"I..." I tried to answer, but my voice stuck in my throat. I felt like if I allowed myself to say the words, I could never take them back. However—

"...What do I think?" In the end, there was nothing I could do but say it. "It's undeniable. It's impossible that it's anything other than the 'calamity.' But..."

"But?"

"*How and why* is it happening?"

"How and why...huh?"

"I mean, that's the question, right?"

Mei didn't need me to tell her that. Still, I couldn't help but make a point of asking.

"That night in July, we returned 'Izumi Akazawa,' this year's 'extra person,' to 'death.' That should have stopped the 'calamity.' Everyone besides you and me lost any memories related to *this year's version of Izumi*, and any recollections they did have of the real Izumi went back to how they were originally. Then in August, there wasn't a single victim of the 'casualty,' right? And yet..."

"*But why? How are people dying again now?*" Mei asked. With both eyes closed, she shook her head slowly, directing her questions inward. "Was *that* not what originally ended the 'calamity'? Or did it stop for a while, only to *start again*? Either way, why?"

She repeated the question and shook her head again.

"I don't know."

She opened her eyes and looked at me.

"I'm sure this is the first case of its kind, so it's only natural that Mr. Chibiki would be stumped."

Her shoulders dropped, and she sighed deeply.

It was painfully obvious that Mei was also at a loss. I had been staring at her face this whole time, but now I couldn't stand it any longer. I had to look away.

3

I kept my mouth closed for a little while, and Mei was also silent... The string melody that had been playing abruptly cut off. Maybe Grandma Amane had stopped the music upstairs, or perhaps there was some kind of problem with the audio.

Suddenly aware of the cool, stagnant air in the gloomy basement showroom, I took a deep breath. Dolls were displayed everywhere throughout the cellar-like space. Out of nowhere, I got the impression that I needed to breathe in their stead... I think it was the first time I'd experienced such a sensation since I started coming to this place.

As I was panting, I was also waiting for Mei to say something.

But Mei being Mei, she was probably waiting for *me* to say something... No, that wasn't it. In that moment, she looked like she was working something out. Still sitting in her chair, she had closed both eyes again. She was perfectly still...perplexed but mulling something over.

Mei stayed quiet for a while longer.

"Um...did anything come to you?" I asked quietly, after she had opened her eyes.

"Hmm?" She tilted her head slightly.

"Oh, um, it's just…"

"I don't know," she mumbled, sighing deeply as she had done before. "Why didn't the 'calamity' stop? Why did it start up again? Ultimately, I don't know." Mei shook her head like she had before. "However," she continued, "there is something that's been bothering me a little."

"Bothering you? What is it?"

"An uncomfortable sense that something is off," Mei said, then placed the tips of two fingers—her middle and ring fingers—against her right temple.

"I think it was around the beginning of May, when that Hazumi girl decided to quit being the 'second non-exister.' When that happened, I told you I thought it would be okay, right? That even if there was one fewer 'non-exister,' as long as you were diligent, it would be fine. That no 'accidents' should happen, as long as you continued to carefully play your role."

Mei had told me as much back then, and I had believed her. However, in reality, in late May, Tsugunaga had went out in a horrible way. On the same day, Takanashi's mother had also died, conclusive proof that the "calamity" had begun.

"Back then, I wasn't trying to be optimistic. I didn't say that just to reassure you, Sou. That's actually what I thought, so I said it. But…"

"…………"

"In the end, that was my mistake. But even so, it was strange. Why did the 'calamity' start at all?"

Why did the "calamity" start at all? In response to Mei's question, I called up *her* words, which were still clear in my memory even now.

"So to solve this problem, I'm sure that finding a 'power balance' will be essential, or so it seems to me, at least."

Her words—Izumi's.

"An 'extra person,' the 'casualty,' has appeared in our class, inviting the 'calamity.' When we established the 'non-existers,' we prevented the 'calamity' from starting. The 'power' of the 'casualty' pulling us toward 'death' is offset by the 'power' of the 'non-existers,' maintaining a balance. That's how I think of it."

Indeed, if I remembered correctly, that was what she had said when we'd met two days after Tsugunaga and Takanashi's mother died.

"For our 'countermeasures' this year, we established two 'non-existers' just to be safe. By doing so, we kept the 'calamity' from starting in April, which means the balance was correct, right? However, once Hazumi abandoned her duties in May, the 'calamity' started. That must mean we're working with a different power dynamic this year."

"Wait…you mean that we're out of alignment with only one 'non-exister'?" I had asked at the time.

"Out of whack, off balance…yes, that's the picture," Izumi had answered. "If we don't increase the 'power' of the 'non-existers,' we won't be able to negate the 'power' of this year's 'casualty.' So…get it?"

So the theory is, if we restore the balance that Hazumi upset when she abdicated by enlisting another "non-exister," it should stop the "calamity"?

By that logic, she had proposed that we work out a new set of "countermeasures"…

"So it's a question of balance of 'power'… Mm, that's what you're saying, right, Sou?" Mei, as usual, seemed to see right through to my inner thoughts.

"And that's what Akazawa thought, so she proposed a new 'countermeasure' of adding a second 'non-exister' again, you said. I remember. Though in the end, that 'supplemental countermeasure' also had no effect…" Mei spoke slowly, as if double-checking her own memory. Then, at last, she pulled her fingers away from her temple. "Let's go back."

Gently sweeping Izumi's voice and face out of my mind, I replied, "Ah…sure."

Mei said, "Back then, in May, I was suspicious. And I was similarly suspicious when I heard that the 'calamity' had started again. Both times, I was asking 'why' and 'how' but…how can I put this, I've got a similar sense of discomfort as you. Something is off; something's strange about all this, somehow…yes, like dissonance between too-similar chords."

Mei herself was having difficulty making sense of her intuition.

I didn't entirely get what she was trying to say, either, so all I could do was put my thoughts into simple words.

"It doesn't make any sense. It goes against the rules. So how? That's basically the question."

"Mm. That's right...but..." Mei responded, her voice sounding unusually anxious.

"In that case—" I began, unable to suppress the feelings that suddenly swelled up inside me like a black mass. "There's no reasoning your way out of this. You talk about rules, but they're not scientifically proven laws of the universe. The 'phenomenon' and the 'calamity' and all that are just terribly irrational things to begin with. No matter how you try to grasp them by teasing apart their peculiar logic, you won't get anywhere. It's hopeless from the very start."

I thought back to a day in late July, after I had moved back to the main Akazawa house from the Freuden Tobii apartment, remembering what Yagisawa had said to me then. At the time, I had gotten irritated and denied it, but now I was repeating it. I was aware of the irony.

"We worked out our 'countermeasures' based on what we thought were the rules, but all our efforts failed. Judging by your experience three years ago, we returned the 'casualty' to 'death'... We went so far as to do that, but in the end, the 'accidents' didn't stop."

I listed our failures with a reckless, almost masochistic relish.

"There's nothing we can do at this point, is there? The information we relied on turned out to be false. Maybe we had it wrong from the very start..."

What we did that night in July, driving Izumi to her "death," might have been for nothing. If I had known that this is what would happen, I don't think I would have chased her like that. If I had given up and surrendered myself to fate from the beginning, without trying to get clever and resist it, or if I'd skipped town like Uncle Teruya...

As I was contemplating this, it suddenly became difficult to breathe.

I inhaled deeply several times. The air was unpleasantly chilly and thin. It felt like my body temperature was dropping with each breath. The dolls on the shelves were whispering to one another with their mute mouths. They pitied me. They ridiculed me. They scolded me. They...

I looked at Mei, begging for help.

She looked back at me with an expression of sadness in her right eye, the one that wasn't a prosthetic... When our gazes met, she blinked slowly and bit her lip slightly.

"Sou." Mei said my name quietly. "I don't think you should be down *here* right now. Let's go upstairs. I'll ask Grandma to make us some tea."

4

We moved up to the gallery on the ground floor, and Grandma Amane brought out some piping hot green tea. I drank it and felt my body warm, recovering somewhat. The music flowing through the building also returned, and I didn't feel suffocated by normal breathing anymore...

Mei barely tasted her tea, then seemed to start pondering something again. I felt too awkward to say anything to her, or actually, I couldn't find the right words, so I just sat on the sofa staring at my surroundings.

Come to think of it—I recalled—*last month, when I stopped by after we went to see the movie, we started out chatting at that round table in the basement, then came up to the first floor, and...*

A doll on display at the bottom of the staircase in the back of the gallery caught my eye.

There was an antique couch beside the stairs covered in a deep-crimson sheet, and the doll was positioned on top of it. It was a figure of a girl, somewhat smaller than life-size, clad in a blue-and-white dress. Apparently, this piece had been stored in a section of the basement for a long time. After the renovations to the first floor, it was moved to a new display area at the start of August.

The doll had been laid down facing upward. Both of its hands were clasped on its chest, fingers intertwined. Reddish-brown hair. White skin. Left and right eyes were wide open, both "Blue Eyes Empty to All." Mouth slightly ajar. It looked like it might start speaking at any moment.

Laid out on the couch like that—the way it was posed so naturally reminded me of a scene from earlier. It reminded me of that day in early August, at Yumigaoka Municipal Hospital. After wandering the bowels of the institution following Izumi's phantom, I'd arrived at a room...

"Sou...Hiratsuka?"

I heard *her* voice from back then. It sounded carefree, yet somewhat frail.

"I'm so happy you came."

"She used to be in a coffin, that one." That's what Mei had told to me when I'd first laid eyes on the doll on the couch last month. "Kirika seems to be very emotionally attached to her. I don't like her very much, though."

I was certain that Mei didn't like the doll because its face resembled hers so closely. I certainly remembered hearing her say as much, at some point, and I could see why she felt that way. At the moment, though, it was the scene in that hospital room that sprang back into my mind...

"Mm, I'm all right. I've been feeling pretty good lately."

There had been a single white bed in the spacious, dreary room. She had stayed lying down on the bed as she greeted Etou and me, who'd come to visit her together.

"In the end, I wasn't helpful at all," I'd heard her say in a desolate tone.

"You were," I think I answered.

"But still, I couldn't do anything..."

"That's not true. Besides, it's all right now. There's no longer any need to worry about the 'calamity.'"

"Really?"

Something had glinted silver as it wavered on the edge of the bedside table...

"Is that really true?"

"The 'calamity' is over," I had said.

That's what I'd believed at the time. I had thought we had no room for doubt.

"I see. Thank you."

I still remembered her smile, slightly relieved albeit somewhat lonely.

"Thank you. I..."

I remembered her smile in that room—Makise's smile.

That day, standing in Makise's room, I had *realized, remembered, and registered* some things...and as a result, I had *discovered a certain solution*. And then, *in order to check my hypothesis*, four weeks ago, here in this gallery, I had...

"Hey, Sou?" Mei asked suddenly.

Caught off guard, I hastily straightened up and stared back as she gazed at me.

After a short pause, Mei asked, "Sou, are you afraid to die?"

Without meaning to, I let out a small noise of surprise. At a loss for how to answer a sudden question like that, I responded without much thought. "Yes, I'm terrified."

"You hate the idea of dying? You don't want to die?"

"I don't want to, I think."

"Mm. That seems about right."

I had no idea what she was after, asking a question like that. At the same time, I wanted to put the same thing to her in response. But I quickly abandoned the idea.

I suspected that she would have a different reply than I did, and it occurred to me that I was a little afraid to hear hers.

"In that case, Sou, I said this once before, but you could just run away, you know?" Mei continued. "As long as you're in this town, the risk of an 'accident' won't go away. If you do as your uncle Mr. Sakaki did years ago and abandon everything to get out of Yomiyama..."

But before she could even finish, I shook my head.

"I don't want to run away," I said.

"But, Sou..."

"I don't want to die, either. So..."

So...? I wondered what the rest of that statement was, but all that came to me were empty words that didn't lead to any kind of resolution.

"I'll try to be careful. I'll avoid anything risky so the 'calamity' won't have a chance to get me."

"I see," Mei mumbled with a sigh. I was aware of the fact that her own position in all this was different than it had been before.

After a little while, it was time for me to start heading home, but I couldn't stop myself from turning to Mei and telling her, "You be careful, too."

5

Doorbell jangling at my back, I left the gallery. I was about to straddle my bicycle, which I had left parked in front of the building.

"Hey, Sou?" Mei called out to me. She had come to see me off. It sounded like she had suddenly remembered something important. "How's that girl, Hazumi?"

"How is she...? Well, yesterday she seemed extremely upset. I think that's to be expected, though, since we got news of Shimamura's death, and they were good friends."

"Do you have her contact information?"

"Like her phone number?"

"If possible, her address, too."

What does Mei want with Hazumi's address?

As strange as it seemed, I didn't give it much thought at the time. I told Mei I would look at the class roster after I got home.

"All right, then will you let me know when you find it?" she requested in the same detached tone as always.

"Um...why do you want it all of a sudden?" I asked.

"Just because." She brushed off the question. "Send it to me later— e-mail is fine. Please."

6

"Hey, is it really true? Did the 'calamity' actually start up again? Didn't it end in July?"

Once we were alone in my room, Yagisawa started questioning me, without even touching the iced tea that Auntie Sayuri had set out for us. Although he didn't have a very angry look about him, his tone of voice and demeanor were uncharacteristically serious.

"Hey, Sou, what's going on? What do you think about this?"

It was the afternoon of Sunday, September 9. I had gotten a sudden phone call from Yagisawa not one hour ago, asking if he could come over. There was no way I could refuse, of course, so I welcomed him in.

As to whether the deaths that month had been caused by the "calamity"—

On Friday, the two of us had gone to see Mr. Chibiki during lunch break. While we were talking, he'd gotten a phone call informing him of Kuroi's death—ever since then, I hadn't had a proper conversation with Yagisawa. It occurred to me that we probably also ought to speak with the countermeasures officers, Etou and Tajimi, but...I just wasn't dealing with it very well.

I wasn't the only one, either.

I had no doubt that Yagisawa, Etou, and Tajimi were feeling the same way.

Mr. Chibiki, too. Faced with the delirium of the class, he had been unable to maintain his usual composure. Though he had just barely managed to keep control by imploring everyone to *"calm down"* and *"hold it together,"* he had been unable to answer those voices that asked, *"So is it the 'calamity' after all?"* or *"Why is this happening?"* or *"What should we do?"*

"I saw Mei Misaki yesterday," I said, averting my eyes from Yagisawa's piercing gaze. "I met up with her and told her everything. She agrees that this is the 'calamity,' just as we thought."

"Oh? Then it's true." He ruffled his long hair and let out a short groan. It sounded almost like a sigh. "Good grief..."

We were sitting in my study-cum-bedroom, facing each other across a small elliptical table. My room was awfully cluttered, and I had been reluctant to invite even Yagisawa in, but it was unavoidable. I didn't want to let Auntie Sayuri overhear our conversation, because even at this point, I still hadn't had an honest conversation with her and my uncle about the "special circumstances of Grade 3 Class 3."

Despite that, they must have suspected something strange was going on. Even if I didn't confide in them, they knew that too many "accidents" had occurred at North Yomi since the spring (indeed, in this very house back in July, my grandfather had died under suspicious circumstances). They had probably been hearing about the whirlwind of events that had been happening since the start of this month, along with noticing that I wasn't acting normally, of course.

In fact, Auntie Sayuri had been asking me every day, with concern in her voice, "Are you all right, Sou?" She had been kind enough to tell me, "If you're ever in trouble, you come and talk to me about anything at all," but aside from that, she didn't meddle. She never pressed me with questions. I was very grateful for how she kept her distance. Even if I did tell my aunt and uncle every detail at this point, it wouldn't solve anything. It would just cause all sorts of grief for them, so I kept quiet.

"But if that's true, Sou..." Yagisawa stopped running his hands through his hair and looked at me, almost scowling. "Then what the hell happened? I thought the 'accidents' were supposed to have stopped. I thought this year's 'casualty' ended in July. It doesn't make any sense, does it?"

"............"

"It's weird, isn't it? It's wrong, for it to go this way. We thought everything through, and you took matters into your own hands, and we made it through the summer break without any incidents, and yet...and yet, here we are. After all that..."

"............"

"What does it mean? What's going on? Huh? Honestly, I can't help but be kinda pissed at you, you know?"

Yagisawa made another low groan, then let out a long sigh.

After that, the two of us were silent for a while.

I drank a little bit of my tea. Most of the ice had already melted. Then I stood up and hunted for the remote control for the air conditioner. I felt like the room had gotten awfully stuffy over the last few minutes.

When I had turned on the air conditioner and sat back down in my original place, Yagisawa looked around and asked, "Where's that photo?"

"Photo?"

"You know, the one you had on display in your old room. From summer vacation in '87."

"Ah…"

1987—summer vacation, fourteen years ago. The photo with Uncle Teruya and his friends at Lakeshore Manor, taken after he'd fled Yomiyama. Far from the reach of the "calamity," they'd spent a few peaceful days together.

That picture…

"I put that away somewhere. Maybe in my desk drawer?"

After Izumi had disappeared in July, it had become sort of painful to have the photo on display. It was an important memento of my uncle Teruya, but now it was also linked to my memories of Izumi at the Freuden Tobii.

But to Yagisawa, this photo of his Aunt Risa, who had died fourteen years earlier, looking happy, must have stuck with him.

"Should I look for it?" I asked. "The picture, I mean."

"Nah, it's fine."

"Your aunt, she died of a sudden illness—is that right?"

"That's what I've heard. I don't know what it was, though." Yagisawa took off his round glasses and pressed two fingers on his right hand to his eyes. He didn't seem to be holding back tears or anything like that. Instead, he just seemed exhausted.

"Kuroi died in an awful way, didn't he?" he said eventually. "And Tanaka's little brother, that was horrible, too."

"Yeah."

"Well, if I'm gonna die," he continued, "I hope the I don't go out too terribly."

"Hang on—wait a second. Just because the 'accidents' are still happening doesn't mean you're destined to die."

"Well, that's true, but..."

"You're an optimist, right?"

"Ah, well, I am, but..." Yagisawa frowned anxiously. "But, man...," he mumbled, then sat there silently for a minute with a serious expression.

"Man"—he opened his mouth again—"is it just hopeless now? Is there no way for us to escape the 'calamity'?" he asked with that same earnestness.

"Well...," I also responded gravely. "There might be some other, completely different approach, but...I don't know what it would be. And so far, no one else knows, either."

"The 'countermeasures' and the 'non-existers' were supposed to keep the 'calamity' from starting in the first place, right? I'm not talking about that. What I mean is, is there some way to end the 'phenomenon' entirely? Like, to lift 'Misaki's' original 'curse' or something?"

"I've heard that it's wrong to think of it as a 'curse,'" I said.

"I'm wondering if there's a spell or something that we could use to avoid the 'calamity.'"

"A spell...?"

"Well, maybe not a prayer or incantation. But perhaps there's something that will keep the 'calamity' from closing in...like a song or something?"

"A song?"

His suggestion seemed crazy, or rather, completely out of place, but I wasn't able to laugh it off entirely.

Yagisawa let out a short sigh, then held his tongue. I held mine as well. Once again, silence descended over the room.

I was the first to speak. "At the end of the day, I think the only way to avoid all danger is to run away, to get 'out of range.' Like my uncle Teruya did fourteen years ago."

"Get out of Yomiyama, huh?"

"In Teruya's year, there was a major incident in May, and a lot of people died all at once," I explained. "My uncle was injured pretty badly, and then the next month, his mom passed... After that, he decided to skip town."

"............"

"But that's not really a feasible solution," I continued. "Even if we explained everything to our parents and somehow managed to convince them to leave, all sorts of pragmatic issues would stand in our way, like where to live and what our parents would do for work. And we're still just kids. There's so much that could stop us..."

"You're right." Yagisawa nodded meekly. "Even if I told them to run, my family is really big. I've got an older sister and three younger brothers. And my dad has to be here for his job... There's no way we can just up and move. Ugggh...but, man..." He pressed his palm into his forehead. "The 'calamity' doesn't just go after us; there's a chance it can hit our families, too, right? So then...ughhh..."

The "calamity" had arrived despite all our "countermeasures." And instead of stopping when we returned the "casualty" to "death," it had started back up again.

Is there really nothing we can do? No way of dealing with this?

I sluggishly mulled over the issue, but no matter how much I considered it, I couldn't find an answer. It felt like I was sunk up to the shoulders in a quagmire of helplessness. It was clear that I wasn't going to just think my way out of this.

"What about you, Sou? You're not running away?" Yagisawa asked. "You could go back to your parents' house in Hinami... Ah, sorry."

I had explained to Yagisawa at some point why I was staying with the Akazawas here in Yomiyama.

"Sorry, man. I just sort of... Well, when I get like this, I—"

The sudden chime of a cell phone interrupted him. I had mine set on silent mode, so the ringtone must have been his.

He pulled his phone out of his jeans pocket and, with his glasses still off, brought his eyes close to the display.

"Tajimi?" he mumbled, then answered the phone. "Hey. Tajimi, right? What's up...? Hmm? Huh, what?"

I couldn't hear the voice on the other end. But just from the changes in Yagisawa's expression, plus the way he responded, I could guess the nature of the conversation.

"...N-no way. No way... Ah, yeah. Yeah, that's right. What do you call it, that...? Oh!"

Yagisawa quietly said, "He hung up...," and tossed his phone on the table. When he put his glasses sitting nearby back on, his hand trembled. His face was extremely stiff, and one side of his mouth was curled upward, almost like he was laughing and crying at the same time.

Before I could ask about the phone call, Yagisawa wailed, "Tajimi's older sister was just in an accident. She was hanging out in Yomi-yama Park with a friend, and that's where it happened."

"An accident...at the park...?"

"I don't know all the details, but Tajimi's sister apparently...died at the scene."

7

The accident occurred at around two o'clock in the afternoon on Sunday, September 9.

The location was Yomiyama Park in the southwest of the city. It was a small, old amusement park rumored to be closing in the near future. On that day, Tajimi's older sister Miyako (nineteen years old, a vocational school student) had visited area with her (female) friend from high school. And when the two of them went on the "coffee cups" ride—

They had turned the handle in the middle of the cup that made it spin, but it rotated too hard. Somehow, the momentum flung Miyako out of her seat and sent her crashing headfirst into another spinning cup. She lost a great deal of blood and passed out. An ambulance managed to get her to the hospital, but she'd died of hemorrhaging soon after.

I had been to Yomiyama Park once, a long time ago—the year that the Akazawa family took me in, Auntie Sayuri and Uncle Haru-hiko had brought me there. It was a difficult period in my life, but I remembered enjoying it—it was the first time I'd ever been to an amusement park. I was pretty sure I'd ridden the coffee cups...

That made it even more disturbing when I heard about what had happened on the news that night. I could see it in my mind, and it was awful... It felt like that feeling of hopelessness was engulfing me.

8

Monday, September 10. It rained all day.

For the past few days, I'd scarcely caught a wink of sleep. When I did manage to nod off, it was light. Today, I arrived at school rubbing my tired eyes once again. I didn't make it in time for the morning homeroom but did make it to my classroom right before the start of first period. When I walked in, I was a little surprised at the large number of vacant seats. But at the same time, it made sense...

A quick look around confirmed about a third of the class was absent.

Tsugunaga and Keisuke Kouda had passed in the first semes-ter. Makise was still hospitalized. Shimamura and Kuroi had died recently. Add to them Tajimi, who was out on bereavement leave after losing his sister yesterday. The seat belonging to Izumi had already been cleared away, so there were now six people's worth of empty chairs. Someone had set vases of white chrysanthemums on Shimamura's and Kuroi's desks.

The fact that more than a third of the seats were without students meant, in other words, that several more people were absent aside from these six—

Tanaka, whose little brother had lost his life last Thursday, had returned from his bereavement leave, but several other people were missing.

I doubt that all of them are out sick, which must mean...

After our first-period math class, Etou came up to talk to me.

"They're scared to come to school; I'm sure of it," she said. "'Related individuals' have been dying one after another, and it's clear that the 'calamity' isn't over…so it's inevitable that everyone's afraid, you know? I feel the same way myself."

"Ah, yeah…I get it," I replied.

"We don't know when or where an 'accident' might happen. People have even died at school. Going to and from there is dangerous, too. So it's safer not to go to class and to lock yourself up at home. Can't blame people for thinking like that, huh?" she asked.

"But no matter how long they stay at home and shut themselves in, the 'calamity' will…"

Take my grandfather, for example. And Shimamura, too. I even heard a story from Mei about a "related individual" who holed himself up on the second floor of his home and died when a huge construction vehicle crashed into it. However—

In the little more than a week since the start of the second semester, five people have already succumbed from "accidents." I do get that some people aren't interested in sitting down and calmly considering the specifics of the "calamity" anymore, though… They'd rather skip class altogether.

"I'm sure that before long, we'll see some people who quit school and move out of Yomiyama, too," Etou said, lowering her voice slightly. "I've heard that it's happened before. My older cousin was really worried about what she should do three years ago—she told me."

"What are you going to do?"

When I posed this question to Etou, she answered in an unexpectedly frank tone. "I don't know. It would feel really frustrating to run away from here after everything that's happened and how hard we tried. I'm a real worrier at heart. That's why I suggested we have two 'non-existers' at the 'strategy session' in March. Just in case, you know?"

"Ah, yeah."

"But obviously that 'countermeasure' didn't work out very well, and once the 'accidents' started happening, I sort of felt like nothing really mattered anymore."

That was the kind of response I'd expect from someone who described themselves as a worrier and who I knew was also a bit of a perfectionist.

"But now, of course, the idea that I might lose my life isn't just frustrating; it's terrifying, too. How about you, Hiratsuka?"

I was slightly at a loss for words when she asked me that. "I...I think it's awful, too. I'm scared. But at this point..."

At this point, the "accidents" aren't stopping. At this point, we can't escape from the "calamity." There's a good chance I'll be swallowed up by "death" as well. And in my case, escape from North Yomi is not an option. So at this point...

"What about Makise, in the hospital?" I asked. "Have you told her what's been going on since the start of the month?" I was suddenly concerned about her.

Etou shook her head slightly side to side. "I haven't been to see her in a while."

"I wonder how she's feeling?" I asked again. I felt conflicted as I recalled the image of Makise, laid out on that hospital bed, all alone.

Etou shook her head. Then she mumbled something, halfway talking to herself. "Honestly, at this point, telling her that the 'calamity' isn't over feels..."

"Impossible?"

She stopped speaking, and this time I saw her nod slightly.

I stared up at the classroom ceiling, full of increasingly mixed emotions.

9

After second period ended, I went over to talk to Yagisawa.

He was still sitting in his chair and glanced up slowly to answer me with a "hey," but his voice sounded awfully frail. His expression was lifeless, and although he made eye contact, he immediately turned away from me the next instant...

What's going on? Is he all right? I was worried for him, but he had an air about him that made me feel awkward asking.

He had been like that after yesterday's phone call with Tajimi, too. Once he told me about the accident, he put on a kind of brooding expression and kept his mouth tightly shut. He even forgot whatever it was he had been about to tell me right before the call came in and refused to say anything more... Eventually, he'd stood up to leave with only a brief remark: "I'm going home."

The news must have greatly unsettled him. I'd felt the same way, so at the time, his attitude hadn't really bothered me.

"I..." Yagisawa had started to say something just as he was leaving.

"Hmm?" I'd asked.

But he'd immediately shaken his head. "No, it's fine. It's nothing."

With that, he'd left in a hurry, but...

"You don't look well," I told Yagisawa back in the classroom. He was still staring at the floor. "Though I don't suppose telling you to cheer up would really be the right thing to do."

"Ah...yeah, you're probably right."

This is the first time I've ever seen him like this, I thought. But I also figured that I didn't need to worry about him. *It's Yagisawa, so I'm sure that he'll be in better spirits by tomorrow.*

Ultimately, those were the only words I exchanged with him that day.

10

During lunch, I went to the secondary library alone. I wanted to speak with Mr. Chibiki (though I didn't know what I planned to discuss or how), but the CLOSED sign was out on the door, and there was no answer when I knocked.

From there, I went straight to the biology club room, which was also on the first floor of Building Zero. It wasn't for any particular reason. I just sort of went... Well, I probably figured that there wouldn't be any club members there during lunch, so maybe a part of me wanted to be alone. At the very least, I didn't want to go back to the Grade 3 Class 3 classroom.

Just as I'd expected, the room was unoccupied.

During our meeting in late August, the biology club had decided that the next step was getting the creatures back in the clubroom by the start of next semester. In spite of that decision, however, we'd accomplished very little on that front so far. I didn't have much hope of progress in the near future, either. That was because the new head of the club, Morishita, was also a member of Class 3—working on that project with him was out of the question.

I pulled a stool from under a long table and sat down.

I could hear the sound of the rain falling outside. Inside, the room was dim, and the air was humid on my skin...but for some reason, I wasn't sweating. It felt like something frigid was burrowing inside my body...

"...Shunsuke."

Shunsuke Kouda's death in June. The scene came back to my mind afresh...but for some reason, it didn't bother me. Maybe it was because a suitable amount of time had passed or because I'd been numbed to "death."

"Shunsuke died back then, and now..."

My voice spilled out of my mouth. It startled me a little.

"What happens to people when they die?"

Ah...that's a question I once asked when I was very young.

"When people die? They can go meet up with everyone else some-where, right?"

Teruya had responded to my question.

"Who do you mean by everyone?"

"You know, all the people who passed before them."

If that's the case, then right about now, Shunsuke is...

Suddenly, I realized what I was thinking and shuddered a little.

No. That's wrong. I mustn't think like that anymore. This isn't a question of whether I was right or wrong, but at the very least, now I know that...

"The thing about 'death' is that it's incredibly empty; it's eternal loneliness..."

These were Mei's words from a summer's day three years ago. And I...

...*Thud.*

"*They drew lots with playing cards, right? That's when Hazumi pulled the joker and it was decided that she was the 'second,' but... Okay, so think back. To before that.*"

Huh? I was surprised. Why did *that* memory suddenly surface?

"*Before the lottery began, someone else tried to volunteer, right? In a small, quiet voice that everyone was a little surprised to hear. Why so suddenly? We all wondered...*"

These were Izumi's words from that night two days after Tsugunaga and Takanashi's mother died at the end of May, giving us conclusive evidence that the "calamity" had begun.

Why am I remembering this? Even as I questioned it, those moments kept playing back in my memory—what was going through my mind at the time, how I responded then, and...

...*Thud.*

"*But ultimately, their offer wasn't recognized, and we went ahead with the lottery, right?*"

"*The cards had already been shuffled, and I think...yeah, Hazumi said in a weird, panicked way, 'You can't do that now,' and immediately started the lottery drawing.*"

"*Ah...yeah. I guess that is how it went.*"

Afterward, Izumi had explained her thoughts on the "balance of 'power'" between the "casualty" and the "non-existers."

Why? Why am I remembering this here, now? I wondered.

Maybe because the topic of the March "strategy session" had come up briefly while I was chatting with Etou in the classroom earlier in the morning. Or...

...*Thud.*

I could feel a deep reverberation coming from somewhere, so low that it was almost outside my range of hearing.

Yuika Hazumi.

Suddenly, that name started to weigh on my mind.

Yuika Hazumi.

She was one of the people who didn't come to school today. We all thought that she was finally back now that the second semester started, but after a week, she stopped coming again, huh?

In relation to that, I vividly recalled how distraught she'd seemed last Friday, when the deaths of Shimamura and Kuroi had been confirmed one after another.

"How? Why?" She had shouted. And then she'd cried, "It had nothing to do with me," and, "It's not my fault." Hazumi shook her head dramatically many times, messing up her short hair. At first, her face had been flushed, but once Kusakabe grew flustered and started trying to soothe her, she had gone through a complete change, and her face had drained of all color...

I wonder what she's doing today? Somewhere that's not at school?

Once I started worrying about her, I couldn't put it out of my mind, no matter how I tried.

I pulled my cell phone from my pocket and called the number I had saved for Hazumi.

11

It took several calls before she picked up.

Hazumi must have known it was me from looking at the incoming call display, because she answered in a trembling voice, "Sou?"

"Sorry for calling so abruptly."

"What is it? Do you need something?"

"No, it's just that..." I spoke as softly as I could. "You didn't come to school today. I was a little worried about what's going on with you."

A moment passed in silence.

"Hmm..." When she spoke, Hazumi sounded somewhat guarded. "You were worried? About me?"

"Well...yeah, I was. You finally started coming to school again, but then..."

"I'm not going anymore," Hazumi said flatly. "I'm not going to class anymore. Absolutely not."

I guess she won't be persuaded, huh?

"Are you at home now?"

"Yes."

"You're going to stay at home?"

"That's right. After all…"

"After all?"

"The 'calamity' never ended, did it? Far from it. Look how many people have died. Ms. Kanbayashi, and Shimamura, and…yesterday, Tajimi's older sister passed, didn't she?"

Hazumi was clearly frightened.

Just two or three months earlier, under the influence of "Big Brother Nakagawa," she had firmly dismissed the "calamity" as entirely unscientific, and yet… I didn't know what had happened between the two of them after that, but I could guess that she was no longer in his orbit.

"If I go outside, I never know when something might happen. So I won't go to school anymore. I don't want to go. Because I don't want to die. If I stay shut up in my house forever, I'll be safe."

I understood why she stubbornly insisted on that. But there was still a risk of being struck by an "accident," even if she stayed locked up in her house and never went outside. Of course, even if I had tried to tell her that, she probably wouldn't have listened. That's how it seemed.

"Mm. I see." That was all I could reply with. "I don't think you have to force yourself to come to class. But I also feel like it's not good to take this too far. I totally understand your fear, but if you let it overwhelm you… What am I trying to say? You could wear yourself out…"

I knew I was probably being too forward, but I was speaking as much for my own reassurance as for hers.

Well, that ends this phone call.

I started to say good-bye, but—

"Wait a minute, Sou." Hazumi stopped me.

"What?"

"Who on earth is that girl?"

I could hear a nuance in her voice that was different than before. The timidity had disappeared, and instead, she was aggressively lobbing her words at me.

"Who do you mean by *that girl*?" I asked her a question in return, unsure of her meaning. "Who are you talking about? Did something happen?"

Another momentary silence. Before long, Hazumi told me these facts.

"Yesterday evening, my intercom suddenly rang. When I answered, someone asked, 'Is this Yuika Hazumi?' It was a female voice that I didn't recognize, and my mama and papa weren't home, so I didn't go out to the entryway. It was late at night, too, so I got kinda scared."

Ah...that was, maybe...

"Even so, I managed to ask her, 'Who are you?' Then she answered, 'My name is Misaki. I'm a friend of Sou Hiratsuka's.'"

So that was her.

"But the thing is, I had trouble trusting what she said. So in the end, we just spoke over the intercom, and then she left. Misaki is generally an unlucky name, too. I was a little curious because she said she was a friend of yours, but I thought she might be talking nonsense. Anyway, it all happened so suddenly, it was kind of creepy."

When we parted on Saturday, Mei had told me she wanted Hazumi's contact information. I suppose it was for this.

But why did she...?

"And then, that same Misaki person from yesterday came to my house again today." Hazumi continued grousing, indifferent to the fact that I was deep in thought and trying to infer Mei's motives.

"It was early in the morning, so Mama was home, too, and she just opened the front door without thinking about it. She didn't even say anything over the intercom first. And when she did, that girl was there..."

Hazumi and Mei had met once before, in May. The location of their encounter was the Izana Bridge, the one spanning the Yomiyama River.

At that moment, I recalled Hazumi crossing the bridge to chase after me and Mei coming over from the other side. There had been a bit of distance between them at the time, but they would have seen each other.

Mei had remembered that instance. But Hazumi didn't seem to have recognized Mei's face from their brief encounter. So…

"The girl had on a high school uniform. Is she an older friend of yours or something?" Hazumi asked.

"Well, something like that, I guess," I answered. "She's really a normal person, though."

"She was suspicious!" Hazumi concluded resolutely. "Her face is so pale, it's creepy, and she had a patch over her left eye… And then when she said, 'You're Hazumi, right?' it was like there was no emotion at all in her voice."

A patch over her left eye…?

"What did you talk about?" I asked gingerly.

"Nothing," Hazumi answered, as if she was commenting on something deeply disagreeable. "She didn't say anything; she just stood outside the entryway and stared right at my face. That's all she did before leaving."

"I see."

"Listen, Sou, what the heck is up with her? Why did she come to my house? What did she want?"

Hazumi piled on the questions, her voice growing much more animated. I wasn't sure how I should answer her, and while I was faltering over it—

The chime signaling the end of lunch break started ringing through the old classroom speaker.

12

The following day, Tuesday, September 11.

I overslept considerably and didn't wake up until after ten o'clock. Second period had already started.

"Don't rush off, Sou."

I had skipped breakfast and was about to leave the house when Auntie Sayuri called out to stop me.

"Are you feeling all right? Have you got a fever or anything?"

"Ummm…I'm fine."

"When you didn't get up, I peeked into your room, but you were fast asleep. Somehow, I felt bad about waking you. You've been going through so much lately, so you're probably exhausted."

"I'm sorry for worrying you."

"You can stay home from school when you're not feeling well, you know."

"No…I'm fine, really," I answered. I didn't want to burden my aunt and uncle any more than I already had. But to be honest, I definitely wasn't feeling "fine" when I left the house.

I hadn't been able to sleep the night before. Every time I was on the verge of getting some rest, I would have a nightmare and wake back up…and that cycle repeated. Night after night, I'd hardly slept a wink. Thinking back on it, it had been that way ever since last Wednesday night, the foggy day when Kuroi went missing.

I was well aware that both my body and mind were utterly exhausted. With the ongoing lack of sleep, I was beyond groggy. That's why I had gotten into bed early last night. But that hadn't stopped my thoughts from running wild…

The Grade 3 Class 3 classroom, with its conspicuous empty seats. The oppressive atmosphere. Yagisawa's listless face. My exchange with Hazumi on the phone. The way most of the teachers tried their best not to make eye contact with the students during class, and how they spoke somewhat gingerly when addressing us…

…After sixth period, our substitute homeroom teacher, Mr. Chibiki, came into the classroom wearing an uncharacteristically severe expression. But the words that he spoke to us were somewhat muffled and weak.

"Frankly, I don't want to think about the 'calamity' starting up again. But I can't deny the fact that since the start of this month, a number of 'related individuals' have lost their lives. So the question is, how should we handle this situation?"

Even when Mr. Chibiki told us this, no one cried or panicked. The response was very blank... No, there was no response at all. The room was silent and still, almost as if "death" itself were now a regular fixture of the room. The only sound was the rain falling outside, like some sort of mechanical white noise...

"How should we deal with this?" Mr. Chibiki repeated the question. "I have no idea," he answered himself, shaking his head side to side.

"But what I mean to say is, we shouldn't let our anxiety and fear get the better of us—that's all I wanted to emphasize. According to the rules of the calamity, one or more 'related individuals' will die each month, but you all—the students of this class only make up a small percentage of the 'related individuals.' You mustn't get obsessed with wondering if you're next. I want you to remain as calm as possible, especially in times like these.

"And there's one more thing about what's been happening this week that strikes me as strange. As far as I know, this is the first time that this many 'accidents' have happened in such a short period of time...so I wonder if after this, they might actually *stop* occurring so often. That seems like a possibility."

Mr. Chibiki wasn't going to offer his students any false reassurances—that was his nature and his policy. I tried to keep that in mind, but all things considered...

"It is also a possibility that our current situation is actually something like an aftershock," he added, squinting hard behind his lenses. It looked like he was mostly trying to convince himself.

"At some point in July, the 'extra person' disappeared, and the 'phenomenon' ended. Consequently, the 'accidents' stopped. That should have been the 'end of things' for this year. Having more 'accidents' at this point defies logic. It doesn't make sense."

Ah, so then—my thoughts started racing—*so then what's happening this year is definitely a "special case." Any rules we thought we knew don't apply anymore. We can't explain it logically. It's an absurd, nonsensical situation that we have no means of comprehending...that's the only way to think about it, right?*

Mr. Chibiki had almost certainly mentioned the word *aftershock* as a last-ditch effort to try to somehow explain what was going on.

"If we think of the 'calamity' as a kind of 'supernatural natural disaster,' like an earthquake, then it's possible that it could have similar aftershocks. That might be what we're experiencing now. This isn't something that's happened before, but this year, there's some kind of rebound, and that..."

It was not a convincing theory. I had no doubt that Mr. Chibiki himself was fully aware of this as he said it.

He looked exhausted and stressed out at the same time...and I could tell that he was starting to lose it just a little.

...He's probably already prepared himself for the worst.

I'd had similar thoughts over many sleepless nights.

Mr. Chibiki, who was subbing for Ms. Kanbayashi in our homeroom after her death, was now an "active member of Grade 3 Class 3." He was one of the "related individuals" who that "calamity" could effect. His position was now completely different than before, when he had been observing the "phenomenon" as an "outsider." So...

On top of his stress and exhaustion, I could tell that he was juggling a great deal of sorrow as well. For some reason, thinking about him reminded me of Uncle Teruya, who had departed this world three years ago.

13

I noticed that I had a missing call in my phone history while I was on my way to school. When I checked, I saw that it had been from Tsukiho.

It was the first time she'd called me in about two and a half months.

There was a notification for one voice message. Tsukiho must have left it. I could imagine what it said, since she had gone out of her way to call me today—the morning of September 11.

I had gotten calls from her this morning last year and the year before, too. To wish me—happy birthday.

I was turning fifteen today.

It was natural for my mom to want to wish me happy birthday. Even when you took our situation for the past three years into account...

Since that day in late June, when I had declared our separation on the roof of the municipal hospital (in front of Mei), my ill feelings toward Tsukiho had diminished somewhat. At the time, Mei had asked me, "...*You love her, don't you? You love her all the same,*" but even I wasn't sure yet if that was really true.

I don't want to hear this message.

I was certain of that, at least. With that thought, I erased it without playing it.

The rain seemed like it would continue falling, as it had all night. It stopped as I left the house, but it was cloudy enough that the weather could turn bad again at any moment. Sure enough, just as I arrived at school, a fine drizzle started falling.

It was a light-enough rain that I didn't bother using my umbrella. I picked up the pace and entered the school from the back gate just before eleven o'clock. Second period would have ended already, and third period had just started.

There were no PE classes happening out on the damp, puddle-covered field, and the huge uninhabited space looked truly desolate. There were several pitch-black silhouettes flying above the school grounds—crows. I stopped briefly to track them calmly with my eyes...and that's when it happened.

My phone vibrated with an incoming call.

Tsukiho again? I thought. But considering the time of day, that wasn't possible. Reassessing, I pulled out my phone. The name on the display was "Yagisawa."

I answered the call. "Hello? Yagisawa?"

I heard his voice. "Sou...you home?"

"No, I'm not. I'm running late, so I just finally got to school."

"What? I was so sure that you would take today off."

"I couldn't sleep last night, so I couldn't get up this morning, that's all. What about you? Shouldn't you be in class now? Or are you not at school?" I asked.

There was a short pause.

"I'm here, but I didn't go to third period."

"So…what's up?"

"Well, I just sorta…" Yagisawa answered evasively, then immediately asked me a question in return. "You said you just got here, right? Where are you?"

"I came in through the back gate…"

"Hmm? Ah, *is that you*?"

"What do you mean?"

Surprised, I looked around instinctively. Maybe he could see me from where he was now.

"Where are you…?"

"I thought you were at home taking the day off; that's why I called you."

"Huh? What do you mean?"

"Well…" He started to say something and trailed off. I could hear his labored breathing whenever he paused…

Before long, he said, "I wanted to talk to you one last time."

"Huh?!"

What is he talking about? What on earth does that mean, one last time?

My anxiety started rising. Panicking, I examined my surroundings again.

Searching for a place where he would be able to see me. A place where he could spot me and recognize me well enough to ask if it was me. *Where would that be?*

"I'm right *here*." I heard his voice through the phone. "On the roof of Building C."

"Huh? Huh?"

Across the deserted school grounds. A three-story gray school building made of reinforced concrete. Building C was the closest one to me. And on the roof…

…*There,* that's *him*.

It was raining harder now, and I strained my eyes to look.

I could see a single human figure standing out against a background of cloudy dark-gray sky. Because of the distance, I couldn't see Yagi-sawa very clearly, but he seemed to be standing on the *outside* of the iron railing that cordoned off the roof.

Is he...?

"Can you see me?" came his voice. "Should I wave?" The figure put one hand up. "Your timing is kinda spooky, man."

"Hang on, Yagisawa—what are you...?" Still pressing the cell phone to my ear, I started jogging through the field. Cutting straight across the grounds was the shortest path to that building.

"Sorry, Sou, but I just...," Yagisawa said, "I *quit*—I'm *running away*."

"You quit? You're running? Wh-what are you—?" I gasped out a response as I ran across the grounds, muddy with rain. "What are you saying? What...?"

"I've been thinking about it the whole time," he answered. "As long as I stay in Yomiyama as a member of Grade 3 Class 3, I can't escape the risk of an 'accident.' And this isn't just a problem for me. My parents or siblings could get wrapped up in it, too. Like Tanaka's little brother. Or Tajimi's older sister. In which case..." He didn't sound worked up at all; instead, he sounded matter-of-fact as he told me, "In which case, *I'd rather disappear now*, I figure. If I do that, my family will be cut loose from Grade 3 Class 3. And since they would no longer be 'related individuals,' there shouldn't be any chance of the 'calamity' getting to them, right?"

"Y-you're kidding..."

I came to a stop most of the way across the school grounds and gazed up at Building C. There was no longer any question about the person standing on the edge of the rain-soaked roof. It was definitely Yagisawa.

"Don't do it!" I was gasping for breath, but I managed to squeeze out the words.

Yagisawa must have been planning to jump from that point. He would leap, end his own life, and save his family...

"You can't! Don't do it!"

Does he not know? Doesn't he know that his plan might not work?

"You can't stop me."

"Don't!"

Like three years ago, when a student died in an "accident" and then their grandparents passed later that year during the school trip…

Isn't he aware of that?

But given the circumstances, I didn't have the chance to explain that to him.

"Don't do it, Yagisawa." All I could do was plead with him with all my heart. "You can't."

"I've already made up my mind."

"Don't! Stop!" This last cry wasn't through the phone. I shouted as loud as I could, directly up at him, where he stood on the roof. "Stop it!"

I was sure that my screams made it to the ears of the teachers and students who were in the middle of class. More than half the classroom windows were open, after all.

Several faces peeked out from the windows on each floor of Building C. I felt their eyes converge on me, looking at me with suspicion.

"Stop it!" I shouted again. "Don't do it, Yagisawa!"

"Sorry, Sou." Through the phone, I heard him sigh and say, "Bye now. You keep on living."

He hung up. Then, the very next moment—

Yagisawa's body, which had been perched on the outside of the railing on the roof, flew into the air. There was no time for me to say anything as *it* soared above the ground—then fell behind the thicket of plants that grew between the sports field and the school buildings and disappeared from view.

14

Several hours after this uproar, I returned back home. Auntie Sayuri already knew what had transpired and worried over me incessantly, but I just answered her with, "I'm fine," and secluded myself in my room in a daze.

I'd witnessed Yagisawa jump in real time. The shock had been overwhelming. I had been literally paralyzed, unable to move a muscle or run over to where he fell. All I could do was stand there, getting soaked by the rain. Meanwhile, someone had reported the incident to emergency services, and before long, police officers and EMTs had rushed to the scene... The whole school was in a tumult.

I remembered watching from a distance as they put him onto a stretcher and loaded him into the ambulance. He'd landed on grassy ground, made soft by the constant rain—he hadn't died on impact.

I'd wanted very much to follow Yagisawa to the hospital, but Mr. Chibiki had found me there and must have guessed what was going on with me, because he called out to me and said, "I'll go to the hospital, so you hurry home today, Hiratsuka. That would probably be best."

"Ah...but—"

"You look awful. Both you and your voice are shaking. How do you feel?"

"I don't know."

"You saw Yagisawa jump, didn't you?"

"Yes. I was running late, and when I got to school, it was just as he..."

"Mm. At any rate, you should go lie down in the nurse's office, or if you feel up to it, you can go straight home."

"But Yagisawa...Yagisawa is..."

"I'll contact you as soon as we know what condition he's in."

"............"

"The police are looking for witnesses and will probably want to hear your story, but for now, I'll intervene as best I can and keep them away from you. Okay?"

"Thank you."

"Be careful on your way home. Don't let the 'calamity' get the better of you."

"Okay."

Ultimately, I had gone home alone around two in the afternoon to wait for Mr. Chibiki's call. The intermittent fits of shaking that racked my body finally tapered off. Strangely, I hadn't shed a single tear. It was as if my emotions had been paralyzed as well.

If I recalled correctly, I got the call from Mr. Chibiki a little after four o'clock. A call came to my cell phone from the municipal hospital where they'd taken Yagisawa.

"He's in critical condition and still unconscious from a skull fracture and brain hemorrhage. He narrowly escaped death, but it sounds like it's touch and go." Mr. Chibiki informed me of Yagisawa's condition in a quiet, subdued voice. "They're not allowing visitors except for family. Even if you rushed over there, there's nothing you could do."

"Really?"

"But why did Yagisawa do this all of a sudden?" Mr. Chibiki sounded like he was mostly asking himself. I was conflicted over whether to inform him of my exchange with Yagisawa over the phone right before he jumped off the roof. In the end, I decided not to, because it was extremely painful to recall.

"Um, Mr. Chibiki?" I asked. "Is Yagisawa's…is *this* also part of the 'calamity,' I wonder?"

"The deaths brought about by the 'calamity' are not limited to accidents and illnesses. They include suicides and murders, too."

"Yes, of course."

"I've seen all sorts. Of course, it depends on the case, but sometimes people other than 'related individuals' do get dragged into it…"

"Do you think he'll survive?" I asked another question.

Mr. Chibiki's answer was unsparing. "Critical condition means it's very serious, even more so if this is a part of the 'calamity.' We shouldn't cling to hope. I know it's tragic, but…"

I imagined the figure of Yagisawa, hovering between life and death in the intensive care unit at the hospital, and my chest started hurting so much, it scared me. Even so, no tears came out. Sure enough, my emotions had been paralyzed.

I should be sad; I should be suffering. I should be anxious and terrified and desperate. And yet, the circuit that connects all those different emotions has been cut somewhere. That was what it felt like.

I also had the bizarre sense that, while my mind was fragmented and confused in the wake of suffering serious trauma, some part of my consciousness was detaching itself from "reality."

I also felt like my heart was starting to break. I couldn't help but recall again the events of the summer of three years earlier.

My heart wasn't that strong to begin with, and it could no longer stand this present "reality," so...

I wonder what will happen once it starts to break, is breaking, has broken? What will become of "me" then? What exactly will "I" be...?

I was caught in a helpless thought loop.

I stayed in my room alone, stuck in a stupor.

15

I only left my room that evening when I was called down for dinner. I ate just a little, without making conversation, then went right back to my room.

Worry. Anxiety. Fear. Suspicion. Doubt. Helplessness. Despair... Countless questions and thoughts were scattered through my mind, but I couldn't bring myself to actually confront a single one. Though I could feel my heart begin to break, it also felt distant, like it belonged to someone else. Like before, I'm pretty sure everything passed in a blur.

What I really wanted was to go to sleep, as soon as possible, whether that meant turning to medication or something else. I resorted to taking twice the prescribed amount of the sleeping pills and sedatives that I had on hand...yet even so, deep sleep eluded me.

During my fitful slumber, it seemed like some parts of my brain were still awake and alert, continuing to ruminate of their own accord. That's how it felt to me, but...

....

...Why?

That was the big question weighing on me.

...Why? Why is this happening?

Why are there still "accidents" even after "Izumi Akazawa," this year's "casualty," returned to "death"?

It was supposed to be over, so why has it been like this since the start of the month...? Ah, why? What could be going on?

Is it because the "phenomenon" this time is a "special case," an "aberration" that even Mr. Chibiki has never experienced before? But what if...what if this is not a "special case" like that? If that was true, what would it mean?

"So to solve this problem, I'm sure that finding a 'power balance' will be essential, or so it seems to me."

I suddenly recalled what Izumi had said.

"The 'power' of the 'casualty' pulling us toward 'death' is offset by the 'power' of the 'non-exister,' maintaining a balance. That's how I see it."

...Why?

"That must mean, in other words, that we're working with a different power dynamic this year."

...Why? Why now, why is what she said...? Why? Why? Why?

Countless "whys" jumbled together, tossing me to and fro.

Or maybe I should take something from this. Something...an answer? But there's no such thing; it shouldn't exist—we've already given up on finding it, and yet...and yet?

...Why?

Why...? Oh, right, at this late stage, Mei Misaki went to see Yuika Hazumi, huh?

"She was suspicious!"

These were Hazumi's words.

"Her face is so pale, it's creepy, and she had a patch over her left eye..."

....

....

...I can almost make something out.

...Thud.

I can't see it clearly. I can almost grasp it—

...Thud.

I can't get a hold on it. Something is... Something's there, maybe something very important...

...Thud.

....

....

...I suddenly opened my eyes.

I urgently needed to urinate.

Legs shaking perhaps from the medicine, I tried to making my way to the bathroom.

Before I got anywhere, I noticed my cell phone, which had been tossed onto the floor beside my bed. When I picked it up, I noticed that the battery was dead. *Come to think of it, I don't think I charged it yesterday or today.* My hazy mind—perhaps also a consequence of the medicine—sluggishly arrived at this thought, and I plugged my phone into the charger...

Once I had gone to the bathroom and done my business, I staggered back toward my room...

On the way, I heard some strange voices.

Weird...unusual voices having a conversation. *They likely belong to Uncle Haruhiko and Auntie Sayuri. They're probably coming from the living room. Maybe the TV is on, too; it kind of sounds like it.*

Even though I was up and moving around, it felt like more than half my brain was still asleep. Despite my fogginess, I went to see what was going on in the living room.

I looked at the clock by the bathroom. It was already past midnight. *At this time of night...?* I wondered why they were still awake.

As I suspected, my uncle and aunt were in the living room. The two of them were sitting on the sofa, watching the television intently. The cat, Kurosuke, was there also, pacing beside them restlessly.

"Sou?" Auntie Sayuri noticed me. "Oh, Sou, something awful's happened," she said, pointing toward the TV. Uncle Haruhiko just glanced at me briefly, then immediately looked back at the screen. I, too, turned my eyes to the television.

The TV screen was showing a striking view of some foreign city. *What is this?*

Some kind of movie? No, that's not it. The news seems to be talking about this as a present, ongoing "event"...

"A passenger plane has crashed into one of the World Trade Center buildings, followed soon after by a second plane. The two damaged buildings have completely collapsed in a terrible disaster..."

New York City?

The World Trade Center buildings?

What they're showing on TV now must be images from right after that collapse.

Under a cloudless blue sky, an incredible plume of smoke rose from the city like a massive volcanic eruption, or perhaps a huge, dark monster with a malevolent will of its own.

"We tried calling Hikari, but the line won't connect," my aunt said with a worried face. "She's living in Queens, so I think she's probably safe, but..."

Hikari was Haruhiko and Sayuri's oldest daughter, who lived in New York City.

"The Pentagon in Washington is up in flames, too. We don't know the whole story yet, but it looks like a large-scale terrorist attack."

Even though I heard what my uncle was saying, I couldn't really respond. It was like I was still more than half asleep.

After that point, I don't really remember what I saw, or heard, or what we talked about. I also don't really remember when I headed back to my room and went to sleep. All I could recall was that no matter how much news footage I watched, and no matter how it was explained, I couldn't help but feel like none of it was really happening.

I wasn't sure whether it would still be real when I opened my eyes in the morning.

Interlude V

Sou,

I called you earlier, but it didn't go through, so I'm sending an e-mail.

Congratulations on your fifteenth birthday.

I think you were nine when we first met, and compared to back then, you've totally grown up. You're strong, and you're kind. Much more so than someone like me.

By the way, I have a theory about the "accidents" that have happened since the start of the month.

Maybe there is something I can do. I've been wavering over whether I should tell you about it or not…but in the end, I guess I didn't need to. Don't worry about it, Sou.

Chapter 16
September III

1

Wednesday, September 12. Third period, math class.

Rrm, rrrrm…

I heard the faint rumbling of the earth right before it happened. I didn't even have time to wonder what it was.

Crack!

The sound and the tremor came at the same time.

The shock, which seemed to be forced up from directly below, lasted just a moment. Then the ground under our feet began to shake, the desks and chairs clattered together, and the chalk fell from the chalkboard tray… *An earthquake?* Even though I realized that's what it was, my body froze in place, and I couldn't react.

The reactions from my classmates varied.

There were quiet and loud screams. Some people leaped out of their seats, while others clung to their desks. Some even tried to crawl underneath them. There were a lot of students who were completely frozen, like me. Even though our responses were different, we all shared surprise and fear.

"Everyone, calm down!" Our math teacher, Ms. Inagaki, was writing on the blackboard just as it happened, and she turned around, still gripping the chalk. "It doesn't seem to be a very large quake. Everything's fine. It will settle down soon."

Just as she'd said, the shaking was already starting to diminish, but still…

One of the pencils I had out on my desk fell to the floor. I looked up and saw that the light fixtures hanging from the ceiling were swaying, but not that dramatically. It certainly seemed like it hadn't been a major tremor, so I began to relax. However, just then—

Crash!

There suddenly came the loud noise of something shattering.

Since I'd already let my guard down, it was terribly disarming. Several screams shook the air of the classroom again.

The flower vases that had been placed on Shimamura's and Kuroi's desks on Monday had fallen. Both of them, together with the white chrysanthemums that had filled them, lay shattered on the floor.

The flower-filled vases hadn't been particularly secure, positioned close to the edges of the desks, and they'd plummeted during the earthquake. It seemed like a bad omen. I had a sinking feeling.

The destruction of the vases may very well have been one of the triggers for the strange situation that occurred in the Grade 3 Class 3 classroom that day.

2

Even fewer students in Grade 3 Class 3 had shown up at school that morning than the day before, down to about half our original number. I'd been among those who had arrived at school on time for morning homeroom. However—

I had *chosen* to go to school that day. Auntie Sayuri had told me that I could stay home if I wanted. But even if I had skipped school and stayed home, I would probably have just shut myself in my room and spent the day depressed. And if I did that, it would cause unnecessary worry for my aunt and uncle…that's what I'd told myself.

I'd been certain that the television in the living room had been on all night. From the time I'd gotten up until I'd left the house, it had been reporting endlessly on the horrible tragedy in America.

According to Auntie Sayuri, she had finally been able to get in touch with Hikari, her oldest daughter who was living in Queens, that morning. Both she and my uncle had seemed very relieved by that, but it had sounded like the chaos at the site of the attack was going to go on for quite a while, so it was easy to tell that they were still very anxious.

The information we'd been getting from the TV news alone had been more than enough to convey the gravity of this incident, which would later be called the "9/11 attacks." It was obvious that America, and the rest of the world, had uncertainty in store. However—

Even after I'd fully awakened, the assault still felt somehow unreal to me. It was incredibly shocking, but it still hadn't registered as something happening in this reality…

I'd been more concerned about Yagisawa's condition and the pressing issue of the "calamity" weighing on my mind. Though no matter how much I worried about either, there was nothing I could do. Everyone else at school that day must have felt the same way, more or less.

"Did you see the news last night?"

"I did. I just happened to turn on the TV, and it suddenly showed those images."

"At first I had no idea what was going on."

"It looked like a scene in a movie."

"My dad was watching with me, and he kept repeating, 'This is really serious!'"

"They've been running special reports all night. I wonder what's gonna happen?"

"It looks like lots of people died."

"They did, tons of them."

"What will become of all of it?"

"It's terrorism, right?"

"That's what they're saying."

"Will there be a war?"

"Maybe…"

Those sorts of conversations had filled the classroom all morning, but on the other hand—

"I heard that Yagisawa has been unconscious this whole time."

"I wonder if he's gonna make it?"

"I wonder."

"If this was also the 'calamity,' it might be difficult."

"But it was suicide, wasn't it? Why would he try to kill himself?"

"The 'accidents' have gotten scarier."

"Suicide is a scary thing. I could never do it."

"You say that, but it was Yagisawa of all people who went through with it."

"I wonder if he left a note or anything?"

"Maybe..."

On the other hand, many students had still been discussing other affairs.

I hadn't felt up to talking about anything with anyone. Instead, I stood alone by the window, staring outside.

Rain had been falling off and on the previous night, but the weather had improved. However, that didn't mean a clear blue autumn sky was stretching out above me. I'd caught sight of a big swelling of cumulonimbus clouds near the mountains, and though it had looked like ordinary summer weather to me, the breeze had seemed to carry an unseasonable chill... Or maybe that was my imagination.

"...I can't."

My ears had picked up on another conversation in the classroom.

"I just can't do it anymore."

"Me either, not anymore..."

"I don't want to come to school anymore, either. I don't want to come, but even when I'm at home, I'm thinking this or that on my own... I feel like I'm going crazy."

"I know what you mean. Why is it like this...?"

"Ah geez, I really can't stand it. I'm terrified!"

"Maybe it's better than the terrorism in New York...but it doesn't feel that way."

"How could it?"

"I don't want to die!"

"I hate this. I'm scared. I don't want to die."

"None of us does."

Me neither.

I don't want to lose my life, either, I'd thought. *But as long as the "calamity" continues and there's a possibility of becoming one of its victims, that risk hasn't gone away. All we can do now is pray for our own safety every day, I suppose.*

Mr. Chibiki looked downright pitiful during homeroom. Obviously he was trying his best to act like a responsible teacher. But he hadn't been able to hide the exhaustion on his face or in his voice.

His voice was incredibly pained as he updated us on Yagisawa's condition, and it had lacked any conviction when he'd told us students not to be pessimistic and to take *"appropriate precautions against accidents and illness."* It was obvious he felt helpless.

"In this situation, everybody is frightened and anxious. If you think it's necessary, I want you to come talk to me without hesitation, no matter how minor the issue seems. Even if it's impossible to resolve the situation, I may be able to offer you some sort of advice, based on my own experience.

"Police will be coming to investigate yesterday's incident, but you don't need to worry about them. It will all settle down soon. Also..."

Then Mr. Chibiki's voice had grown somewhat more intense. "...Starting yesterday, members of the press have been spotted around town, but you shouldn't talk to them, even if they ask you questions. Even if you were to tell them about the 'calamity,' they would just write it up as a curious story in some irresponsible article. There would be no use to it. Besides..."

Here, Mr. Chibiki's voice grew yet more intense as he continued. "Even if they make a fuss over it for a while, *they will soon forget.* The rest of the world, and even the people of Yomiyama, will quickly vanish from their minds. Anyone without a direct connection to the 'phenomenon' at North Yomi or the 'accidents' won't hold on to memories of the 'calamity' and any related events *for very long.* It's not a natural circumstance, you see? So no matter how worked up they may get about it, it's only temporary, and their awareness will quickly fade. In my nearly thirty years of observation, that's how it's always been. Presumably this, too, is related to the 'alterations' and 'falsifications' that the 'phenomenon' brings about."

3

Between first and second period, a student showed up to school late—Hazumi.

I'd been a bit surprised to see her.

When I spoke to her on the phone on Monday, she was very insistent that she was not going to come to class anymore, so...why is she here?

After second period, I had looked over at Hazumi, and our eyes had met. She turned away awkwardly but didn't stand up from her seat.

I had gone over to her desk by the window and tried to speak to her. "I thought you weren't going to come anymore. Did you have a change of heart?"

Hazumi had stared silently out the window for a long while. "I'm scared. Somehow being home alone is just as frightening. If I turn on the TV, every channel is showing nothing but the incident in America...and it's scary."

Her face was extremely pale. Upon closer inspection, she seemed much more haggard than before.

"You told me about it on the phone the other day, but Misaki came to your house, didn't she?" The question had been weighing on my mind, and I hadn't been able to stop myself from asking.

Hazumi had continued staring out the window and only nodded wordlessly.

Then I'd asked another question. "You said that Misaki had on an eye patch when she showed up, right? When you went out to the entryway, did she take it off at all?"

At last, Hazumi glanced up at me. "*She did.* She took it off, and she stared right at me."

"And then?"

"That's it."

"She didn't say anything?"

"I did hear her mumble, 'I see,' but that was it."

Stopping to picture the scene, I'd been able to understand why Hazumi had been creeped out. But even so, my mind had raced, wondering what had happened.

If Mei had been wearing the eye patch over her left eye, then she'd likely been wearing the "doll's eye" in her left socket. Then she'd taken off the eye patch to "look" at Hazumi.

Just what was she up to?

It couldn't be…

At that point, a nagging suspicion had bubbled up in my mind of its own accord.

It couldn't be… No, but…

Nothing had been clear.

The chime signaling the start of class had played, shaking me from my thoughts, and then third period had begun…

4

The earthquake hadn't been that serious, but the two flower vases had fallen off the desks and broken.

Vase fragments and flowers were scattered across the floor, along with spilled water. Several students left their seats to clean up the mess of their own accord. They all moved somewhat timidly.

One student gathered the fragments with a broom and dustpan, another wiped the wet floor with a mop, and another bundled up the scattered flowers and set them back on the desks… At a glance, it looked like their movements were coordinated and focused.

The students cleaning up did their work in silence, and the other students watched them attentively. Everyone's expressions were incredibly stiff. Though we had recovered from the shock and fear of the earthquake, it was obvious that the surprise of it had caused a surge of fresh anxiety to spread through the classroom.

In the midst of all that—

The one who realized the first little change was none other than me.

I suddenly became aware of a dissonant sound and looked around the room, wondering what it could be. What I saw there, one of the white chrysanthemum flowers that had been picked up off the floor and set on a desk—

A single black insect was resting there.

What's that?

I strained my eyes, and it became clear.

"A fly..."

The words rushed from my mouth reflexively, and one of the girls who had been cleaning (Fukuchi, the class representative) let out an, "Oh no!"

Normally, a single fly in the classroom wouldn't cause much of a stir. But considering everything that had happened, it was really ominous and unsettling to see one sitting on the flowers set out in tribute to the dead...

"Oh no," Fukuchi repeated, "when did that get in here?"

She waved the fly off with her hand. The faint sound of its wings as it left the flower petal made it to my ear. And then, immediately afterward—

Suddenly, a different noise, dozens of times louder than the fly's wings, was audible from somewhere.

Someone shouted, "Wah!" It was a boy sitting in a seat by the windows. When I looked—

Right outside the open window was some kind of huge, unstable black mass... Quickly, I realized what it was. Flies. Dozens of them, no, hundreds, flying together in a swarm. Right at that moment, they started to pour into the classroom through the window.

The class burst into chaos.

In the middle of it, in my head, suddenly—

Bzz—, bzzzz——bzz.

There was a high-pitched vortex of fluttering wings. It was separate from the buzzing I was hearing in reality and seemed to overtake it for a moment...

Bzz—, bzzzz——bzz.

Is this...?

Is this the sound from three years ago? A flashback to that disgusting experience in the basement of Lakeshore Manor? And I only just finally managed to stop thinking about it so often this past year...

Bzz—, bzzzz——bzz.

The harsh noise seemed to surround my whole body and reverberate through my brain. Whether I wanted it to or not, the sound was calling to mind the vivid memory and terror of "death"...

The students were in an uproar. Since the windows to the corridor were all open, some people frantically tried to drive the swarm away. A few bugs flew out of the room, but many remained.

"Nooo!"

I heard a scream, and when I turned around to look, I saw it was coming from Hazumi. She was batting at her hair and clothes with both hands as flies pursued her.

"Why...oh why?! Leave me alone!"

Kusakabe rushed over to Hazumi, who was almost in tears, and the two of them drove the insects away together.

Eventually, Hazumi's agitation subsided, but—

Bzz—, bzzzz——bzz.

Even though the chaos in the classroom had finally settled down, I could still hear the high-pitched buzzing in my mind. I shook my head hard and squeezed my eyes shut, but it just wouldn't go away.

Dropping back down into my seat, I put both elbows up on my desk and rested my head in my hands. The endless droning of wings was joined in my mind by the odor of "death." I knew that it couldn't be real, but I felt like I was losing my grip on "reality." I pinched my nose shut with one hand.

"Um...teacher, I'm..."

Just then, I heard someone make an anguished appeal.

5

"I'm, um, not feeling..."

The complaint was coming from a girl named Ichiyanagi. She sat in the very front desk in the second row over from the corridor. Only her back was visible to me from where I sat.

"Oh?" Ms. Inagaki answered. "If you're not feeling well, go to the nurse's office…"

But before she could finish her statement, Ichiyanagi's figure disappeared from sight, accompanied by a dull thunking noise. Perhaps she had tried to stand, and her legs had given out. She'd keeled over in her chair and collapsed to the floor.

"Oh! Are you all right?" Ms. Inagaki rushed over with a panic stricken across her face.

However, as she did—

"I feel bad, too."

"Me too."

"And me."

…One after another, students started complaining about feeling unwell.

"It's hard to breathe," whined a boy whose shoulders were rising and falling furiously, as if he had just finished running as hard as he could. "It hurts, I…"

"Something smells weird," remarked one girl, Takanashi, pressing a handkerchief to her nose and mouth. "Hey, you smell it, too, right? The weird stench. It's making me feel kind of sick."

"Me too. It's…" The boy who answered her as he stood up was Morishita, the new head of the biology club. "It's suddenly gotten worse."

He took several tottering steps toward the window, but before he got there, he put both hands on his upper abdomen, fell to his knees, and began to vomit.

Several other students tried to stand on unsteady legs and collapsed. Many others remained seated, facedown on their desks and suffering from headaches.

What about Hazumi?

I looked over to her with concern and found that she, too, was lying limp with her face planted on her desk.

Kusakabe must have noticed the offensive odor, too, because she was holding her handkerchief against her mouth. Etou had left her seat and gone over to the windows on the corridor side, and now the upper half of her body was hanging out over the sill, and she'd stopped moving. Even Tajimi, who had come to school despite losing his older sister on Sunday, hadn't found the strength to get out of his seat, and now he sat crouching beside his desk.

Clearly, something strange was going on.

Almost every student in the classroom was now doing poorly. Ms. Inagaki just stood there in earnest confusion, watching it all happen...

We had fallen into a state of mass hysteria.

So many deaths in such a short time since the start of the second semester—the "calamity" had stopped for a little while, but it obviously wasn't really over. The fear and anxiety of our situation had been building and building, and then the earthquake, and the broken vases, and the swarm of flies... These ominous events had pushed our stress past the breaking point, manifesting as real, physical symptoms. It wasn't clear whether everyone had been affected all at once or if the symptoms had spread like a contagion.

I was only able to make sense of the situation later, after it was all over. At the time, I'd been too engrossed in the pathological chaos of the classroom to understand it. I had been swallowed up by the hysteria.

"What the hell is this?" I heard someone yell. "What's going on? Are we all about to die here?"

That's ridiculous!

But even as I was thinking that, I had been sitting there the whole time with both hands on my desk, positioned as if I was going to stand up from my chair but basically unable to move beyond that. The high-pitched whine continued to reverberate around inside my head. The disgusting smell of "death" wasn't going away at all; nausea and vertigo assaulted me. It felt like the person I knew as "me" was gradually slipping away from "reality"...

At some point, I must have passed out. The only other thing I remember is a chorus of ambulance sirens.

6

"...Sou?"

I opened my eyes upon hearing my name to find Izumi Akazawa. I was in a familiar place. It was her apartment in the Freuden Tobii.

"So as I was saying, the important thing in the end is the balance of 'power,'" Izumi insisted. She looked rather upset.

"The balance of 'power.'" I realized that it was my own voice repeating her words back to her. She was—Izumi Akazawa was this year's "casualty," and I had returned her to "death" that night in July, so of course, the girl sitting with me now was not my real cousin. She must have been a reproduction of my own mind...

"You've got the resurrected 'casualty' and the 'non-existers' established as a 'countermeasure.' The balance of those two seats of 'power' is surely—"

"Surely?" Even though I knew this wasn't reality, that it had to be something like a dream, I felt a sort of sense of impatience as I asked, "Surely what?"

Izumi's expression changed to a sad smile as she turned her back on me.

"*Think*, Sou," she said. "Think and *remember*."

"...Sou?"

I heard my name and opened my eyes to see Mei Misaki. I was in a familiar place. It was the Freuden Tobii again, in the room where I had lived for close to four months.

"So I had a sister born on the same day in the same year as me—a twin sister. We were fraternal twins, but we looked a lot alike...," Mei said quietly.

"But she died before me, in April three years back. Of illness."

Ah, this is...this isn't reality, either. It's not happening now; it's in the past. If I remember correctly, this happened in June when she visited my apartment. It's not a dream—it's my memories playing back in my mind.

That evening, Mei had told me her "life story," something she had barely ever spoken of before. From hearing her tale, I had learned of the true relationship between Mei and Kirika, and…

"Aah," Mei groaned as she intertwined her fingers and stretched both arms straight up. "I'd rather not have any family or blood relatives to worry about, but I'm still a child, and children can't just run away. And while I'm stuck here, wishing I could run away, I, too, will inevitably grow up."

I don't want to grow up. That had been my urgent wish as an elementary schooler—at least up until that summer three years ago. *But now… I wonder…? How do I feel about that?* The very same thoughts echoed again in my mind. And then…

"Listen, Mei? Can I ask you just one thing?" I inquired. "It's that twin sister you told me about earlier. What was her name?"

"Her name…" Mei moved her lips. "She was…"

In broken syllables, she told me the name. "She was… ■… ■ ■… ■ ■ ■."

But I couldn't hear what she was saying. I couldn't read her lips, either.

Mei's figure suddenly melted into the darkness, leaving me alone in my confusion. Then I heard whispering in my ear.

"*Think,* Sou."

I could only hear the voice.

Is this Izumi's… No, is it Mei's?

"Think and *remember.*"

7

I woke up in bed.

For a moment, I didn't understand what was going on, but an instant later, I realized that I was in a hospital room. I could recall hearing the sound of ambulance sirens just before I blacked out. Someone must have noticed the crisis in our room and called emergency services, and now…

I tried propping my upper body up slowly. Though my head was still a little fuzzy, I didn't feel particularly unwell… Well, there was a dull pain running from my right palm into my wrist. When I examined the area, I saw there was a bandage wound around my hand. I must have injured it when I'd lost consciousness and collapsed. My left arm had an IV needle stuck into it, and when I moved it, a slight pain ran up that side, too.

"How are you feeling?" someone asked me. A nurse had just stepped into the room. She was an older woman but still several years younger than Auntie Sayuri.

"Ah…fine. I think I'm all right."

I caught sight of her name, "Kurumada," on her ID tag.

"Does the wound on your hand hurt?"

"No, not that much."

Ms. Kurumada came over to my bedside, checked on the state of the IV drip, then spoke to me like she was comforting a child. "I'll be done with this soon, okay? Then I'll call the doctor in."

"Um…where am I?"

"In the municipal hospital. Someone called us about a bunch of students getting sick and collapsing."

"So everyone's here, then?"

"Yes."

I looked around the hospital room.

It was for a single patient. Atop the single bedside chair sat my bag. Someone must have brought it along when they transported me here.

I couldn't see the clock, so I asked the nurse what the time was. Ms. Kurumada informed me it was 1:45 in the afternoon.

"Where is everyone else now?"

"We're having the students with minor symptoms rest in one of the large rooms on the sixth floor. Those who collapsed or came in with injuries were put into whatever private rooms were available for more serious treatment."

"So everyone's all right, then?" I couldn't help myself from asking. "There was nothing life-threatening…?"

"Everything's fine on that account," Ms. Kurumada said with a kind smile. "I heard there was a disturbance over an offensive odor— is that what happened?"

Even when asked directly, I couldn't quite give an answer. Really, at the time, I didn't know what I could have possibly said.

"Okay, all done here," announced Ms. Kurumada as she pulled out my IV line with skilled motions. "Now then, you rest here, just like this."

The nurse departed, and once I was left alone in my private room, my ears picked up a long, low rumbling.

Is that thunder? But it's been sunny all day...

Apprehensively, I peeked out the window. I couldn't see even a sliver of blue sky. It was so dark that it was hard to believe it was still daytime.

I shuddered, full of dread. It seemed like a terrible omen. Then I began to shake again.

8

Despite being told to rest, I had no desire to lay there motionlessly.

I got out of bed and pulled my cell phone out of my bag where it sat on the chair.

There were two missed calls in the history, both from Auntie Sayuri. The school must have reached out to her. She had called my phone directly, likely worried sick.

I had to let her know that I was all right, so I pressed the button to call her back. However, the only thing I could hear was some kind of terrible static, and the line never connected.

Maybe the reception is bad...

I stuck my phone into my pants pocket, then left the hospital room to go relieve myself. Though I was a little unsteady on my feet at first, that went away after a moment.

I must be all right now.

My room number started with the digit 5. When I examined a

display on the wall, I discovered that I was on the fifth floor of the hospital ward. The pediatric area, apparently.

I found a bathroom quite a distance from my room and did my business. I tried calling Auntie Sayuri once again from there, but yet again my efforts were fruitless—all I could hear on the other end was static.

Just as I was about to quietly return to my room—

"Huh?" I let out a noise of surprise and stopped in my tracks.

I was standing in a small open room like a lounge that joined two corridors. It was about half the size of our classroom, and it had several sets of tables and chairs. In one section of the lounge stood a large television. A special news report on the present situation in America was playing on screen, but the sound had been muted. In front of the TV—

A very young girl was standing there, alone. Her back was toward the screen, and she tilted her head to the side as she looked at me.

"Hello," I said out of curiosity. I recognized her. "You're Kiha, right?"

I think I'm right; her name is Kiha. The second-grade daughter of Dr. Usui, the head doctor at the "clinic"...but...

The girl was wearing lemon-yellow pajamas instead of the usual uniform she would have donned on her way home from school. Which meant—

"Are you staying here?" I asked without thinking. "Is something the matter?"

The girl—Kiha—ignored my question.

"I'm worried about Papa," she said quietly.

"Huh?" I didn't understand. "Your father? What's—?"

Before I could ask what was going on, Kiha silently turned around and walked calmly over to one of the windows in the back of the lounge space. I followed after her, growing concerned.

I had absolutely no grasp on where this space was located in the confusing labyrinth of the hospital ward, so I didn't know where the window was positioned exactly or even which direction it faced.

Only one section of the window was open, and Kiha paused in

front of it. I followed her over, and when she stopped, I looked out to see where she was staring.

It was even gloomier outside than it had been when I'd looked out the window of my room earlier. It was so dark that you would think it was nearly sunset. Though the low rumbling of thunder was absent here, the shrill cry of the wind filled the air in its place. And there was another noise, completely different from the gale. It was not a noise of the natural world. It was dreadful—harsh and grating.

Is it some sort of explosion? A helicopter?

Kiha was looking directly out the window. She said nothing, didn't move at all.

"Hey, what's wrong?" I asked quietly. "Is something…?"

"The wind," she replied.

"Huh? What about it?"

"The wind," she repeated, extending her right arm in front of her. I stepped up to stand beside her and gazed out at the dark sky where she was pointing. When I noticed her expression, my breath caught in my throat.

Both her eyes were open wide. Her irises were a different color than they had been just a moment ago. They were now a strange shade of dark blue with little rivulets of silver running through them.

"That girl…"

Suddenly, something Dr. Usui had told me about his daughter at some point in the past came back to me.

"You know, that girl's always had something a little strange about her."

"The wind is coming," Kiha announced. She looked possessed. She spoke in a hollow, flat voice, like she wasn't really the one doing the talking.

The wind is coming… The wind is coming?

As soon as she said that, the sound of the gale shifted abruptly. The constant, high-pitched whine was replaced in an instant by a terrific, thunderous boom, as if all the sound had been gathered together and pressed into a single, massive din. It was terrifying, but it still did not prepare me for what came next.

The illumination outside also rapidly faded. Before my eyes, the sky grew dark as night, as though a wave of inky blackness had swept over the world all at once.

And then came the wind, accompanied by a horrendous tumult, like the bellow of some gigantic creature.

A great gust blew in through the open window, sweeping Kiha off her feet. She let out a short scream as the winds literally blew her small body away, sending her sprawling across the floor.

The gale buffeted me as well, and although it did not blow me away, I was forced to take several steps backward and then drop to one knee. Unable to stand, I resorted to using my hands and knees to brace myself against the force of the squall.

I could hear people in the hospital (several adults and two or three children) screaming. Pamphlets and other papers that had been sitting on tables and counters swirled through the air in disarray.

Somehow or other, I managed to stand up and made my way toward the window, moving against the wind. I was thinking that I had to at least close the open window. However—

Bam!

A dull, violent noise rang out nearby. Another shriek came from someone's mouth. I nearly shouted, too, in my surprise.

Bam!

The same sound came again.

What is that? What on earth is happening now? As my head was in chaos with these questions—

Bam! Wham! B-bam...

The clangor persisted, reverberating from somewhere beyond the bank of windows before me. It sounded like something was colliding with the glass over and over again.

Once I reached the windows, the source of the noise became clear. Birds. From the color and size, they were probably pigeons.

Maybe they were being blown about by the sudden gale. Or maybe they were trying to escape it. Perhaps the sudden change in weather had taken them by surprise. Whatever the case, a flock of frenzied pigeons was swarming about the building's windows, crashing into them again and again. Some of the birds bounced off the glass and flew away, but many plummeted motionless to the ground, or stuck to the windows, writhing and bleeding. The windowpanes were smeared with gore and run through with cracks. It looked like the glass might shatter at any moment.

Argh, what on earth is happening outside? What's going on around this building right now? What's next?

I recalled a day in early May when a sudden hailstorm had struck the school in the middle of the late Ms. Kanbayashi's science class. It was right after Hazumi had renounced her role as a "non-exister" and insisted that we acknowledge her. The hail poured down like bullets and shattered a window, after which an injured crow flew into the classroom…

This time, there was no hail. There wasn't even any rain. And yet the ferocity of the terrible gale was unlike anything I'd ever seen.

The roar of the wind was inescapable. A lone pigeon fluttered in through an open window, battered by the gusts. By that time, a few hospital staff members had noticed the commotion. Several people screamed, and the bird flew off down the hallway and disappeared.

I saw one of the nurses take Kiha by the hand and help her stand up.

"What happened, Kiha?" I heard the nurse ask. "Are you all right? What a surprise that was! Okay, let's go back to your room, shall we?" I was somewhat relieved to see the girl obediently follow the nurse's suggestion.

I fled from the area near the windows. My knees were quivering. It felt like the temperature in the room had suddenly dropped, but at the same time, it seemed like it was someone else who noticed it, someone who was not "me."

Argh, what is this feeling…? Oh…

It felt as though the gale had blown half of "me" away, leaving another "inner" part of "me" exposed somehow.

So if things stay like this, I…

Just as I began to sense those disturbing thoughts overtake me, once again, several people screamed at once.

The lights in the hospital flickered before suddenly giving out.

9

The blackout lasted only a few seconds. Power was almost immediately restored, but even after the electricity came back, the lights continued to flicker. There was no way to know for certain, but the violent winds had probably caused some problem with the electrical system.

Turning my back to the disturbance near the windows, I set off down the hallway. I was still beset with the bizarre sensation that some part of "me" was not "inside" but "outside" myself.

Should I go back to my room? Or should I look in on everyone who's in that big hall on the sixth floor?

I walked down the corridor, vacantly musing to myself.

Prompted by the sudden violent weather or the problems with the lights, people were emerging from their rooms and going every which way. I heard a number of cell phones getting calls. I heard the cries and shouts of children. I saw adults stopping staff members and grilling them about the situation. What had been a quiet afternoon in the hospital until just a few minutes earlier had abruptly been replaced by a complete clamor.

The lounge I had just moved from probably wasn't the only place where pigeons were crashing into windows, for as I walked down the hallway, the din of the wind engulfed me. Windows had probably broken in other areas as well. At any rate, it was a bizarre situation. And surely the problem wasn't isolated to the fifth floor. The whole ward was probably dealing with the same craziness right now.

Despite the chaos, half of "me" was still wondering—*What was going on with that girl Kiha earlier? Did she notice the wind was coming and tell me at the perfect time? Or...?*

She said, "I'm worried about Papa." And she was obviously hospitalized for some health problem herself. She left her room on her own. But what about her "papa," Dr. Usui...?

Oh, I get it, I realized. *Maybe Dr. Usui is in this building now? With all the students they brought in, he was probably called over from the psychiatric ward to help examine them.*

Maybe that's what she meant by "worried"?

Just what is she worried about? What kind of worry? What on earth did Kiha Usui mean...?

I think I'll go to the sixth floor after all rather than return to my dorm. If I go to the sixth floor, I might be able to see Dr. Usui. And if I see him, I'd better tell him how Kiha was acting earlier.

There was a floor map exactly where I needed one. I found the marking for the central elevator and figured out where it was in relation to my present position.

As the lights continued to flicker, I moved down the hallway at a cautious pace. After rounding who knows how many corners, I arrived at the elevator lobby. However, neither of the two elevators was operating. A consequence of the power outage earlier, no doubt.

Several adults were gathered in the lobby, and anxious voices asking, "What was that?" and "What's going on?" filled the space. They all sounded very irritated, or upset, or nervous...

"Hiratsuka?"

Just then, someone called my name. I spotted a familiar black-clad figure in the hallway across the lobby. It was Mr. Chibiki.

"I heard you were in a room on this floor. How are you feeling? Okay now?"

"Yes, I'm all right," I replied.

"Is that so? Good."

"How's everyone on the sixth floor?" I inquired.

"They mostly seem to have calmed down," Mr. Chibiki replied. "Though it's hard to get much information, what with everyone's parents complaining."

"What do you think happened during third period, Mr. Chibiki?"

"Well, I heard the whole story from Ms. Inagaki. Apparently, the disturbance was caused by some sort of foul stench—however, it turns out that nothing smells at all, so it was probably a byproduct of group hysteria or something similar. The teachers who examined the other students were of the same opinion."

"Okay." I nodded, recalling the moments of confusion before I'd lost consciousness. The bandaged wound on my right hand throbbed with dull pain. "I'm glad everyone made it through unharmed."

Mr. Chibiki nodded back at me. "Mm-hmm. But it's not calm here, either, is it?" he remarked, frowning sharply. Looking up at the flickering lights in the ceiling, he continued. "Somehow, these…"

"Pigeons," I informed him. "Just now, a whole lot of pigeons crashed into the windows and caused a big uproar."

"A bird strike against the hospital windows, huh?" Mr. Chibiki frowned even more severely. "And the weather has been odd for a while, too. It's not raining, but it's as if this place—as if the hospital, and all of Yumigaoka—was suddenly swallowed up by a massive storm."

Do these strange circumstances mean that students of Grade 3 Class 3 somehow brought the "calamity" with them to the hospital?

I'd like to think that would be impossible, but after all the strangeness surrounding the "calamity" this month, I don't think anything would surprise me.

That's how it felt, and I was horrified.

"What will you do now, Mr. Chibiki?"

"I was planning to head back upstairs."

"All right, I'll come with you."

I can go back and get my bag from my room later.

"The elevator doesn't seem to be working, does it? Well, the stairs are this way." Mr. Chibiki led the way, and we headed up to the sixth floor.

10

Halfway up the stairs, we ran into a female student going down the steps. It was Hazumi.

"Ah!" We both gasped simultaneously.

"What's the matter?" Mr. Chibiki asked her calmly.

"Um…I'm frightened," she answered, looking Mr. Chibiki in the face. "I'm not feeling unwell anymore, so…"

"Oh, but, Hazumi—"

"If I stay in that room with everyone, something else scary might happen. Since we've been in there, the lights have gone out, that terrible wind shattered a window… I'm too scared to stay there."

"It's dangerous outside because of the strong wind."

"I'll be in the first-floor lobby. It's less scary there."

Refusing to listen to anything further, she jogged off down the stairs. I couldn't help but sense some kind of unspeakable danger surrounding her, but—it occurred to me that she was hardly alone there.

Everyone who'd suffered a *breakdown* during third period, myself included, was still very much at risk. Even if our outward wounds had been treated, even if we were no longer showing any symptoms, the danger lurking within each of our minds had not yet disappeared—

We came out into the sixth-floor hallway, and I followed along behind Mr. Chibiki. Just like on the fifth floor, the lights overhead were unstable, and pockets of raucous noise blared throughout the corridors.

After following him around several corners, Mr. Chibiki stopped briefly and pointed to the end of the long hallway. "It's down there. The hospital said they had a large room that wasn't in use…" He trailed off.

Suddenly, there was a crash, a furious sound, like something had been destroyed with terrific force. A violent tremor seemed to shake the whole building.

Another earthquake?

That was my first thought, but it was obvious that that was not the case. This wasn't a natural disaster. Instead, it seemed more like the accident I had witnessed last Wednesday, when that huge chunk of concrete had fallen from the building that was being demolished…

People were curled up on the floor in the hallway, holding their heads in their hands.

"What was that just now?" Mr. Chibiki grumbled. "It was kind of like—" I didn't hear the rest.

People started wailing and screaming, crying and bellowing.

"This is bad." Mr. Chibiki broke into a run.

I followed after him. I still didn't know what was going on. When I reached the end of the hall, I froze in place, confronted with a disastrous spectacle.

The light fixtures had shattered, scattering broken glass everywhere. The air was hazy, filled with a whirl of dust and debris, along with a musty, chemical odor and the smell of something burning…

Mr. Chibiki came to an abrupt halt.

I stared with eyes wide open.

I could hear screams and frantic footsteps coming from up ahead. Figures were rushing out of the haze, one after the other.

Students wearing the North Yomi uniform. First one boy, then three girls, then another boy…

"Ah, Mr. Chibiki, it's t-terrible!" the first boy shouted to our teacher—it was Morishita, from the biology club. His face and hair, shirt and pants, were filthy. All the other students were in the same state.

"What was it?" Mr. Chibiki asked. "What happened?"

Morishita turned toward us as if to answer but was pushed aside by the three girls behind him, who shoved him about as they rushed past us.

"I can't do this anymore."

"Not again!"

"We have to run."

"We've got to get out of here!"

I heard the students shouting.

"A helicopter suddenly—" Morishita called out frantically. "I think it probably crashed into the window of the room next door. The wall and ceiling collapsed, and it took our room with it…"

A helicopter?

A helicopter crash?

I was stunned. I had no words.

The vehicle must have been caught in the gale and blown out of control. But for it to crash into this building, on this floor, into the room beside the one where everyone from my class was staying of all things…

"…The helicopter is really messed up. The broken rotor blades flew off, and the room's a wreck, too. It's awful, just…terrible."

"Any injuries?"

"I think so. But we have to get out of here. Everyone's freaking out; there's nothing we can do…"

As we were having this exchange, people continued streaming past us. There were students from our class and unrelated adults, too. Some people had frantic expressions like Morishita, while others wore faces blank with shock… Then, before long—

An ear-splitting explosion jolted the building. I guessed that the fuel tank in the damaged helicopter had caught fire.

I could make out some flames flickering on the other side of the haze. A wave of intense heat washed over me.

"It's no good—run!" Mr. Chibiki ordered us loudly, and we turned on our heels in a mad rush.

The flickering lights dimmed completely, and the windowless hallway was plunged into darkness. The fire alarm started wailing.

Patients and their visitors rushed out of their rooms, joining the confusion in the corridor. There were doctors and nurses there, too, but they had no hope of directing the maddened crowd. The hospital ward was quickly consumed by panic and confusion.

11

After that, my mind grew more and more unstable, and my hold on reality became strangely fragmented.

I knew for sure that I was turning, thinking that I had to escape. Then I was running off down the hallway. But it was only half of "me" making my body move like that. My other half was still "outside" myself; even as I was jostled about in the growing mayhem of the place, I felt as though I was watching myself from a slight distance.

People were running every which way as they attempted to escape the pitch-black corridor. It sounded like everyone was shouting. Then the emergency generator kicked on, although only a few of the emergency lights actually seemed to be in working order. To make matters worse, the smoke from the fire that had occurred down the hall was beginning to spread.

The scene grew more and more frenzied. It was on the verge of devolving into total madness.

I could see the elevator lobby on the other side of the crowd, but the elevators must have still been out of order. When people saw this, everyone started streaming toward the stairs. The stampede surged around several inpatients with obviously limited mobility, and I wondered what on earth would become of them. Part of "me" was watching the situation as if from outside, while at the same time, some other "me" was pushing through the crowd in an attempt to flee, keeping low so as not to inhale any smoke.

I had long since lost sight of Mr. Chibiki.

The light from the emergency lamps was dim and spotty. I could hardly see a thing. There was an announcement running on the hospital PA system—I thought it probably had something to do with the emergency, but I couldn't make out what it was saying because the hallway was much too noisy.

In the midst of all this—

The crush of bodies streaming toward the elevator lobby knocked me about. Then I felt someone push me, and I staggered. Then another person ran into me, and I lost my balance entirely, falling face-first into the floor. People stepped on my back, my legs, shoulders, and arms... Unable to stand, I rolled over onto my side and curled up on the floor to protect myself from the surging crowd.

While I was on the ground, half of "me" was overcome by an intense fear.

I recalled the dreadful footage of the American terror attack that had been running on TV since the night before. The airplanes crashing into the buildings and exploding, the fire breaking out and spreading, then finally the buildings collapsing... In my mind, the shocking spectacle coalesced with my current situation. I was certain that the hospital was going to crumble to the ground just as those buildings in New York had. It was a powerful and entirely irrational fear.

I'm sure it's not just me, thought half of "me" dimly. *I'm sure that*

almost every person here is imagining the same thing, whipping them-
selves up into a frenzy. That's why they're like this...

But another part of "me" couldn't stop to think. *Gotta run away,*
run, run away. Run fast! If we dawdle, this building could collapse at
any time, and we'd all die. We'll die. We'll die!

I rolled across the floor, and at some point, I took a powerful blow
to the chest, knocking the air from my lungs...then I briefly blacked
out.

...Aching all over, I finally sat back up.

The smell of smoke hit my nose with more of a sting than before.
Flustered, I took off down the hall, keeping my head low. By this
time, however, I had no idea where I was or where I was headed.

Suddenly, I caught sight of an EMERGENCY EXIT sign.

I didn't see anyone near it, but I did not hesitate. Rushing over
toward the sign, I lunged for the gray iron door beneath it. I grabbed
the bar with both hands, threw my shoulder against the door, and
pushed it open.

I fell through to the other side and briefly blacked out again.

...The space was incredibly dark.

There were no windows. There was but a single, dim light fixture
in the ceiling. In the sparse gloom, I could just make out the emergency stairs extending downward to the lower levels.

I couldn't see any light farther down the staircase. It was like it
was being swallowed into the depths of the earth. But at that point,
it would have been dangerous to go back the way I'd come. I couldn't
stop moving forward.

My mind made up, I began to descend.

There were no signs of anyone else.

Has this stairwell been somehow forgotten by everyone? Or maybe
there's some kind of problem with it...?

At this point, it was too late to think about it. I had to go down
these stairs regardless; I had to escape the building.

I wanted to hurry, but as I descended, the light vanished, leaving

me in darkness. With one hand against the concrete wall, I continued down the stairs one step at a time. After making it about one
level down, I was completely blind.

It was at this point that I felt the fragmentation of my consciousness, which had started when the "wind" on the fifth floor struck
me, finally resolve itself. I sensed that the half of "me" that had been
knocked "outside" by the wind had now returned. I was a singular
being once again. But it also seemed as though I'd lost my sight in
the process.

Looking forward or back, left or right, I couldn't see anything—
only stark, utter blackness. Naturally, I couldn't see where I was
walking, either. Nevertheless, I still had to get down the stairs, so I
groped along with my hands and feet.

Curiously, no outside sounds made it through the walls of the stairwell. The smell of smoke didn't follow me down, either, cut off by the
iron door above. But for precisely those reasons, I couldn't stop there...

I descended the staircase in blackness.

As I went down, an eerie sensation sprouted inside me.

*I know I'm still definitely inside the hospital, but it feels like these
dark stairs are cut off from the real world somehow. As I go down floor
by floor, am I sinking into a world consumed by even greater darkness?*

But I wasn't able to ruminate on those strange thoughts for very
long.

After going who knows how far down, I finally missed a step. I
frantically tried to catch myself, but I couldn't do it... I began to fall.

I had no idea how far I fell or where or why I stopped. I think I hit my
head hard on the way down, but I didn't have time to register the pain.

Once again, I blacked out.

12

"*Think*, Sou."

I heard a voice.

"Think and *remember*."

What's that...? Ah, again? Is it the voice of Izumi Akazawa again?

A dream?—I thought and opened my eyes, but even after I opened them, there was only darkness. I couldn't see Izumi.

"*Think*, Sou."

Darkness and the voice, which repeated the same words.

"Think and *remember.*"

I'm not sure what I'm supposed to be thinking about...

I stared into the inky black.

I'm not sure what I'm supposed to remember...

What?

And how?

I continued peering into the deep darkness. Suddenly, a pale light shone from some source I couldn't see, gently illuminating a *certain object.*

It was a huge set of scales. There was a long balance bar with two plates hanging from it, one on either side. It was the only thing I could see, suspended there in the void.

"So as I was saying, the important thing in the end is the balance of 'power.'"

Izumi's voice came to me again.

Balance. The balance of "power" between the "casualty" and the "non-existers"... Is that *what this scale is trying to show me?*

While I was contemplating this, a ring of luminescence, like a spotlight, illuminated a space to my left to reveal a single, naked, ball-jointed doll. Its gender was ambiguous, and its bare white skin was somehow captivating. For some reason, its head was covered with a black hood.

Next, another light beamed down onto a space to my right. This time, it revealed two similar dolls. Both had their heads covered in the same hoods...

Then, an invisible hand began to move. It lifted up the doll to my left and the two to my right and placed them on the left and right plates of the scale.

After tipping slowly for a moment, the balance stopped, its bar horizontal.

These are…
The left is the "casualty."
The right are the "non-existers."
Is that what this is?

The "casualty" that appeared this year in Grade 3 Class 3, Izumi Akazawa, was the doll on the left.

The "non-existers" who were set up as a "countermeasure" were the dolls on the right. One of the two was me, Sou Hiratsuka, and the other was Yuika Hazumi.

Thus, the "power" of the "casualty" and the "non-existers" was in a state of equilibrium. This "balance" had lasted from April until the start of May. The "calamity" had been prevented as long as both sides were in alignment.

However, one week after the start of May, Hazumi had renounced her role as a "non-exister." The invisible hand removed one of the dolls from the right-hand plate, and the scale tilted dramatically to the left. The balance of "power" had changed, and the "calamity" began. First, Ms. Kanbayashi's older brother died, then Tsugunaga, then Takanashi's mother…

In order to restore the skewed equilibrium, Izumi had proposed an "additional countermeasure," but around the end of May—

A new doll appeared. This was Makise, who had volunteered to be the "second non-exister" in Hazumi's place. The invisible hand picked up the doll and placed it on the right-hand plate. But the balance of the scale did not change.

The "calamity" had not stopped, and at the end of June, the brothers Shunsuke and Keisuke Kouda and their parents had died. The *retroactive* "countermeasures" could not stop the "calamity" once it had started. Once the balance was broken, it couldn't be restored. And then—

The "countermeasures" were discontinued.

The invisible hand removed the two dolls from the right-hand plate. Only the single figure on the left remained, and naturally, the scale tipped even farther in that direction. The "calamity" would not let up. However—

Now the invisible hand moved again and removed the hood from the doll still sitting on the left-hand plate. From underneath the hood, Izumi's delicately constructed face appeared.

The hand lifted the doll. Unseen forces tore at its torso and limbs, quickly breaking it into pieces, which faded away into darkness.

That night at the start of July, the "casualty" Izumi had returned to "death." With her disappearance, the balance should have been restored. And yet—

I stared at the scale, looming out of the darkness.

There was no longer anything on the left or right plates. With nothing on either side, it should have reached an equilibrium, and yet—

There were the rapid deaths of many "related individuals" in September. The "calamity" had not ceased. Which meant...

The scale still tipped to the left. Even though there was nothing on either plate...

Why? I asked myself as I stared at the balance.

Why? Why? Why?...

"As long as you do your job as a 'non-exister,' Sou, I'm sure everything will be fine."

I recalled Mei's words from some time ago, in April.

"By designating someone as the 'non-exister,' we can account for a 'casualty' appearing in the class and keep the roster at its original number. That way, balance is maintained. That's the original meaning of the 'countermeasures'—they're a charm. As long as you do your job, the class should still be protected from 'accidents.'"

At the time, Mei had seemed very confident. We had both thought that even if Hazumi quit being a "non-exister," the balance would be preserved, with one "casualty" against one "non-exister." And yet, reality had proved different. Hazumi abandoning her role had been enough to start the "calamity."

"That's the power dynamic *we're working with this year."*

Izumi had given me her opinion on the subject.

"Wait...you mean that we're out of alignment with only one 'non-exister'?" I had asked.

"Out of whack, off balance…yes, that's the picture. If we don't increase the 'power' of the 'non-existers,' we won't be able to negate the 'power' of this year's 'casualty.'"

That's how Izumi had answered me, and at the time, I'd agreed with her, but…now I probably needed to rethink the meaning of the power balance.

Why? Still questioning, I kept staring at the balance scales.

Why was Mei's prediction wrong?

Why was the balance of power wrong this year?

Why? Why? Why?

…As I repeated the question, staring at the scales, something appeared on the left plate, as though it had coalesced out of the darkness—something I had *never seen before.*

It was a doll, its whole body painted pitch-black.

…It can't be.

The instant I saw it, a cold chill ran up my spine.

13

"Think, Sou."

Izumi's voice came to me again from somewhere.

"Think and *remember."*

The scales that had been floating in the darkness disappeared, and as they vanished—

…Thud.

A *certain scene* played back in my mind.

I was in the Grade 3 Class 3 classroom on the third floor of Building C. Nothing was written on the blackboard. There were desks and chairs, lined up in neat rows. But none of the students moved to sit in their places.

This is…

Yes, this is the classroom on April 9, after the opening ceremony for the first semester.

On Ms. Kanbayashi's order, everyone sat at their desks except for me. One student occupied each place. The number of seats was exactly right. In other words, there was nowhere for me to sit.

...We were one desk short.

"*Think*, Sou."

I shook my head slowly as the voice repeated.

"Think and *remember*."

...Thud.

I remembered thinking at the time that we had one too few desks. Everyone must have had the same thought.

So...no, wait. Ah, what was it? Just now, something...

...Thud.

...Something's out of place.

Something feels wrong about this...

...Is that really what happened?

Was there really one desk too few that day?

Everyone was in the classroom, and then the "extra person," the "casualty," Izumi was there, too, so... Ah, wait!

That's wrong. *I'm wrong. I was wrong. It* wasn't *everyone. Because Makise didn't come to school that day. She was in the hospital from April on. In which case...*

With her absent, there should have been one too many desks in the classroom. Even with the extra student, Izumi the "casualty," the numbers would have evened out, so there should have been exactly the right number of desks. And yet...

...What could it mean?

Why didn't I notice such a blatant irregularity before?

...Thud.

The same low reverberation from earlier rolled over me, outside my hearing range. As I felt the strange vibration, I grew totally disoriented.

In this peculiar "world," where the "phenomenon" can freely alter memories and records, how am I supposed to figure anything out? How can I know anything for sure?

"*Think*, Sou."

And yet, Izumi's voice repeated again.

"Think and *remember*."

14

I felt my cell phone vibrate and woke up with a start. Apparently, I'd lost consciousness after missing a step on the stairs and falling. I had no idea how long I'd been out.

Despite opening my eyes, my surroundings were still pitch-dark. I was lying facedown on the cold, hard floor. That was all I knew.

I fished my phone out of my pocket and looked at the display. It read: "Incoming call." The vibration continued. The caller was—

Mei Misaki.

I hurried to push the answer button and held the phone to my ear. *Ksh-ksh-ksh...* Beneath the static, I could hear her voice.

"...Sou? Are you okay?"

I wonder if she knows about everything that happened to our class and the disaster at the hospital just now? Maybe she heard about it somehow and is calling to see if I'm safe?

In that moment, there were so many things I wanted to ask her. But I didn't exactly have the luxury of time on my side.

"Mei." I wrung out the word. "Did you figure it out already?" When I didn't get an answer, I continued. "Why did you go visit Hazumi?"

Ssh-ssh-ssh, ksh-ksh-ksh-ksh-ksh... Terrible static filled the line. Before I knew whether my words had actually made it through to Mei or not, the call went dead.

I sighed and lowered the phone from my ear. I looked down at the display. Its faint light pushed back the darkness slightly.

I had fallen onto a landing between sets of stairs. When I looked around, I saw a gray door right next to me. I could see that it had a sign on it that read <3-F>.

Should I keep on going down these stairs? Or should I...?

After some hesitation, I extended a hand toward the door.

15

The hallway on the third floor of the hospital was also dim, illuminated only by the sparse light of the emergency lamps. I didn't see anyone else around. Everyone must have already escaped to a lower level.

I couldn't hear the fire alarm anymore. There was no smell of smoke. But I couldn't imagine that the crisis on the sixth floor was over already, so it seemed dangerous to stop where I was.

From knee to elbow, from shoulder to hip…I was throbbing with dull pain. And my head was pounding, too, on the top left, where I'd hit it during my tumble down the stairs. The bandage that had been wound around my right hand had come loose, and blood was oozing from the wound on my palm, which had reopened. The injury was larger than I thought it was, and there was a lot of blood.

Catching my breath, I stood there alone in the eerie silence and glanced around. Just then, in the corner of my vision, a pale human figure stirred.

Who? I thought. But a moment later, I accepted *it*.

"I see."

So pale…and yes, that's the North Yomi summer uniform. I saw the skirt flutter, so it's a girl.

The figure had her back turned to me. She paused at the corner of the corridor ahead. And then she gently turned back for a second to look at me. It was dark, and she was quite far away, so I couldn't see her face clearly, but I murmured, "Ah…of course."

It was definitely *her*. It was Izumi.

The ghost of Izumi Akazawa, who should no longer be in this world…

Wait, I'm looking at a phantom right now. Just like that time in August, the 8th, I think it was, when I spotted her in the first-floor lobby of the hospital and followed after her.

Izumi rounded the corner and disappeared. I followed her again and turned the same corner. I could faintly make her out in the gloom ahead, several meters down the hall. I broke into a jog and followed. She continued down the hallway, around another turn. I chased her.

I persisted with this nightmarish repetition for a little while. I was trying my best to catch up to her, but no matter how fast I ran, the distance between us never closed an inch, and before long, I eventually lost sight of her...

I had no idea where I was or the path I'd taken to get there. Just like that time in August, it was like I had wandered into some kind of enormous, ghostly labyrinth, and eventually—

Before I knew it, I was standing in the dead center of a long, familiar corridor.

I don't want to say that I was led there by Izumi's "ghost." At the end of the day, *she* was nothing more than a phantom created by my own mind. Without thinking about it, I had sought out *that hallway*, which I knew had to lie somewhere on the third floor of the ward.

Honestly, I'm not sure which explanation is easier to accept, but either way...

I know this place.

I had been there once before, after chasing Izumi's specter back in August.

This is—this hallway is...

The hospital was made up of two sections: the "main building," which combined the medical offices and the inpatient ward, and the "auxiliary building," which housed the psychiatric and neurology departments. This was the corridor that joined the two. They connected on the first and third floors, and this was the third-floor passage...

Of course, I knew *that hospital room* was ahead of me. I felt like I had to go there now. My thoughts were still muddled up, and though I was starting to put the pieces together, I couldn't yet see the whole picture.

Windows lined both sides of the passageway, but very little light shone through. Outside, it was still as dark as night, and on top of that, most of the lights were still out—

The wind was flowing violently again. It blew without interruption, making a distinctive high-pitched scream. Like countless people wailing. I could also hear the sound of the rain. I wasn't sure when it had started, but raindrops were battering the roof, walls, and windows with frightful force. However—

In the moment, all those sounds seemed incredibly distant to my ears. Almost as if this hallway were an otherworldly tunnel that had been partitioned off from the rest of reality.

I steadied my ragged breathing and began to press forward. As I advanced, a voice echoed through my head. It wasn't Izumi's.

"*Think*, Sou."

This time, it was Mei who spoke.

"Think and *remember.*"

I continued on.

…Thud.

As if illuminated by flash bulbs, suddenly I recalled many different scenes that had taken place and remembered my own thoughts at those times.

Ah, yes, this is like that strange sensation that came over me on that night in early July, when I was chasing Izumi's fleeing ghost.

…Thud.

…April 21, Saturday.

The day of my first visit to the "clinic" at this hospital since starting my third year of middle school. I'd already seen the doctor, and I was passing through the corridor, heading toward the lobby of the first floor of the main building, where the cashier's window was located.

The world had gone black for a second, along with a low, reverberating *thud*. But it was really only for an instant…and then the next moment, some information had surfaced in my memory.

Since the beginning of April, one student in Class 3 had been continually absent because she was in the hospital—I didn't know any of the details, but apparently, she needed to be hospitalized for a long time, so it was hard for her to attend school. That student was Makise…

…What does this mean?

An uncomfortable feeling swelled up suddenly in my mind.

It is possible that my memories from that time *have been...?*

...Thud.

...Sunday, May 27.

That evening, Izumi and I had spoken in my apartment.

"You remember what happened at the 'strategy session' at the end of March, right?" she had asked. *"When we decided who would be the 'non-exister' if this year turned out to be an 'on year'?"*

Her words had spurred me to recall an earlier scene in March, when the class was discussing who would bear the burden of being the "non-exister." I had raised my hand, and Etou had asked if that would be enough, and we had decided on adding a "second" that year. And then, after that, the rest of the class had held a lottery with those playing cards...

"They drew lots with playing cards, right? That's when Hazumi pulled the joker and it was decided that she was the 'second,' but... Okay, so think back. To before *that."*

Izumi had narrowed her almond-shaped eyes as if she was looking at something far away.

"Before the lottery began, someone else tried to volunteer, right? In a small, quiet voice that everyone was a little surprised to hear. Why so suddenly? We all wondered..."

When she'd said that, the scene in March more than two months prior had unfolded in my mind, as if revealing itself out of the darkness.

That's right—I had thought at the time. *Something like that did happen.*

I had finally remembered that someone else, besides me, had volunteered to accept the role of the "non-exister," and that I'd been a little surprised when they had...

In the end, that person's offer had been dismissed, and the lottery had been carried out as originally planned. And then Hazumi had drawn the card and become the "second non-exister," but...the other student who had volunteered was Makise.

Even when I had heard the name Makise, even when I had been reminded that we'd already met at the "strategy session," I had never been able to clearly recall her face. She was a feeble, inconspicuous girl... That was all I had been able to remember at the time.

Ah...this, too, could it be?

These memories, *could they also be...? Maybe...*

16

As I continued onward, I thought back on other things.

When I'd encountered her on August 8, Etou had been standing in front of *the hospital room* at the end of this very hallway, holding a modest bouquet of flowers.

"I'm here to visit someone," Etou had said. *"She was in the hospital ward in the main building before, but they told me she switched rooms. The layout of this place is kind of confusing, so I got pretty lost before I finally found it."*

And now, a familiar door, the door to *that hospital room*, was just ahead of me.

I had passed through the corridor connecting the main building with the third level of the annex, where the psychiatric patients had once been housed.

"Come on in."

I recalled hearing a girl's voice from inside the room last time I was there. *Right. I'm sure I've heard this voice before*, I had thought at the time. *It belongs to the girl I met at the "strategy session" in March...*

"Hiratsuka...Sou? I'm so glad you came."

I'd been drawn in by that voice, which had had a carefree quality despite its frailty, and entered the room after Etou, but—

...Thud.

When I did, a low reverberation came out of nowhere, and the "world" had gone black for just a moment...

...Thud.

I finally arrived in front of the hospital room. As I stood there staring at the unassuming cream-colored door, I thought. I tried to think.

I wonder if she's in this room right now? Or if she evacuated because of the uproar in the main building and isn't here any longer?

No, she's here.

Without any good reason, I felt certain of that.

She's here. I'm sure she's still here.

In that case, what should I—what should I do?

I stood stock-still in that spot as the moments passed. I opened and closed my eyes several times and took a few deep breaths…and then I pulled out my cell phone.

"*Think*, Sou.

"Think and *remember*."

I was thinking, and probably in the process of remembering. The faint silhouette that was the cornerstone of the problem was coming into focus. However—

I had no way to determine whether that shadow was real or phony. So…

I gripped my phone with my right hand, sticky with my own blood.

If only Mei were here, I thought. But that was an impossibility. It was a weekday, and at this time of day, she would still be in school. I wasn't sure where she'd called me from earlier, but even if I sent her an SOS with my phone right now, she probably couldn't get there in less than thirty minutes, or maybe an hour.

"It's no use," I grumbled, adjusting my grip on my phone. As I did, inspiration struck.

I'll ring up Koichi Sakakibara.

If I call him, maybe…

I pulled up Koichi's phone number from my address book and hit the call button with a prayer. Thankfully, this time the reception wasn't bad. After several rings—

"Hello, Sou?"

Koichi picked up.

"What's the matter? Is something…?"

"Sorry for calling you suddenly," I interjected. "Just answer my questions without asking anything back. Please."

"What…the heck?"

He sounded surprised and bewildered. No surprise there.

"I heard something from Misaki about you having trouble again?"

"Sakakibara. Regardless of what you heard, I need you to answer the questions I'm about to ask. Please."

"Hmm? Okay, got it."

"They have to do with what happened three years ago." Straining to keep control over my voice, I tried to sound as reserved and dispassionate as possible as I posed my questions. "Three years ago—do you remember the name of Mei's twin sister, who passed away in April of 1998? Can you recall it?"

At the moment, I couldn't remember what it was. Even though I was certain that Mei had told it to me that night in June, when she'd come to visit my apartment and shared her "life story," I could not produce that name, no matter how hard I tried. I wasn't sure when I'd forgotten it.

I had no way to confirm it at the moment, but I suspected that Mei herself was in the same situation...

But if I ask Koichi, I think he might remember.

He'd been "out of range" for a long time, far from Yomiyama. Plus, he bore the special distinction of being the person who had returned the "casualty" to "death" three years earlier. That meant he had the unique privilege of retaining his memories of the "extra person" even after everyone else had forgotten them. He seemed to remember more than most when it came to the "phenomenon" and "calamity" of three years ago. Koichi Sakakibara was the one.

"Mei Misaki's younger twin sister, who was originally the daughter of the Fujioka family. That April, she died in the hospital... I remember her, Sou."

I wondered whether he sensed anything unusual in my behavior. Koichi answered my question without interrogating me about the reason behind it.

"Her name was Misaki."

"Ah..."

"Misaki, spelled with the 'mi' from the word for *future* and the 'saki' from the word for *flowers blooming*. Misaki Fujioka."

I pulled my phone away from my ear and lowered my voice. "Oh..." My eyes fell on the nameplate hanging beside the door to the hospital.

The patient's full name was written there in sharp, angular letters. It said MISAKI MAKISE.

17

"Hiratsuka...Sou? I'm so glad you came."

A memory from the afternoon of August 8 played back in my mind, the day when I had just so happened to run into Etou, and she'd insisted that I go with her to this very hospital room.

There had been a single bed in the dreary, spacious room. A girl had turned to greet us, still lying on the bed—Misaki Makise. Etou placed a flower bouquet on a small table near the window. I had been surprised to see a sturdy-looking iron lattice fitted over the window...perhaps as a relic leftover from when this room was part of the psychiatric ward. Actually, it wasn't until I saw the lattice that I had finally realized that this was a room in the annex, which was connected to the rest of the hospital by a passageway.

"In the end, I wasn't helpful at all."

She had sounded lonely when she spoke. At Izumi's suggestion, Makise had volunteered to replace Hazumi as the "second non-exister," but it hadn't amounted to anything, so...

"That's not true," I remembered answering.

"But still, I couldn't do anything..."

"That's not true," I remembered repeating. "Besides, it's all right now. There's no longer any need to worry about the 'calamity.'"

"Really?"

Makise had raised her voice somewhat as she asked but continued lying where she was, sideways in the bed.

"Is that really true?"

I had been standing a little far from the bed, so I hadn't been able to see her face clearly. But on the edge of the nightstand, something had caught my eye, *glinting silver as it swayed*.

A cell phone strap. The strap had dangled off the side of the table where her phone sat...and I had seen that silver mascot before. The design was based on a famous mythological creature from Okinawa.

It was a *shisa*, the same as the souvenir Mei had brought me from her school trip...and *that was when I'd had a realization*.

I almost let out a gasp, then quietly approached the bed.

"The 'calamity' is over."

That's what I had said before taking a good look at the face of the girl who turned to glance at me—

I remembered being shocked. The girl before me had been awfully gaunt, and with different hair, but *her face had been almost identical to Mei's*. They definitely could have been related.

But that couldn't have been the first time I had noticed the resemblance...because I had also met her at the March "strategy session." Surely, back then I had also seen her face and noticed her resemblance to Mei.

Then I'd recalled that yes, I *had* seen her and noticed that before.

Simultaneously, I had also remembered spotting Kirika at the hospital several times. Only it wasn't actually her. The woman I had seen was Mei's birth mother, Mitsuyo. Her surname had been Fujioka once, but two years earlier she had divorced, then remarried and moved into a house nearby, which was one of the reasons why she had started occasionally reaching out to Mei that spring.

Then a thought had crossed my mind.

Maybe the surname of Mitsuyo's new husband was "Makise"? And...that's why this girl in the hospital is named "Misaki Makise"? Because she also changed her name when her mother got married, from "Fujioka" to "Makise." She must have moved as well, over to this part of town, and transferred to North Yomi for middle school...

Mitsuyo has been coming here because her daughter has been hospitalized since April. She's not coming to receive medical treatment herself; she's visiting her daughter. Could that be what's going on?

Besides the twin sister who died three years ago, Mei also has a sister who is three years younger than her. I heard that from someone once. This girl—Misaki Makise, I'm almost certain she's Mei's "younger sister by three years."

That was what I'd thought when I had visited her room. And at the time, it had seemed completely true to me.

The fact that she had the same *shisa* phone strap as the one I'd received from Mei had been almost enough to convince me. But at the time, I hadn't said anything to Makise herself to confirm my suspicions. For some reason, I had hesitated to bring it up the first time I'd visited her hospital room.

Even then, though, something had been weighing on my mind. I had been thinking about *how unnatural Mei's speech and conduct had been on that crucial day in July.* The question had been bothering me ever since Izumi had returned to "death" and disappeared—
—on July the 5th.

It had rained all day that day. By the time Mei called me, the sun was already started to set. The moment I had heard her voice, I'd known immediately that something was wrong. Mei definitely seemed different somehow. She had always been standoffish, never one to let her feelings show. But as soon as I'd heard her voice, I could tell that her composure was broken.

…On that phone call, Mei had said to me:

"We have to hurry. That's what I was thinking, and I…"

Then she had asked me if I had *"a photo that shows as many members of your class as possible."* When I had replied that I had the group picture taken on the day of the entrance ceremony, she had asked:

"I don't suppose you could come show it to me now?"

Per her request, I had immediately set out for the "Blue Eyes Empty to All, in the Twilight of Yomi" gallery where she was waiting, carrying the photo, but…

Her voice and mannerisms that night had seemed agitated and desperate. I had never seen Mei act like that before.

But after her phone call with Koichi in Mexico, Mei seemed to have lost her conviction and resolve to use the "power" of her "doll's eye" and return the "casualty" to "death," and maybe that was why...

That night, we had used Mei's "doll's eye" to determine that Izumi was the "casualty," and the two of us had chased her down and returned her to "death." That should have ended the "calamity" for the year—that's what we had believed at the time. But—

Even after it was finished, questions had continued to weigh on my mind. Why had Mei rushed me like that? Why had she seemed so impatient?

"Why are you in such a hurry tonight?"

I remembered asking Mei the question directly.

But her answer was: *"...I don't know why."*

"You don't know why...you're in such a hurry?"

I had asked her again.

And her answer was: *"I have a bad feeling..."*

At the time, it had felt like Mei was hiding something. Something had definitely seemed off about the way she was talking.

Maybe—an idea struck me.

Maybe, that day, Mei—maybe July 5 was actually when Mei learned that her little sister, Misaki Makise, was a member of Grade 3 Class 3 at North Yomi?

She hadn't known before then. Her mother, Mitsuyo, may have told her that Makise was ill, and Mei had said she even went to see her in the hospital, but the topic of school and her sister's class had never come up. They hadn't talked about it at all, not about her transfer to North Yomi or about the special circumstance of Grade 3 Class 3, nothing.

However, on that day—on July 5—maybe that was when Mei had finally found out the truth. I didn't know how it all went down, but she'd probably heard it from Makise herself.

That was the reason why. That was why Mei was acting like that...

In my memories, I discovered the answer to a question that had been bothering me for a long time, an answer that I could confirm with another recollection.

...Mid-August, after our dinosaur-film-festival outing—

I had left Yagisawa after the movie and dropped by the doll gallery on the way home. In that familiar basement space, I had prepared myself and then started *that conversation* with Mei. I laid out the facts as I had witnessed them, plus my own thoughts about what was going on, and listened to Mei's explanations, then confirmed how various things fit together...

On July 5, Mei had indeed learned that her younger sister by three years, Misaki Makise, had transferred into North Yomi, and moreover, that she was a member of Grade 3 Class 3. The news caught her off guard, and she panicked. After all, if her sister was in my class, that meant that Mei herself could be a victim of the "calamity," as well as her biological mother, Mitsuyo, since they were both "related individuals." I'm sure that Mei was most concerned about her younger sister, though.

The fact that she hadn't known any of this had come as a great shock. So she'd panicked. And that evening, driven by the thought that she had to stop the "calamity" as soon as possible, she had called me...

"Oh..."

Without realizing it, I let out another noise. I was still staring at the nameplate that read MISAKI MAKISE. I extended a hand toward the door of the hospital room.

When I had visited this room on August 8, I had met Makise and then *realized, remembered, and registered*—I had awakened to a whole series of facts and memories and the connections among them. All of them were actually part of a "false reality" that had been altered or invented by the "phenomenon."

Is that what's been going on? Is that really it?

My hand reached the knob. It felt unpleasantly cold. Without knocking, I opened the door.

18

It was even gloomier in the room than it had been in the hallway.

All the lights were out. But even though it was as dark as night, there was still a tiny bit of light coming from the window. I could just barely make out the inside of the room via that faint illumination.

The bed stood stark and pale against the darkness. And I could see a figure of a girl lying on it.

The girl on the bed didn't move at all, even when I entered the room. Maybe she was sleeping. Or maybe...

Despite the chaos going on in the hospital, the girl had been left here on her own. That was certainly unusual, no matter how far her room was from the main building.

Everything seemed too contrived, like the setup for a cruel game being played by some entity outside our world... It gave me chills to think about.

Outside, the wind howled and the rain pummeled the ground ceaselessly. But the noise seemed far away somehow, as though the corridor that had brought me to this room had also taken me to another plane of reality.

I took two or three steps toward the bed, trying not to make any noise.

She was lying there faceup, with her eyes closed. I could see her chest slowly rising and falling.

In the end, I've been asleep this whole time, too...

But now that I'm here, what should I do...?

"Sou."

That was when I heard a voice.

It didn't come from the girl on the bed. The owner of the voice was somewhere behind me. She had been standing in the shadow of the open door, so I hadn't noticed her at all.

"Ah...!"

I nearly screamed when I saw who it was in the semidarkness. It was an awful surprise. Though I was quickly relieved to see—

"...Mei?"

Standing there was Mei Misaki.

She was wearing her high school uniform. And over her left eye was a white patch...

"Ah...um..." Keeping my voice down, I said, "Earlier, you called me..."

"Mm-hmm."

"Was that…from here?"

"Yes. I heard about the mass transportation to the hospital, so I thought maybe that meant you were here, too. I was worried that you might have gotten caught up in everything going on. We got cut off right away…but I'm glad you're safe."

"Um…don't we need to evacuate?"

"This room is far away from everything, so I think we're okay," Mei said as if it was no concern, taking a step toward me.

I asked, "When did you get here?"

"Quite a while ago."

Did she cut class? Or maybe she slipped out partway through the day.

"Mitsuyo came to see her today, too. But she already left."

She stayed in the hospital room even after Mitsuyo left, and…?

"You called Sakakibara, didn't you?" Mei asked. "Just now, in front of the room. I heard you. And I understand why you called him."

"…All right."

Mei stared at me. She was very close. "So?" she continued. "What did Sakakibara say?"

"Um, he…"

"My twin, who died in this hospital in April three years ago. *What did he say her name was?*"

As I suspected, Mei can't remember her name, either.

With a crushing feeling in my chest, I answered, "Misaki… He said her name was Misaki Fujioka. That was the name that Sakakibara remembered."

Even when she heard that, there was no conspicuous change in Mei's expression.

"I see." She nodded slightly. "I knew it," she mumbled softly, as if saying it to herself.

Then she looked over at the bed where Misaki Makise was sleeping. Watching her, I asked quietly, "When did you realize?"

"Last Saturday, after I talked to you," Mei answered dispassionately. "Back then, when I said I '*didn't know,*' that was the truth. But something was bothering me a little…"

Sure enough, Mei had said something like that. She had told me about feeling sort of strange or uncomfortable.

"It was all about the balance of 'power,' right? Like Akazawa said." Mei inhaled deeply, then took a step toward the bed.

"Akazawa returned to 'death' in July, but the 'calamity' didn't stop. Why…?" Mei mumbled the question, as if to herself, but I answered.

"Because *there was more than one 'casualty.'* And that was almost certainly because we added a second 'non-exister' to the 'counter-measures' this year. In doing so, *we destroyed the balance, and a 'power' moved to correct it. The 'second casualty,' who appeared in the middle of everything, was…*"

As I spoke, I was working it all out in my head.

I figured that Mei had gone to see Hazumi because she was searching for the "second casualty." When she had looked with her "doll's eye" at that group photo of the class that I brought her on the evening of July 5, she had identified Izumi as a "casualty," but not every member of the class was present in that photo, which had been taken the day of the entrance ceremony. *There were three students who weren't there.*

One of the three was me, since I had accepted the role of a "non-exister," and one of them was Hazumi, the "second non-exister." And the last was Makise, who was absent because she had already been hospitalized.

In my case, Mei had used her "doll's eye" on me early on and confirmed that I was not the "casualty," so that left Hazumi and Makise. She went to see Hazumi first. She met her, looked at her with the "doll's eye," and checked whether she was a "casualty"…

As usual, Mei seemed to see straight through my thoughts, and she added, "I didn't see the 'color of death' around Hazumi. So that meant the only one left was *this girl.* That was my thinking."

She closed her right eye and paused briefly.

"That's what I thought, but I also thought it couldn't possibly be… I couldn't make up my mind right away."

That's only natural. It's understandable.

But…despite that, today, Mei must have made up her mind, resolved herself in some way, and come here alone.

"Have you checked yet?" I asked. "Have you looked with the 'doll's eye' already?"

Mei nodded silently, then abruptly removed her eye patch. With the figure of the sleeping Makise reflected in the exposed "doll's eye," the "blue eye, empty to all," she said, "After Mitsuyo went home... she wasn't sleeping yet, but I looked at her like this."

"Did you see it? The 'color of death'?"

"I did. I see it now, too. Clearly."

"So..."

"But still, I hesitated," Mei admitted, sounding anguished but stubbornly quiet. "I kept on second-guessing myself; I was really perplexed. Was this girl really a 'casualty'? Did I even have a sister three years younger than me in the first place? Were my memories false? Did 'false memories' really exist? ...I didn't know what I was supposed to do."

Mei approached the hospital bed. I stayed where I was, dumbstruck.

On the table beside the bed, there was a fruit basket, which Mitsuyo had probably brought with her on her visit today. Beside the basket was a stack of several white plates. And beside the plates was a paring knife.

"Thank you, Sou."

Mei stopped walking and glanced back at me.

"Thank you for calling Sakakibara. And for asking him about her name."

She turned back toward the bed and took the blade in her right hand. In my mind I was shouting at her, but my throat seized up, and nothing came out—

"The only younger sister I have is the half of me who died three years ago—Misaki Fujioka. I never had a sister three years younger than me..."

I could barely understand her murmuring.

"...which means that you don't exist."

Gripping the knife with both hands, Mei leaned over Misaki Makise where she slept.

My mind screamed at her to relent. Part of me wanted to do

something, to rush over and stop her, but another part was holding me back, refusing to let me move an inch. In the end, I did nothing.

The knife swung down straight at Makise's chest.

There was a dull sound. I saw a dark stain begin to spread out across the bed. Makise opened her eyes. She looked surprised, but she didn't try to resist. She didn't let out a single groan. Like a doll that had already lost its "life." Like one of those girls on display at the "Blue Eyes…" gallery, laid out on a deep-crimson bed.

Mei pulled the knife out and then immediately drove the blood-stained blade into Makise's throat.

For a second, I thought I saw an expression like a faint smile pass over Makise's face, but it might have been my imagination. At the same moment, her lips trembled slightly, and she looked like she was trying to say something. However—

Mei did not relent. She sliced through the blood vessels at the base of Makise's pale throat, severing the thread of her false life. Without hesitation. Without mercy.

Outroduction

Allow me to lay out the facts that came to light the following day.

The fire that broke out in the inpatient ward of the Yumigaoka Municipal Hospital on the afternoon of September 12, 2001, was extinguished before sunset that same day. The flames burned through more than half of the sixth floor, as well as part of the roof and the fifth floor, but thanks to strenuous firefighting efforts as well as the relentless downpour, the damage was prevented from spreading any farther.

Regarding the helicopter crash that caused the blaze, the sequence of events leading up to the accident is still under investigation. The aircraft in question was owned by Hoshikawa Aviation in the prefectural capital, Q** City. On the day of the crash, it had apparently been chartered by a certain newspaper company. The current theory was that they were probably flying in to cover the mass-hospitalization incident caused by an uproar over an offensive smell at North Yomi, which had been plagued by a series of student suicides and accidental deaths. Much remains to be seen.

The helicopter pilot, as well as the reporter and cameraman who were riding along, all succumbed in the crash. There has been talk that one of them was actually a "related individual" to someone in Grade 3 Class 3, but so far, no details or information on the veracity of that rumor have emerged.

The helicopter collided into the north side of the sixth floor of the inpatient ward. In what could be called the silver lining under a dark cloud, it struck the linen room, which was unoccupied at the time. That said, the linen room was next to the large hall where the students of Grade 3 Class 3 were being housed, and two people died when they couldn't make it out in time. Their identities have been confirmed as follows:

•Ruiko Etou......Female student. Countermeasures officer.

•Seiya Nakamura......Male student. Soccer club member.

The other students and a number of parents and guardians who had come to the hospital escaped unharmed or with minor injuries. Including the patients and staff members who were not "related individuals," four people died in the hospital in addition to the three in the helicopter, and twenty-odd people sustained major or minor injuries.

†

Personally, I was very relieved to learn that my psychiatrist, Dr. Usui, hadn't been harmed.

As I'd suspected, he'd been examining the students on the sixth floor of the main hospital building that afternoon. However, he'd apparently left just before the madness started. And his daughter, Kiha, who'd been so worried about her father, also made it out okay.

Even so—

I can't help but wonder about Kiha's strange behavior that day.

Dr. Usui had always said that there was something a little off about his daughter, and I wonder if that had anything to do with what happened. I think I'll wait for the right moment and ask him more about that.

†

I do need to finish describing what happened in the hospital room.

The knife pierced Makise's carotid artery. Mei was instantly covered in blood, which even splattered on me. As her hospital bed became a sea of blood, Makise passed, returning to "death." With her death, the "otherworldly presence" I had sensed in that place also disappeared.

Once she was gone, the roaring wind suddenly quieted, and the rain began to taper off. I could hear the hospital-wide announcements calling for evacuation.

In any case, Mei and I left the hospital room together and went down to the first-floor lobby of the annex building. Several staff members greeted us and told us that the fire in the main building seemed to be dying down. However—

Not a single person mentioned the fact that our faces and clothes were caked with blood.

I have to imagine that *it must have been completely invisible to them.*

Mei didn't speak a single word while we were there. She didn't try to talk to me, either. She, too, seemed to have transformed into a lifeless doll.

The room on the third floor of the annex had been out of use for a long time. Obviously, there had been no patient by the name of Misaki Makise staying there. That version of reality had already taken hold of everyone, with the exception of Mei and me.

Nothing was found in the room—not Makise's corpse, nor the blood-soaked knife and bedding, and any documents indicating that "Misaki Makise" had been hospitalized since April also vanished. The same thing happened to the memories of people connected to her, from the staff at the hospital to her own mother, Mitsuyo...and at school as well, of course.

Just like when "Izumi" disappeared in July, not a single student or teacher remembered "Makise." Everything was altered or falsified to be consistent with the new "reality" in which she had never existed.

†

In the end, more people lost their lives to the "phenomenon" than in an average year. All our efforts to prevent the "calamity" had been in vain. It had claimed many victims before we managed to stop it. There was nothing we could do.

It was the most sinister year in the history of the "Yomiyama phenomenon." That's how it will go down.

But even in the middle of everything—

A sole piece of good news reached me three days after the disaster at the hospital.

Yagisawa, who had been hovering between life and death in the intensive care unit, regained consciousness the day after the blaze. He was moved out of critical condition, and his recovery afterward also apparently went remarkably well. I heard the word *miraculous* fall from his doctor's mouth.

"They say you'll be able to go see him before too long. Apparently, there won't be any lasting damage, which is also 'miraculous.'"

When Mr. Chibiki told me that over the phone, tears began to fill my eyes.

After some major deliberation, I had confided in him about what had happened that day in the hospital room. I explained how even after "Izumi Akazawa" disappeared, the "calamity" hadn't stopped because of the "second casualty."

"So from now on—really this time—we shouldn't have to worry about any 'accidents,'" I asserted with confidence. "This year's 'phenomenon' has totally run its course. It's undoubtedly finished; there won't be any more…"

Mr. Chibiki seemed utterly exhausted, but he silently listened to my appeal to the end. Then he answered me with a single word: "Understood."

I wasn't sure how much of my story he believed, but at any rate— he was sure to recognize this as fact once September ended and we made it through October without incident.

†

September 30, Sunday afternoon.

The wound on my hand, as well as the bruises and scratches that covered my body, had mostly healed, and for the first time in a while, I went for a walk on the path beside the Yomiyama River. Partway down the path, I went over to the riverside and sat alone on a bench, where I found a peaceful moment for the first time in a long while.

There was a refreshing breeze blowing through the perfectly clear sky. I saw a swarm of red dragonflies gracefully flitting about. I heard the chirping of crickets. On the river's surface, there were several Eurasian teal ducks that had just arrived to pass the winter.

On the opposite shore, a cluster of red spider lilies bloomed. The flowers were a vivid deep-crimson hue, almost disturbingly red, as if their petals had been stained by the blood of all those who had lost their lives in "accidents." As I watched them swaying in the autumn breeze—

My thoughts inevitably turned to the events of the past half year. Once again, I pondered over the "truth," as I understood it then, having ruminated about it on countless occasions.

At the time of the "strategy session" in late March, when I had volunteered to be this year's "non-exister," after which the class decided to choose a "second non-exister" at Etou's suggestion—*at that time, "Misaki Makise" did not yet exist.*

The memory of Makise volunteering before the lottery to choose the "second" was a "false memory" the "phenomenon" had planted in our minds after the fact...

On April 9, the day of the opening ceremony for the first semester, "Izumi Akazawa" had appeared in our class as the year's "extra person," otherwise known as the "casualty." *At that moment, too, Makise did not yet exist.* There were one too few sets of desks and chairs—that's what we had thought at the time, and our perception was correct.

We had understood that this year was an "on year," and Hazumi and I were to play the roles of "non-existers." Following precedent, two sets of old desks and chairs had been carried over to our classroom from Building Zero. No desks or chairs had been removed in exchange, so in doing this, the classroom came to have one extra set, and...

The year's "countermeasures" of having two "non-existers" versus one "casualty" had functioned quite well. There were no "accidents" in April.

However—

In the meantime, the "phenomenon" took an unexpected turn. By establishing two "non-existers," we had caused an imbalance in the "power dynamic." In order to correct the balance, which was tipped too far toward the side of "life," a "second casualty" had appeared. You could even say that the appearance of this "second" was *a side effect of our excessive "countermeasures."*

The "extra person," the "casualty" who joined Grade 3 Class 3 during an "on year," was resurrected randomly from among the people who had lost their lives to previous "calamities." But they always come back as a "member of Grade 3 Class 3," and "reality" is altered so that everyone automatically accepts them as such. Everything changes to account for their presence.

However—

The "casualty" has to come back at the apparent age they were when they died. They aren't supposed to get younger or older when they are "reborn." That means the resurrections aren't entirely random, since it would be impossible, say, for an elderly person who had died in a past "accident" to blend in with the other students.

The person brought back as the "second casualty" was "Misaki Makise," who'd died three years ago in April, at the municipal hospital.

This "phenomenon" was able to happen because her mother, Mitsuyo, had divorced and remarried, then moved into the North Yomi school district last year. But Makise hadn't appeared in our classroom at North Yomi. Instead, she'd been "reborn" as an "inpatient" at the hospital where she had spent her final days three years earlier—in the same room where she had died.

April 21. After visiting the "clinic" for my first appointment after starting Grade 3, the "fact" that there was a student hospitalized there had surfaced in my mind in the corridor while I was on my way to the first-floor lobby of the hospital building. That was probably the moment that the "false memory" of "my classmate named Makise, who has been absent from school and in the hospital since the beginning of April" lodged itself in my mind.

The "second casualty" absolutely did not exist from the start.
In the middle of April—probably around the 20th, she had *materialized.*

Not in the classroom, like usual, but in the hospital. True to form, however, she was a member of Grade 3 Class 3.

When Makise appeared, people's memories had been altered, going far back in time. I'd said that Makise was there for the "strategy session" in March and that she had volunteered when we were choosing the "second non-exister"—but *that recollection*, too, was a "false memory" that we all began to share once she appeared. Etou had even been given "false memories" of her friendship with Makise since her transfer to our school at the end of last year.

Around this time, our perception of the desks in the classroom was also altered accordingly. We had brought over two old desks from Building Zero for the "non-existers" to use, so there was an extra. In our minds, the desk that Hazumi had vacated became the desk that belonged to "hospitalized Makise"—everyone suddenly took that as the truth. When I look back on it carefully, the details were inconsistent, but no one had noticed. It's likely that some kind of "power" was working to keep us from seeing something that we should have otherwise noticed.

So a second "casualty" appeared, putting the "power dynamic" between them and the "non-existers" in equilibrium. That balance had collapsed at the beginning of May, when Hazumi quit "not existing," kicking off the "accidents."

Come to think of it, the fact that Izumi was the one who proposed the new "countermeasure" to address the "calamity" once it started and the fact that we'd entrusted Makise with taking over the role of the "second non-exister" in place of Hazumi were exceptionally ironic turns of events.

It was the end of May when Izumi and Etou had visited her in the hospital to make the request. And it was several days later when Izumi had come to the "Blue Eyes…" gallery and met Mei for the first time. Now I understand why Izumi had been so surprised and bewildered back then.

I'm sure that when she saw Mei's face, Izumi had noticed how much she looked like Makise, who she'd just seen in the hospital. I'm certain that's why she reacted the way she did...

We made it through June, and in July, we had established that Izumi was a "casualty" and we had returned her to "death." But even after "Izumi Akazawa" had disappeared, there was still "Misaki Makise," the "second casualty." The balance was still tilted toward the side of "death," resulting in the "accidents" that continued into September...

By the way...

"Misaki Makise" was originally "Misaki Fujioka," Mei's younger twin sister. Misaki had existed in this world until April, three years ago. After that, she'd been resurrected as a member of Grade 3 Class 3. In order to resolve any inconsistencies and make everything coherent, a "false memory" stating that "Mei has a sister three years younger than her, in addition to her twin sister" had been planted in people's minds, but—

There was a small problem with that.

Since the changes and falsifications had not altered any facts about "Mei's twin sister, who died three years ago," it turned out that both her "dead twin" and her "little sister who she was three years older than" were both named "Makise."

So when I had asked Mei the name of her twin, she had answered (finally, after what I now realize was an oddly long pause, looking back on it...) that her name was "Misaki." *Immediately after that,* both of us had forgotten the name. The "phenomenon" must have changed things—this is something else that I now easily grasped in hindsight.

....

....

...I had been lost in thought for a long, long time. When I realized that it was now 4:25 in the afternoon, I hurried to my feet.

We had promised to meet at 4:30, at the pedestrian bridge a little farther down the path, the Izana Bridge.

If I run, I think I'll just make it.

There was no one on the bridge when I got close. I walked on with a feeling of relief and arrived exactly on time.

A figure appeared on the other side. It was her—Mei Misaki.

†

I hadn't seen Mei, or heard her voice, since the 12th of that month, when everything crazy happened.

After that day, she hadn't answered when I called or replied to my e-mails, and I wasn't going to go uninvited to her house in Misaki, so...

But the evening prior, I'd gotten an e-mail from Mei.

"Tomorrow at 4:30, at that bridge on the Yomiyama River—" it said.

Mei was dressed in a black blouse and skirt, an outfit that looked like mourning clothes. As the sun was sinking in the sky and the scenery was taking on a faint red tinge, we each walked toward each other and stopped in the middle of the bridge, facing each other.

"Are you well?" Mei was the first to speak. "Have your injuries healed?"

"Yeah, mostly."

"Going to school?"

"Starting next week, actually."

"Yagisawa survived, huh?"

"Miraculously, apparently."

"That's great."

"Yeah."

Mei's voice and tone were no different than the girl I had always known. Her face was nearly expressionless, but that wasn't unusual, either. Even so, I was very nervous as I asked, "Um...what about you?"

"Hmm?" Mei tilted her head a bit, then nodded slightly and answered, "I'm fine now."

She slowly closed, then opened both eyes. She wasn't wearing her eye patch. She had a prosthetic, black with brown flecks, in her left eye.

"I haven't been able to get *her* off my mind ever since it happened," Mei said. "But I stopped trying to force myself not to think about it."

"Um...can I ask you something?"

"What?"

"Makise was in the hospital, so how did you...? What I mean is, how did you end up meeting and talking to her?" I asked.

"Through my mother," Mei replied. "I heard about her from Mitsuyo, and I would go visit her sometimes and even call occasionally. I ran into you once at the hospital, right?"

"Ah, yes."

Once, I had caught sight of Kirika (who was actually Mitsuyo) in the hospital. Then Mei had found me, and the two of us had gone up to the roof...

"That was one of the times I was visiting. I think that day I was with Mitsuyo. But back then, I didn't know yet that she was a member of Grade 3 Class 3 at North Yomi. I didn't even think to ask...but we went over this during summer break, didn't we?"

"Ah, yes we did," I replied, and mumbled, "sorry..."

Mei had insisted that she was fine now, but the memories still had to be painful for her.

"You don't need to apologize," Mei said in response to my mumbling.

"Ah...but—"

"After several years, I'll forget about it, whether I want to or not."

Then Mei looked down at the flowing river and pressed her chest against the handrail of the bridge. I stood beside her and placed both hands on the railing.

I thought carefully about what we should discuss.

There were so many things I wanted to ask her.

For example—that day on the 12th, what had the two of them talked about when Mei went to visit her sister's hospital room, in the time between when Mitsuyo left and when Makise fell asleep? What was Makise thinking, and how did she pass the time alone during her long hospital stay? What on earth had Makise tried to tell Mei in that last moment before her death, when she opened her eyes as the knife plunged into her chest?

But I decided to keep all these questions and more to myself for now.

So then, what should we talk about?

Something less important. Something inconsequential.

But the more I pondered, the harder it got for me to say something.

Ah, that's it—how about the e-mail I got from Mei on the night of the 11th?

That was the day that Yagisawa attempted suicide, and by the time I'd gotten home, I hadn't had it in me to even turn on my PC, so it was the 13th before I realized that I had an e-mail from her. As one would expect, I had been happy to get her message congratulating me on my birthday.

I should thank her again... No, but when she wrote me that e-mail, Mei was definitely already...

Looking down from the bridge, I saw the beautiful image of the setting sun reflected in the river.

But—I thought—on that night not even three months ago, there was a violent, turbulent current running under this same bridge. And Izumi tossed herself into it from about where we're standing now...

Recalling that event was still painful, even now. As Mei had said, a time would surely come when both the memory and the pain would fade and disappear, whether I wanted them to or not.

"There's just one thing stumping me...or rather, something that's been weighing on my mind." Finally, at last, I opened my mouth.

"What?" Mei responded as I glanced at her profile.

"Why did we make it through August without anything happening? The 'second casualty' was still around, so why did the 'accidents' stop for August?"

Still looking at the river, Mei mumbled, "I wonder...why did they?"

Musing aloud, I asked, "Was it taking a breather for a month after one of the 'casualties' disappeared or something?"

"I guess that's possible, but...I don't know." Mei tilted her head uneasily. "It is an 'unnatural natural phenomenon' to begin with, after all. Honestly, it might just be really fickle, like the weather."

"Fickle? You're kidding..."

I started to say something, then held my tongue. Mei also made no further attempts to discuss the issue.

†

"That reminds me..."

After a silence that went on for a short while, this time it was Mei who opened her mouth to speak.

"I got a call from Sakakibara the other day, and he said he's coming here during the holidays in November."

"He's coming?"

"So when he does, he wants to get together, the three of us."

We had enlisted Koichi Sakakibara's help at every important point along the way. Honestly, I was extremely grateful for his assistance. If I saw him, not only would I want to offer him my thanks but also pick his brain about a bunch of things.

"Sakakibara came to Yomiyama last year and the year before during Obon. Apparently, he wants to come in November because he wasn't able to make it for Obon this year."

"...Huh."

"He wants to visit the grave of someone important to him."

"Someone important?"

I didn't know who that could be. But the idea made me feel sad, almost jealous.

An important person. I wonder whether I have any of those, living or dead?

I glanced at Mei again, then up at the darkening sky. Listening carefully to the sound of the gently flowing river, I casually wished that we could stay there like this forever.

"I think I'd better be getting home for today," Mei announced at last. "Kirika's been a little high-strung again, you know."

"Does it have something to do with Mitsuyo?" I asked, but she didn't reply.

"Did you hear anything from Tsukiho, after all that?" Mei inquired abruptly.

I answered with a sigh. "She's called so many times."

"Have you talked to her?"

I shook my head silently.

"You haven't answered the phone?"

I nodded silently.

"Not even once?"

When I nodded wordlessly again, Mei said, "I see," and smiled for the first time since we'd met up today. "I think you should do whatever you want, Sou."

After that, as we were parting, she brought something else up. "Oh, that's right...," she started. "I feel like I mentioned something about this before, but do you want to visit Lakeshore Manor someday soon?"

"Huh?" Surprised, I averted my gaze.

But Mei stared straight at me. "When I went to Hinami over summer break, I checked out the house. It's still there, the same as always, but... Sooner or later, it's probably going to be demolished or sold off."

From the tone of her voice, I could tell that she was informing me of this in earnest. I slowly turned back to her. She was still staring straight at me.

"Sometime soon...say, next spring or something," Mei said. "Of course, we would keep it a secret from everyone. Let's go just the two of us and explore the house. How about it? Want to?"

I didn't know what expression to make in response to her enthusiastic questions...

"Everything's okay now, right, Sou?"

I nodded silently at her next statement.

Let's go have a look. Let's go, yes, and make a report to Uncle Teruya, I thought. *I'll tell him that Grade 3 Class 3 at North Yomi had a really difficult time, that the "calamity" struck hard again this year. And that I didn't run away. That's what I'll tell him.*

I brought together my fingers and made a pretend camera viewfinder for the first time in a long while. I centered it on a puff of cloud floating in the evening sky, then clicked the pretend shutter closed. When I did—

A low, faint reverberation echoed from somewhere. And then, for just a second, the red of the sunset glow that painted the scenery seemed to be obscured by darkness… Panicking, I searched for Mei. But there was no need, since she was right where she had always been—beside me.

"See you later," Mei said and turned to leave. As I watched her black figure walk slowly away across the bridge, fighting my desire to chase after her, a gust of wind suddenly blew around me. I felt a chill that didn't belong in an autumn breeze, and it made me shiver—just a little.

—The End

You have been reading
"Another 2001"

Part 1 Yuika Hazumi
Part 2 Izumi Akazawa
Part 3 Misaki Makise

written by Yukito Ayatsuji

This work was serialized in the following issues of *Shosetsu Yasei Jidai* magazine. November 2014–April 2015. June 2015–September, November, December. February 2016–August, October, November. January 2017–July. August 2018–February 2020. Revisions and amendments were made for publication as a single volume.

All individuals, groups, and events in this book are fictional. (Editorial department)

Afterword

This is actually the first long novel I've written in seven years, since I put out *Another: Episode S* in 2013.

The idea for this book came to me not long after I finished penning *Episode S*. I had been working on a different concept for an *Another* sequel for a while, but I decided to put that idea on hold and write this one instead. I started serializing it in *Shosetsu Yasei Jidai* magazine in autumn of 2014. At the time, I had planned to finish it up in two years, three at the longest, if all went well, but as usual, my prediction was entirely too optimistic. Writing it was really rough going, and I ended up having to suspend serialization for a whole year, so it took more than five years before the serialization was finished. After that, I had to somehow polish the manuscript, which had grown to a considerable length, into something satisfactory. Then, as soon as I had finally managed to publish it in this format—

As I was writing, I felt like I was constantly anxious about whether I would be able to make an interesting novel and about whether I would get this one done. That was probably because, in a certain sense, the stories I had written before had taken a very different structure. On top of that, I was no longer a young man and had little confidence in my stamina or vitality. As the serialization dragged on, I was (quite earnestly) haunted by anxiety over what would happen if I should drop dead before completing the work. To be honest, I'm incredibly relieved now.

It probably goes without saying, but allow me to give a little bit of background on the story's historical setting.

Another and *Episode S* were set in 1998. As the title indicates, this book is set three years later, in 2001, so the cell phones that appear in the story are, naturally enough, flip phones (now we would call them retro). At that time, it wasn't yet common to use phones to exchange e-mails, and the "photo mail" service had just started to take off that summer—a new feature allowing devices with cameras built in to take pictures and send them to other users. "E-mail" largely referred to messages sent using a computer, and Internet lines were still mostly narrow-band... That's the era we're dealing with. Circumstances have changed quite a bit in the past twenty-odd years.

I'm so happy to have you visit the Yomiyama of 2001—both those of you with memories from those days and those who will simply have to imagine them.

Anyway, back to 2020, a year of ongoing history-making chaos, when an unexpected pandemic has covered the entire world in the blink of an eye. The fact that this happens to be the same year during which I am publishing my first long novel in seven years must be some meaningful twist of fate.

It's an unsettling, shameless book in which people die one after another at the hands of an irrational "calamity"—but, well, if somehow you can forget our stressful "reality" for a short while and enjoy yourself a little in this fabricated world, that would bring me great joy as an author.

As I touched on at the beginning of this afterword, I have a concept for one more sequel to *Another* (probably the last entry in the series). I've laid several bits of groundwork in this book that would lead into that sequel, but...the truth is that at this point, I haven't decided when I'm going to write it or even if I can. I'm a bit worn out, in body and mind, so I think I'll take a step back from Yomiyama for a while to pull myself together and wait for the right moment.

Lastly, the acknowledgments.

To all the successive editors at *Shosetsu Yasei Jidai* responsible for keeping up with the writing of this book over a long period of time—Mai Fukushima, Ryou Nakamura, Makoto Ishibashi. When it was time to turn the story into a single volume, the aforementioned Ms. Ishibashi, as well as Kaoru Ichiji, lent me their assistance. And to my good friend of many years, who I should call my general adviser on this whole series, Aki Kaneko. To the cover designer, Kumi Suzuki. And to the many other people to whom I am indebted in a myriad of ways. I thank you all from the bottom of my heart.

Summer 2020
Yukito Ayatsuji